THE PEN NAME PROJECT

LEIGH CREEK

Hardcover ISBN: 979-8-9880600-4-8

Paperback ISBN: 979-8-9880600-3-1

Ebook ISBN: 979-8-9880600-5-5

Book Cover by Amanda Hawkins at Eternal Geekery

Edited by Jamie at copyediting.by.jamie@gmail.com

Formatting by ECC Publishing (Elizabeth C. Cabrera)

Published by ECC Publishing LLC (the imprint of Elizabeth C. Cabrera)

www.eccpublishing.com

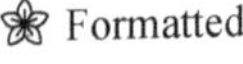 Formatted with Vellum

CONTENT WARNING

For the full, detailed list of content warnings for this book,
please visit the author's website:
www.eccpublishing.com/the-pen-name-project.

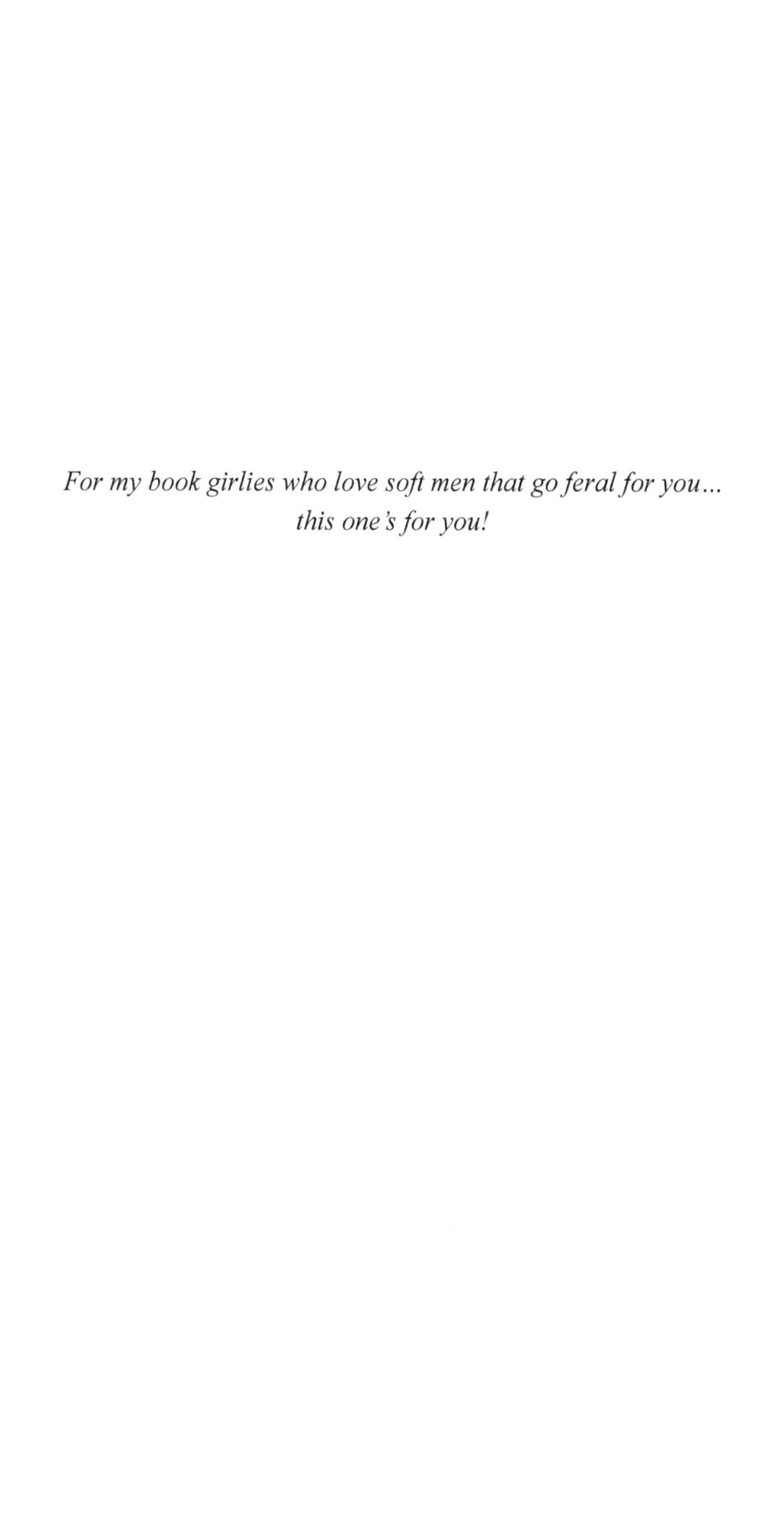

*For my book girlies who love soft men that go feral for you…
this one's for you!*

CHAPTER 1

SAM

*O*f all the things Samantha MacMillian expected today, getting pulled out of her writer's block by hearing the word "smut" was not one of them. But who was she to look a gift horse in the mouth? If it meant a light at the end of the tunnel for this predicament she was in, she'd take it.

She was set up in her favorite cafe a few blocks away from her apartment, her gaze fixed firmly on the blank page glowing at her from the screen. The relentless and much-dreaded blinking cursor taunted her with each passing second, a flashing reminder that if she didn't start coming up with something soon, she was in trouble.

She hissed out a groan as she rubbed the back of her neck to ease the tension there. Blinking a few times to shake the sleep out of her eyes, she began the torturous mental loop that had accompanied her every day the past few weeks.

How was she supposed to know that after publishing the last book, the well of ideas she'd had for something new would dry up?

Her popular detective mystery series had finally

wrapped up last year with its final installment, a thrilling conclusion that had been well received by both critics and readers. But after she wrapped up the press releases and book tour for it, when her publisher had asked her what was next, she quickly realized that she didn't *have* anything planned next.

If only she could time travel and slap that stupid contract out of her hand. It had seemed like such a good idea at the time that she didn't even consider the scenario she would end up in.

While she was still in process of writing the fourth book in her series, her publishers generously offered her a brand-new contract for whatever else she wanted to write. After her mystery series had wrapped up with the planned ninth install-ment, she'd have free reign to write, well, anything she wanted. A creative person's dream come true.

She'd already expressed back then that once she was done with this series, she wanted to take a break from writing mysteries, and they had been excited about the prospect of her creative flair in a new genre. It was a smart business deci-sion on their end. Sam was basically a guaranteed payout for them, as every single one of her books had hit the New York Times bestseller's list at least once.

That said, in her excitement about writing something completely new, she failed to realize what a creative slump she would enter immediately after publishing the last book.

Her book tour wrapped up just shy of a year ago, and she still had nothing to show for it in terms of her next project. Her publisher had been more than patient with her, something she was eternally grateful for. She'd told them that she wanted to take a bit of time off to decompress from the whirl-wind that the past few years had been. She'd started writing her first book right before she'd graduated from college, and as she was now pushing thirty, she'd had little time for herself.

They'd extended the contract to allow for her to have a much needed break, but she knew that her grace period was swiftly coming to a close. She'd have to give them something soon, or she'd be breaching her contract. But the second she'd started to brainstorm ideas, absolutely nothing came. It was like she'd used all her best material on her mysteries, and now there was nothing left.

A reminder popped up on the screen, temporarily distracting her from her spiral and causing another groan to escape her. She had almost forgotten about the video call. Granted, it was a weekly occurrence, and normally she looked forward to it, but with absolutely nothing to tell her agent, Angel, she wasn't exactly leaping with joy.

She gave a languid stretch before getting up and walking over to the counter. Another cup of coffee might help wake her mind up, or at least that was what she tried to convince herself as she waited for her order.

The Oak House was her favorite coffee shop in downtown Durham. Not only was it one of the closest coffee shops within walking distance of her apartment, it was relatively quiet during the daytime, so she could work in peace. Plus, Sam couldn't help but adore the cozy atmosphere embedded into each inch of the space. Coffee shop during the day, craft beverage lounge at night—the ambiance alone was unmatched.

Sam collected her iced latte from the barista and went to sit back at her table, nestled comfortably in the back corner of the space. She allowed herself to sink into the comfortable leather seat as she gazed outside. Every time she came to work here, she always picked the same spot. It was far enough away that even the morning rush didn't disturb her, and it had the best ambient lighting of the entire space. It also didn't hurt that the floor-to-ceiling exterior window perfectly displayed the bustling downtown activity outside, currently showcasing the pitter-patter of a late spring shower as it created a sheen of water on the ground. It was the perfect kind of peace that almost made Sam forget her troubles.

Almost.

As she settled back into her seat, a familiar name popped up as a new text notification dinged.

> We still on for dinner tonight? I can pick you
> up from the complex if you want?

Sam smiled involuntarily, the movement tugging at the freckles speckled across her nose. It wasn't like they hadn't *just* spoken half an hour ago—before he'd gone into the office earlier and about this very topic—but her best friend was anything but subtle when he had his mind set on something.

And though he would never find this part out, there was a high likelihood that her car would never leave the shop again after she'd taken it in a few months prior.

> Yes on dinner, no on the ride, I told you I'm
> fine to take the bus

She was in the process of saving up for another car, so the bus would have to do for now.

She could practically hear the groan from there when his response quickly came back, choking back a laugh as she read it.

> Ugh, fine, just sit FAR FAR away from the
> sniffer this time

Smiling at the inside joke, Sam set down her phone. She

was jolted back to reality, however, when the tell-tale jingle of the incoming video call started blaring through her laptop's speakers. The suddenness of it caused her to nearly spill her coffee, an expletive leaving her lips as she placed the cup on the table and quickly placed her headphones on to limit the sound spreading to the rest of the building.

"You're early," Sam half-scolded as Angel's face lit up her laptop screen.

Angel feigned shock as she placed a finely French-manicured hand on her chest, the subtle jingle of her gold bracelets accompanying the gesture. "Only by five minutes."

"That's five minutes I could've spent in peace and quiet," Sam teased, seeing the immediate frown appearing on the screen.

"Someone hasn't had enough coffee in their system yet, I see. Or do I sense bad news on my horizon?"

Sam sighed, rubbing the back of her neck before reaching for her coffee. "Both?"

"You're lucky I love you."

Sam chuckled. "You love me because I'm your best client."

Angel glowered at her. "Alright, I may be your agent *now*, but you forget I've been putting up with your antics for *years*."

This time Sam let out a genuine laugh. It was true, technically, Angel had first been her roommate back in college. It was only her good fortune that Angel had decided after graduation to move up to the Big Apple to work in publishing. The two of them had spent hours talking about books, Angel acting as a soundboard for the ideas Sam had for her first mystery novel, which she'd started working on at the time.

It was sometimes hard, seeing Angel all prim and proper now, with her Manhattan-esque fashion sense and polished appearance, when a few of the memories Sam held dearest were the times when the two of them were sitting in their dingy little university student apartment, eating cup ramen.

"Still," Sam said as she leaned back in her seat, "it doesn't hurt that I'm also your bestselling client."

"No, it certainly doesn't," Angel conceded before quickly adding, "luckily for you, though, because any other agent would be throttling you right about now."

"I still have time."

"You have three months. To write an entire book. From scratch. And not a mystery," Angel reminded, a smile gracing her lips as she reached for the sleeve of her blush-colored blazer and deftly rolling it up to her elbows.

Regardless of the time of day, Angel almost never looked less than a million bucks. She possessed a sense of fashion that Sam couldn't help but envy, always appearing so effortlessly put together and professional no matter what she had on. She'd been that way since they'd met during their freshman orientation almost ten years prior, the only major change to her wardrobe now being a larger budget.

It was a far cry from the raggedy pajama set she often remembered Angel wandering around their old apartment in. A stark reminder of how different they were—Angel now all posh New York City girl who came from a rural town in North Carolina, while it felt like Sam had hardly changed at all. The same old type-A homebody who preferred the comfort of the local coffee shop down the street from her apartment over exploring most of the downtown area she lived in.

"Should we have another brainstorm session?" Angel asked as she leaned back in her office chair, the view of downtown Manhattan peeking in over her shoulder.

The claw-clip ponytail that Sam had haphazardly pinned

up that morning finally relinquished the thick waves of rosy-blonde strands from its confines, unable to hold back another second longer. Sam groaned in frustration as she pulled the strands back, smoothing out the edges with her hands. "I don't know if another one is going to help. We tried that last month."

Angel shrugged. "Then what's the harm in trying again?"

Other than her pride, Sam couldn't think of any other good reason. "Fine, I guess we can attempt it."

"Alright, great," Angel said as she scooted forward in her chair toward the screen. "How about instead of trying to brainstorm story ideas right now, like we did last time, we just brainstorm a genre to try? It would be a bit less pressure and still at least gives us some progress for today."

"How very manager-sounding of you." Sam laughed.

Angel rolled her chocolate-colored eyes dramatically. "Did I also mention that because I've known you forever, you're also my biggest pain in the ass client?"

"Sorry, sorry, you're right. Let's brainstorm. Whatcha got?"

"That's more like it. How about fantasy? I remember you trying to write one a long time ago. Maybe that could be a good direction?"

Sam chewed on the idea for a second before shaking her head. While she did love a good fantasy, she wasn't sure if she could summon the kind of creative flare and world-building needed to get through something like that.

"Historical fiction, then? It's a bit of a broad net but maybe something in that realm?"

Sam shook her head again. "I don't even really like to read those that much, so I don't think I'd enjoy the process of writing one."

"Literary fiction?"

"Same thing but also even broader of a net."

"Science fiction?" Angel suggested, a bit of impatience starting to creep into her voice.

"While I'd love to say I'm smart enough to come up with something ingenious for something like science fiction, I don't think I have that kind of creative brain power, either," Sam admitted, quickly taking another sip of her latte.

"Fair. How about a thriller? Your mysteries were all murder mysteries, so maybe something that leans farther into the thriller element?"

It was a tempting thought. It was familiar enough that she wouldn't have to venture too far out of her comfort zone to create something, and it would still technically be separate from the mysteries she'd been known for. It could work.

Then again, the whole pitch she'd given to her publishers when they came up with this arrangement was that she wanted to write something completely new and different from what she was known for. A thriller felt like a cop-out.

"Definitely something I'd like to circle back to, but I think it hits a little too close to what I've already done for it to be really unique."

"You're not taking this very seriously," Angel chided.

Sam laughed. "I promise I am."

"Alright," Angel said. "How about horror? It might reflect your love life?"

Sam scowled. "My love life isn't a horror novel, thank you very much."

Angel laughed. "I beg to differ. Do I even have to remind you of that terrible date you had with that guy a few months ago? What was his name again?"

"I'd rather not write something that you immediately associate my love life with," Sam quickly said, changing the subject. She already had enough things to worry about without having to add *him* to the list. "Besides, you're one to talk."

"At least I've been on more than one date in the past five years. Though we both know *your* hangup," Angel commented, looking narrowly down her slender nose at Sam.

"Oh shut up, are you going to help me, or are you going to just sit here and make fun of me?"

Angel's smile widened. "I rest my case. Though, with as many romances you read in your free time, maybe you could write a romance? Hell, you could even write a smutty romance. Maybe then you'd be getting laid, even if it's just in the book."

In that moment, it felt as if a lightbulb flickered to life—so much so that Sam felt stupid for not thinking of it already. Why on earth hadn't she thought of a romance?

It was her favorite type of novel to read when she needed to chill out and relax, but she'd never really pictured herself being able to write one herself. The series she'd just wrapped up had a minor romantic subplot, and even that had felt like she had no idea what she was doing. Her readers had apparently eaten it up with vigor, though, if the number of fanfiction stories and artwork she'd been sent over the past few years were any indication.

It would be another thing entirely, however, to write a book with romance at the forefront. And a smutty one at that? While the idea wouldn't have tempted her much at the start of her writing journey back in college, the thought was now titillating enough that Sam was practically drooling at the opportunity to explore.

It checked off so many different boxes that it felt like she'd be stupid *not* to dive into it. It was something she enjoyed reading for fun, so she wouldn't be forcing herself into a genre she wouldn't even pick up herself. And it was different enough from her other work that her publisher would probably agree that it met her contract. But, most importantly of all, it was the first time in quite a while that she felt genuinely excited to start writing again. She felt the spark that had so eluded her for the past year.

Angel was about to be very thrilled, especially since it was technically *her* idea.

"Hello? Are you still there?" Her agent's voice broke through Sam's thought bubble, and she realized she'd been silent a lot longer than she'd intended.

"Angela Louise Smith, I could kiss you!" she declared excitedly, quickly suppressing her volume when a few other customers glanced in her direction.

"What? What did I say?"

Sam leaned back in her chair, her decision firm in her mind.

She was going to write smut.

CHAPTER 2

SAM

"You really like the romance idea?" Angel asked, looking a little smug. As long as it had been since Sam had had an idea for a book, she was more than happy to indulge it.

"I do," Sam replied before taking another quick sip of her coffee. "What do you think?"

Angel pursed her lips thoughtfully, her hand absently rubbing her chin. "You know, I said it in jest, but as much smut as you read in your free time? I'm more surprised that neither of us came up with this before."

"So am I, if I'm honest."

"Do you think you'd be comfortable writing sex scenes?"

Sam blinked at the screen a few times. "I think so. Why wouldn't I be?"

"You have to know what to do during sex, more than just reading about it," Angel said, trying but failing to hide a laugh.

Most of Angel's other big-name clients were in her preferred genres of choice for representation, fantasy predominantly, so her being Sam's agent likely had more to do with the fact that they were friends than anything else. A fact that bit her in the ass more often than not, now notwithstanding.

Sam frowned. "I could just find another agent who won't pick on me all the time you know."

Angel feigned shock as she placed a hand on her chest. "After all we've been through? Besides, who else would put up with your antics as much as I do?"

"Fair point."

"In all seriousness, though," Angel continued. "As much as I tease, I genuinely think a romance might be a good direction for you. With your writing style and attention to character detail, I think you might be able to pull it off."

Sam relaxed back into her seat, relieved. "It will take a bit of work, but I think it'll be a fun project."

Angel nodded, her movements smooth as she turned and reached for something off-screen. The soft sound of water pouring filled Sam's ears as Angel returned into frame, taking a sip from the large, crystal-clear glass that looked almost as expensive as Sam's rent. "Alright," she started after daintily placing the glass on the table, an imprint of her signature cherry-red lipstick staining the exterior, "give it some thought, and let me know when you have a story, so I can pitch it to the publisher."

Sam held up a finger as a sudden thought occurred to her. "Well, before you do, I have one other thing."

"And that would be?"

"I don't think I want to publish this under my current name."

Angel raised a perfectly groomed eyebrow, the sharp angle accentuated by the distinctive cut down the middle of her brow line and further reminding Sam that she needed to make an appointment to get her own busy eyebrows waxed soon. "You don't?"

"I think if I'm going to write smut, I'll want the flexibility a pen name will provide. The publishers get to have two for the price of one, so to speak. That way, I can continue writing other stuff under my real name if I want to and keep this stuff separate."

Another thoughtful nod. "I suppose that makes sense. Do you want it completely untied to yourself, or can it be known that it'll be a pen name? Might be a tougher sell without your brand tied in at all, especially since this would mean an amendment to your contract."

Sam scrunched her nose, seeing the freckles dotted along the ridge of it dancing it time with the movement in her reflection. "If it'll help convince them to keep me around, we can give them whatever they want. However, we can make the case that if we release this under a pen name, detached from my brand, that it will work to their advantage if the book turns out flopping."

"Good angle. Well, I'll be here in New York until the end of the week, then I'll be traveling. Think you might have at least a rough story idea by the time I get back?" Angel asked, flicking her dark-russet bob over her shoulder.

"That's right; I forgot that was coming up. How long will you be in Seoul again?"

"Can't live without talking to me that much?"

Sam laughed. "No, just so I know when to have the idea to you by."

Angel scrunched her nose at Sam before smiling again. "I'll only be there for a few days for my friend's wedding, but let's say you have an idea for me in a week's time?"

Sam chewed on her lower lip in concentration. There weren't any other events she had to attend, no book tour to fly around for, no personal holidays she had planned, or anything else like that. She had a few administrative tasks to do, but she could finish those relatively quickly to focus her attention on this.

Finally, she nodded. "I think so. I should have something by then."

"Good. And I'll also keep you posted on when I'll be heading your way for a visit. I know how much you miss me," Angel purred playfully and offered a wink.

Sam did miss her. While she had plenty of company with her best friend, Charlie, who lived only a few floors above her, she definitely missed having a bit of girl time with Angel. Though, in addition to her advanced style, Angel had also grown accustomed to the hustle and bustle of New York City life that wasn't quite as busy and active as downtown Durham, North Carolina was.

And Sam wasn't sure if she had the stamina to keep up with how often Angel loved to go out.

Sam laughed. "Always will."

"Though, I need you to miss writing more. Get to it! I need you busy as a bee there."

"I'm not your only client; it's not like you aren't rolling in cash over there," Sam remarked with a wry smile. "I thought you could've used a break from me."

"True, but you're the only client I actually *like*, so don't leave me hanging."

"I bet you say that to all your clients," Sam teased.

"Only you, babe. Is Charlie back from that conference of his by the way? I forgot to ask earlier."

Sam nodded, fighting the smile that followed. "He texted me when he got back to his apartment last night."

"Cool. Tell him I said 'hi' when you see him later. Now, scoot. Get to work!" Angel tossed back, offering another wink and a wave before the screen went black.

Sam's gaze lingered on her computer for a few moments before taking off the headphones she'd been wearing.

The soft clink of ice resettling into her nearby cup drew her focus back to her coffee. The melted cubes swirled within the milky liquid invitingly, a reminder of her significant lack of caffeine at the moment. She scooped her cup up to take another healthy swig.

A sense of excitement coursed through her as her thoughts lingered on her conversation. This felt right. It had felt like such a long time since she had genuinely felt this excited about starting a new project, especially one that hadn't been meticulously crafted and plotted out in advance with a predetermined storyline and conclusion. The possibilities suddenly felt endless, causing the creative flame within her to flicker back to life with renewed enthusiasm.

She snatched her bag from beside her to retrieve her notepad, barely held together from old age and usage. There were plenty of ideas she'd jotted down over the years in this thing, so it was time to start actually going through them to find something that she could work with.

It was still early enough in the afternoon that she knew she'd have plenty of time to think and work before her dinner plans with Charlie.

She couldn't wait to tell him about all of this.

CHAPTER 3

CHARLIE

If anyone had told Charlie that his week was going to take a dramatic turn for the better, he'd have laughed and told them *not likely*. Charlie wasn't a grumpy person by any stretch of the imagination; really, he wasn't. In fact, most people who knew him at work would agree that he was one of the more friendly engineers they'd met. Most of the others he worked with survived mostly off of snark, copious amounts of caffeine, and junk food hidden in the cave dwellings they called their cubicles.

But this hadn't been a normal week for Charlie, and it also hadn't helped that his day at work had been more stressful than usual. He'd been gone for the first few days of the week for a conference and had returned to a pile of cases waiting for him to handle.

Tick, tick, tick.

His gaze shifted back to the clock hanging above his office door. The metallic silver of it captured the light pouring in from the window behind him.

It had been one of the few perks that he'd been given when he'd *temporarily* taken on the manager role, but he feared it would be a more permanent installation if he kept avoiding the other managers. It was flattering that they'd wanted him for the position, but their persistence was starting to become annoying, considering that he'd already turned it down twice already.

Managing computers and the data lab, that was one thing—but managing an entire team of people? No, thanks. Charlie was much more comfortable with the silence and peace that being in the lab brought him.

Computers, he understood. Data towers, piece of cake. It was like an intricate puzzle each time a case floated his way. A lot of people might not agree, but things were simple. Codes, trial and error, simple math. Things Charlie could put together. He was *not* a creative kind of guy, unlike his best friend who was on the complete opposite end of that spectrum in every way imaginable.

An image of her flaming strawberry-kissed hair fluttering around her face came to his mind, and he struggled not to smile.

In reality, he normally never watched the clock so carefully. He liked his work, but he was ready to leave. He'd been counting down the time—essentially since the moment he'd walked in the door that morning—until he got to see her. And he was impatient for it.

Tick, tick, tick.

Three, two, one. Shift over.

Charlie practically threw his belongings into his bag in hopes he could leave before anyone tried to talk to him. The other unspoken perk of having his own office was that he could easily sneak out. Being the height and stature he was, it had always made it difficult to navigate. Gone were the days when he would have to shimmy out of a cubicle, issuing an apology to his neighbor when he'd once again bumped into their cubicle on his way out.

He gave a curt wave to a few coworkers lingering near a water cooler in the back, sauntering quickly to the elevator before any of them tried to call him over to chat. Normally, he wouldn't think twice about going over and making conversation, but he needed out.

A relieved sigh hissed between his lips as the elevator doors closed behind him, looking at his reflection in the shiny metallic surface. The graphic tee and jeans he had on wouldn't be a problem where he was going, thankfully, so he didn't need to worry about going home to change first.

The bite of the upcoming change in seasons hit him as he walked outside into the parking lot, a chill in the breeze that hinted at the lingering coolness of the preceding months. Charlie despised the reminder. Always had, always would, and if that made him seem like a grump, he didn't particularly care.

While most people were really settling into the season—enjoying the last hints of winter that blended into milder spring temperatures—it had never brought on happy memories for him.

And it *certainly* didn't help that it wasn't too long before—

Charlie's phone rang out from his pocket. He continued on the path toward his car but answered the call anyway, seeing the familiar caller ID flashing on the screen.

"What do you want, Peter?" he huffed.

A scoff on the other end. "Why is that the first thing you say to me? No '*He*y, big brother, it's nice to hear from you.'"

Peter always had a knack for calling him at the absolute worst times. Today was no exception, but he knew this wasn't just a casual check-in.

Charlie rolled his eyes. "Okay. Hey, big brother, I just talked to you yesterday, and nothing has changed since then. Better?"

"I know I just—"

"I haven't changed my mind," Charlie interrupted. "If Mom insists on forcing participation, I'm not going at all."

The bigger reason why Charlie's week hadn't exactly been pleasant. He rarely fought with his family, particularly his mother, who he adored more than anything. However, he had his boundaries, too. He was allowed to lay them out just like everyone else, and she was crossing a major one with her request.

"She said if any of us brought a date, she wouldn't force us to do it. She's not cruel; she just doesn't have a lot of volunteers for that part of the auction," Peter said, the warm depth of his voice more high pitched than normal—likely nervous that he wouldn't change Charlie's mind.

Charlie shrugged as he opened his car door, the dark-blue SUV he'd had since he was a teenager, and threw his bag into the passenger seat. "Well, all three of us aren't dating anyone that I know of, so that seems highly unlikely."

Peter sighed in a way that Charlie could practically see him rubbing his temples, like he always would when he was stressed. "I could care less whether you do the auction at all; really, I don't. But you can't *not* come at all."

The phone call switched over to the speaker system as Charlie started up the car. Anything to distract the thoughts already threatening to rise to the surface. "I don't *have* to be there, you know. It's not like it would be the end of the world."

"True, but you know how much it would devastate Mom and Dad if you don't," Peter stated. Charlie rubbed a hand through the rough stubble of his beard, the feel of its scratchiness against his hand helping to ground him.

He hated that his brother was right but grumbled anyway. "You're almost as good at guilt tripping as Mom is, but the answer is still no."

"Is it worth breaking her heart over?" Peter asked.

Charlie's eyes met with his own in the rearview mirror, the depths of blue that normally looked so vivid now appearing dull, almost discolored in the current lighting. Right on point with how he felt with that jab.

He knew it would. It always would when it came to this. He just seemed to be the only one in the family who didn't feel like throwing a fucking party on arguably the worst day of the year. Charlie's grip on the steering wheel tightened, causing his knuckles to turn white.

"You know… you can always talk to me," Peter continued when Charlie didn't say anything. "This time of year is, well… it's tough for all of us. But you know you can—"

"Yeah, yeah, I know," Charlie said quickly, not eager to enter this rabbit hole again. "Now, I gotta go. I have somewhere to be."

"Oh?" Peter asked, sounding intrigued all of a sudden. "What are you and *Sam* up to tonight?"

Charlie's body heated at the name, but another eye roll felt inevitable. His hands released their death grip from the steering wheel.

"Dinner. Now, go bother our other brother if you have nothing better to do. I'll think about it, alright?" he snapped, tapping to end the call before Peter could protest.

Stopped now at a red light, Charlie took a moment and closed his eyes. Yeah, his week could've been better. But at least he knew that it was about to get at least a fraction better.

CHAPTER 4

SAM

The sun dipped just beneath the horizon when Sam hopped off the bus later that day, the last few golden rays of light stretching upward and signaling the finality of the work day.

She glanced down at her watch to ensure that she would be on time, forcing herself to slow her pace when she did. As it seemed to be tradition these days, her trademark of habitually overestimating how much time she would need to get to her destination proved accurate once again.

After having to make a quick stop at the bank, exactly ten minutes ahead of schedule, she had more than enough time to walk to the restaurant. In fact, she decided to take a moment to eagerly embrace the approaching dusk as the wind kicked up around her, forcing her to tuck a lock of hair behind her ear.

It had only been a few days since she'd last been able to see Charlie, so she was a bit surprised just how much she'd missed him. Though, to be fair, they *had* been practically glued at the hip since they met as children.

The memory flashed in her mind, and she absently rubbed her hand over her heart.

The two of them, all gangly long legs and buck teeth in desperate need of braces. Awkward as ever, but with one shy smile shared between them as their mothers chatted in the whole food aisle at the supermarket, the rest was history.

A gust of wind forced her out of memory lane and back to her conversation with Angel earlier.

Her notepad was already brimming with ideas from her earlier burst of creative energy, overflowing with hastily written chicken scratch that she knew even she would have a hard time deciphering later. Whether any of these ideas would actually work as a romance, she wasn't sure yet. She'd most likely have to start from scratch, but she'd managed to scrawl a few new ideas in there.

A dull throb radiated from her temples, a result of all the caffeine she'd guzzled down earlier.

If she could just—

"Well, look who's here already!" A voice called from behind her, jolting her from her thoughts. Sam turned, instantly recognizing the voice as her face broke into a wide smile.

Charlie walked toward her as he exited the nearby parking garage. He quickened his pace to catch up with her but easily closed the distance between them with a few long strides. She raced forward, all but throwing herself into his waiting arms as he lifted her feet off the ground and hugged her.

"You're back!" she exclaimed.

Charlie laughed and gave her a quick squeeze before lowering her back to the ground. "I was only gone for a few days."

She shrugged, a little embarrassed by her reaction. "I know, but it's boring around here without you."

She sometimes hated how true that was, but being her best friend meant that the significant amount of time they spent together was void without him there. But more than that, she just missed *him*. Not that she'd tell him that. He'd just get an ego about it, or worse, poke fun at her for it.

"Aw, I missed you too," he teased, an almost knowing twinkle in those blue eyes of his.

"I thought you'd hit more traffic coming this way," she said to change the subject, her hand rising to shield her eyes from the few rays of light that managed to slip around him.

Leave it to Charlie to be one of the only people in this city who could make *her* feel short. Standing at just under six feet tall herself, it was a difficult feat in and of itself. But as he was an entire head taller than she was, he was one of the few people that pulled it off. Coupled with the fact that he was built like a linebacker, it was enough to make her feel small in comparison.

Charlie shook his head, running a hand through the soft waves of his light-brown hair. It appeared almost golden with the way the sun hit it. "Not as bad as usual. I left a few minutes early, so *someone* didn't have to wait too long." He affectionately nudged her with his shoulder as they turned to walk the remaining distance to the restaurant.

"You know me, chronically early. Have a good day?" she asked.

The smell of his cologne filled her senses as the wind shifted in her direction. It was earthy, the kind of smell that immediately flashed images of a log cabin out in the woods right at the peak of fall. It was one he'd been wearing since he was old enough to buy his own cologne—and one that always made her think of him whenever she smelled anything similar to it.

"About as good as can be expected. You know how much

I love having to be at the office," Charlie joked, mimicking a rope strangling him with his free hand and eliciting a giggle from her. "You take the bus again?"

She nodded slowly and eyed him. "You really do hate me taking that bus, don't you?"

"Can you blame me? You're too stubborn to accept rides from me often; I have to practically bear wrestle you into the car the few times you even hint you'll accept my help, and I really don't like to think of you sitting next to some crazy person," he defended.

She rolled her eyes. "That was one time, *one* time, and now you'll never let me hear the end of it!"

"As I shouldn't!" he protested, giving her shoulder a gentle squeeze. "It was just about the only time you let me drive you around after that because you were so freaked out."

It wasn't that she didn't *like* being carted around. It was obviously more convenient than trying to rely on the bus. But while they lived in the same apartment building and spent a lot of time together, she hated relying on him too much.

"Yeah, well, I'm fine now, so stop worrying about it. You are such a worrywart."

Understatement of the year. Despite being the youngest son of the Backman family, Charlie radiated the protective aura that was typically associated with older siblings—a mantle happily handed down to him by his *actual* older siblings.

"One of us has to be. Will I ever be able to convince you to get another car?" he asked.

She shook her head, offering him a determined, albeit defiant, smile.

While the downtown area of Durham was walkable to a certain degree, the rest of the area required larger means of transportation, meaning she often didn't venture too far outside of the city unless she called a cab or was going with Charlie somewhere. Her own car had been stuck at the repair shop most of the year since… well, after what had happened to it.

"Nope! I work remotely anyway, so it's not like I have a commute to worry about, unlike *some* people."

Charlie scowled at her. "Ugh, fine. Someday, though, I'll wear you down. Tell me about your day at least."

She shrugged. "You know how it's been."

"I'm sure you'll come up with something soon. Talk to Angel lately?" He offered one of his trademark dimpled smiles. The flutter in Sam's chest forced her to let out a sigh to cover it.

"Yes, I talked to her earlier today. She sends her love."

"What'd she have to say?"

She shrugged. "Oh you know, the usual. She's gonna be in South Korea for her friend's wedding soon, so she'll be MIA for a bit."

"And when is she coming down to visit us?"

Sam laughed. While Angel had been Sam's roommate in college, Angel and Charlie had gotten on thick as thieves. If there was anyone who would be able to keep up with her friend's energy level, it was Charlie.

"She said she'd let me know after she gets back to New York."

"Good. You guys have any progress with book stuff?"

Sam eyed him. "Maybe…"

"Oh, tell me! What do you have up your sleeve?" Charlie asked as he quirked an eyebrow at her mischievously.

As they rounded the corner together, the mint-colored brick of the burger joint came into view, its facade perfectly juxtaposed against the traditionally red-bricked exterior of the building opposite it. A perfect contrast—and a perfect distraction to put their conversation on hold until after Sam satiated her growling stomach.

"I'll tell you about it in a minute. Let's get food sorted out first."

Charlie hissed out a sigh, aiming a playful pout in her direction. He let her go first as they got to the front door, so he could open the door for both of them, ushering her in with a grand wave of his hands.

Few things had changed since they were kids, Charlie's sense of humor being one of them. She sashayed past him, flicking her long hair over her shoulder as she did.

The two followed the long red arrow drawn on the floor, which led to the order counter near the back of the restaurant. Charlie loved coming here, so Sam could practically feel him buzzing with excitement as they made their way past waiters and other patrons.

The hiss of the brewery equipment, sheltered behind the glass wall immediately to the right of the entryway, reverberated through Sam's ears and piqued her interest. She briefly entertained the idea of ordering herself a beer to go with the burger she would most definitely be getting but decided against it.

She inhaled the heavenly aroma of grilling meat and salt that permeated the air. A delightful departure from her previous location's lingering coffee scent. The sweet and bitter combination melted away into a savory aroma that already had her mouth watering.

In all the excitement of the day, she quickly realized that she'd forgotten to eat much of anything. The thought was punctuated by her stomach growling angrily, loud and persistent. A sound that didn't seem to escape Charlie's sharp hearing as he stood next to her.

"You are absolutely hopeless, you know that?" he teased after they placed their orders and made their way to a table.

Sam immediately claimed the seat facing away from the window and draped her bag over the back of her chair for safekeeping.

"I may or may not have forgotten to eat. Besides, though," she added pointedly before quickly sticking her tongue out at him, "mind your business."

"Mature," Charlie chided but almost immediately stuck his tongue out at her in return.

The waiter flounced by them, placing their plates in front of them before quickly scooting away with the other orders on his tray. The food looked as good as it smelled, and Sam immediately scooped up the cheeseburger she'd gotten and took a big bite.

A giggle nearby caught her attention, and Sam glanced over to see a few girls, probably fresh from the salon down the street, whispering amongst themselves. Giggling behind their hands and whispering to one another as they glanced in Charlie's direction. They were less than subtle about it, but Charlie seemed none the wiser. Eagerly chowing down on the burger in his hands.

Sam fought an eye roll. It was far from the first time it had happened, and who could blame them? Charlie had really grown into his features. The once awkward set of his jaw had morphed into a sharp jawline that Sam sometimes wondered if he could cut someone with it if he wasn't careful. It was barely hidden by the thick five o'clock shadow that almost never went away. Even down to how that growth spurt he hit when they were kids had made him more like an NFL linebacker than the gangly-limbed child he once was.

Yeah, Charlie was an attractive guy, so she couldn't blame those girls for staring.

She just hated the light burning sensation in her chest whenever it happened.

"Oh, by the way," she said, "my phone number changed again. I'll text you the new number in a bit."

Charlie scrunched his eyebrows as he swallowed. "Why'd you change your number again? Isn't this like the third time you've changed it recently?"

"I've just been indecisive about the phone service I wanted to stick with, and they keep making me change my number every time I go to a new provider. Now, tell me about your conference. How was it?" she asked quickly before he questioned her.

He shrugged, the muscles of his shoulder rising enough that it raised the sleeves of his T-shirt and deposited it further up his arm. The light and breezy material was a stark contrast to the muscles that laid underneath.

Damn, she really needed to take him up on going to the gym.

"It was alright," he said with an absent wave of his hand as he shoved his phone back in his pocket. "It was mostly a bunch of presentations on earnings and projections, though I did manage to sneak into the table discussion they were having on some of the new technology they want us to try out next quarter."

"Anything that interested you?" Sam shoved another handful of fries into her mouth.

Charlie, having taken an enormous bite from his burger, held up a finger as he chewed, causing her to laugh. A laugh that was quickly cut off when she felt her phone vibrate in her pocket.

She froze for a moment before pulling it out long enough to see a new text message appear on the screen. It was from another unknown number, so she immediately silenced her notifications and shoved it back into her pocket before she could see the content.

She knew who it likely was but didn't want to deal with that right now.

Charlie shrugged again, thankfully not seeing the exchange. "Not particularly, but I work in the lab most of the time, so I'll only see the implementation of these things. I should probably at least be familiar with them."

She swallowed down a few gulps of her drink before continuing. "That makes sense. Did you do anything else while you were out there?"

"Not really," Charlie answered. "I went to eat with a few of the other guys at some of the restaurants at our hotel. It was a packed schedule, so we didn't get to sneak out much."

"You didn't check out that book convention you mentioned before?"

He shook his head. "Nah, any time someone tried to sneak away, one of the managers would drag us back unfortunately."

Charlie's curiosity about her work never seemed to diminish, despite the years it had been since she'd published that first book. It was understandable given the disparity between their professions—a clash of creativity versus practicality. Her, the novelist, and him, the computer engineer. Yet his interest extended beyond the boundaries of careers and even went beyond their friendship.

A dedicated reader himself, Charlie devoured mystery novels like his life depended on it, which only *happened* to include the ones she'd written. At least according to him.

"I'm sorry, Charlie, I know you were looking forward to it," Sam said earnestly, seeing the disappointment flash in his eyes, an emotion that betrayed his smile.

"Well, I wasn't there with who I would've wanted to go

with, so it's no big deal," he replied, throwing a wink at her. "Anyway, are you going to tell me about whatever it is going on with your book stuff, or am I gonna have to drag it out of you?"

Sam gestured with her hand as she quickly chewed. "I have a loose idea of something that I want to start working on, though I still don't know the plot or anything like that. It's completely different from what I'm used to writing, so it'll definitely be a fun challenge."

Charlie chuckled. "I'm waiting with bated breath."

"I've decided to write my first *smut* novel," she announced, waggling her eyebrows for dramatic effect but making sure she kept her volume down, so the people around them didn't overhear.

Charlie raised a thick brow at her. "Very nice, MacMillian. Sex sells. Have you ever written anything like that before?"

She shrugged her shoulders. "Well, no. Angel and I brainstormed a few different genres I could try, and when she suggested a smutty romance novel, it just sort of clicked."

"Question, does watching porn count as research for something like that?"

Sam buried her face in her hands, peeking through her fingers to see Charlie watching her with amusement, those dimples of his on full display with that cocky smile of his. "Oh my God, you are such a *guy.*"

CHAPTER 5

CHARLIE

*C*harlie absolutely wasn't going to think about the fact that Sam was going to write a romance novel, a *smutty* romance novel. Nope, he was definitely not going to think about that today.

Except… he was.

It was *all* he could think about.

Imagining her sitting in that cafe, innocently typing away as she wrote out some explicitly sexual scene, had him shifting in his seat. She read romance novels in front of him all the time. It wasn't as if this was a brand-new fact. It was one of her favorite things to read whenever they hung out at either of their apartments. He'd read whatever latest mystery had just come out, and she'd be nose deep in some romance.

He remembered a few years before, when he'd picked up the book she'd been reading after she'd run to the bathroom. Mostly out of curiosity, as it wasn't a genre he typically read, but also because of how she'd practically kicked her legs out and giggled as she read.

But, as they say, curiosity killed the cat.

He'd had to excuse himself to the bathroom immediately

afterwards to hide how red his face was from what he read on the page. The thought that she'd been sitting there next to him so innocently but was actually reading something like *that*, possibly getting all hot and bothered by it, so close to him… Yeah, he'd had to cool off for a bit afterwards.

So, he knew exactly what kinds of things Sam would be writing about. It shouldn't bother him. If it were anyone else *but* her writing it, he didn't think it *would* affect him nearly as much.

Charlie wasn't sure of the day he knew for certain that he was head over heels in love with his best friend. For all he knew, it was the day that this freckle-faced redhead flashed a brace-filled smile at him on the day that they met. But it was long enough now that he'd gotten *very* good about concealing that fact.

And aside from a moment or two, like the incident with the book, topics of a more sexual nature just weren't things they really talked about. So, it wasn't exactly as if it were something he had to be constantly on the offensive for.

Probably for the best, in Charlie's case at least.

"Sam is off limits, you hear me?" The words echoed in Charlie's memory—his mother's, about a week after Sam's parents' funeral. *"That girl has been through enough. She doesn't need you three jackals causing her any trouble."*

If only his mother really knew what a pickle she'd put him in, maybe then she wouldn't have enforced that stupid rule. He couldn't blame her; it made sense with a bunch of hormonal boys running around the house. But still… if he hadn't waited so long to be out from under that, maybe then things would be different…

A vibration shook his phone as it teetered precariously on the edge of his office desk. His mother's caller ID flashed on the screen of her incoming call, but Charlie let it ring. He was still a bit sore after their last conversation. He'd call her back like he always did. This time of year just made him more sensitive with his family.

The phone stopped vibrating, but not more than a few seconds later, incoming texts lit up the screen.

Hey sweetie

I know you're probably ignoring me right now, and that's fine.

I just want you to know I love you — Mom

Charlie rubbed his forehead. He couldn't bring himself to respond right now.

This time of year always managed to sneak up on him, no matter how much he tried to prepare for it. They say time heals, but it still felt just as raw as it had all those years ago.

To distract himself from the uncomfortable emotions starting to rise, he turned his attention back to his computer screen. Or at least, he tried to.

The glare that had made his mind space out in the first place still glowed against the backdrop of the contrasting black coding screen behind it. It was nearly the end of the work day, so Charlie wasn't sure whether it was worth even fighting. If push came to shove, he could always finish up on his laptop back at his apartment.

Once he made it to the elevator, managing to skirt the managers successfully once again, he pulled his phone out to shoot a quick text to Sam. He was about to press send when he stopped, glancing at the old number still displayed at the top. That's right, she'd given him her newest phone number when they were at dinner. He clicked to switch it to the correct one before pressing send.

It was odd that she had changed her number so many times this year. She'd claimed it was about changing service providers, which might've made sense the *first* time she'd switched. She was now on the third new number this year, and something about it just… didn't sit right with him. He couldn't put his finger on exactly why, but something about it felt off.

Charlie just hoped that her car would get out of the shop soon, so he wouldn't have to worry about her on that damned bus all the time. It had been there for so long at this point, though, that he wasn't sure she'd ever get it back. What could possibly be wrong with it for it to stay there that long, he had no idea. At this point, Charlie would happily just buy her another damned car if it meant she was safe.

That's all he cared about really. As long as she was safe and happy, everything else be damned.

He tried to shake it from his mind as he slammed his car door behind him and turned the key in the ignition. The SUV hummed to life, the vibration of the engine somehow soothing him as his hands gripped the steering wheel. The music he'd played on the way to work that morning blasted through the speakers at full volume, which Charlie normally would have scrambled to lower, but today, he let it go. At least this way, the loud music might drown out all the noise in his head.

The rough stubble spreading out across his chin scratched roughly against his hand as he rubbed it, trying to shake the feeling of unease sneaking in. He was probably overreacting like he usually did. It didn't help that he was on edge more than he usually was because of his family, so he tried to tuck those worries about Sam away. She was fiercely independent, always had been, but he hoped, at least, that if something was going on, she would tell him.

She was still his best friend, after all.

As he pulled into his usual spot in his apartment complex's garage, his phone vibrated with a few more notifications. He didn't need to look to know they were from his mother—the string of vibrating notifications nearly causing his phone to fall from where he'd perched it precariously.

His head slumped back against the headrest. He'd have to figure out what to do about the charity at some point. Despite his argument with his mom, he knew he'd eventually cave in and go.

He just really needed to think of a way to get out of the bachelor auction.

She'd said that if any of them brought a date, she wouldn't make them participate. He wasn't seeing anyone at the moment, so he'd have to come up with something if it meant he wouldn't have to be paraded around like fresh meat at the butchers.

 But he wasn't going to stress out about that right now.

Instead of heading straight home, he decided that he would stop by the apartment gym. Maybe then he could work off some of the unease and frustration from the day there.

CHAPTER 6

SAM

*A*s Sam settled into her seat the following morning, she finally felt ready to get started with her book.

She started thumbing through the pages of her notepad, carefully scanning each page for any of the hundreds of ideas she'd jotted down there over the years. None of them were wordy or robust, no paragraphs detailing a play-by-play of what she'd been thinking, merely a few words strung together in an attempt to convey what she meant. To anyone else, it likely wouldn't make a lick of sense.

She figured, however, that by process of elimination, she could narrow down to at least one storyline that would work. She'd already started striking out any redundant storylines to what she'd already written, nixed nonsensical verbiage that likely had stemmed from some vivid dream she'd had that, in the moment, had made complete sense but no longer seemed to even be written in the same language, and axed any ideas that she didn't think would work well as a romance.

In total, she had six ideas left to mull over.

She'd arrived just after the coffee shop doors had opened, even earlier than her usual arrival time there, in hopes that she'd pick an idea and get started working on a rough outline to present to Angel when she got back from her trip.

But unfortunately, her mind kept drifting back to those text messages.

A groan rumbled through her. Knowing how much work she had to do, she wished more than anything that she could just not think about that and go about her day.

After she'd gotten back from dinner with Charlie last night, she finally had to scroll through a string of texts, all from different numbers.

She had taken screenshots of all the texts saved off to the side, in the little folder she'd created when this whole disaster started.

The cop she'd spoken to last, though less than helpful in most senses of the word, had at least given her his phone number in case things escalated. She hoped more than anything that she wouldn't have to use it, but that folder with *his* name plastered on the front of it was starting to grow thicker by the day.

She attempted to return her thoughts back to her mission at hand. Review notes, pick an idea, start on an outline. In that order.

The cup of hot coffee, another deviation from her usual iced latte, was perched off to the side—something to warm her up despite the dreary weather outside as rain continued to tap against the nearby window. The dull roar of nearby passing cars as they splashed through the forming puddles reverberated through the quiet space around her.

The perfect kind of atmosphere for a writer, if Sam had to voice her opinion on the matter. Sure, she could always write in her apartment. It was one of the biggest perks of not having a nine-to-five to rush to. She could write from wherever she wanted to.

The problem was, as she discovered pretty early on, that she worked best with some structure to her day. Leaving her to her own devices often ended up in long stints in bed, watching Netflix.

It had taken some practice, but she'd managed to create her own little schedule that suited her needs quite nicely. She got ready, walked to the Oak House to grab her morning coffee, and set up shop at whatever table was free.

Damn it, her mind had drifted again.

She blinked the tiredness from her eyes and flipped the page. Down near the bottom of the page, she came upon an idea that finally excited her. The story could be fairly simplistic without sacrificing a good plot. There were an endless number of subplots that could be added to create further depth to the characters without it feeling forced. And, naturally, there were ample opportunities for spicy scenes— something she looked forward to just because she'd never actually *written* anything like that before.

It was perfect.

Her debut smutty romance.

She began formulating a to-do list and snatched her laptop from her bag. First important milestone: an outline. It wouldn't need to be nearly as intricate or detailed as her other books had required, but it would definitely help her to plan things out.

Her fingers hovered over the keyboard as another thought suddenly occurred to her, giving her pause.

What in the hell did she know about *real* romance?

Hell, it had been literal years since the last time she'd had sex with anyone.

Sam couldn't even remember the last time she'd even been on a date with anyone. Well, beyond the one she went on a few months ago. And given she knew exactly how *that* situation was going, she wasn't sure she was an authority in the romance realm.

Sure, she knew what she liked when she was *reading* a romance, but this was different. She was the *writer* now. She was the one who would have to come up with the romantic situations, the intimacy, the *spice*. What the hell did she have to use as reference material?

The world was at her fingertips, but she lacked the ink to form the words on the page.

She slumped in her seat, already feeling defeated, as her head fell back against the headrest. Why hadn't she thought about this before? Was the chance of trying something completely new so tempting that she'd overlooked this glaringly obvious roadblock? Hell, Angel had teased her about it with the horror-genre comment. Why hadn't that been a red flag that this plan was doomed to fail?

Yeah, this was going to put a huge damper on things. How could she possibly write something with a believable and compelling romance if she hadn't the faintest idea what that would entail in real life?

Calling Angel to back out of this was extremely tempting. She could always go back to the drawing board and think of something else, right?

She pulled up the calendar on her laptop to see if she could schedule a call but quickly remembered that Angel was already out of her office—likely halfway across the world already.

What were the odds Angel *hadn't* already hinted at this idea to her publisher?

Knowing her? Less than likely.

Fuck, this was bad.

Alright, she could handle this. She'd dealt with worse

situations than this, so she could figure this out. She just needed to do some research, that was all.

Then again… there was already a high probability that she was on some FBI watchlist for her browser history when she was working on her murder mysteries, but how the hell could she *research* romance?

No, that wouldn't work. Maybe some more… hands-on experience would be the way to go? A hook-up could give her the experience she would need? Something fleeting and casual, where they went their separate ways afterwards? She could admit she wasn't the biggest fan of the idea, but it could work in a pinch.

Yet the more she chewed on the thought, the less appealing it became.

The only sexual encounter she'd ever had was a one-night stand back in college, and it hadn't exactly been anything that she'd write home about. She'd been drunk and feeling particularly in her feelings about a *certain* individual, who she definitely shouldn't still be having feelings for at this point, so she wasn't sure if she would be thrilled to try that out again. If it hadn't worked then to get rid of her feelings, it likely wouldn't work now.

No, she concluded after a few moments, that wouldn't work.

She could try actually dating someone. She had never tried dating apps before, but she could try going out with someone there?

No, she really didn't like that idea either. Not only did she not have the kind of time it would take to develop an entire-ass relationship right now, but she also wasn't sure how comfortable she'd be able to get with someone if they were only going to meet up a few times at most.

Besides, it wouldn't be fair to them knowing that it

wouldn't work out in the long run. There was only one person she'd ever truly had feelings for, so it felt unfair to put someone else through that.

And after the last real date she'd been on, which she was still dealing with the consequences of, she wasn't too sure she wanted to put herself through that all over again and risk the same outcome.

She was jolted from her train of thought by a large hand snapping in front of her face, causing her to jump in her seat. She blinked a few times and glanced up to see Charlie standing there in front of her, seeming more than amused by the absent look on her face.

"You alright?" he asked, a chuckle in his voice as he lowered himself into the seat opposite hers.

"What are you doing here? I thought you were in the office today," she asked defensively as she all but slammed her laptop shut.

"Easy, tiger." He laughed. "I thought I'd work remotely today and join you, if that's alright?"

Sam relaxed her shoulders and took a deep breath before responding. "Yeah, of course. Sorry."

"Are you okay?" he asked, shoving his laptop bag to the side and leaning forward on his elbows toward her.

It forced her to look up at him, leaning toward her with a curious quirk of his eyebrow. She was reminded once again of the rain outside, seeing that his hair was damp, causing it to appear darker than usual. Absentmindedly, she grabbed some of the napkins near her and pushed them toward him, so he could dry off.

"Yeah, I'm fine. I was just deep in thought."

A twinge of embarrassment flickered through her body as her mind returned to her previous train of thought.

She had never been ashamed by her lack of experience,

nor had it been a particularly pressing issue. She was perfectly happy with her life, her friends, her career, and dating someone hadn't ever been something she'd been that interested in. It was only at Angel's insistence that she at least tried to go on a date to get out there.

It was the only reason she'd gone on that stupid fucking date months ago.

All that said, this was definitely going to put a hindrance on writing a whole book with a convincing romance.

"What are you thinking about so much? I feel like you left the building already, and I just got here," Charlie said, waving a hand in front of her face.

The beige knit sweater he had on was pushed up to his elbows, which she could have sworn he hadn't been wearing moments ago when he walked in. Eyeing the black jacket slung over the seat next to him, though, she felt a little less crazy as she focused back on him.

"Book stuff," she answered finally.

Charlie nodded as he pursed his lips. "Oh, very fun. Know what your book will be about already?"

She lifted a shoulder in a half-hearted shrug. "Sort of. I have a general idea but need to start working on outlining it and stuff."

Technically, she needed to solve her little research problem first, but he didn't need to know that.

"Let me know when you finish it. I'd love to read it," he said, throwing her a wink. She couldn't help but smile at that, responding by gently kicking his leg underneath the table.

"I didn't take you for a romance reader."

He shrugged. "I'm not usually, but I would if it was yours. That's beside the point. What's going on in that head of yours? Not like you to completely space out like that."

"Really, it's nothing. I just hit a bit of a… roadblock," she said carefully, "and I need to figure it out. Don't worry."

She wasn't sure how else to phrase it, but it only seemed to make him more curious.

"Come on. Tell me!"

When she remained silent, Charlie sighed and propped his elbows on the table again dramatically, flashing her one of those puppy-dog expressions he was notorious for. The one that somehow made his blue eyes stand out even more than usual, like the sun reflecting off the ocean's surface.

Damn him. He was good. "You're getting too good at that, you know."

He grinned. "I've had a few years of practice. Now, spill. What's up?"

"It's just… I came up with this idea to write a *smutty* romance," she said, lowering her voice to a whisper, "but I kind of realized that I don't exactly know much on the subject."

Charlie's eyebrows shot up, as if he hadn't expected that level of honesty. Neither had she, to be fair. It was both a gift and a curse that he was so easy to talk to, so really, he only had himself to blame.

He covered his mouth with his fist to conceal a laugh, only making her regret saying anything at all. "Romance experience?"

"Don't laugh. This is a serious problem! How can I write something that people will enjoy if I've never really gone through any of it myself?"

"You're worried you won't be able to write romance… because you haven't experienced much romance firsthand?"

"Exactly!"

"Hm," he hummed. "That is an interesting problem to have."

"You *asked*! Don't patronize me."

Charlie held up his hands defensively. "I'm not; don't worry. I thought you read a lot of romances, though? Shouldn't you be an expert by now?"

She jutted her chin out at him at the comment, earning a laugh from him. The sound was warm and familiar enough that it sent a trill of heat up her spine. "I do, from time to time, but it's different *reading* about romance and *writing* it. I need to do research."

"Research? You want to research... romance?" he asked incredulously.

"Yes, research," she hissed. "See? Now I wish I hadn't said anything. Go back to work if you're just going to tease me. I have a lot to figure out."

Charlie laughed, reaching across the table and rustling her hair before she smacked his hand away. "Oh, come on. Don't look so stressed."

"How can I not be? I've already talked to Angel about it, which means she's *definitely* already mentioned it to my publisher. So, even if she hasn't formally proposed anything to them, they already know that this is the direction I'm going, so it'll be nearly impossible to back out now."

He shrugged. "So? Just tell them you decided to go in a different direction if you're not feeling up to it."

She closed her eyes to take another deep breath. She'd already word vomited more than she needed to with him. The last thing she needed was to make it worse. Angel was the only one who knew about the crunch she was under with her contract, and she didn't need Charlie worrying like he always did.

"You know how I get when I make up my mind," she said instead. "I've got it stuck in my head to write this book now. And you know how much research I've done for some of my other books. So, it would make sense that I'd need to do the same here, right?"

"I guess so, but how does one do research on something like romance?"

She threw her hands up in frustration. "I don't know. That's what I'm trying to figure out! I need to work with someone who is willing to go out with me and show me what dating is like right now without making it weird or expecting anything out of it. Like, how on earth am I supposed to propose that to some random guy? Like, 'Hey, I need experience for a book I'm writing. Are you open to dating me for a bit until I'm done, and then we can part ways for eternity?' Not to mention the research I need to do for the more physical aspects of a relationship—for the spicier scenes—like, what am I supposed to do?"

Charlie blinked a few times at her, and it was then that she realized that, once again, she needed to button her lip. "You're serious?"

She tried to ignore the heat that suddenly flamed in her cheeks at the odd look he was giving her. It wasn't one that said he was wondering whether she'd grown another head or if he needed to check her into the nearest mental institution like she might've expected. But she couldn't quite place exactly what it was.

"Yeah, so?" she asked, a little defensiveness seeping into her tone. "You got any better ideas?"

CHAPTER 7

CHARLIE

cross the table, Charlie's gaze was fixed on Sam, his mouth slightly open as he struggled to find something, *anything*, to say. In all the years he'd known her, all the years she'd been a writer, this was definitely the first time any of her research endeavors had caught him off guard like this.

Over the years, there were few topics that they hadn't discussed, as any close friends would. However, romance had remained relatively untouched between them.

And there were certainly reasons for that, at least on his end.

"Seems a bit extreme for a romance novel," he said, hoping for a teasing tone to mask the hint of strain in his voice.

She dramatically tossed her hands up once more. "Well, it's not like I have a lot of options right now. But wouldn't it be, like, any dude's dream for a girl to have him take her out, no strings attached?"

"And if they expected sex in return for their efforts?" he asked.

She'd accuse him of being overprotective again. And he

couldn't deny it—he definitely was. But the thought of her meeting up with some stranger online to do *romantic* research of any kind left a bad taste in his mouth. And for more than one reason.

Her doing that kind of research with *anybody* caused his chest to burn uncomfortably.

Her eyes didn't meet his. "It's not like we're kids anymore. If I want to have sex, then I'll have sex. If not, I'll tell them to piss off. Seems simple enough to me. Besides, I want to focus on the romance aspect first before I even *touch* the sex stuff. If I even consider that with someone… Gotta learn to crawl before I run and all that."

Charlie nodded thoughtfully, as any good friend would in this situation. What she said did make sense, albeit in that unique, authorly way of hers that sometimes escaped him. She was trying to write a novel, after all. She always did a lot of research when she was writing anything. That was just how she was—meticulous, methodical, leaving no stone unturned in her quest to make sure every piece of the puzzle fit together perfectly.

Though, he didn't like that analogy for this particular novel.

She often teased him that he only read her books because they were friends, but it was only a small part of it. She never believed him whenever he told her that she was just *that* good. He'd devour every page of her books even if he had no idea who she was.

So, naturally, it made complete sense that she'd want to do research, to fill the blanks of her own knowledge. Still, he couldn't shake the feeling that, knowing her, she didn't fully grasp the complications of what she would be getting herself into. There was a vast difference between traveling to visit the city she was writing about, or digging through the local library's treasure trove of historical documents, and a living, breathing man.

"Are we including psychopaths in your research, or are we hoping for a surprise?" he asked.

Her lips stretched thin at the thought. "Hadn't thought of that."

She let out a resigned sigh, a faint hiss escaping her lips like a balloon deflating after a lackluster birthday party. "Then what am I gonna do, Charlie? My options are limited. I just need help figuring out romance stuff. How can I possibly create a believable love story if I've never even been on a proper date?"

This woman was going to kill him.

He allowed a moment of silence to linger between them, both lost in thought.

What she needed was a friend, someone she could trust without fear of being taken advantage of. Someone who would support her through this without making her feel weird in the process, and there was only one person he trusted to do the job.

"Then let me help you."

It was the perfect solution, to him at least. She could safely conduct whatever research she needed to without worry, and he got to spend time with his best friend.

He knew from past experience that she didn't like him in that way, and it wasn't exactly like he hadn't fantasized about how he would want to romance Samantha MacMillian since the day he'd met her. So, as long as he could muster the strength to shove his own feelings aside, it would be a walk in the park.

She blinked a few times, attempting to hide the surprise that flickered in her eyes. "What?"

"What? Wouldn't it make more sense to hang out with

someone you already know as opposed to getting to know some stranger? You said so yourself—you need someone who isn't going to be weird about it. Who better than me?"

"Are you serious?"

He'd never been more serious about anything in his life.

He shrugged. "Why not? I'm your best friend, aren't I? Besides Angel at least."

"Of course you are, but that's exactly it, you're my best friend. Wouldn't it be weird?" she asked.

"You already are weird," he teased, loving the way her ensuing laugh lit up her face. It was easy to see how much it eased the tension that had been building there all morning. "Look, it won't be awkward. It'd probably be a lot easier doing this with someone who knows the whole situation, who knows *you*, and wants to help, right? Besides, I don't like the idea of some guy getting a whiff of what you're doing and taking advantage, that's all."

Who else could serve as a human battering ram should the occasion call for it?

Sam nibbled on her lower lip. "I don't know, Charlie... I could easily make you feel really uncomfortable with something like this."

"I can assure you that there is little chaos you could cause that would make me uncomfortable. Besides, you need the experience, right? I'm available for hire."

The light caught the flecks of gold centered around the middle of her irises as she laughed, like sunlight chasing the horizon across an endless meadow of rolling green hills. "For hire? We went from a friend helping a friend to hiring myself my own Pretty Woman?"

Charlie laughed. "I get Julia Roberts level? Wow, I'm honored."

She pursed her lips at him, studying him for a moment. "I don't know. I might've been a little generous."

"No, no, you can't take it back now. I'm gonna put that on my business card from now on."

"You're impossible. But I don't know, Charlie, this would be a lot to ask of you. This isn't just helping me comb through some reference textbooks. This would be... I don't even know what to call what this would be," she said slowly, as if searching for the correct term.

Charlie wasn't sure of what the proper term for what they were discussing would be, but he knew of a term he knew she would find interesting. At least if her ramblings of some of the romances she'd tried to explain to him were any indication.

"Fake dating?"

"Fake dating," she repeated, scrunching her nose as if she were trying to taste how the words sounded while she mulled it over. "Yeah, I guess it would be, essentially. We'd need to go out on dates and do couple-ish things, so I can add them to my notes, but we wouldn't actually be dating..."

"See? It could work," he confirmed with a smile.

She shook her head, leaning forward to lower her volume. As she did, the smell of soft florals tickled his nose from her perfume. "The going on dates stuff, maybe, but the more... *physical aspects* of dating would be something I'd have to explore to a degree as well. And that's the part I don't know if you'd be comfortable with."

Charlie fought down the shiver that ran down his spine at the thought.

"Let's take it one step at a time, then. See what we're both comfortable with. The worst that happens is that you feel weird, decide to scrap the idea, and go back to the drawing board, right?"

She stared down at the table momentarily, lost in thought, before looking back up to meet his gaze. "I don't know… I'd feel bad asking you to do all of that just for some stupid book thing of mine. It's a lot to ask *in general.*"

It was almost hilarious because Charlie knew, with alarming certainty, that he would do just about anything she asked of him.

But she was stubborn, especially when it came to asking *anyone* for help, let alone him.

"Tell you what. I have an idea," he proposed, leaning further forward onto the table between them. "We can make it an exchange. I help you, you help me. We both get something out of this. That way you don't feel so bad about me helping you out."

She raised an eyebrow but leaned in, mirroring him as he could see the curiosity pique. "Okay, I'm listening."

"You know that charity gala my parents are throwing?"

She nodded. "Yeah, your mom mentioned it the last time I talked to her on the phone."

"Yeah, well, as part of it, she wants me and my brothers to join the little *bachelor* auction that they'll be doing."

Sam laughed, attempting to cover it by throwing her hand over her mouth, but failed miserably. "You're joking."

"I wish I was, but she said that if I had a *date* with me, she wouldn't force me to participate."

Sam's face lit up. "So, if I went with you as your date…"

"Then I don't have to be auctioned off like cattle," Charlie finished, nodding.

She giggled and smiled. "It's for a good cause at least?"

He frowned, lowering his voice a bit. "It is, but you know why I would prefer to just be left alone, *especially* for that night."

He didn't add more, knowing that she of all people would

understand what he meant. "So," he prompted, her softened smile promising, "what do you say?"

"When is it?"

"Three months."

She was on the precipice of saying yes. He could see the word practically forming on her lips, but she held off. Her resolve was wearing down with each passing second. He went in for the kill, so to speak.

"Samantha MacMillian, will you fake date me?" Charlie asked, offering his hand in what he hoped was a grand-looking gesture.

She laughed, slowly reaching forward, taking his hand with hers, and shaking it. "I will."

CHAPTER 8

SAM

Sam eased onto her bed, gazing up at the ceiling.

She would explore the contents of her notepad again in the morning, when she had more energy, but for tonight, she would just let her imagination take hold. If anything came up, she could always add it to the list. It had always been one of the easiest methods for her to come up with story ideas anyway, so she didn't think a romance would be that much different.

When another idea happened to pop in to her head, she swiftly sat up, reaching for her notepad on the bedside table to jot down a few simplistic notes.

It hadn't been that long since she'd gotten back to her place after dinner with Charlie, leaving the evening young for her to kick back and relax for the remainder of the night.

It had been a particularly interesting encounter on the bus with *the sniffer*—as Charlie had not-so-affectionately nick-named him—so he refused to let her take the bus home at night whenever they went out for dinner. It had stirred up more than one argument in the past whenever Sam tried to agree on the condition that she gave him money for gas, which he steadily refused every time. But Charlie was persistent when it came to this kind of thing.

So, tonight was no different. Logically, she'd known it would make no sense and that it would be stupid to refuse him since they lived only a few floors apart from one another, but the little voice in the back of her mind tried to argue. And unless she wanted to tell Charlie the *real* reason why she was hesitant to get another car, she knew she needed to just suck it up and accept the help when he offered it.

If it were anyone else that acted the way he did, whenever he had any inkling that trouble was afoot, she would tell them to stick it where the sun doesn't shine. She'd been taking care of herself since she was young, so she didn't need anyone trying to baby her now.

But with Charlie, it was different.

Deep down, she knew that he was only trying to look out for her. She was his best friend too. If the roles were reversed, she'd be the same way. But, at the same time, it was that very reason why there were certain parts of her life she couldn't share with anyone right now.

Even Charlie…

Especially Charlie.

Fully engaged with the most recent idea she'd come up with, reality rang to life when her phone chimed next to her. She picked it up and glanced at the caller ID, suppressing a groan as she did.

The fact that her aunt even bothered to call at all usually was signal enough that she probably needed something.

Part of her wanted to ignore it, let it go to voicemail for her to deal with later. She had been in such a good mood with everything else that she hated to spoil it, but she knew she would have to deal with her at *some* point. Her aunt could be very persistent when she needed something, and so, she decided to get it over with.

She adjusted her position on the bed, sitting up and leaning back against the wall to make herself more comfortable.

"Hey, Aunt Emily," she said, trying to force some enthusiasm into her voice but failing.

"Hello Samantha," Her aunt chirped happily on the other end, her name fully enunciated with an over-exaggerated 'uh' sound at the end. The word foreign on her aunt's tongue, as if it tasted bitter with the lack of use. Then again, with how often they spoke these days, it wasn't too surprising. "I'm just calling to check in and see how you're doing. I was talking to someone the other day about that last book you wrote… Oh, what was it? That one you published last year… I think it was a mystery or something, right?"

Sam blinked a few times, surprised. "It was the last book in my mystery series, yes."

"Ah, that's the one! Anyway, we were talking about that, and I realized I hadn't talked to you in a while. How are you doing? I hope you're well."

"I'm a little surprised you were talking about my books at all… But I'm doing alright. How about you?"

"Oh, we're doing just splendidly! Thanks for asking. And why wouldn't we talk about your books, dear?" her aunt hummed excitedly on the other end.

Sam blinked a few times. Her books? *Dear*? Okay, something was definitely up.

"Well, considering how our last conversation on my work went…" Sam started, trailing off at the end as the memory of that conversation already had heat prickling her skin. It had been a few years *since* that conversation, but even remembering it was enough to make her want to hang up.

Her aunt laughed, somehow sounding posh, as if she were trying to embody a golf clap in the sound. "Oh, that was so long ago I'm surprised you even remember that."

"It was a pretty memorable one considering that you told me to never bring the topic up again because you didn't want to be reminded of... Oh, how was it that you put it...?" Sam mulled the memory around in her mind for a moment before finding the exact words. "Oh, that's right. You didn't want to be reminded that the niece you *practically raised* was chasing such a pipe dream, and you said that I needed to get a real job if I didn't want to end up on the streets, whoring myself out for rent."

"Oh, dear, you exaggerate, and don't be so crass. You know how much I hate it when you use bad language like that."

It was the ultimate irony that her own words were considered *bad language*, but Sam decided against fighting her on it. She'd never win that debate anyway.

"We haven't spoken in months, Aunt Emily. What do you want? You never call me these days unless you need me to do something."

The dissatisfied click of her aunt's tongue felt momentarily satisfying before she spoke. "Did my sister not teach you *any* manners before she died? How dare you speak to me that way!"

It felt like a punch in the gut, one that consistently subdued her, even when she didn't mean for it to. It was more effective than a slap across the face.

"Sorry."

"That's better. You might have only been six when they died, but I *know* my sister taught you better than to talk me that way. I know *I* taught you better than that," Aunt Emily snapped. "Took you in when no one else would, sheltered you, put a roof over your head, made sure you had the *best* education. And what did you do with it? Wasted it on an *English* degree."

There's the Aunt Emily she lived with for all those years. It was no wonder she spent most of her time over at Charlie's house growing up.

Her aunt continued, the words tumbling unrestrained out of her mouth. "To think that Tommy ever looked up to you and wanted to be anything like his older cousin is beyond me, with how you've turned out."

Yes, she wanted to say, what an angel that menace of a cousin was. The one who reveled in the fact that he could do no wrong, while anything that ever *did* go wrong at home instantly became *her* fault.

A fact he eagerly exploited more than once.

The word vomit didn't stop there as her aunt simply took a quick breath and continued. "So ungrateful for everything we've ever given you and you…"

Sam lifted the phone away from her ear and held it out, letting her aunt continue with her rant as she placed the phone on the nightstand and went to grab the cup of water she'd placed there earlier.

She took a couple of healthy sips to satiate her throat, which had started to feel like the Sahara desert.

Once her throat didn't feel like it was constricting in on itself, she picked the phone back up. Her aunt was continuing to rant on the other end until Sam finally let out a heavy sigh.

"Are you finished?"

Her aunt paused mid-sentence, and the sound that reverberated from the other end of the phone could only be described as pure disgust. "You haven't changed one bit!

Here I was hoping to have a civilized conversation with my niece and ask to help her *participate* in something exciting with the family, but I guess I was just dreaming that you would ever be anything but nasty about it."

Sam sank back into her spot. Ah, there it is. There was a reason for the call, but the reins on Sam's own temper felt pulled taut as she steadied herself to take a deep breath in. If there had been anything she'd learned over the years, it was that engaging in a screaming match with her aunt wouldn't accomplish anything other than ruining her day.

"After you've just spent however long it's been insulting me? Forgive me if I'm not leaping with joy."

"What an ungrateful, useless—" Her aunt hissed before the line went dead.

Rain clouds veiled the setting sun, getting rid of the little light that had been warming her apartment. A chill settled through her limbs, brought on both by the encroaching storm and the dread stirred up by her conversation.

It wouldn't be the last time she heard from Aunt Emily, especially if she actually did need something.

Forcing the thoughts from her mind, she flicked on the lamp next to her bed to prevent being totally swallowed up by the darkness.

Despite the outrageously expensive rent, she loved her little one-bedroom apartment. The floor-to-ceiling windows lining the outer wall captured the sunlight at the perfect angle, allowing swaths of natural light into the space. Not to mention the spectacular view of downtown Durham. The merging of modern high-rise buildings bleeding into the backdrop of the rustic brick buildings from a time past was uniquely beautiful in a way that always made her glad that she lived there.

Her stomach grumbled again, hunger rearing its head

once more even after the meal earlier that evening. She sat up and walked over to search the contents of her refrigerator, making a mental note as she did that she needed to grab some groceries soon.

She knew exactly what her stomach was craving at this time of day, her mouth watering when her eyes landed on the bowl of strawberries sitting off to the side. Still bright and inviting despite having sat in there for a few days.

There would never be a time that Sam would tire of strawberries. In her opinion, they were the superior fruit of choice by a mile. Juicy and perfectly plump, the best blend of a sharp citrus punch and a delicate sweetness that was hard to find in other foods.

Her collection of strawberry-inspired items had grown over the years, something she'd started back when she was a child. Though it had taken a hiatus in her time living with her aunt's family, her collection had grown quite extensive at this point, and she always felt like she was on the hunt for more.

She eagerly pulled the bowl out of the fridge and grabbed the can of whipped cream from the side door, another staple that she ensured she had in reserves.

The bitter sweetness of the strawberry combined with the artificially sweetened cream. Natural deliciousness that took weeks to cultivate and grow smothered in goo with more fake chemicals in it than she cared to think about. The irony.

After double checking to make sure she locked her front door, a habit she'd recently developed, she settled back into the comfort of her bed, placing the bowl in her lap and squirting a healthy portion of cream into the bowl. She scooped up the first strawberry she laid eyes on and let her teeth sink into the sweet delight. Fighting a moan of pure delight as the gush of flavor hit her tongue.

Without thinking, she grabbed her phone with her free

hand and scrolled through to one of her recent chats with Charlie. Her thumbs tapped at the keys as she took another bite of strawberry.

> Aunt called today. Celebrating with a bowl of strawberries and cream

She tossed the phone back onto the bed, not expecting to hear back until later. Charlie had his gym bag tucked away in his car for after work, so she figured he'd be busy for a while longer until a sudden notification alert dinged her attention back to her phone.

Someone needs to put that woman on a leash

Preferably with a muzzle

Sam smiled down at her phone.

> If my uncle had the balls to, I think he would, but she's had him on a leash of his own for far too many years to start now

You alright?

The pattern felt familiar at this point, unfortunately. Phone call with her aunt, as no one else in her family bothered to talk to her at this point, bowl of strawberries, text Charlie or Angel for a sanity check, rinse and repeat.

> I will be after I demolish this bowl of strawberries

I can beat 'em up for you if you want?

Sam laughed wryly, feebly attempting to prevent herself from spitting the bite of strawberry out of her mouth.

No physical violence required at this time

The immediate offer for violence should be concerning but I'm not complaining

You know me, all bark and no bite

Ok, mostly bark, some bite

That aside though, you sure you're ok?

Yeah, you just know how she can get under my skin when she starts ranting

The fact that Charlie's parents had a Christmas stocking for her from how much time she spent at their house, just to avoid being around her own family, said enough. It didn't hurt that Charlie's mom and her mom had started to become pretty good friends before her death, so she had an open-door policy for Sam that was more appreciated than Sam thought she even knew.

I know, don't sweat whatever she said — you are a much better person than she or that little shit Tommy could ever dream of being

She smiled down at her phone once again, feeling a sense of calm wash over her. She couldn't quite pinpoint exactly how he did it, but Charlie always seemed to know exactly what to say at times like this. Though, the years of practice probably didn't hurt.

Thanks Charlie

Anytime

Are you working from the office tomorrow or remote?

Remote, meet in the coffee shop?

Yep!

My offer for violence still stands, though, if you change your mind?

Your aunt deserves a firm boot up her ass

Knowing her, she'd probably like it

Kinky

❧

"So, I've given our arrangement some thought," Sam announced as she plopped into the seat opposite Charlie's the following morning, "and I think I have a plan."

She'd been up most of the night coming with ideas—to the point that she'd only closed her eyes for a few minutes before her alarm had gone off. But she was too excited for that to bother her today, her mind racing with all the things she was going to write.

When Charlie had knocked on her door, so they could walk to the cafe together, she'd instead yanked him into her apartment and shoved him toward her couch. They had a lot to talk about, and she didn't know if she'd want the people wandering in and out of the coffee shop overhearing them.

Charlie blinked a few times in surprise as he landed on the couch. "Well, good morning to you too."

"Good morning," she said quickly as she grabbed her notepad, "I was up last night working on my outline and…"

"Did you even *get* any sleep?" Charlie interrupted as his eyes narrowed at her, as if the bags under her eyes were large enough to spot from space. "And don't bother lying. I hear the coffee pot brewing."

She'd put the pot on only a few minutes before his arrival, thinking she had more time before they left.

"I was too excited to get much sleep, but that's besides the point—"

"Coffee first. I'm not sure either of us are awake enough for this yet," he interrupted again, moving to stand before she pushed him back down. She hurried into the kitchen to beat him there, with more energy in her system now simply with the promise of caffeine.

While her little coffee pot was nothing compared to the fancy drinks from their favorite shop, she couldn't help but inhale the delightfully bitter smell drifting up from the now-steaming pot. A contented sigh escaped her before she reached for two mugs from the cabinet, laced the handles through her fingers, and grabbed the pot with her free hand.

Charlie yawned from the couch, stretching out as she placed the items on the coffee table in front of him. A hint of his stomach showed as the fabric of his shirt lifted to reveal the sprinkling of hair leading down to his…

She blinked a few times, feeling her face heat as she quickly placed a cup in front of him and poured the liquid into it for him. Turning back quickly, she poured some milk into her own cup, knowing Charlie took his black.

"Alright," Charlie said as she came to sit in the lounge chair opposite him, "what did you want to talk about? You look about ready to bust at the seams."

She shot a frown in his direction as she started flipping through her notepad. "You agreed to help me, so you're gonna have to deal with all that comes with it."

"Is this where I see the writer behind the curtain? I've seen you as you've written your other books, but are you going to pull a Dr. Jekyll and Mr. Hyde on me? One minute, you're your normal self, and the next, you're jumping up on the table, declaring our next adventure?"

Her frown deepened. "You really love to hear yourself make a joke, don't you?"

Charlie grinned. "Come on. That was funny."

Her frown slipped a bit as she fought a smile. "Okay, only a little. But we're officially fake dating, so I need you to take this seriously. I need to explain everything I've been thinking, and then we can set up some ground rules."

"But—" Charlie started but was silenced when she raised her hand up, palm facing him.

"I came up with a rough plot last night that I think will work really nicely as a romance. I'm going to just give a general idea of what I'm thinking for the book, and then we can discuss the nitty-gritty for our end. Now, the plot is gonna revolve around my two main characters meeting in a coffee shop and hitting it off—"

"What do you know, we do that all the time. Done."

She ignored him and continued. "They're going to go their separate ways after exchanging numbers but expect the other to call first, so they go a while without talking. But *then* they're going to both be invited to a mutual friend's wedding that they'll be involved in, and they'll end up being paired together for the wedding..."

Charlie raised an eyebrow at her. "Wedding stuff? Is there someone we know getting married soon to help with that? Or are we taking an impromptu trip to Vegas?"

"Well, no, obviously, I'm just telling you about the story, so you have an idea of what I'm working with and so we can prepare dates and stuff."

"Yeah? Like what?" he asked, leaning forward to take a peek at her notepad.

"I mean a lot of different stuff, but I haven't decided on what activities they're gonna do just yet. I just have a framework of what I want, and I'll fill in the blanks as we go."

"I see," he said, looking a little more amused than she cared for at this time of day.

"I think I'm going to have it be a destination wedding to some tropical island for a couple of weeks, so—"

"I don't know if I can afford a trip to Vegas *and* the Bahamas," Charlie interrupted again. "You're gonna have to pick one."

"Shush! Let me finish!"

He chuckled, grabbing his cup and taking a healthy swig before holding his hands up in the air in defeat. "Sorry. Please continue."

"Anyway," she huffed, "the purpose of it being a destination wedding is that they'll have to be around each other on a regular basis in between wedding stuff. They're gonna be forced to share a room together so that it's forced proximity and all that."

Charlie raised an eyebrow at her, an unexpectedly roguish glint in his eyes that caused her chest to flutter. "Are you suggesting a slumber party, Sam?"

She swallowed as her entire body clenched. How the hell was she *already* struggling with this? No, she had to focus.

She swatted his shoulder with her notepad to deflect.

"That's not what I'm suggesting. Again, if you don't stop interrupting me while I'm explaining everything, we won't get anywhere!"

When he made a zipper motion across his lips, she continued. "I'm still ironing out all the minute details, but all of that was to say that I think I have a plot line that will work, and I've narrowed down a few activities we can do that will help me."

Charlie made an un-zipping motion. "Sounds great, but what does that mean for us fake-dating? And do you want to be around me all the time like your couple? How exactly do we work forced proximity into something like this?"

Sam rolled her eyes. "Well, obviously we can't do that, but we can do other stuff together that a normal couple might do."

"Gotcha," Charlie said, nodding. "I can work with that."

This next part was what Sam was least looking forward to out of fear that this alone would cause him to immediately back out. Not that she'd blame him. "The other part, and this is the part we need to establish right off the bat, is some of the physical stuff."

Charlie quirked an eyebrow up at her. "The *physical* stuff?"

"Yes," she said as she sat forward more and lowered her volume a bit. "If we are, in fact, fake dating right now, we need to establish what boundaries we have. This whole thing is to help me get an idea of how romance is, which is obviously going to involve that kind of stuff, so I need to know what both of our boundaries are. And you have to be completely and *one hundred* percent honest."

Folding his arms across his chest, Charlie nodded. "Alright, that's fair. You first. You're the lead in this. What are you comfortable with?"

Though she knew how Charlie was, she was a bit surprised he was so relaxed about the whole thing. While she had been flustered about this part of the conversation most of the night, and while she had babbled on so much about the *plot* of the book, he seemed very cavalier about the prospect. She wasn't sure if that made her feel more relaxed, as well, or more nervous.

"So, I think things like hugs and regular touching aren't outside the bounds of how we usually are…"

"Right," he agreed.

"…But I think some of the more *romantic* kinds of physical touch, such as cuddling and kissing, are things I'm open to," she said, keeping her eyes on him for any hint of discomfort.

"Okay. I'm open to those as well."

The relief she felt was temporary as she continued, blurting everything out as fast as she could to alleviate the nerves swirling in her gut. "Good. But as I am writing a *smutty* romance novel, eventually I will have to get to the sex scenes for that. I think drawing a hard line at sex itself is where I'm at, but I might be open to other, more… sexual things… as we get further into fake-dating each other. However, I want to discuss that more once we get more comfortable with this."

God, she wished she could just drop dead from the embarrassment that flooded her veins. In addition to everything else she'd worked on that night, building the courage for this exact moment had been what she was preparing for.

She knew that she had to have faith that Charlie would tell her if he genuinely didn't feel comfortable with any of this, even if it meant calling off this whole thing. She trusted him that much at least.

Charlie shifted in his seat, and for a split second she was

terrified she had indeed made him uncomfortable. Immediately preparing to apologize, she ran through the hundreds of things she could say to let him know that backing out now was completely okay and she would figure something else out.

Instead, he surprised her when he smiled and nodded. "I'm open to that as well. You just have to promise that you'll be honest with me, as well, alright? Nothing happens if you don't want it to, regardless of your book stuff. Deal?"

When he extended a hand toward her for a shake, she let out an anxiety-filled laugh, relief wafting out of her in droves.

It was almost embarrassing for her to realize that there was little Charlie could do to her that she'd say no to, but instead she breathed out a sigh of relief and shook his hand.

"Deal." She adjusted herself to alleviate whatever tingling was happening in her body. "Alright. Now one other detail."

"I'm enraptured to hear it."

"Well, I was thinking it would be kind of awkward if we kept *talking* about this little experiment of ours. I want it to be as organic as possible, so it doesn't feel forced, you know what I mean?"

Charlie nodded slowly. "I think, but please elaborate."

"I think we should operate under fight club rules for it."

Charlie raised an eyebrow and laughed. "Fight club rules? I didn't know violence was involved in this."

"I more so meant that *we don't talk about fight club* mentality. I think a similar idea would work here. The more we talk about it, the more 'in our heads' we'll be about it. So, as long as we make sure we're not making the other uncomfortable, we just act as organically as a couple as we can. Think you could handle that?"

He shrugged. "Doesn't sound like a bad idea. Alright, fight club rules."

"Perfect. I was also thinking that it might also be a good idea if we make a trip to the bookstore together after we get done with work today."

He cocked his head to the side with a grin. "The bookstore?"

"Yeah, that way I can pick up a few books with some similar tropes and such that I might want to include. For research."

He laughed, the deep timbre of his voice resonating warmly in the air. "Is this just an excuse to get more books?"

It hadn't been that long, maybe just over a month, since they'd last ventured over to the bookstore. As often as the two of them ran through books, it was a relatively frequent occurrence.

"Would you complain either way?" She laughed.

"Not in the least," he said, folding his arms across his chest and relaxing back into the couch. "I just finished off the book we got the last time we were there. Could always do with more. Besides, if I'm going to be a good fake boyfriend, who am I to turn down a book date with my fake girlfriend?"

Despite the way her stomach flipped at the way he'd said that, she smiled. "You can't; it's mandatory now."

He chuckled. "Fair enough. In the meantime, I think we should plan something else, our first official fake-date so to speak. Do you have plans for Saturday night?"

She thought for a moment before shaking her head. "Not that I know of."

"Perfect. You want to get dinner?"

She pursed her lips. "What'd you have in mind?"

"That little Italian place over in Morrisville? It's a bit on the nicer side without requiring either of us to dress up too much. Figured it'd be a nice spot for a date," he replied.

"That sounds great!"

He grinned, the edges of his mouth crinkling into his dimples. "Cool. Say I pick you up at seven?"

Sam laughed. "Charlie, we live in the same building. How would you be picking me up?"

"Okay, by picking you up, I meant more that I'll come by your apartment, so we can walk to my car together. Jeez, spoilsport."

<h1 style="text-align:center">CHAPTER 9</h1>

<h2 style="text-align:center">CHARLIE</h2>

"What is this one about again?" Charlie asked, finding himself standing in the middle of the romance book section later that day. The book that she had shoved into his hand as she reached for another revealed little other than the shirtless man embracing a scantily clad woman on the front cover. Sam had provided little information as she continued stacking books into the basket that she had grabbed on their way in.

She was on a mission, it seemed, and he was just there for the ride. Though, he wasn't sure he'd have it any other way if it meant she continued looking as positively exuberant as she did now.

Charlie was much more of a mystery reader, with the occasional fantasy thrown in for good measure, so his exposure to romance novels was limited. His only knowledge of them was through Sam, who went through them like candy and would excitedly try to explain them to him once she would finish, so he had to admit that he was curious.

When she'd been explaining everything to him that morning, he hadn't wanted to admit that he had tried to do some research of his own the night before. Hoping to find some light reading material that might help him in this new role of his, as he had to admit that being a fake boyfriend was out of his circle of knowledge.

He had managed to stumble on a few titles that seemed popular on social media and downloaded a few for him to read in his free time. It wasn't much, but it was a step in the right direction if he wanted to do this right. He had to admit that proposing this whole fake-dating arrangement between the two of them had been a spur-of-the-moment thing, but he was finding the whole situation exciting.

But, oh God, when she'd talked about what things she was willing to do with him, he'd had to adjust himself in his seat to prevent her from seeing exactly what effect that declaration had on him.

The fact that she'd said she was open to kissing him, much less anything remotely sexual down the line, and he'd had to restrain himself from throwing her down onto the table and immediately having his way with her. He'd become accustomed to the occasional flaring desire like that over the years, but it felt as if a bottle of soda had been shaken up and the cap was being torn open now.

"That one is a popular forced-proximity romance from what I read online," she finally said excitedly, tossing another book onto the stack. "I wanted to get a few titles that would align with some of the topics that I'll be touching on to get a good frame of reference."

"Uh-huh," he said, his eyes roving back to the cover in front of him, "and shirtless guys throwing women over their shoulders is a good frame of reference?"

Sam glanced at the cover with a smile. "Hey, don't knock

it until you try it. Who knows, that romantic lead could be an absolute stud and not just a long-haired Fabio."

He held up the cover next to his face, pouting his lips to mimic the fuller lips of the man on the cover. "Do I meet the qualifications of a romantic lead now?"

She laughed as she rose from where she had been crouching, leaving her basket on the floor and rolling up the sleeves of her pale-green button-up shirt—a color that perfectly complemented her eyes. The garment hung loosely on her frame, obscuring whatever contours her body held beneath. Unlike the pair of skinny jeans that accentuated the gentle curve of her hips in a way that…

Charlie cleared his throat and distractedly picked up another book on the shelf, as if it had caught his attention.

She gently pushed past him to venture further down the aisle. "You joke, but these older covers have some deceptively good material in them."

"I don't doubt that. I'm just not sure why Fabio has to be shirtless on the front?"

She laughed again and turned to look up at him. "It was just a trend at the time. The trend now is cartoon covers. See here? Most of these have some variation of a cartoon couple on the front."

As if to prove her point, she handed him another book. It was a top-down view of a beach scene with a woman holding up a book over her head while the man sat back on a towel. Simple but effective.

"I think I like these better," he said, flipping the book over to scan the blurb. "It's a bit more subtle."

"I think I do too. I love that old adage, *don't judge a book by its cover*, but clearly, whoever said that wasn't in publishing," she mused as she flashed him a wide grin.

It was a smile so purely her that Charlie couldn't help the surge of affection it created. It made him want to touch her, even in a small way, just to get even a fraction of that light bubbling out of her in droves.

She was in her element here. One of the places she felt most herself, most at home.

It reminded him of the countless hours that they'd spent at the dingy little library they had back home. The one so old and decrepit that it was nearly falling apart at the seams, but that somehow only managed to add more character to it. It had been both of their sanctuaries when they were teenagers, when being home was the last thing either of them had wanted to do—instead getting lost in the worlds created by others.

And now, standing there and watching her excitedly pointing out books, he couldn't help but smile and silently thank his lucky stars for this opportunity, however strange it might've been. Anything just to help keep that light inside of her alive.

He knew she didn't feel the same way he did about her. She'd made that apparent years ago, but that didn't matter. He was pretty sure there would never be a day that the sun didn't rise and set in Sam's eyes.

"Show me more, then," he instructed, bringing himself back to reality and reaching to take her hand in his. He used his other hand to scoop up the basket off the ground and pulled her along behind him, heading to the next aisle.

Her mouth opened as if to protest, but instead, she closed it when he laced their fingers together. Her hand felt so much smaller in his than he thought it would. Her fingers were always so long and slender, delicate and pale, as if she'd taken special care not to mark them in any way to preserve her writing capabilities. It was silly, probably, to think that way, but when he'd spent so long wondering what they would feel like, it made those finer details more readily apparent. But now he simply liked how her hand felt in his. How, despite the fact that she was tall herself, his hand engulfed hers.

"What else are we looking for?" he prompted, lowering her basket back onto the ground for her to have easy access.

A touch of pink colored her cheeks as he looked down at her, and he couldn't ignore the irresistible urge in his gut to tease her. "Oh, don't tell me Miss Smut-Writer is getting embarrassed because she's getting her hand held?"

Sam's face immediately scrunched, and her brows furrowed together.

"Shut up," she grumbled. "It's not like this is the first time I've held your hand, asshole."

Even grumpy, she was the cutest thing he'd ever seen. "I know. Then your fake boyfriend holding your hand should be a breeze, right?"

Despite her sour expression, a hint of a smile cracked through to the surface. "You're the worst."

"I know, the absolute worst. That said, however… I'm literally begging you to be honest with me if something I do makes you uncomfortable, okay? I mean it. No being brave and toughing it out, deal?" he instructed, giving her hand a firm shake with his and all but refusing to release it unless she asked him to.

She rolled her eyes. "Alright. I won't."

"Promise?"

She groaned, but the smile betrayed her. "I promise."

Charlie eyed the stack of books in her basket. By his count, there were least half a dozen there. He did the math and made sure his wallet was in easy reach for when they eventually headed to the front to check out. No way was he letting his *fake girlfriend* pay for these on their first outing.

He was going to have a little too much fun, he feared, calling her that.

"Are you even going to read all of those? Seems like a lot to read in such a short amount of time."

She shrugged. "Probably not, but it wouldn't hurt. Might help me with any future books I write—if I decide to write more romances at least."

"You're the expert," he teased, nudging her shoulder with his affectionately.

"Well, if I were the expert," she replied, nudging him back, "I wouldn't need your help, would I?"

He chuckled as she bent back down to browse more books on the bottom shelf closest to her. As she did, a notification chimed from his pocket. He placed the book in his hand on the nearest shelf and dug his phone out, seeing the text message displayed on the screen.

> Peter said that you're already trying to back out

> If I have to do it, you have to as well

> Please don't make me drive over from Raleigh to beat you up

Charlie suppressed the eye roll that threatened to surface, knowing he should've called his mother after he and Sam had agreed she would go with him.

> Relax, Tyler, I'll be there. But I'm still not doing the auction

Don't be an ass about this

> I can't, I have a date. Mom said we didn't
> have to do it if we went with a date

You got a date?

Charlie looked over to check on Sam, seeing her busily retrieving another book.

> Yes, am I not allowed?

You are, just surprised is all

Who is it?

> Nosy

Do I know this person you're supposedly
bringing? I swear to God if you're just
making this up to get out of the auction I'm
gonna deck you

Charlie sighed, rubbing the tension suddenly building between his eyebrows.

> Yes, you know her, now can you drop it
> please?

Ah, I see

Tell Sam I said hi :)

Charlie shoved his phone back in his pocket with a quiet, aggravated grunt. He made a note to call his mother after he got home.

"Hey," Sam suddenly said, snapping him out of his thoughts as she pointed toward a book perched on the top shelf, "Can you grab that for me? I'm tall, but I don't think I can reach it."

He looked up to see the book she pointed at, up on one of the display shelves above the rest. It appeared to be one of the newer releases, a stack of identical copies propped beneath it. He stretched over her to snag the spine of the closest copy to his reach between his fingers. He pulled it out as gently as he could, so as to not disturb the display.

When he pulled back, Sam was staring up at him, a faraway look in her eyes that intrigued him, but then he immediately realized that he'd effectively pinned her body between him and the shelf.

"Sorry! Did I squish you there?" he asked, a bit concerned when she blankly stared at him before blinking a couple of times.

She cleared her throat. "No, I'm fine. Sorry. Was just lost in thought."

The irresistible urge to tease her overtook him, seeing the flustered look plastered to her face. He lowered his head a fraction and grinned. "What were you thinking about?"

"N-nothing!" she stammered out, shifting her gaze to the side and avoiding his eyes.

Yeah, he was definitely going to have too much fun with this if it meant getting to see this side of her.

Sam snatched the book he held in his grasp and ducked underneath his arm. "Thank you for grabbing this!"

Suddenly turning on her heel, she reached into her bag and whipped her phone out, typing away on it as she started walking away and effectively leaving Charlie behind in the dust.

"Hey!" he called out, grabbing the forgotten basket of books and following after her. "Everything okay?"

She nodded, not taking her eyes off the screen. "Yes! Perfect! Sorry. I just came up with a great idea for a scene, so I wanted to jot it down before I forgot."

"Uh-huh. Got everything you need, then?" he asked, lifting the basket up. "We should probably head out. It looks like they'll be gearing up to close soon."

A few more taps on the screen and she tucked her phone back into her bag. "Yeah, I think that should cover it for now."

"Good. Let's go," he said, scooping her hand in his again before she could argue and pulling her toward the closest cashier. Any excuse to touch her at this point now felt like a gift Charlie was going to exploit as frequently as he could.

He handed the basket and his credit card to the cashier before she could fetch hers out of her wallet.

"Charlie! You don't need to pay for those!" she protested.

He'd been planning on buying anything she put into that basket the moment they'd walked in, so he simply shrugged and leaned back against the counter. The loud beep of the scanner punctuating each bar code. "Oh, shut up. Let me do this. Besides, the dress you'll have to get for that charity is probably going to be a hell of a lot more expensive than this, so don't worry about it."

She groaned, biting her lip before folding her arms across her chest. Yep, he definitely would never tell her how much he loved it when she pretended to be angry like this, which she absolutely was with that mischievous gleam in her eyes.

It took everything in him not to lower his gaze to her lips.

"Is this what I have to look forward to being your fake girlfriend? Are you gonna spoil me and pay for everything?" she asked, trying and failing to sound innocent.

He chuckled. "I might. Is that all it takes to romance you? A shopping bag full of books?"

"Hey," she defended, leaning back on her heels, "you're fake dating a bookworm. That's on you."

He laughed again. "I suppose that's true. Though, what should we call each other throughout this? Fake girlfriend and fake boyfriend feels a little clinical."

She shrugged. "I don't know what other titles we would use. Not everything is going to be super romantic, but I'll see if I can think up something for us to call each other in the meantime. Writing a book can be extremely tedious, so I'll be jotting down a ton of notes most nights after we get done with our dates."

He hated how much hearing her use the word "date" in reference to him sent a little tingle up his spine.

"And it's not *clinical*," she continued. "It's logical."

He frowned. "You're already making it very hard to want to romance you."

She finally laughed then, the sound easing his nerves. Pure music to his ears.

As he turned, something happened to catch his attention out of the corner of his eye. He stepped to the side, peering over Sam and the cashier to look out the window. It was dark outside at that point, making it hard to really see, but it looked like it was… someone standing there? Standing directly opposite the glass and just glaring inside, though most of him was shaded by the lack of street lamps in the area.

"You okay, Charlie?" Sam asked, leaning the same way he was as if to see what he was looking so intently at.

He turned back to the window, seeing that no one was standing there any longer. Or maybe no one had been there? He wasn't sure, blinking a few times as the exhaustion from the work day started catching up with him. He craned his neck, trying to see if anyone was further down the street, but it looked as if no one was there. Odd.

"It's nothing, don't worry," he reassured her, accepting his credit card back from the cashier. "You ready to walk home?"

Sam held her bag up excitedly, nodding enthusiastically. "I am now! Thank you!"

"You're welcome. Now, come on. Let's go," he said, taking her hand once more in his and heading outside into the cool night air.

CHAPTER 10

SAM

Sam turned another page as she sank deeper into the pile of pillows she had arranged on her couch. With her nose firmly buried in her book, she had started the morning reading, occasionally jotting down notes as she did. Although, her notes were sparse, as she had gotten absorbed into the story, deciding after only a few minutes to abandon the notes altogether until she finished reading.

She had specifically chosen this book because it was a bit shorter than the others that she had gotten with Charlie the day before, so she knew she could finish it more quickly. With her appetite for reading, she often found that she breezed through books effortlessly. Hence the growing collection on the bookshelf in her bedroom.

It had been a while since she'd actually sat down to read just because she wanted to. The stress of trying to come up with another novel had weighed heavily on her, so much so that trying to do much else had felt like a chore. But now, she decided that she'd take advantage of the cozy Saturday morning and enjoy herself a bit.

She'd managed to prop herself up enough to watch the

sun rising in the distance earlier, cup of coffee in hand. It had been one of the biggest reasons she'd even moved into this apartment building in the first place, the view. When she'd graduated from college, she'd already published the first book in her series, so she was lucky enough to have the kind of money to afford a place like this. It was a one-bedroom apartment, but it was vastly more expensive than most of the other buildings in the area. She hadn't planned on getting something with this kind of price tag, but when she had toured the apartment and been shown the view, she'd immediately run down to sign the lease.

The little box-shaped room she'd stayed in when she lived with her aunt hadn't had any windows, so having a living room with wall-to-ceiling windows was the kind of upgrade she hadn't known she needed until she'd moved in.

Then again, the place hadn't exactly been a hard sell in the first place when Charlie had only moved in a few weeks prior in a two-bedroom apartment just a few floors above this one.

Sam lowered her book and looked out across the horizon as her mind quickly wandered to their outing to the bookstore the night before.

Heat immediately pooled in her stomach as she thought of how it had felt being encased by Charlie's body as he had reached for that book above her. It had surprised her just how casual he had been about the whole ordeal, and a bit more surprised that her body reacted the way it had when he did.

She'd quickly made up the excuse that she had gotten an idea for a scene just so she could get away and walk it off.

What the hell was she doing?

Charlie had been more than convincing when he proposed this whole fake-dating thing between them, and she had been so swept up in it that she couldn't say no. Especially when he'd asked to use it as an exchange to go as his date for the charity.

Even the memory of how it had felt just simply having his body that close, in this new context between them, felt dangerous.

She had long ago stamped her feelings for him down, the memory of the conversation she'd overheard between him and Peter echoing in her mind. She'd accepted that she'd have to keep herself in check wherever Charlie was concerned. Hell, it was the whole reason she went on that godawful date months ago, just hoping that there might be the faintest of faint hopes that she could get *over* this silly little crush of hers.

And now? She was going to have to work overtime to make sure that no matter what happened, that she wouldn't mix her real feelings up with exploring this fake-dating scenario.

She was so lost in thought about the whole ordeal, in fact, that when her phone began to ring on the table, she didn't think twice but to pick it up to answer. Not even bothering to check the caller ID in the process.

The word "hello" barely left her mouth when reality slammed back into her, the voice on the other end exhaling as if they had been holding their breath. "My *god* you have been impossible to get ahold of."

Sam's entire body clenched in on itself.

"Paul…"

"You keep ignoring me! I've tried texting you, calling, emailing, nothing gets through."

She immediately went into autopilot as she acted immediately, using this opportunity to add something incredibly concrete to the folder. Her hands shook as she quickly scurried to grab her laptop, throwing it open and hunting down the recording feature as she sought to put the call on speaker. Hitting the recording button at the same time.

She placed the phone on the table next to her laptop where she thought the audio would come through clearly. "Because I don't want to talk to you, Paul. I told you before that I want you to leave me alone."

A hint of confusion came through as he laughed. "You don't mean that."

She didn't fight the shiver as it raced down her back uncomfortably. "I really do, Paul. We had *one* date and that was it."

"But," he said more emphatically, "we had such a connection?"

What she would give to turn back time and decide against the whole date at the start. "No, Paul. You spent the entire date talking about yourself and interrupting me anytime I tried to say anything. There were no sparks, no connection. I told you that I didn't want to go out with you again, and you won't take no for an answer. It's that simple."

"We are just meant—"

"No," she said more clearly, fighting the tremble in her voice. "I've lost count of how many times these past few months that I've told you that I have no interest in seeing you again. I've already contacted the police to let them know that you are harassing me, and what you did to my car, so I'm *begging* you to please just leave me alone."

There was a short pause on the other end, and for a second, Sam feared she'd said too much. What was it exactly she should say in such a situation, she wasn't sure. All she knew was that the past few months of his constant texts and calls, even after she'd blocked his original phone number and the dozens of others he used to try and get ahold of her, the number of times she'd had to change her own phone number just to avoid him, had been stressful. She'd barely been able to focus these past few months, worrying that he was going to show up out of the blue, like he had back with the whole car incident.

How he'd known she was away for a book signing of her last release, she had no clue. She'd already cut contact with him by that point. But when she'd got back and found her car all but totally trashed, it hadn't taken a genius for her to figure out who could've done it. But because she didn't have any definitive proof that it was him, with no cameras in that area of the parking garage, there was little they could do about it.

Charlie knew that something had happened to her car that made it basically unusable, but exactly what that was had been something she'd purposefully kept from him. Even when she'd called him to come get her that night. It had been in the shop so long that she wasn't sure it would ever drive properly again. A fact she tried hard not to think too much on, considering it was what little she had left of her parents.

"I didn't do anything to your car," Paul said sharply.

She couldn't help but scoff. "I don't know anyone else who would've slashed all four tires, poured sugar and God knows what else down the gas tank, and written… well, all of those awful things on it."

"There are bad people in this world, Sam! All the more reason you need me around to make sure that you're safe."

"The only person I don't feel safe around, Paul, is you. I have people in my life who make me feel plenty safe, so I—"

"Oh," Paul interrupted, "like that tall guy yesterday?"

Her brows furrowed as she looked down at her phone. "What are you talking about?"

"Yeah, I know about *him*. Here I thought we had something special, something *exclusive*, but you're out with some other guy. You were at the bookstore with him last night."

Sam's stomach clenched in her gut. "How would… You weren't… Are you *following* me now, Paul?"

"I'm making sure to protect what's mine. You are *mine*, Sam, and I will watch over you until you come to your senses and…" Paul said before Sam abruptly cut him off by immediately ending the call. She tossed her phone onto the couch, as if touching it would scald her.

A creeping fear, shooting up her spine like a lightning bolt, encased her entire body. It pinned her to the spot momentarily as she tried to learn how to breathe once more.

Realizing the camera on her laptop was still running, she reached a shaky hand up to end it. Saving the file with all of the rest in Paul's folder.

It had been a fear of hers for a while that he would eventually start escalating more; she just didn't think it would already be happening.

She'd developed the habit of double, triple, checking her front door every day. An extra precaution just in case he *did* get to this level, but a small part of her had hoped that if she ignored him long enough, he would just lose interest. She'd thought it had been working, as it had been a week since she'd heard from him. Until dinner the other night with Charlie, that is.

A naive hope now.

A little voice in the back of her mind told her to call Charlie, but she immediately silenced that. Charlie was already helping her with this whole thing with her book. The last thing she needed was to add additional stress with *this* whole situation as well.

She didn't need help.

She could handle this.

She could take care of herself. She'd been doing it this long, after all.

Now that she had this recording, she could send it to that cop. Maybe then they would finally grant her that restraining order she'd been asking for. At least it would be a step in the right direction.

She retrieved her book from where she'd set it down earlier, turning to the page she'd left off on. With each word scrawled across the page, she knew that she could lose herself to the beautiful and enchanting world unfolding before her. A temporary oasis from the shadows that loomed in the corners of her reality.

*he knock on the door came promptly at ten minutes before seven. Exactly ten minutes before Charlie had said he'd arrive, and decidedly, ten minutes too early.

She really shouldn't have waited until the last minute to get ready.

Her brain had been fried from her earlier call, making it difficult to focus on any kind of writing, so she'd resorted to reading for the remainder of the day. It wasn't until she finally managed to tear herself away from the ending of the most recent chapter she'd read when she realized the time and had rushed to get ready.

All she'd needed to do was to finish fussing with her hair and makeup. She'd managed to curl her hair into loose beachy waves that cascaded down her back and had just opened a tube of lipstick when she heard the knocking.

In her haste, she'd run to unlock the front door, so Charlie could let himself in when he arrived, but given her conversation earlier, she froze in her spot.

"Charlie?" she called out, crossing her fingers that she hadn't made a huge mistake.

"Yeah, I'm a bit early," she heard from the front door, Charlie's familiar voice floating down the hall toward her. "I hope that's okay?"

A sigh of relief escaped her. "The door's open! Let yourself in. I'm finishing up in here, but I'll only be a minute!"

The sound of the door clicking shut loudly from the next room confirmed he'd heard her, and she resumed. She did a little spin in front of the mirror, watching as the skirt of her dress danced and twirled around her. She didn't often wear dresses, as most of them rode too high on her tall frame, but she could appreciate their appeal. The black tulle fabric around her cascaded down her figure, showcasing a femininity that she didn't often embrace so openly.

It had been a birthday gift from Angel on her last birthday, when Angel had last come down to visit. Despite the plunging neckline that had initially given her pause, the dress was adorned with a cute little strawberry pattern that Sam simply hadn't been able to resist.

"You really shouldn't leave your door unlocked like that, you know," Charlie scolded, his voice carrying down the hall like an admonishing echo that already had her smiling. He definitely wasn't wrong, but she wouldn't give him the satisfaction of being right.

"Relax. I only unlocked it when I started getting ready, so you could let yourself in while I finished getting ready. Worked out in our favor this time, didn't it?"

"*This* time."

"You're such a worrywart. But sorry, I'll be out in just a minute. I'm just putting on a few last-minute touches," she called out as she opened the container where she kept her earrings. Her eyes were drawn immediately to the pair of strawberry studs that would perfectly match her outfit.

"Take your time. I know I'm a bit early," he called back.

Her smile reflected back at her in the mirror, a mix of sudden nerves and anticipation dancing in her green eyes. She pictured Charlie sitting at her kitchen table, patiently waiting to take her on a date, a fake-date. It all seemed so absurd that under different circumstances, it probably would have sounded completely insane.

Satisfied with her reflection, she fluffed up her hair once more before grabbing the pair of earrings. She brought the first one to her ear, attempting to snap it into place as she walked out of the bathroom. The pair of heels she had already chosen clicked across the hardwood floor as she made her way into the kitchen.

As she attempted to secure the other earring in place, she saw Charlie standing there waiting for her, leaning back against the kitchen counter with one hand behind his back.

It gave her pause as she took him in, unable to stop herself from admiring the picture he made. He looked fresh, clean cut. The usually wavy locks of his hair were combed back neatly, a few loose strands framing his face in a way that somehow, combined with the trimmed cut of his facial hair, perfectly accentuated the sharp cut of his jawline.

He looked as if he'd stepped directly out of a magazine.

The dark navy material of the casual suit jacket he wore was slightly opened at the front, showing off the crisp white dress shirt he had on beneath it—a color combination that suited Charlie remarkably well. With the top button of his dress shirt undone, she caught a glimpse of the sprinkle of dark chest hair just below. It made her vacantly wonder what it would feel like if it were to tickle her face if…

No, down girl.

"You look nice," she said simply, unsure of what else to say without her voice betraying her.

His smile further illuminated his face, sharpening his features. "You look beautiful."

Beautiful. He thought she looked beautiful. He'd told her that a few times before in the past, but for some reason the word clung to her like a second skin.

"Thank you," she replied, realizing with a hint of shyness that she still hadn't hooked her other earring into place, having come to a stop mid-motion when she'd seen him.

She began fussing with it again to keep herself from staring. Charlie in his regular clothes was enough to cause distraction, but this? Deadly. Even the smell of his familiar cologne flared in her nostrils as she passed by, the scent of citrus and pine like a warm embrace that forced her to button her lip to prevent a delighted sigh from escaping her.

At least it had its usual effect in calming her nerves considerably.

"I seem to have a theme tonight with the strawberries. I hope you don't mind?" she commented quickly.

When he didn't respond, she turned, surprised to see him watching her. His eyes roved over her, as if he were studying her. If he saw that she was now watching him, too, he made no inclination. Sure, she knew this was probably the first time that he'd seen her in a dress in a few years, but there was something about the way his eyes studied her that suddenly made her very aware of his presence.

She'd told him that she wanted these dates to feel real, to feel like even though they were "fake dating" that she wanted them to act like a normal couple might.

And the way his eyes felt on her body suddenly felt very real.

She cleared her throat. "Charlie?"

He blinked a few times and shook his head before meeting her gaze. She could feel the heat practically pulsing in her cheeks, but she hoped that it wasn't obvious.

Charlie grinned as he fiddled with the collar of his shirt. "Sorry. What'd you say?"

"I-I said that I apparently had a theme with the strawberries tonight, and that I hoped you didn't mind," she repeated.

His smile softened. "I'd expect nothing less with you. Besides, I like it. The color looks nice on you."

Noticing that he still had one arm behind his back, she nodded at it as she finally finessed her earring into place. "What's that?"

Another couple of blinks before Charlie moved, revealing a handful of sunflowers he'd kept behind him. Bright and vivacious in his grip.

"Oh, Charlie, they're beautiful!" she exclaimed, giddily accepting them from him. "Let me put these in some water real quick."

He nodded. "Of course."

She gathered the flowers from him, sneaking a quick whiff in as she plucked a vase from under her kitchen counter. She'd take proper care of them when she got back, but she wanted to make sure they didn't wilt in the meantime.

The momentary distraction also helped her to steel her nerves once more. She could do this. This was what she had wanted for her research. She just needed to keep it together.

That said, she couldn't help but smile down at the flowers, fluffing them out a bit as she settled them into the vase. Even if it was a sort of girlish notion, it made her happy. No one had ever gotten her flowers for a date before.

"You didn't have to get me these, Charlie," she chided, not meaning a word of it.

He followed behind her, leaning against the kitchen counter opposite her. "What is a good first date if not preceded with flowers?"

She couldn't help but giggle. "Quite the romantic, aren't you?"

"I'd like to think so, not that I've had too much practice these days."

She filled the vase with water, bunching her eyebrows together. "I guess that makes us two peas in a pod. When was the last time you went on a date anyway?"

He shrugged. "I don't know, a year or two ago maybe?"

"Anyone I know?" she asked, ignoring the slight flare of jealousy that cropped at that. She, of all people, had no reason to feel that way given the situation with Paul.

"Nah, just lasted one date. I think I've just been so satisfied spending time with you that I haven't really felt the urge to date."

She returned the smile he gave her then, sharing in the sentiment. "Why sunflowers by the way? Isn't the traditional flower for dates roses?"

"Sunflowers are your favorite, though, so it made more sense," he replied, opening the front door and stepping to the side. "Ladies first."

Yeah, this man was going to be trouble, she could tell already.

CHAPTER 11

CHARLIE

In a strange way, it hadn't even occurred to Charlie that he should feel nervous about being on a date with Sam. Mostly because he knew in his gut that this was, in fact, not a real date. He had assumed it would be like any time they had dinner together.

But now he knew how naive he'd been.

The flowers had been a bit of a risk, but if Sam was looking for romance, flowers were a start. He'd ordered them from the florist down the street from work, grabbing them on his way back home to get changed.

He hadn't even had to sweat the choice on what to get her. It wasn't as universally known as her love of strawberries—a fact evident by the collection of strawberry-themed items she had at home—but he knew she liked having them in her apartment when they were in season.

He'd gone straight to her apartment after changing and cleaning up a bit, despite knowing that it would make him early. He'd been so confident that things would go smoothly. That is, until he'd caught sight of her emerging from the bath-room, fidgeting with her earring.

That dress.

It was a long black number with sheer sleeves puffed out at the shoulder and adorned with little cute strawberries pressed into the fabric that felt so very… Sam. Beautiful was the understatement of the century, but it was all he could muster at the time.

Though, Sam could wear a sack and still look divine.

It was, however, completely unlike something Sam would normally wear, and with that dangerously low neckline, Charlie knew he was already in trouble. Plunging down just low enough to tease and revealing a hint of cleavage that strained against the fabric, it took most of his strength to *not* look every chance he had.

He held the menu up in front of him like a shield, determined to keep his gaze away from that neckline at all costs. She deserved exponentially more than him acting like… well, like such a *guy,* as she would put it.

They had fallen into a relatively comfortable silence as they tucked into the appetizer. Her phone had dinged a few times as they had sat down, which had seemed to annoy her a bit, and Charlie could only guess it was her aunt, though he couldn't be sure. She seemed a little more stressed as she apologized and yanked her phone out to respond, so Charlie simply watched her.

She worked her lower lip between her teeth as she typed, unaware that he was watching her so carefully.

He couldn't help but wonder if she was even aware that she often did that whenever she was deep in thought. It was a habit he'd noted over the years that always seemed most prevalent when she was trying to figure something out. Usually book-related, but he doubted she was texting with Angel with the way that little wrinkle appeared between her eyebrows.

His eyes began to wander down, landing on her lips. Her lower lip popped forward from beneath her teeth as she released her hold on it. He was enraptured by the way their fullness immediately came back into shape. Full and oh-so-inviting, her lips began to move and he suddenly wondered what her lips would taste like with that cherry red lipstick she had on…

"Charlie?" she prompted, smiling at him as if she'd been trying to get his attention.

Dammit.

He blinked a few times.

"Sorry," he apologized swiftly and cleared his throat. "I was thinking about something at work. Everything okay?"

She nodded, her eyes darting off to the side as she adjusted herself in her seat. "Uh, yeah, I just had to send someone some files I had."

"Gotcha. You talk to your aunt since she called last?"

"No, thankfully not, but I wouldn't be surprised if I heard from her again soon."

Neither would he. He hated the chokehold that woman seemed to have over Sam, but he understood that it was a… complicated relationship to say the least. He tried not to pry too much, but he remembered the blowout they'd had back when they were in college and still held his own personal grudge about it.

"What do you think she wants anyway?" he asked carefully.

Sam shrugged. "Probably something for Tommy, knowing her."

"After the way they treated you?"

She chuckled, trying to appear unaffected by the situation, but Charlie could see the lingering sadness hiding in those green eyes of hers. "You know how she is."

"Why do you still put up with them?"

She shrugged again. "They're the only family I have left, so it would feel weird just completely cutting them out of my life, even if I hardly ever talk to them these days."

"Why?" Charlie prompted, though he wasn't sure why he wasn't dropping it and leaving it be.

She pursed her lips, staring off into the distance for a brief moment before turning her attention back to him and shrugging once more. "My grandparents on my mom's side died before I was born, and my dad's parents died when I was in college. Cutting them off just feels … I don't know, it just feels like completely closing that part of my life. Like, as shitty of a family as they are, they are all I have left."

Charlie hated that. She deserved so much better than the hand she'd been dealt.

Even before their big blowout, Sam often would come to his house, crying after some fight or another that she'd had with them. It was part of the reason his mother had become so protective over her. Especially after Erica…

"You deserve better than that," he said, forcing himself to take a drink before he continued pushing. "But anyway, how is the book writing going?"

"Good!" she replied with a soft smile. "I started actually writing yesterday. We don't have to talk about that stuff right now, though. I don't want to bore you."

He shook his head. "You could never bore me, Sam."

The truth, if he had any to offer at the moment.

Every second he spent with her always felt like a gift, and that was just as true now as it had always been. She was the one thing he wanted more than anything, but she was also the one thing he could never have.

Regardless of his feelings, however, he would always care

about her. She was, at the end of the day, his best friend. And that fact would never change.

The waiter traipsed over to the table, thankfully saving him from saying or doing anything else, and popped open a bottle of wine for them.

"So, I've been doing some thinking..." she said as she collected her glass.

"About?" he prompted.

"It was what you said when we were at the bookstore, about it feeling a little awkward about what to call each other. I know we said fight club rules, but I agree calling each other fake girlfriend and fake boyfriend is a bit awkward. Maybe we should come up with a name or something else to call each other exclusively for this?"

He pursed his lips, leaning back in his chair. "That's not a bad idea."

She nodded and scooted forward, glass of wine in hand. "Right? It'll help make this feel a bit more natural, which is the whole point."

He smiled. "Alright. What should we go with, then?"

"It should be something you would call a romantic partner but something we would normally never call each other."

There were a thousand names he'd love to call her, but he quickly pulled out one from the list. "How about babe?"

"Babe?"

He shrugged. "Yeah, it's a common name people call their partners but isn't something we say to each other."

She leaned back, resting her glass of wine against her lips as she chewed on the idea. After seemingly coming to a decision, she gave him a nod of finality and grinned. "I like it! It's cute and feels personal without being too weird. Are you sure you're okay with it?"

He'd call her whatever she wanted if she smiled at him like that again. "Yeah, it works for me."

"Good. Alright, *babe*, tell me about work. Let's not talk about book stuff anymore. This is a *date*, after all," she said before taking a sip of wine.

A delightful tingle at the name shot up his spine, and he had to lean forward and rest his elbows on the table to distract himself from just how much he was going to enjoy hearing her call him that.

He shrugged. "It's been alright. Nothing too exciting to report."

"Oh, that's not true, and you know it. You told me recently that you were up for a possible team lead role, right?"

"Yeah, they made the offer earlier this week."

"Oh, Charlie, that's great!" she exclaimed, reaching forward to pat his arm a few times. "Are you gonna take it?"

He shrugged again. "I don't know. I don't know if I want to."

"Why not?" she asked.

"It'd mean longer hours and more responsibilities. The pay increase would be stellar, I won't lie, but I'm not sure if I want to bother."

She smiled. "What do you want, then?"

He leaned back in his seat, relaxing into the conversation a bit. "I think I'm pretty content where I am, honestly."

"You haven't thought of doing anything else?"

It had been a while since he'd really thought about what he wanted beyond his current role. In actuality, this wasn't the first time he'd been offered the role. It had been proposed to him last year, which he had turned down to focus on helping to get the data lab center fully up and running at the time.

But if he really thought about it, he still leaned toward

turning it down again. The happiest time he'd had at his job recently had been when he'd been working in that data lab.

"If I had to choose," he said carefully, "I think if there were any lead role I would want, it would be in the data center lab—maybe even run the lab at some point."

She took another sip of wine before responding. "I'm not super technical. What's the difference between the two?"

"I wouldn't be managing people so much as I would be managing equipment and the couple of people who work in there. I'd still be the same level as a team lead, just with less of the hassle. I'm not so great at managing people."

She reached forward and gently smacked his arm again. "Don't say that. You're great with people."

He chuckled. "Managing people in a technical setting is vastly different from managing my idiot older brothers. Trust me."

She tried to stifle her laughter by covering her mouth with her free hand, but the sound bubbled out anyway. It echoed against her palm as she struggled to contain it, as if she were afraid of disturbing the people around them. A smile tugged at his lips as he watched her, enjoying the way her laughter was a balm to his soul.

Samantha Macmillian's laugh was, and had always been, his favorite sound.

They'd basically fought over who would get the check when it came, but luckily for him, Sam had been distracted by the cheesecake that they got to split, so he'd managed to sneak the waiter his card before she could protest too much.

He hadn't been necessarily surprised at how easy the date

had gone, but then again, it wasn't like they didn't regularly spend time together already. They could sit and talk to each other for hours with ease, so that part had been easy.

But as they pulled into the parking garage back at their apartment complex, Charlie couldn't help but feel those nerves swirling in his gut. He didn't want this to end. It was their first outing as a *fake couple*, and he wanted to live in the moment, even for a few minutes longer.

There would be many more outings to come, so this wouldn't be the last. He knew this, but he didn't care. He wanted more time. Even if it was to admire how incredible she looked tonight, he would find any way to stretch this out.

So, when they got out of the car and started walking toward the complex, Charlie stopped and turned toward her. "You up for a walk around the block before we head up? It's a really nice night out."

It was the best he could come up with, but it definitely didn't hurt that it was, in fact, an absolutely gorgeous evening. Sam had commented on it during their drive home, and Charlie had wholeheartedly agreed. Stars gleamed above them like diamonds strewn across a velvet sky, not a cloud in sight as the sky stretched, unhindered, for miles.

When she smiled at him and nodded, he quietly let out a sigh of relief. "Any place in particular?"

He shrugged. "Just around the block?"

"Works for me," she said, deviating from the path and toward the nearby sidewalk.

The brisk night air kicked up a gentle breeze around them, and the usual dull roar of nearby traffic was notably absent, making the atmosphere more peaceful.

Charlie almost wanted to kick himself for not thinking of the walk earlier, where he could have taken her somewhere a bit nicer. A bit more scenic than just outside their apartment complex. Even just driving a bit further over to the Tobacco Trail would have worked, but he tried not to think too hard on it.

He tugged her arm until she was away from the edge of the sidewalk, instead taking his place there between her and the road.

"So," she began as they turned the corner that led out of the garage, side by side, "what all should I prepare for with this charity event? I only have a few vague details on what to expect."

He cleared his throat as it inevitably tightened. "Oh, you know, those two spared no expense this year setting this up."

Sam grimaced before wrapping her arms around herself. "I can't believe they decided to do it *on* the anniversary this year. You doing okay?"

He shrugged, keeping his gaze forward. "I'm fine."

He really wasn't, but that wasn't something he was in the mood to elaborate further on—especially with this topic. This time of year was always hard enough as it was, but having some elaborate event he had no choice but to go to certainly didn't help things.

His guilt always felt tenfold on that day every year.

"But you know my mom is," he continued. "Once she gets an idea stuck in her head, it's really hard to talk her out of it."

Sam offered a gentle shrug with a small smile. "I think it's just her way of coping, Charlie."

"Yeah, well, I'm sure she'll text you the details now that she knows I'm taking you as my date," he said, trying to change the subject as quickly as he could. "But enough about that. This is a date. Aren't we supposed to be talking about first-date kinds of things?"

Sam watched him for a moment, as if she was studying

him, but thankfully accepted the topic change. "I guess you're right. We didn't really do much *first-date* kind of talk at dinner, did we?"

"I don't think so, but now that I think about it, what kind of first-date talk do people usually do?"

She pursed her lips for a moment, rubbing a hand hastily up and down an arm. "You know, I don't really know. It's been a while since I've been on a first date—"

He felt a hint of guilt that he selfishly liked that he'd essentially had her to himself all these years, unable to keep the grin from spreading across his face.

"But," she continued, "I think first dates are usually for people getting to know each other, and you and I already know each other really well."

"This is true," he said as he shrugged out of his jacket, taking it and draping it over her shoulders. She opened her mouth to protest, but he held up his hand. "Don't *even* start. You're in a dress, and it's a bit chilly now."

She attempted to suppress a smile but failed miserably as she leaned into him.

"Anyway," he said as they rounded the corner, heading back toward their complex, "now that we have done our first outing, what are you thinking in relation to your book stuff?"

She smiled. "We're heading back home. We can be done with that aspect for tonight, Charlie. You've done your duty, so you're officially off the clock."

He was tempted to ask her what if he didn't *want* to be off the clock but decided against it.

"Humor me. I want to really get into the writer's mindset here, so I can help make the most out of this," he said, earning a laugh from her. "I did some reading myself, but I'm not exactly a writer, so I don't know what kind of things you have planned for your book."

After he'd gotten back from the bookstore the other night, he'd decided to download a few of the titles that she had gotten. He still had the receipt, so it wasn't hard to locate them on his Kindle. He'd gone into work the next day exhausted, having chosen to stay up most of the night reading one of them, but it had been worth it. At least he had *some* semblance of what she was thinking, considering she'd picked the title for her own research.

"You did your own reading?" she asked, a softness in her eyes that made his heart swell.

"I picked up a copy of one of the ones you had in your basket. I figured if I wanted to be a good fake boyfriend, I should at least have an idea on what to expect."

"That was really sweet, Charlie. You didn't have to do homework for this."

There was very little he *wouldn't* do for her, but he didn't think offering that in this moment would be the wisest choice.

He shrugged, a bit more sheepishly than he intended. "I wanted to. Anyway, back to my line of questioning. When you're writing, do you like to develop your characters before you put them onto the page? Or do they get more fleshed out the more you write?"

"Depends, I guess. For the mystery series I wrote, I had those characters fleshed out before they ever came alive on paper, but with this book, I just have an idea of the characters and am letting them guide me."

He nodded thoughtfully. "Interesting…"

"Why?" she asked, looking amused. "Are you looking for writing tips, Charlie?"

It was his turn to laugh. "I told you, I'm trying to get into the writer mindset. Gotta be prepared for whatever you throw at me."

She returned a nod, seemingly satisfied with his answer. A

comfortable silence slipped into place between them as they neared the complex. He closed his eyes for a moment, letting it all in. Enjoying that comfortable silence as it stretched between them and knowing he didn't have to fill it awkwardly as he would if it were anyone else. But that was just the way things were with Sam.

He felt as her hand found his in the quiet, and he tried not to let his excitement get the better of him. He gave her hand a gentle squeeze as they continued walking together. Their fingers laced together naturally, as if they were the perfect fit.

His hand enveloped hers, so precious and fragile in his grasp that he worried if he squeezed too hard, he'd hurt her.

It was far from the first time he'd ever held her hand, though he could clearly remember the first time as if it were yesterday. It was right after her parents had died in that accident, and she had to move in with her aunt. Sam often kept her emotions close to her chest, something he had tried easing out of her for as long as he could remember. But on that day, he'd noticed in between classes that she had snuck off somewhere, so he'd gone to look for her.

The funeral had been the day before, so he'd kept a closer eye on her than normal, but when he finally found her, she was underneath the gym's bleachers. Sitting on the floor up against the nearest wall, her legs pulled up to her chest, quietly sobbing into her knees.

Words had never been his specialty, typically opting for a smart-ass comment most of the time to make someone laugh, so instead, he'd sat down next to her. He'd taken her hand in his, lacing their fingers together, and simply sat there next to her as she continued crying. They'd stayed there until she felt better.

Returning to the present, Charlie briefly mulled ideas over for their next date, a plan already beginning to take shape in his mind. It went a little off script from what she had mentioned before, but he was confident she would love it.

When they finally reached her apartment door only a few moments later, Sam paused to fish through her purse in search of her keys. Seemingly disappearing into oblivion into the vast void of her bag.

"So, how did I do overall?" he asked as he stood in front of her.

"Highest marks, *babe,*" she said, sending his heart fluttering a bit. "You are the best fake boyfriend I've ever had."

He waved her off dramatically, earning a giggle. "Oh, you're just saying that."

"No, no, you are so far the reigning champion," she said, finally pulling her keys out of her bag. "Well, thanks again for tonight. I had a lot of fun."

"Good. I'm glad. What should we plan for next?"

She shrugged. "Can I get back to you on that?"

"Sounds good to me," he replied, his eyes lowering to her lips. The undeniable urge to kiss her was far greater than he ever expected in a moment like this. He often had the urge to kiss her, well before they ever agreed to this, but he'd gotten quite good at restraining that. Right now, however, it took almost everything he had not to.

Her lips were so wonderfully inviting, puckered ever so slightly from a fresh application of whatever lipstick she'd reapplied before they'd left the restaurant. Beckoning him as his vision seemed to hone in on them, the rest of the world evaporating from view.

"Are you… Are you going to kiss me?" Sam quietly asked, uncertainty and intrigue reflecting in her eyes when his gaze shot up to meet hers. His body suddenly felt as if it were on fire—in the most delightful way possible. His skin burned with a desire that roared to life.

"I was thinking about it," he admitted honestly. "I know we agreed already, but remember that nothing happens if you don't want it to."

She licked her lips, her breathing a little heavier than it had been seconds prior. "I know."

"Don't push yourself if you're not comfortable." He took a small step toward her, the precious space between them feeling electric.

She shook her head slowly, her voice barely above a whisper as she took the remaining step toward him until they were barely a breath apart. "I'm not."

Their eyes were locked on one another, and despite the heat pooling in his veins, he searched for something, anything, that indicated that he shouldn't kiss her. Any hint of hesitation or restraint and he'd back away.

But when he found none of that, instead seeing the same intensity in her eyes that he felt, he brought a hand up to rub her cheek with his thumb affectionately. She watched him, as if she, too, were studying him, but she leaned into his touch. As if the pull she felt were as magnetic as it was for him.

Her eyelashes fluttered shut as he lowered his face toward hers, before his lips pressed against hers.

It was soft at first, experimental. Their lips barely touched a whisper before his hand moved once more. Snaking around to hold the back of her neck and pulling her toward him even more until their bodies were flush against one another.

It was far better than anything he'd ever imagined.

His fantasies were a pale comparison to the real thing.

He hungrily deepened the kiss as he angled his lips more firmly against hers, desperately clinging to some hint of rational thinking so he didn't throw her over his shoulder like an absolute caveman.

He knew what this kiss was, what it really meant, what it

was really for, and despite the desire and want licking at his heels, by God he was going to control himself. For her sake. He would *not* lose her because he couldn't keep himself in check.

He forced himself to finally pull back, giving her lips once last, soft peck. His hand was still on the nape of her neck as he watched her eyelids flutter back open. Gauging her reaction for a moment to make sure she was alright before giving her a soft smile.

"Good night, Sam," he said, giving her a final kiss on the tip of her nose before releasing her and turning on his heel. Leaving her standing there, he made his way quickly down the hallway, turning the corner to head toward the staircase.

Damn.

CHAPTER 12

SAM

Sam watched the cursor blink on her screen a few more times before she let out a heavy sigh. She'd been staring at it for at least the past twenty minutes, but she couldn't find it in herself to concentrate on writing. Her mind kept wandering back…

That kiss.

Her lips still tingled from the softness of Charlie's kiss, his lips fitting so perfectly against hers like a long-lost puzzle piece. It was a whisper of a touch at first, but slow, exploratory pecks that softened each time their lips greeted one another. The way his hand snaked around the back of her head to pull her closer, deepening the kiss.

It was true that she'd spent most of the night thinking about it, only pulling away from it by forcing a writing session in to distract herself last night.

A hint of panic settled in her gut over the whole thing, knowing that if a simple kiss like that would cause her to blush like a sinner in church, she was going to be in a lot of trouble. How on earth would she be able to keep her composure and actually try to focus on getting notes for her book when her body wanted to melt into a puddle at Charlie's feet?

Angel's words lingered in her mind, but she tried to brush them off swiftly to focus back on the words on her screen. It might have been a long time ago, but she knew Charlie still felt the same way. Nothing had changed between them, and even if he had kissed her like that, it wasn't because he genuinely wanted to. He was being a good friend to help her, just so she could write a good book.

Besides, he would've told her if his feelings *had* changed… Right?

No, Charlie had always been honest with her. He would've told her if things had changed for him. He wasn't one to keep many things from her. He told her just about everything, things he hadn't told anyone else before. It was why they were such good friends to begin with. He rarely spoke about Erica these days, but he had opened up to her once or twice about it, so she knew without a shadow of a doubt that they were comfortable enough with one another to share anything.

Well, even though she didn't tell him about how *she* felt… But that was only because she knew it would make him uncomfortable, knowing he didn't feel the same. The last thing she wanted was for Charlie to distance himself from her because she made things awkward between them. If they could survive a silly little fake dating experiment like this, they could survive anything.

The more she tried to convince herself of that, however, a deeper, more persistent fear hovered over Sam like a dark rain cloud, calling out to her from the depths.

Things between them had always been the most stable part of her life, knowing he would always be there. This could change things between them, and that frightened her more than she initially thought it would.

She could lose him if she wasn't careful.

Before she could dwell too much longer on the thought, her phone rang. She picked it up without looking, immediately regretting the decision when the familiar voice came through. "Samantha, dear, I hope you're in a better mood than you were last time we spoke?"

Sam fought to contain the groan before it slammed through the phone receiver. Aunt Emily, of course. As if she didn't have *enough* problems in her life right now.

"It's about the same as last time," she replied honestly.

Aunt Emily tsked on the other end. "And here I was hoping you would apologize for how you behaved before. I suppose I thought too much of you."

This time Sam didn't fight the laugh as it bubbled out of her. "Me, apologize? I wasn't the one who went on a tangent on how *awful* of a person I am, according to you."

"You exaggerate, dear. I was simply making a point."

"A point that I'm a terrible person?"

Aunt Emily scoffed. "A *point* that you have received a lot of blessings from our family, and it's time you started to act like it."

Sam sank back in her spot. "Where should I send my eternal gratitude to?"

"Don't get smart with me, young lady. I'm still your aunt, one of the only family members you have left!"

"As you keep reminding me," Sam grumbled. "Which you manage to forget when you bring up my *education*, as you did last time we spoke, that I've already paid you back what you and Uncle Ron spent to send me to school. Remember? Sent you a huge check for it? Ringing any bells?"

Another indignant scoff. "Well, that is *expected*, Samantha, don't you think? Your uncle and I are not made out of money, and with how you wasted your education on that useless English degree, I think we were owed our money back."

It was laughable how much of a point of contention her degree had been at the time. But she wasn't sure she should've been surprised at all. Her aunt didn't take kindly to her disobeying the *plans* she had laid out for her.

Sam had been told most of her life, ever since she moved in with her aunt's family basically, that she had two options in life. If she wanted an education, she would have to go to a college that they approved of and get a degree in accounting, so she could eventually work for her uncle's law firm. Or, option number two, they would set her up so that she could marry rich like her aunt had—most likely to the son of someone that her uncle wanted to go into business with.

Her freedom of an *actual* choice with her life had been stacked against her from the very beginning.

"What is it that you want, Aunt Emily? You mentioned last that you had something you wanted my *participation* in, so what is it?"

The other end was silent for a moment, and it almost gave Sam a sense of satisfaction, knowing Aunt Emily was likely trying to collect herself to at least *pretend* to be pleasant for a moment. Which meant she definitely needed something.

Ever since that huge blowout when she was in college, the only time her family ever bothered to reach out was if they needed something. Most of the time, she would decline, though once or twice, she'd been guilted into helping in one way or another.

"Tommy wants to write a book," Her aunt finally announced.

Stunned silence forced Sam to clap a hand over her mouth before another shocked laugh escaped her. "You're joking."

"I would think you would be *thrilled* your cousin would want to follow in your footsteps," Aunt Emily said curtly, venom laced in her words that Sam could recognize too easily.

Unbelievable.

"Well, considering how you and Uncle Ron acted when I got into writing, color me surprised that you sound so… supportive now," she said slowly.

What surprised her almost as much was trying to imagine Tommy writing a book. When he'd spent most of his life being handed everything he ever wanted on a silver platter, thinking of him putting in the time and energy to write anything was almost fiction in and of itself.

Her aunt cleared her throat. "He shows promise, and I think he could really make some good money."

She wasn't going to mention the extensive process of *getting* a book published and simply sighed again. "And how would I be participating in this exactly?"

"Didn't that little friend of yours you went to school with go into publishing?"

Sam held the phone out, as if it had shocked her, staring at it with indignation. Oh, this was priceless. After all these years of giving her shit for being an author, all of a sudden when Tommy wants to do it, it was up to Sam to roll out the red carpet for him?

It was her turn to scoff when she put the phone back to her ear. "You want me to put in a good word for him." A statement, not a question. She didn't need the question. It was the only thing that made sense.

"Well, of course," her aunt stated, as if it were the most obvious thing in the world—as if she was more surprised that

Sam hadn't *already* immediately started calling everyone she knew.

"Aunt Emily," she started as calmly as she could muster, "it's not as simple as saying, 'Hey, my cousin wants to write a book. When should he come in to sign a deal?' There are steps that he's going to have to take in order to get to a point where he would talk to an agent. I can walk him through what he needs to do when I have a—"

"I should've known you would make this as difficult as humanly possible."

"Me?!" she exclaimed. "You know you can't just snap your fingers and get what you want, right?"

"Excuse me? How dare you speak to me that way! I know your mother—"

"—raised me better than to speak to you that way. I *know*," Sam finished for her, letting her irritation bubble out of her. Sam surprised even herself at that one, though she immediately felt a sense of euphoric pride for not letting that guilt trip hit the way it normally did.

There was a long pause on the other end of the phone. An eerie silence that Sam should have taken advantage of by hanging up the phone, and she regretted not doing exactly that when Aunt Emily finally regained her composure.

"We're the only family you have, Samantha," Aunt Emily finally said, "and it would do you some good to remember that if you're not careful, you'll run off anyone left to give a shit about you."

&.

The sky opened up just in time for Sam to make it back to the coffee shop. After her call with her aunt, she decided to head there to get some more work done because it didn't seem possible at her place. Her aunt's words spun around in her mind like a greyhound on a racetrack, so she'd thought some fresh air would do her good. Raindrops pattered insistently against the glass window, the sound rhythmic and calming as the once-calm sky churned with dark clouds.

It was the perfect kind of atmosphere for her to pick up the book she'd last been reading, curl up in a comfy chair with a cup of hot coffee, and take in the relaxing atmosphere of the quiet cafe. But she had a lot to do.

She shrugged out of her jacket and tossed it, and her bag, onto the back of her seat. Her hair hung in tangles around her shoulders, a combination of the wind and rain wrapping them in tangles and clinging to her neck. She reached for the hair tie wrapped around her wrist and gathered it into a messy ponytail, emphasis on the messy. A little delighted sigh whizzed out of her when the cool air of the cafe greeted her heated skin after the humidity outside.

Pulling out her laptop and notebook, she set to work. But only after a few words tapped away on the keyboard, Sam's mind began to drift.

You'll run off anyone left to give a shit about you.

No, she was absolutely not going to let her aunt ruin her day.

Blinking a few times to snap herself out of it, Sam set back to work. Her fingers flew over the keys as words poured out of her in a deluge. If there was anything she could be grateful for, it was that, while her mind was preoccupied with everything she had going on, the words that started to pour of her never faltered.

It felt like a release in and of itself.

Right after her parents had died, her aunt had shoved her into one of those grief counseling sessions. It was just a single session, just to evaluate to make sure Sam was sane and wouldn't cause trouble at home, or, at least, that was how her aunt had put it.

It was honestly the one good thing her aunt had ever really done for her.

The counselor had encouraged her, in the short time they had together that one summer afternoon, that if she was having a hard time expressing her emotions, she should try writing. She had told her that she could write about what she was thinking, how she was feeling, write a letter to someone she was having a hard time confronting, or she could make up complete works of fiction to process those things. Basically whatever worked for her.

Sam often wished she could remember the name of that counselor, so she could thank her, as it not only turned out to be the thing she loved most and had made a career out of but it was just about the only way she *could* really get out her thoughts in a cohesive way.

She was so distracted by the story as it began to unfold in front of her that she didn't notice someone settling into the spot across from her. "Did you know when you're so focused on writing, you scrunch your nose a little? It's the cutest fucking thing I've ever seen."

Sam froze, recognition running up her veins like ice.

As if her day couldn't possibly get worse, the universe saw that and decided to throw in a nice cosmic joke.

Paul shot her a crooked smile from across the table, causing her to reflexively flinch in her seat. He looked the same as he had the last time she'd seen him, on that disastrous date. The dark waves of his black hair were combed back neatly, the matching black thick-rimmed glasses perched over a pair of bright hazel eyes, now piercing her, as if he were trying to skewer her into place. He was attractive—at least he had that going for him—but it had been his attitude and mannerisms that had initially turned her off.

"Paul… what are you doing here?" she asked, trying to force any fright out of her voice. She refused to let him think he scared her, even if he really did right now. This was confirmation enough for her to know, without a shadow of a doubt, that Paul was following her. It wasn't just phone calls and texts anymore.

He leaned forward casually, as if they were old friends. "I wanted to see you. You won't respond to me through calls or texts, so I thought I'd just join you for coffee."

Sam cringed back in her seat, closing her laptop as she tried to discreetly begin packing her things away. If Paul noticed, he made no indication. He simply watched her, enraptured, as if he were hung onto whatever words she offered. But she'd met guys like him back in college, the ones who were so full of themselves that any hint of rejection would cause them to immediately turn sour.

"I think I was just about to leave," she said, collecting her now packed bag in her hands.

"No, please don't leave," he said quickly, immediately reaching across the table and grabbing one of her hands. "I can't stand not seeing you every day. You can't leave now!"

Sam ripped her hand out of his grasp and quickly shimmied out of her seat. "Paul, I've lost count of the number of times I've told you that I don't want to see you!"

She shot out of her seat, slinging her bag over her shoulder as she made her way toward the exit. She wasn't sure where she was gonna go. She certainly didn't want him following her home, but she wanted to put as much distance as she could between them.

Paul jumped up out of his seat and stood in her path, grabbing her arm, more firmly than he had her hand, and held her there in place. She winced under the pressure of his grip but tried to pull away from him. "Paul, let me go."

"You can't just walk *away* from me, Sam. You and I belong together! All you need is some time to realize that, and everything will be fine. Just give us a chance, I *promise* you'll feel what I'm feeling too!" he huffed out, desperation leaking into his voice.

When she went to push him away, he snatched her other arm with the same pressure.

She'd been creeped out by him before, yes. The calls and texts had been extremely unnerving and had frightened her at just how persistent he'd been. But she thought she could handle it. She *had* been handling it. She'd sent those recordings and screenshots over to that cop she'd spoken to before.

It was now, however, with the intense gleam in his eyes, that she felt genuine fear.

Her eyes flashed over to the two baristas standing behind the counter, their attention fully on her, as if they'd already been keeping an eye on the situation. As soon as her eyes met with the taller male barista, he leaned over to say a few words to the other barista, a teenage girl, and started making his way toward them.

"Is there a problem here?" he asked firmly, coming to stand next to Sam.

Paul, a good few inches taller than the barista, but level with Sam, puffed out his chest a bit and tried to shoot him a reassuring smile. "Oh, no, we're fine. My girlfriend and I, here, are just having a discussion."

Sam shook her head vehemently. "I'm *not* your girlfriend Paul. Please let me go."

"You heard her. She's asked you to let her go. I think it'd be a good idea for you to listen to her."

Paul scoffed. "This is none of your business. This is between her and I. Buzz off."

His grip only tightened painfully, causing Sam to let out a yelp and pull back harder from him.

The manager, who Sam had only seen a handful of times, rushed over to stand at her other side, flanking her. She hadn't seen him come out of whatever back office he'd been tucked away in, but when she looked over to see the teenage girl standing behind the counter, holding her phone up in front of her, Sam had never been more grateful.

"I'm gonna have to ask you to leave," the manager instructed. "Let go of her before I have to call the police."

Paul ignored him, turning his attention back to Sam with a new viciousness in his eyes. "Just come home with me, Sam, and we'll sort this all out."

"I'm not going anywhere with you. Not now, not ever," she spat back, managing to release Paul's grip on her arms with the help of the barista next to her.

The next few moments were a blur as Sam stood there, the manager and the barista all but having to shove Paul out of the store as he immediately launched at her. He reached for her, but the manager deflected and grabbed onto him, the barista grabbing onto the other side to keep him away.

A string of curses flew from his mouth, accusations and threats so vulgar and graphic that it made Sam want to gag. She closed her eyes momentarily, feeling a bit lightheaded at how quickly the exchange happened, but by the time she finally was able to open her eyes, Paul was gone.

"I told him I already called the cops, and he bolted," the manager explained when he returned, seeing the confused look that must've been on her face. "They should be here soon."

"Are you okay?" the teenage girl asked, reaching forward

to gently touch Sam's arm. As if she sensed how lightheaded she still felt and wanted to make sure she didn't crumple to the floor. A tempting notion at the moment, but Sam quickly tried to recover, hating the concern plaguing all of their eyes.

"No, no, I'm fine. Thank you," she assured them, turning her attention to the girl. "Would you, would you mind sending me the video you recorded?"

"Of course! I'll send it to you, and I'll be sure to give it to the cops when they get here. I think I see their car pulling up now," the barista said, gently rubbing Sam's arm. Despite being well over a foot shorter than Sam was herself, she'd have been lying if the motion didn't make her feel at least a little safer.

"Is there anyone you want us to call for you?" the other barista asked.

Charlie. She wanted Charlie. His name was on the tip of her tongue, but she wasn't going to say that right now, despite how much she might have wanted to. Right now, she wanted to get herself together.

"I'm okay for now. I'm just gonna clean up in the bathroom if that's okay?" she said, her voice sounding weaker than she thought it would.

When she closed the bathroom door behind her, she leaned back against it and held back a sob, refusing to let it out and desperately trying to calm her tattered nerves.

"I'm okay. I can handle this," she whispered to her reflection in the mirror.

Sam repeated the same mantra she'd been repeating to herself over the years, hoping that it would help calm her. She repeated the phrase several times until the words rang in her ears, to the point where she was almost able to believe it.

If she were honest though, all she wanted in that moment

was to retreat to the safety of her bed, to sleep until the chaos of the world faded away around her.

If this didn't grant her a restraining order, though, she didn't know what would.

Charlie probably wouldn't kick her ass for not telling him sooner about this, but Angel certainly would, so that was a cross she would have to bear in the future. She wasn't sure if she had the strength to deal with all of that right now.

Her fingers dug into the flesh of her arm as she hugged herself.

She wanted Charlie.

The need to have his arms around her clawed at the back of her throat until she almost choked on it.

He was still at work as far as she knew, but she began thinking of excuses to see him. Everything, anything, just to feel his comforting touch. In that moment, she didn't care if she took advantage of their arrangement to do it, she just needed to be with him.

An idea struck, and she shot him a quick text before tucking her phone back into her pocket. She'd have to clean herself up after giving her statement to the cops waiting on the other side of the door but all in due time.

For now, she'd give herself a few moments to herself in this bathroom.

Only then did she let the tears she'd been fighting roll down her cheeks.

CHAPTER 13

CHARLIE

Thursday ushered in an odd kind of peace that Charlie found himself in desperate need of. Not just because it was so tantalizingly close to the weekend but because he knew it would help take his mind off of things.

Work already hadn't been great, with an unexpected outage that had caused pandemonium the entire day. But that hadn't been the worst of it. It was the phone call he'd gotten on the way home from the office that sealed his foul mood.

The last thing he'd needed was an extra dose of guilt heaped onto his plate.

Charlie got along with his brothers, for the most part, but some days were more of a challenge than others. Despite the slight age gap between the three of them, they had gotten along well growing up. Other than the usual brotherly antics that came along with having two rough-and-tough older brothers, things had been relatively normal.

Their dynamic had changed thirteen years ago, and it hadn't really been the same since.

Peter tried, as he and Charlie spoke at least once a week

on the phone to check in with each other, and Tyler had his moments, but it all still felt a bit strained.

Tyler had called as Charlie was packing up to leave the office, complaining about the unfair workload of helping out with the charity. It wasn't Charlie's fault that Tyler had bitten off more than he could chew, but Tyler had a knack for really pushing buttons when it came to this time of year.

They'd argued back and forth for a while until Charlie eventually had to hang up on him. He'd call him back later when he cooled off a bit.

He supposed everyone in his family had different ways of coping. It was par for the course. His parents had started a whole charity to make something so awful into something positive, Peter decided to channel his grief into working at a non-profit that supported some of the same causes his parents' charity did, and Tyler pretended like nothing was different the entire rest of the year but would get super agitated with literally *everyone* the month of.

Charlie, on the other hand, preferred if everyone didn't make a whole spectacle of it every single year—having these huge elaborate celebrations around the anniversary were just about the last thing he wanted to have to deal with.

It had been thirteen years, and the only positive thing he had gotten over those years was that the four of them had stopped looking at him and seeing her. The pained looks in their eyes diminished with time to the point that it felt like only recently that they started to see Charlie as a whole individual again.

And that certainly didn't ebb the guilt that consumed him every year.

So, when Sam had messaged him to see if he wanted to catch a movie, a romantic comedy that had only just come out, he'd been more than happy to accept the invitation. If anything, to take his mind off reality for a bit and spend time with the one person who seemed to understand him.

Sam and Erica hadn't been close like she was with Charlie, as Erica ran with a different crowd, but she had known her well enough. She was Charlie's sister after all.

He remembered how young he was when he and his family had gone to Sam's parents' funeral. The way he'd watched Sam from where his family stood, wanting more than anything to walk over and hold her hand. Tell her everything was going to be alright. Comfort her and wipe away the few tears she'd allowed to slip down her cheeks.

And then how, ten years later, when the roles were reversed, Sam had done the thing he couldn't and had stood next to him. Holding his hand quietly as they'd lowered Erica down into the ground.

It's your fault.

He quickly dismissed the thought before it could latch on too tightly. The familiar ring of it caused a headache to pound between his temples as he pulled into a parking spot. He'd insisted that he picked Sam up from their apartment building to take her to the movies himself, instead of her catching the bus again from the coffee shop. Despite her protests otherwise, and despite the throbbing in his head, he didn't regret his decision.

He shot off a quick text to let her know he was there before leaning forward and resting his head against the steering wheel. A few deep breaths and his churning stomach would soon settle.

Locking himself away in his apartment for the rest of the day had been a tempting thought, more than tempting actually, but he'd decided against it. Despite his mood, he knew that he'd feel infinitely better spending time with Sam.

A sudden rush of heat surged through his body thinking of her—and remembering the other night.

He'd kissed her.

He had actually kissed her.

Her lips were as soft and inviting as he had always imagined, fulfilling every dream he'd ever had about them. It had been short and sweet, literally forcing himself away from her before he'd made a complete fool of himself. It had taken just about all of his strength at the time to do it, to turn around and walk away when he'd wanted nothing more than to shove her back against the wall and kiss her until she was delirious from it. But he had to keep a level head.

He knew that she hadn't kissed him because she *actually* wanted it.

It was for her book.

And if he needed to continuously repeat that mantra to get through this, he would. He could do this. He *would* do this, for her.

When Sam bounced into view from the apartment complex exit, waving at him, Charlie finally felt himself relax. The sight of her never failed to brighten his mood.

She looked stunning. Her hair cascaded around her shoulders, her usual waves appearing more refined than usual. Loose curls framed her face, blending seamlessly with the natural waves that rippled like silk in the light.

He swallowed thickly at the pair of blue jeans she had on, her hips swaying with her movements that made it nearly impossible not to follow. The pair that Charlie always had a hard time distracting himself from, especially if he was walking a few paces behind her. It made him appreciate the coffee-colored knitted pullover she had on —an odd pick he had to admit with the warmer temperature today — hoping it was loose enough that he wouldn't be able to get a good view of her ass.

Despite how much he might want to.

He raised a hand in greeting as she grabbed the door handle and jumped inside, the sweet smell of whatever perfume she'd put on immediately wafting in his direction. It was sweetly feminine and familiar, like walking through a field of daisies on a warm, sunny day.

"Thanks for picking me up, Charlie. I appreciate it!" she exclaimed as she pulled the seatbelt across her chest and clicked it into place. Close up, Charlie could see the hints of brighter blonde strands bouncing effortlessly around her shoulders—usually lost in the sea of copper but highlighted perfectly in this light, like little rays of sunshine hidden in the fire.

"Of course. Had to save you from seeing the sniffer again." Charlie laughed, affectionately reaching over to tousle the loose strands of her hair. He was unable to help himself, causing her to playfully swat his hand away with a laugh. When she did, he noticed a bandage wrapped around her forearm poking out from beneath the long sleeves of her sweater.

He nodded at her arm. "What happened there?"

She froze for a fraction of a second before rolling her eyes. "Oh, you know how clumsy I am! When I was curling my hair for our little movie date, I ended up dropping the curling iron by accident and burnt myself a bit. It's fine. Don't worry."

His chest warmed. "You didn't have to curl your hair for me."

"Only for you, *babe*," she teased, giving him a little wink as she did.

Damn it, he hated how hot that was—and how hot it was

to hear her call him that. Even if it was what they had agreed on. He adjusted himself in his seat, distracting himself by shooting a smile at her and pulling the car out of the garage.

He cleared his throat, which suddenly felt thick. "As long as it wasn't the sniffer getting too handsy, I guess it's fine."

"I haven't taken the bus in a bit, so we're safe there. You two will never be friends, though, huh?" Sam sighed.

Charlie chuckled. "As long as he leaves you alone, we're best of buddies. Now, what movie are we seeing again?"

She shrugged. "It's just some romantic comedy. I saw an ad for it earlier and thought it sounded interesting."

His eyes glanced over at her, noticing that her smile seemed a bit forced. "Were you working out of the cafe today?"

Sam fiddled with her hair. "I was. I didn't stay too long, though."

"Why? You love that place."

She shrugged again, more curtly. "I was working from home earlier this morning and decided to go over, so I just stayed long enough to drink some coffee and then headed back home. My stomach started to feel a bit sour. I think I had a little too much caffeine without a lot of food."

"You want to stop and grab something?" Charlie offered, scanning to see what was available.

"No," she answered quickly. "You know this place has more food than I could handle. I'll just order something when we get there."

The theater Sam had chosen was a bit further out of Durham than usual, closer to downtown Raleigh, but it was one of the only theaters they ever liked going to.

It was a chain, but it was a movie lover's dream theater, with movie memorabilia crammed into every inch of the lobby and hallways leading to each screening. If Charlie were honest, though, he just liked it because the seats were comfortable, could be reclined back, and they had dine-in food and drink options that were served seat-side.

The theater was empty, aside from the two of them, when they eventually made their way inside, which made sense given that it was a Thursday afternoon. Charlie was grateful for the quiet that could never be found there on a weekend. It made the atmosphere feel more cozy—exactly what he needed.

Sam led the way to their seats, holding her phone in front of her as she did to check the seat numbers.

Exactly as he feared would happen, his eyes trailed down the curve of her spine, past the pullover, and down to the tight jeans she'd put on. Those damned hips of hers were at it again. Nothing about the movement was different than how she usually walked, but it was the way these jeans managed to hug every inch of her.

He wondered if she knew what an incredibly nice ass she had. Sam never complimented her own appearance very often, so he doubted it. An absolute shame, if he was allowed to have an opinion on the matter, because she really did. Perfectly curved and just enough of a handful that Charlie's palms itched just thinking about it.

Sam whirled around in front of him, nearly stumbling over her as his eyes finally released their hold on her rear end and shot up to her face. Where she was already looking more than amused up at him.

"You okay?" she asked before pointing to the two seats next to them and lowering herself into one.

"Yeah, sorry. Just lost in thought," he shot off quickly, wondering distantly if leering was part of their agreement.

She giggled, but something caught his attention when she turned to face the movie screen. He couldn't quite put his finger on it. It was just something in her eyes that made him feel a bit uneasy.

"You sure you're okay?" he asked as the theater lights began to dim.

She blinked a few times and looked over at him. "Yeah, why?"

"I don't know. Something seems to be on your mind."

She shook her head, her body leaning against his as if surrendering to the gentle pull of gravity. "I'm fine. I promise."

Her head found a comfortable perch there on his shoulder, a content exhale escaping her lips to tickle his ear.

The movie began playing on the screen, but neither of them seemed to be paying it much attention. Their hands had found one another in the dark, on the joint arm rest of their seats, seeking the comfort that the other held in the quiet space between them. Where words didn't exist, the movements of their hands did, an unspoken conversation taking place.

Charlie brushed his thumb across her knuckles, following the line from there down to the fingertips and back up.

The feeling of her hand in his silently echoed the various things he loved about her. The smooth and almost porcelain-like quality of her skin, like those soft edges she so often tried to hide. The sharp sting of her nails as they playfully dug into his hand, like the sharpness of her tongue when it was needed. The warmth radiating through her hand, like the pure ray of sunshine she could be, lighting up his entire world.

He didn't want to stop touching her, caressing her, feeling her skin against his.

Sam pulled Charlie's hand into her lap, her fingers tracing lazy circles along the curve of his palm. It was a featherlight touch, but it kicked up sparks of electricity that skittered along his skin and forced the hair on his arm to stand up on end. It *felt* electric, sitting there with Sam's head on his shoulder and her hand teasing his.

It all felt so natural, as if this was how it was always meant to be, and the thought caused Charlie to choke on the sense of yearning clawing desperately at the back of his throat.

CHAPTER 14

SAM

"I love… *everything*… about this!" Angel all but shrieked from the other side of Sam's laptop screen.

The following morning, Sam had decided to set up shop at home to work on her book when Angel had messaged her. She was back from her friend's wedding, so the two immediately hopped on a video call to catch up.

When the topic of the book inevitably came up, Sam gave her the general pitch of what she had decided to work on. As Sam had walked her through the details, she tried to slyly make mention of the fake-dating experiment with Charlie, so she could better research the romantic elements, and… well… Angel took the ball and ran with it.

"I've *always* said that you two are absolutely fucking adorable together!" Angel squealed, clapping her hands together excitedly.

Sam pinched the bridge of her nose. "And *I've* always reminded you that Charlie and I are just friends. I needed help getting a better idea of how to build a realistic romance, and Charlie offered to help. Don't make it weird."

Angel rolled her eyes. "I still don't know why you two haven't just fucked and gotten it over with already."

Sam, mid-sip of her coffee, rushed to cover her mouth before she had the chance to spit the liquid all over her screen. "Jesus, Angel, a bit of warning before you say shit like that, please?"

"Do you honestly forget that I know you really well?" Angel continued. "I might not be Charlie, but come *on*!"

"What?" she asked, wiping her mouth.

"You can *not* sit there and tell me that you don't still feel a certain type of way toward him and that if he *kissed you*, which I'm still fucking squealing about, trust me, that he doesn't feel the same way?"

It was Sam's turn to roll her eyes this time, and she shifted uncomfortably. "I told you before, he doesn't feel the same way I do, so it's a moot point. We promised to make it realistic for research purposes, so Charlie's just being the good guy that he is and is doing exactly what I asked him to do."

"Oh God, this again…" Angel groaned as she rubbed her temples.

"What?" Sam exclaimed.

Angel rested her head in her hands and leaned toward the screen. "A wild idea here, but do you think maybe, just *maybe*, what you overheard him saying back when he was… what… fucking thirteen?… Well, however old he was, that maybe he's *possibly* changed his mind since then?"

Sam sighed heavily. Every time Angel brought the topic up, she made the same argument, but Sam knew what she'd heard, and she respected Charlie enough to respect how he felt. It didn't matter that they were just teens when he'd said it, and that she'd accidentally overheard him telling his older brother Peter when he'd questioned Charlie on the topic. His words were pretty clear. *She's just my best friend. Nothing more, nothing less.*

It had stung at the time; she could admit that. It *still* stung on occasion when she herself struggled with her own feelings. She'd hoped that her feelings would fade with time. But, if anything, they only flourished more over the years.

And after he'd kissed her, she'd frustratingly spent most nights since thinking about it.

"The point is," Angel continued with an exaggerated lull in her tone, "that there is a remote possibility that you're being ridiculous not talking to him about how you feel. That maybe Charlie only suggested this whole thing because he didn't want you doing this with someone else?"

If only, Sam wanted to say. If there was anything she'd learned living with her aunt and aunt's family, it was to never expect more than what was offered. And even then, question why it was offered in the first place.

She didn't have to expect the worst if she never asked in the first place.

With Charlie, as childish as it might sound, she feared that voicing that long-hidden desire would change everything. Whether for the better—or for the worse.

Her biggest fear was that it would ruin everything.

"I regret ever mentioning this," she muttered.

Angel smiled and laughed. "Who else are you going to talk to about stuff like this with? You're like a sister to me."

An air of professionalism slipped into place for only a moment before she laughed once more. "Look, I know we don't live with each other anymore and can only see each other once in a while, but I still *care*. And *more* than just as your agent. We're friends first. You know that I love you. I just think that denying something that could be absolute magic won't make you as happy as you think it will."

Sam rubbed her temples to ease the dull ache growing there. "Look, at the end of the day, we have a tight deadline for this book, right?"

Angel sighed, sounding defeated. "Right."

"So, having someone helping me with, arguably, one of my weakest points when it comes to writing a romance, is really helpful," she said as she pulled her notebook out of her bag and waved it in front of the screen, "I lost count of how much I've written so far just from the two outings we've had."

"Outings? Is that what we're calling it these days?" Angel chided with a wink.

"My *point*," Sam emphasized, ignoring the grin on her friend's face, "is that these *dates* we're going on are really helping me. And me going to that charity thing with Charlie is going to really help him."

Angel nodded. "That's right. That's coming up around the same time as your deadline is. How's he holding up?"

Sam shrugged. "You know how he is this time of year. He doesn't like talking about it."

"True, though I'm sure his parents deciding to throw some elaborate party *on* the anniversary itself doesn't help."

Sam simply nodded in return. "I'm glad I can help at least, even if it's small, like getting him out of the bachelor auction part of it."

"Probably won't hurt just having you there with him, period," Angel added.

"Anyway," Sam said, "I wish I hadn't said anything, but I suppose it'll be good to have you on board with it since it'll help with my writing process."

Angel gave her a sharp wave, a new French manicure briefly flashing on her delicate fingers as she did. "When you guys get married, do I get to pick my own maid-of-honor dress? Or are you gonna stick me in some frilly pink number?"

"Angel—"

"I'll need a date to your wedding, and I guess Peter will probably be a groomsman, so it would only make sense to go with him."

Angel was rich for giving her a hard time about Charlie when the long-lasting tension between her and Charlie's older brother had been going on so long that Sam could feel it from where she was.

But she wasn't in the mood to go tit for tat at the moment.

Sam groaned. "This is serious! I need to be able to talk about this without you being all weird about it."

"Fine, fine. You win," Angel conceded, lowering her voice to a more serious tone as she continued. "Then if you really want to do this fake dating thing with Charlie, I have a suggestion I think could work for you." The golden hoops dangling from her ears, accentuated with little white pearls at the bottom, clanged against the side of her neck as they stilled against her.

The change was so sudden that Sam quickly flipped to a new page and grabbed her pen. "Okay, what is it? What are you thinking?"

"Now, this might be a bit more of an advanced activity —but I think with some practice, the two of you could really get some great feedback for a specific part of your book."

Sam nodded along excitedly. "What is it?"

"It's the ancient art of sexual intercourse. Try it. I'm sure you'll love it. I hear it's been a while for you," Angel teased, waggling her eyebrows at her and immediately dropping the serious look.

Sam shoved the notebook away from her, snatching up

her coffee instead to take another drink as Angel cackled in the background. "You're the worst."

"Hey, if it means you might get some good dick out of it at least, what are you complaining about?"

Sam once again choked on her drink, this time so suddenly that it caused her to cough violently as it sucked down the wrong pipe.

"A-are you trying to kill me?"

"No, but if you're into choking you might want to call—"

"I'm hanging up now. Goodbye!" Sam called out before all but slamming the laptop shut.

Sam really had her work cut out for her.

CHAPTER 15

SAM

Exhaustion wrapped around Sam's body as she placed her laptop on the kitchen table. She had chosen to stay up late once again, inspired by yet another surge of creative energy. She was working on a crucial part of the book, as it would set up the tone for everything that followed, so she believed that if she could get it just right, the rest of the story would flow effortlessly.

It had taken a while, but as she read back what she'd written, she felt a sense of satisfaction. It was still only the first draft, so nothing was set in stone, but it was a good start.

Beyond that, however, she was also aware of the fact that there was more at stake than simply capturing readers' attention. If it failed to impress her publisher, she'd be in trouble with her contract, and she may as well flush everything she'd worked so hard on down the toilet.

"No pressure or anything," she whispered at the screen with a touch of humor.

As the first trickle of light poured in through her window, Sam squinted at the glare now bouncing off her computer, the tension that had built up in her muscles a palpable reminder of exactly how long she'd spent hunched over the keyboard.

She groggily pulled herself out of the kitchen chair and sauntered over to the coffee pot, desperate for the hit of caffeine.

A short break wouldn't hurt.

With the weekend now upon her, she had all the time in the world. Freed from the weekly constraints of the administrative tasks she needed to do, she could fully immerse herself in her work with little interruptions.

As the coffee machine hummed to life, Sam gravitated toward the nearest window to open it, letting the gentle cool breeze through. It woke her up, the feeling of drowsiness that had enveloped her disappearing in an instant.

When the machine signaled her coffee was ready with a cheerful ding, she decided to take a few moments to watch the sun rising. She filled her cup, pouring milk on top to soften the taste until it was at the brim, and headed over to the couch. She easily nestled herself in, the steam rising from her cup to tickle her face and accompanying the warmth against her palms.

There wasn't a cloud in the sky to distract her from the vibrant hues painting the horizon. It became the perfect canvas, a mixture of pinks, oranges, reds, and yellows blending seamlessly in a pattern only nature could craft.

The natural playlist from her neighborhood drifted in with the breeze, adding to the ambiance. The steady hum of cars on the street below her continued in waves as the nearby traffic light switched from red to green. Leaves from the nearby park skittered across the road, accompanied by the thrum of voices as people passed by.

She felt at peace.

The rest of her problems could wait. Even if it was for the

briefest of moments, when her mind settled long enough to break free, she wanted to luxuriate in the morning.

Sam was more of a morning person to begin with, so she had grown used to being the first one up on any given day. Her mother had been the same way, often rising before the sun did.

She remembered the mornings when they got up together to watch the sunrise together, usually on the weekends. Her mother would have a cup of coffee in hand and would make Sam a cup of hot chocolate, so she had something warm to drink.

She remembered the quiet. The serenity of something as simple as the sun rising at the start of each day. The warmth of her mother's smile.

It was rare she thought of such things the older she'd gotten. Life had taken over as she had learned how to navigate it without both of her parents. When she had finally managed to get out from under her aunt, she often would find herself exactly like this—sitting and watching the sunrise.

The mere thought of her aunt in that moment soured her mood slightly, remembering the texts she'd purposefully tried to ignore that she'd gotten the night before. It only had confirmed that the only reason she'd reached out to her was to get something. To *put in a good word* with her publisher for her cousin, Tommy, who apparently saw his cousin's success and thought he could do it *even better*.

Sam scoffed at the idea, knowing the kind of work ethic Tommy was capable of. Which, for lack of a better term, sucked. If it were up to Aunt Emily, however, she'd try to convince anyone willing to listen that Tommy was the next great American novelist.

Lost in thought as she mulled over exactly what response she should send to her aunt, if any, a firm knock echoing from the front door ripped her back to reality. The sound startled her, causing the cup she held to slosh dangerously with the still piping hot liquid inside. She muttered a curse and set the cup on the coffee table to avoid disaster.

Who on earth could be at her apartment at a time like this?

Sam froze for a moment. Could it be Paul? After she'd given her statement to the cop the other day, she'd been afraid that he would show up. She'd hadn't left the apartment much since, but whenever she did, she double, triple, *quadruple* checked her locks multiple times through the night, just to be sure.

He hadn't shown up, thankfully, but the thought was in her head now.

She crept toward the door, making sure to scoop up her phone to have it at the ready as she walked carefully and tried not make any noise. If it was him, she didn't want him to know she was home.

She knew she should've told Charlie beforehand. He was going to…

She peered through the peephole to catch a glimpse of whoever was on the other side, and a sigh of relief rapidly tore from her.

Sam swung the door open, a hint of frustration now tugging at her features, as she glared up at Charlie.

He was smiling, a warmth to it that matched the warmth of the coffee cup she'd put down only moments ago. Without a word, he immediately extended an iced coffee and crumpled brown bag toward her, as if reading her mind.

She accepted the items from him with an eyebrow raised at him suspiciously, her stomach grumbling appreciatively from the enticing smell.

"Do you realize what time it is?" she asked, ushering him inside.

He chuckled as he followed, closing the door behind himself. "Good morning to you, too, babe."

She ignored the hairs that raised on the back of her neck from hearing him call her that. It had been her idea to start calling each other *babe*, but it affected her far more than she thought it would.

To distract herself from the fluttering in her chest, she pulled a fresh bagel out of the bag. Her mouth watered at the way the steam rose from it in delightful little tendrils. Fresh out of the oven.

"Your bribery will only get you so far," she teased, taking a healthy swig from the iced coffee in her other hand and practically moaning in delight. "Is there a special occasion for this visit? I know you're an early bird, as well, but this is early even by *your* standards."

Her gaze shifted over to him as he leaned casually against the kitchen counter, his arms folding across the black shirt that hugged his chest. Noting his ensemble, she raised her eyebrow further at him.

He had a pair of mustard-colored khaki pants on, instantly an odd choice as Charlie almost always wore jeans. The pair of hiking boots he had on thumped against the floor as he adjusted himself to grin at her, the same pair that he'd gotten a few summers ago when she'd forced him to finally replace the previous ones.

He looked rather… outdoorsy.

It was a look, she noted, that suited him quite a bit. His five o'clock shadow appeared heavier and more noticeable than it had the other day, the beginnings of a beard Charlie always tried to fight growing in nicely and making his face appear more rugged. That, combined with the outfit, made him look like he'd fit well in a log cabin by the lake.

His eyes were far too bright for this time of the morning as he chuckled. "Yes, actually. It's time to get those gears moving. We have plans for today."

Her eyebrows shot up her forehead. "It's early on a Saturday. What could we possibly have planned? Was I part of this planning process?"

She'd been so busy working and writing that she had to think for a minute if there was anything that they had planned that she could've possibly forgotten about. Nothing came.

"I found a place that I thought would work well for another date, and I took some creative liberties and planned it out. So, hut-hut"—he motioned at her—"get moving."

She blanched at him. "You're joking, right?"

"Nope. Now, hurry up. We're burnin' daylight," he instructed, waving her off in the direction of her bedroom once more.

She rubbed her eyes, sleep creeping back in at the edges. "Is this an outdoor activity? I assume so with your boots on."

"Yep, we'll be outside. It's supposed to get warmer later, so hurry and get dressed so we can get on the road."

"Charlie," she whined. "It's early, and I'm not sure if I'm ready for any surprises. Can you just tell me what—"

Before she could process it, he quickly snatched the iced coffee from her hands, holding it at bay from her. "I'm holding this hostage until you get changed. Wear something for warm weather with some tennis shoes or something."

Sam eyed him, feeling her resolve melting away at the dimples poking out behind the wide smile spread across his face. Damn it, she loved his smile. It was like a weapon when he wanted her to do something.

"Do I need to bring anything?" she finally asked.

Charlie shook his head. "Not really. Maybe some sunglasses and a hat if you feel so inclined?"

"Makeup?"

"Not unless you really want to put it on. We'll be outside. Now, *get*!" he ordered, shooing her.

Sam trudged to her bedroom, willing the caffeine to start kicking in. She closed the door behind her and went to the closet to find something. She was still wearing the pair of yoga pants and baggy shirt she typically wore to bed, so she'd have to dig through her wardrobe to find something suitable.

After a bit of deliberation, she opted for a pair of jean shorts, a sports bra, and a sunny yellow tank top. Simple but comfortable. It didn't hurt that it was also still clean, as she was in desperate need of the next laundry day.

When she emerged from her room, she gave a demonstrative twirl to make sure he approved.

He laughed, his eyes lingering for a moment before he spoke, narrowing on her arms. "Did you burn both arms?"

Sam caught herself before asking what he meant, looking down at the matching bandages on both arms, covering the bruises that had started to form there. It had only been a few hours when the spots where Paul had grabbed her had started to turn yellow and purple. She'd bandaged both arms to prevent anyone from seeing the marks, particularly Charlie, and she was glad she had now.

He'd accidentally already seen one, and the lie that had spilled from her lips had been easy. Mostly because it was a lie by omission.

She really did burn herself trying to curl her hair. It just hadn't been where the bandages were.

She rolled her eyes and laughed. "Yeah, I was clumsy. I accidentally dropped the curling iron and flailed a bit to try and catch it, managing to burn both arms in the process. Sounds like something I'd do, huh?"

He looked hesitant but nodded slowly. "Yeah, just… be careful next time, will ya? Would like to keep you around in one piece."

"Yeah, yeah, I know," she teased, relieved he didn't push further. "Is it okay if I bring my laptop? I might want to run to the cafe later to get some writing done after we get back."

"That's fine. You ready to go?" he asked, extending her iced coffee toward her.

"Yep! Let's go… wherever the hell we're going," she replied.

She checked the door twice as they left, making sure that it, in fact, had locked behind her. Even opting to check it a third time before she was satisfied to walk away, afraid momentarily that the morning fog lingering in her head was messing with her.

As they reached Charlie's SUV, he stepped ahead of her, theatrically opening the car door and offering her a hand inside. Despite the eye roll she gave him, she couldn't hide the smile that accompanied it. Sam accepted his hand and eased into the passenger seat.

"Alright, what do we have planned?" she asked, the car thrumming to life as the air conditioning wheezed and forced the familiar scent of Charlie's cologne into her senses. A welcome smell that not only mercifully drowned out the effect her morning breath had as it was blown back into her face but sent a familiar longing coursing through her.

"If I told you," he answered, "that would defeat the purpose of a surprise, wouldn't it?"

"Okay, give me this at least," she begged. "Is it nearby?"

"No, it's about a forty-five minute drive."

She nodded thoughtfully. "Will this be an all-day excursion?"

He shrugged. "Depends. But most likely not. Don't worry; you'll get your writing time."

"And you can't tell me what it is?"

"Nope," he replied with finality.

He tucked his arm behind the headrest of her seat as he turned to look over his shoulder to back the car out. The position caused the muscles in his arms to flex as he began to slowly pull out of the spot. She couldn't quite put her finger on exactly why, but something about the position was incredibly sexy. It could've been that it showed off the toned muscles of Charlie's arms, his time in the gym paying off in spades.

Maybe it was just the way his arm behind her headrest felt intimate, familiar in a way she couldn't quite put into words.

Or it could've even been the straining tendon of Charlie's neck that flexed at him looking over his shoulder. If Sam listened to the intrusive thought that just blasted into her mind, she'd lean over and lick her tongue along the ridge of it.

That thought caused her to nearly jump out of her seat.

Good Lord, she was no better than a man.

She cleared her throat and looked out the window, as if she were suddenly fascinated by their surroundings. The car turned out of the garage and onto the nearby street, the sound of the stereo coming to life as it connected to Charlie's phone.

"One tiny hint?" she pleaded.

Charlie chuckled but shook his head once more. "You're not gonna break me."

"Fine." She pouted and took a sip from the coffee Charlie

had returned to her. "Do you want me to DJ while you drive?"

"If you want. I figured we could talk on the way there, but you can also play DJ if you'd rather."

If she could bribe him to tell her where the hell he was taking her, she'd talk the rest of the trip.

"Talking works," she said.

"Give me a status update on the book, then."

She laughed. "A status update? You're not Angel in disguise, are you?"

Charlie made a dramatic show of looking down at himself before scowling. "Last I checked, I'm not a tiny Korean woman."

"She'd kick your ass for calling her tiny, you know."

"I have no doubt about that. That's why I'm not calling her tiny *to her face*." He chuckled. "What did she have to say when you told her about the book?"

"She was excited about it, said the premise sounded good and that she can't wait to read the first couple of chapters," Sam answered, carefully leaving out the things Angel had said about her and Charlie.

She was already struggling this morning and didn't need the help.

Charlie smiled. "I told you she'd like it."

"She's a romantic at heart, I think," Sam said.

"Nothing wrong with that for sure," Charlie confirmed as his hand reached over quickly and flicked something off her knee. "Sorry, there was a bug on there."

She wanted to ask if it had been a butterfly because it had apparently flown away from her knee and gone into her stomach, Fluttering about rapidly in there like some blushing virgin who had never been touched before.

It was embarrassing how swift it was, and she definitely

wasn't sure what the hell her body was doing. It was a bit alarming, but she'd be lying if she didn't admit that she'd liked it. A lot.

In fact, she wanted him to put his hand back—to rest it on her leg as he drove. She chewed on the idea for a moment before reaching over and grabbing his hand, dragging it back over the center console and placing it on her thigh. Higher than where it had been moments before on her knee.

He seemed a bit surprised for a fraction of a second, though whether because she'd grabbed his hand so suddenly or because she'd put it on her thigh, she couldn't tell. Whichever the case, his hand immediately relaxed against her, giving her thigh a gentle squeeze.

It was far more intimate of a touch than the two of them had ever shared, well, besides that kiss, which Sam was definitely trying not to think about right now in fear that her body would further disobey her higher brain function. But it was a struggle.

Goosebumps prickled to the surface where his skin made contact with hers, the warmth of his hand on her cool skin causing it to practically sizzle in the most delightful way.

Charlie, on the other hand, appeared completely calm. In fact, his eyes had gone back to focus on the road, and his thumb started to gently rub back and forth where it rested. As if it were the most natural thing in the world to him.

Dammit, maybe the physical contact part of this was a bad idea...

The little voice in the back of her head didn't care, though. She wanted Charlie to touch her. Even if it wasn't real, she could at least pretend that it was. It was a dangerous game to play, but she wasn't going to worry about it now. Not with Charlie's hand touching her like his hand was made to fit there on her thigh.

"You okay, babe?" he asked, and though his eyes remained on the road, she could see the almost cocky smile spreading.

So, she simply nodded and reached forward to cover his hand with her own. "I'm great."

❧

The two had gotten lost in conversation for most of the drive, with Sam hardly noticing the passing miles until she felt suddenly drawn to the window.

It was an endless sea of green oak trees, standing strong and proud as they lined the roads and disappeared into the rural land surrounding them. A lush green field came into view, drawing her attention away from their conversation, the greenery punctuated with a speckling of bright-red specks hidden within the foliage.

The less buildings there were, the more vegetation sprung out of the ground.

She and Charlie had grown up in a small town about an hour and a half west of Durham, so it wasn't as if she were unused to so much nature around her. In fact, seeing so many oak trees like this made her wonder whether Charlie's parents still had that massive one out in their front yard. The one with the driveway wrapped around it and the tire swing dangling from one of the thick branches above.

There had been many summers spent swinging on that tire.

Living in the middle of the bustling downtown area of Durham had made her forget what that felt like. It wasn't nearly as chaotic as downtown Raleigh or—God forbid— New York City, where Angel lived, but it was enough to forget the day-to-day sensations that living more rurally provided.

It was a welcome change in scenery.

The crystal-clear blue sky above them made the almost-completely-risen sun to sparkle across the land—only the faint glow of the horizon keeping its full effects from taking hold. The perfect sort of day for whatever outdoor adventure awaited them.

Charlie pulled off the main road, turning Sam's attention to a large pavilion in front of them—a gravel parking area coming in between it and the road. The red tin roof in front of them shimmered under the warm rays of the sun, yellow posts rising from the concrete beneath to hold the roof up. Nestled beneath it, on the far-left side of the pavilion, the tan-brick exterior of a small building could be seen with a row of ice cream options out on display.

Once Sam was able to read the signs posted nearby, she excitedly clapped. "A strawberry farm?"

Charlie grinned. "It's not an apple orchard like you'd mentioned, but I figured you'd like this better."

"It works *so* much better! Are you kidding me?" she declared.

Charlie threw his car into a spot closest to the building, and Sam all but ripped her seatbelt off. She couldn't even remember the last time she'd ever set foot on a strawberry farm, and she couldn't wait to get her hands on them already.

The sound of Charlie's laughter followed her, cut off as she slammed the door behind her excitedly. The crisp morning air flooded her lungs, a hint of moisture lingering in preparation for the oncoming warmth expected later that day.

She clapped her hands together as Charlie made his way around the car. "This is perfect! What a great surprise!"

"I figured you'd like it."

She turned to thank him, to tell him how much fun this was going to be, but the words caught in her throat. His smile was warm, his dimples crinkling into his cheeks. The effect of it lit up his entire face, and not just from the sunlight.

There was a heart-aching gentleness in his eyes that she hadn't seen before, affection welling up there, as if watching her jumping around excitedly was enough to brighten his entire day. She'd only seen that look once, back when her parents were still alive.

It was how her father looked at her mother every day.

And there was Charlie, looking at her as if she were the most precious thing in the world to him. It was the kind of look that most little girls dreamed of in their happily-ever-afters—all swimming in the depths of Charlie's ocean-blue eyes.

That had to be wrong, though... He was just happy about surprising her… right?

"This is *amazing*!" Sam finally blurted when she realized she was staring at him.

He laughed. "Well, I can pat myself on the back later. Let's get started."

It took them only a few minutes to check in and get their baskets before they were walking out into the field, patches of red speckles around them in the brush. Her mouth began to water at the very sight of them. Store-bought strawberries were delicious, but boy, was she thrilled to taste a freshly picked one.

They veered off to the right, distancing themselves from some of the other guests that had arrived around the same time they did. Charlie affectionately nudged her shoulder with his, offering her an encouraging nod forward. She didn't need any further permission, immediately rushing to take the lead and practically bursting at the seams.

She stooped down in front of the first bush, eyeing the selection of lush strawberries it contained.

It appeared to be the perfect time for them to be plucked, their coloring *just* right with the perfect shade of red. Each of them were plump and juicy looking, practically begging to be picked and devoured.

A mission she was more than eager to accomplish.

It seemed a shame to let the beauty of them go to waste, so Sam pulled her phone out of her pocket. Angling the camera just right, she clicked a few pictures of the particularly thick bush she was crouched in front of.

"There it is," Charlie said as he squatted down next to her.

She tapped the button and took another picture. "There what is?"

"That smile."

She rolled her eyes to hide the flash of embarrassment that coursed her and bumped his leg with hers. "Yeah, yeah, celebrate your victory by helping me pick these. How can you not be drooling over these babies? They're perfect!"

He chuckled and gestured toward her phone. "Here, give me that."

"What for?"

"To take a picture of you, I need to document that look on your face."

She laughed. "I'm not giving it to you, then!"

She held the phone away, a pointless effort with his long arms as he easily reached over and attempted to snatch it from her grasp. "It's part of the experience. Now, hand it over."

After putting this together for her sake, a picture suddenly didn't feel like a big ask. She sighed but relented, letting it slip from her grasp. "Fine, but just one!"

He positioned the phone in front of him, making a few

adjustments to his angle until he seemed satisfied. There were a few faint clicks from the device as he started instructing her on what to do next.

If she'd had any mind to scold him for taking their attention away from the strawberries next to them, it completely dissipated seeing the happy expression crinkling the corners of his eyes.

It *was* the most fun she'd had in quite a while, and she was grateful that he would think of doing something like this just for her.

The whole reason she'd wanted to go see that movie with Charlie the other day had little to nothing to do with her book, their experiment, or even the movie itself. She'd just wanted to be with him. It was one of the few times she'd felt safe since then, and while she knew she would have to tell him what was going on at some point soon, a twinge of fear kept her mouth shut.

Charlie was far from an angry person, but he *was* protective. What if he got angry at her for not saying anything sooner? Would he get angry for putting herself in that situation in the first place? Her mind raced with each new doubt and fear that popped up, an endless spiral of *what if's* that she choked down.

She'd tell him this weekend, she resolved. She just wanted one more day, one more peaceful and fun day with him before the chaos lurking in the shadows came creeping in.

Charlie spun around and extended the phone outward, leaning back with a playful peace sign aimed at the camera with her hovering just inches behind him. He gently jabbed at her with his elbow until she finally relented, scooting closer and offering a peace sign of her own.

The two descended into a series of goofy poses to make

each other laugh, which worked wonders. The two were nearly in tears when her phone started to ring in Charlie's hand.

Another number she didn't recognize flashed on the screen.

She snatched the phone back from him and quickly sent the caller over to voicemail. She excused the abruptness of it on a spam caller, but Charlie watched her carefully as she returned her attention back to the bushes in front of them.

Sam quickly developed tunnel vision as she plucked only the largest strawberries she could find. Allowing her mind only to wander to figure out all of the delicious, sweet treats she could make with her spoils.

A strawberry jam, maybe? Oh, a fruit parfait would be perfect with how fresh these were. Even just a simple bowl of strawberries and cream had her nearly drooling. She'd have to run to the store later to get another can or two to go with it, but it would be so very worth it.

A soft munching sound prompted her to glance over to catch Charlie eating one of the strawberries he'd just picked.

"Charlie!"

He looked at her curiously, mumbling around the bite in his mouth. "What?"

She giggled and gently shoved him. "You're not supposed to eat them yet!"

"Says who?" he asked before taking another massive bite to finish it off. "Isn't that like… half the fun?"

"You're supposed to pick them and save them for later!" she argued. "Otherwise, this place would be littered with half-eaten strawberries."

Charlie laughed. "I'll put the stem in my basket, so I can toss it out when we get back. Try one. Live a little!"

As she started to protest about her very detailed order of

operations for appropriate strawberry picking etiquette, he leaned forward and plucked what was undoubtedly the largest strawberry she'd seen that day.

"Try this one," he offered, holding the massive strawberry in front of her face.

She pushed at his hand. "I'm saving them for later!"

"Then I'm giving you one of mine. Come *on*, just try one. Take a bite. It won't kill you," he promised, holding the strawberry steady in front of her.

When she continued to regard him with skepticism, he pushed the strawberry forward and nudged it against her lips. She was so caught off guard by the gesture that when she went to protest once more, Charlie seized the opportunity and pushed the strawberry into her open mouth.

"Bite," he instructed.

She did so obediently, despite the blood suddenly rushing to her face.

"Good girl."

Oh Lord. If it wasn't for the incredible flavor as it burst across her tongue, an indecent sound would have strangled its way from her at hearing Charlie call her a *good girl*.

The strawberry was, indeed, one of the most delicious strawberries she'd had in a very long time. The usual bitter tartness was minimal and replaced by a strong, sweet citrus taste that took hold of her. Despite herself, she beamed at Charlie as she nodded in approval.

"See?" he teased, tossing the stem into his basket. "Told you."

She was about to comment on the residue left behind on his fingers, the juice causing a trail of sticky reddish liquid to trickle down his hand. She followed the line as it continued, dripping down his strong forearms and almost reaching his bicep. The urge to lick him was again pervasive, and she vaguely wondered why this was now the second time recently that she'd wanted to lick something from him.

But it was pretty hard to do much thinking when Charlie brought his hand to his lips and quickly sucked the juice off, a light smacking sound accompanying each finger. A quick drag of his tongue down his arm as it chased the liquid, reaching the tail of it before it reached the crook of his arm.

Heat burned her skin as she watched, the simplicity of the gesture somehow vastly more erotic than she'd have ever expected. Each moist pop sent an unexpected shiver down her spine. A dangerous pooling of heat spreading between her thighs as an image of something *else* he could suck flashed in her mind.

She fiddled with her hair to distract herself. Charlie didn't appear to be the least bit fazed by it, instead giving her an almost shy-looking smile before turning back to continue plucking from the nearby bush.

That had been... unexpected...

And very, *very* hot.

"So... What are you gonna do with your share?" she asked, her voice a touch higher than she intended it to be.

"These are all for you."

She turned. "What?"

Charlie laughed, flashing her a smile. "You didn't think I'd have it in me to rip these suckers away from you, did you?"

"Oh, Charlie, you should at least keep the ones you picked!"

He shrugged. "I like strawberries but not nearly as much as you do. Besides, I did this because I knew it would be something you'd enjoy. You know, like the good fake boyfriend that I am?"

Yeah, that didn't help the heat still pulsating between her thighs.

"You're a little too perfect, babe, you know that?" she said casually, reaching forward to collect another strawberry.

Understatement of the century, honestly, considering how casual Charlie had been about the whole day. As if it were just any day and not the sweetest date she'd ever been on. Fake or not.

"You think?" he asked.

She nodded, plucking another strawberry to inspect. "I know so. I can always tell how hard you're trying, no matter what you're doing. You pay attention, and you're very thoughtful. I mean, come on. Taking the person obsessed with strawberries to pick them for the day?"

He laughed again, the infectious kind that made her want to laugh along with him. "I just wanted to make you happy, that's all."

Her heart clenched in her chest at that, the tenderness and sincerity ringing true to who she knew Charlie to be.

Her best friend, who had always looked out for her, even when she hadn't wanted him to.

Her best friend, who offered to help her with her book because he knew she needed help and wanted to make sure that she wasn't taken advantage of.

Her best friend who—she was starting to realize at an alarming rate—she didn't *just* have a crush on.

Dammit.

"You're very good at it," she replied honestly. "I just hope that you've had fun too? I'd hate if you did all of this just for me and didn't at least have fun."

Their eyes met once again, the softness she'd noted earlier when they first arrived coming back. A softness she needed desperately not to read too much into.

"I'll always have fun when I'm with you," Charlie said with a wink, looking both cocky and yet entirely serious about his statement.

She cleared her throat and reached for her next strawberry. "I'm just not sure how you've remained single so long. You're a catch, you know."

The words came out before she could catch them, but she refused to look at him, too embarrassed that she'd let the words slip in the first place.

He paused, and for a second, she worried she shouldn't have said anything, but instead, he chuckled. "I could say the same about you, you know."

At that, she snorted. "I'm a mess, Charlie. Most men wouldn't touch me with a ten-foot pole if they knew what was good for them."

The truth if she had any to offer. Other than her more obvious answer—that she had no interest in any other men, other than the one next to her. She was well aware of the fact that she could be a lot to deal with.

"I wouldn't say that," he answered, standing up with a grunt and extending a hand out for her. "Let's go. I think we've picked this area clean."

CHAPTER 16

CHARLIE

*B*ringing Sam here was one of Charlie's better ideas. He couldn't deny that the surprise, however, hadn't been entirely for the purest of reasons.

The stress of relaying calls between Tyler, Peter, and his mother for planning purposes was wearing down on him. He'd decided to surprise her with this to distract himself from all the chaos going on with that area of his life. He knew it would help him focus on something good, something he looked forward to.

The sensation of Sam's lips lingered, electricity dancing across his fingertips from where her lips had touched.

All he'd wanted today was one thing—one thing that could drag him from the depths of all the thoughts and feelings that had been plaguing him all week.

That smile.

Sam's smile was one of the only things that could bring him back from the precipice, and he had selfishly wanted it by any means necessary.

When he got that smile from her earlier, the one that gave

her an almost ethereal glow, everything felt right with the world again.

He hadn't been thinking about what effect seeing her eat that strawberry would have on him.

The puckering of her lips, the sucking sound she made so her bite wouldn't fall, the swift movement of her hand to catch any juices before it could escape down her chin, that little half-covered groan she'd made when it hit her taste buds…

Practically orgasmic to witness.

He had pulled his hand away to suck the juice from his fingers, hardly even noticing the juice that had trailed most of the way down his arm, before she could see exactly what that little groan she made did to him.

Thank God they'd both been squatting.

His thoughts turned to what she said to him before, desperately finding anything to relax his body. The comment had made him want to simultaneously laugh and scream at the same time.

How was he single, indeed.

The answer remained there, untouched between them, however, as plainly to him as if he would've stamped it across his forehead.

How could he *possibly* think about another woman when she would always be the one thing he ever wanted.

Peter had been suspicious of him about it more than a few times growing up. He would tease him about it, as brothers do, often relentlessly. But despite Charlie's protests and denials, Peter seemed to know better.

It wasn't until they had both moved out and gone to college that Charlie thought he might be able to have the opportunity to ask for more. See if there was a chance she might feel the same. That is, until he'd accidentally overheard her talking to Angel about it one night back when they'd been hanging out at Angel and Sam's apartment.

He knew then that any chance he might have had was long gone.

The fact remained, however, that Charlie loved her regardless of whether or not they were together in that way. He'd likely always carry that torch for her, but he loved her enough to keep things the way they were.

Another fact cropped up at the same time.

This situation was destined to burn them both if they weren't careful. He knew that, but part of him didn't *want* to care about it. Let them go up in flames together; he'd welcome it. All he wanted was to burn with her. Scorch them both until they were completely ruined for anyone else.

That was a fairytale. At the end of the day, he knew what this was between them right now, and he needed to keep reminding himself of that every chance he got, or he would be the only one to get burned.

Sure, they'd always been a bit flirty with one another. He wasn't a complete idiot. But that was all it had ever been, *flirting*. Nothing more. He would always be *just a friend*, or at least if what she'd told Angel back in college was to be believed.

With their baskets filled to the brim, they strolled back over to the main building. The pace slow as they enjoyed the warmth surrounding them, delaying the inevitable end of their outing—but they weren't about to leave just yet. Charlie wanted more time, even if it was just a few minutes.

This place wasn't only known for their strawberries; they had fresh ice cream in the adjacent building, so he knew exactly what to do next.

"Here, take these over and snag a table for us," he instructed as he pointed to the group of picnic tables to the left of the pavilion, beneath an open wooden canopy. "I'll grab us some ice cream and join you in a minute."

"Oh, Charlie, at least let me pay for this…" She started before he held up a hand to stop her.

"Nope, I got this. This was my surprise, after all. Let me spoil you a little, hm?"

He gave her a gentle push, watching in amusement as her gaze flickered in that stubborn way of hers. She wanted to protest further. He could practically hear the words tumbling out of her mouth, but she didn't.

She turned on her heels, both baskets in hand, and headed to one of the picnic tables.

He, in turn, went the opposite way. Pulling open the screen door and walking up to the counter. He ordered two cones, a chocolate for him and a strawberry, of course, for her.

Glancing over his shoulder through the glass window separating him from the picnic area, he watched as Sam comfortably settled down at one of the tables toward the back. Her gaze was fixed firmly on her phone as she sat down. The shade from the umbrella centered on the table helping to ease the squint of her eyes as she began typing away.

He relaxed back against the counter, folding his arms across his chest. The cashier behind him hummed as she worked, the song choice a familiar one that he couldn't quite remember the last time he'd heard.

He mulled it over for a moment before the realization hit him.

A memory flashed by, so vivid and unexpected that he could practically feel the heat of the car as it had driven away.

Erica rolling her window down and leaning out, the sound of this song blaring through the speakers as her friends chattered behind her. The affectionate wink and finger to her lips as they had driven away. A memory he had replayed countless times over the years.

She'd known he'd keep her secret.

And he'd regretted it every day of his life ever since.

He swallowed the growing lump in his throat and pushed the memory aside. He'd gotten very good at trying to forget, but with the anniversary fast approaching, it was always more difficult.

It was the last thing he wanted to be thinking about right now.

Luckily, the cashier called out to him, holding out two generously endowed cones toward him. He was here, with Sam. They were on a date, regardless of the circumstances surrounding it. It was still a date, and he was determined to show her a good time. She deserved that much.

He swung the screen door open on the other side of the building, circling around to head to the table.

Sam was standing now, appearing to be engrossed in a phone call now. Her animated gestures, aimed at no one in particular, made it appear to be a less-than-pleasant conversation. There were only a few people in the world he knew of who could sink their teeth into her like that, and the thought of it had him fuming.

What could her aunt possibly want with her now?

There was little that the two of them hadn't talked about over the years, but her family had always been something she intentionally spoke little of. Not that he blamed her, as she reversely never pressed him on the topic of Erica, so he tried simply offer a sympathetic ear whenever she did open up about it.

His interactions with her aunt, and her aunt's family, had been scarce, as they rarely indulged in anything, or anyone, that mattered to Sam. The handful of times he *had* been around them in person felt like too many.

Her aunt and uncle were the kind of snooty people that others would avoid at parties in fear of the constant one-ups every conversation seemed to bring with them. A constant battle for superiority in every action, every word.

It always left a bitter taste in his mouth, but it was part of the reason why she spent so much time at the Backman family home back then.

If there was any testament, however, to exactly how much his mother had grown to love Sam as one of her own, it had been about a year or so before they were scheduled to graduate from high school. Sam and her aunt had a particularly nasty fight, over what he couldn't recall her ever saying, and she had shown up at his front door.

The look on her aunt's face, when she had finally shown up to try to drag Sam back home and his mother had gotten a hold of her instead, was priceless.

He slowed his pace, so as not to intrude on her call, despite his peaked curiosity.

Her gaze darted toward him as he approached, her hand hovering over the speaker. She mouthed an apology to him and accepted the cone he offered.

"I'm hanging up now," she said with finality as she practically slammed her finger onto the red call button, looking back to him with a soft smile. "Sorry about that."

"Don't be. I can take a guess who that was."

She paused for a second before she rolled her eyes and settled into the spot across from him. "She's relentless and opportunistic, I'll give her that."

"What'd she want?"

She shrugged, taking a tantalizing lick of her ice cream that forced Charlie to dial into her voice like his life depended on it. "She's been on me about putting in a good word in with my publisher."

"For who? Her?"

"No, Tommy."

"*Tommy?*" Charlie asked incredulously. Anyone who wanted to read a book written by that spoiled brat needed their head examined.

Sam giggled. "I know. I had the same reaction when she told me. But apparently, according to both of them, since I was able to make a career out of it, it must not be *that hard*, and he wants to try his hand at it and get a few bucks out of it."

That protective instinct of his wanted to lash out, curling around him with a fist-like vice, but he took a steady breath instead. If anyone knew how hard she'd worked over the years, had seen all the sleepless nights she'd spent writing, the countless hours she'd spent hovered over one of her books with a bright-red pen, it was him.

The mere insinuation that she was anything less than a literary genius was not going to fly for him.

"She sure changed her tune," he offered simply, swiping some of his ice cream into his mouth.

Sam scoffed this time, trying to appear dismissive despite the hurt lingering in her eyes. "Are we shocked? If it's something I want to do with my life, it's stupid and pointless and doesn't bring *the family* any prestige. The second Tommy hints he wants to do it, I'm suddenly under obligation to help."

"Tommy? Write a book?" Charlie shook his head. "I'm pretty sure not all the lights are on where he's concerned."

She stifled a laugh by taking another lick of her ice cream. "No, I'm still convinced that he didn't get into Stanford on his own, but let's not worry about them right now. There's something else I wanted to talk to you about."

"And that would be?"

Sam's eyes softened on him. "How are *you* doing? Really. I know the anniversary is coming up, and…"

Charlie held up a hand to stop her. This was the last thing he wanted to talk about today, and he wasn't about to let it ruin his day. "Stop. I'm fine, I promise."

"I don't want to push; I just want you to know you can always talk to me about it if you—"

"Thanks," he quickly interrupted, "but I promise it's not necessary."

Sam considered him for a moment before she sighed and changed topics. "This has been a really fun day, Charlie. I can't tell you how much I appreciate you setting this up."

She flashed that sunny smile of hers at him, and his body immediately relaxed. *There it is.*

"As much as I'd love to toot my own horn, this was literally nothing, Sam," he replied with a laugh. "Five minutes of research and a bit of a drive is nothing. I'm just glad you enjoyed yourself."

She shrugged. "I don't know, not a lot of guys I know would even think to do anything like this."

"And that is painfully sad."

Her laugh further warmed her features, causing the freckles across her nose to dance in the sunlight. "Come on, let me toot your horn for a bit."

"Oh, if you insist. Though, if you think this is going above and beyond, babe, I have a lot of work to do as your fake boyfriend."

She leaned back, raising an eyebrow at him. "I don't know. This is already a pretty high bar to beat."

He laughed this time. "And where is the bar usually? In hell?"

CHAPTER 17

SAM

The entire drive back, Sam didn't want to think about the phone call.

She cursed herself for even accepting it in the first place. It wasn't a number she recognized, but she thought it might've been that cop calling to give her an update. They were on the lookout for him, as he would definitely be going to jail for what he had done, but he'd essentially disappeared.

She should've known it would be Paul.

And he wasn't just pissed off about how the whole situation at the cafe went down. He was *livid*. So angry, in fact, that she had hardly been able to barely make out half of what he said. Ranting and raving about how she was ruining everything, about how she was his, about how he needed to *show* her that she was his.

That last part frightened her.

She didn't want to find out what he meant by that.

She watched the passing scenery out the window as she held onto Charlie's hand, their fingers laced together. The feeling was more comforting than arousing, as it had been earlier.

There was no avoiding it now—she'd have to tell Charlie. Not that she wasn't going to before, but now she couldn't dilly-dally about it.

Tomorrow. She would tell him for sure tomorrow. She'd invite him over to her place to talk and hang out, and she'd explain the whole situation. Start to finish. No details spared. He deserved that much, at least.

Just… not now. Not today.

The day had been such a wonderful escape. It was exactly what she'd needed without even knowing it. She wasn't ready to face reality just yet.

One more day before things tumbled back down.

Charlie's thumb rubbed across her hand soothingly, his eyes on the road but a smile crinkling his dimples the way she loved. She watched him out of the corner of her eye, not wanting to let on that she was essentially staring at him in hopes of distracting herself from her thoughts.

He really was an incredibly handsome man, frustratingly so in her opinion.

His seatbelt stretched across the muscles of his chest, more well defined now from his time at the gym. Charlie had always been a bit self conscious about how tall and lanky he had been when they were growing up, but he had absolutely put the work in to grow out of that.

It would almost be an insult *not* to admire his hard work really.

And admire she did. She couldn't help it.

Looking at him for a beat too long, however, began to stir something in her. The way the sunlight poured onto him through the sunroof, giving his light-brown hair an almost golden glow. The sharp cut of his jawline at this angle. The toned complexion of his arms flexing as he turned the wheel onto another street.

Heat pulsed down her body and buried itself between her legs, creating a heartbeat of its own.

Charlie gave her hand a squeeze before he released it, instead going to rest his hand on her thigh as he'd done on their drive over earlier that morning. She was surprised that she hadn't already burnt his hand with the heat prickling up from within her.

Why on earth was simply *looking* at this man turning her on this much?

She ran her tongue over her suddenly parched lips.

His thumb repeated the motion from when he'd held her hand moments before, rubbing a gentle line across her thigh soothingly. Both a comfort and torture all at the same time. She wondered what it would feel like if his hand went further up, dipping below the edge of her shorts toward her…

"You okay?" Charlie asked, an amused chuckle in his voice, as if he could read her thoughts. An instant wave of embarrassment washed over, afraid that he somehow *had* read her mind.

When had they parked?

Sam blinked a few times to bring herself back from whatever dream-like state she'd lulled herself into.

"Yeah," she dismissed as she fiddled with her seatbelt. "Sorry. I was just thinking about some notes I need to add in."

He flashed her a smile. "Have fun today?"

She couldn't look him straight in the eye, not after her train of thought seconds prior, but she laughed. "How could I not? This was literally tailor-made just for me. Of course I had a blast. This was a great idea, Charlie."

He chuckled. "What can I say, babe? I know you well."

"That you do."

"Don't thank me yet," he said after they both hopped out

of the car and began walking into the apartment building. "You don't know what I have in store next. I could be lulling you into a false sense of security."

"Ah, yes, the calm before the storm. I'll be sure to keep my eyes peeled," she teased, walking quickly to beat him to the staircase. The last thing she needed right now was to walk behind this man where she could easily ogle his ass after her previous thoughts.

"You should. I'm very mysterious, you know."

She paused to laugh. "Right, you, Mr. Mysterious."

"Don't joke. I could be, you know," Charlie tutted behind her.

"You're too nice. I think you'd have cracked under the pressure if you hadn't shown up at my apartment so early in the morning and had I been more persistent with my line of questioning. I was an easy target."

Charlie made a dramatic stabbing motion into his chest. "You wound me. I totally pulled it off. And besides, at the end of the day, you had fun. That's all I really cared about."

Sam fought the tightening in her chest as they continued up the stairs, feeling a bit relieved when they finally reached her floor. Yet, at the same time, she didn't want this to end. She wanted more time with him, *needed* more time.

They moved away from the landing, her apartment just around the corner and down the hall, when she met his gaze. All that softness, all the gentleness, greeted her once again. It wasn't unfamiliar, but it felt far more intimate than it had before.

"Well, either way, thank you for today, Charlie. I had a really good time," she said.

"You're welcome," he answered, taking a small step toward her.

Her breath hitched as he stood there, as if to gauge her

reaction, but didn't move an inch further. Watching her until she licked her lips nervously. "Are you going to kiss me now?"

Why on earth was she asking him that?

It wasn't as if it were the first time he'd kissed her, but thinking he was about to do it again had caused her brain to short-circuit. She wanted to apologize but instead heard him chuckle instead, a heated intensity there.

"You know, next time, you're going to have to not narrate that, right?" he teased, but his voice sounded thicker, a bit husky.

The hint of humor laced in his statement did help to calm the nerves firing rapidly in her veins, so she forced a shy smile onto her face. "I know, sorry."

He took another small step toward her, instinctively causing her to take a step back, watching his eyes as she followed his lead until she felt the wall against her back. He lowered his forehead to hers, able to more closely see the faint touch of pink starting to color his cheeks. "Tell me what you want, Sam. Don't tell me what you *think* I'm gonna do. Tell me what you *want* me to do."

His voice was barely above a whisper, the tickle of his breath against her cheeks. Everything in her screamed for him, for his hands on her body, for his lips on hers. Anything to relieve this inferno ignited between them in that moment, shooing that shyness away and replacing it with something else entirely.

Her eyes never left his. "I want you to kiss me."

The corners of his mouth tugged up into an entirely too smug grin for her liking. "*How* do you want me to kiss you?"

"There are options?" she asked, the last word squeaking out when Charlie moved to press a kiss against her neck. It was gentle, his lips hardly touching her, but it already had her toes curling.

"Of course there are," he murmured quietly. "There are always options."

This was definitely a side to Charlie she'd never seen before, but damned if she didn't love every second of it. Racking her brain to desperately find the words she wanted to say.

"Are-are you flirting with me right now?" she sputtered out, feeling a bit stupid for saying something that felt fairly obvious now.

He hummed low in his throat. "Maybe. Remember, don't narrate."

She nodded slowly, capturing her lower lip between her teeth when his lips went from her neck to her ear. His teeth nibbled the lobe before he placed another quick kiss just below it.

"Now, answer the question," Charlie ordered, placing a quick kiss to the tip of her nose when he pulled back, a smoldering look in his eyes that threatened to burn her alive if she wanted.

And boy, did she.

If he wanted flirty, she could give him flirty. "Kiss me like you mean it, then. Don't be such a fucking gentleman about it."

Her words surprised even her, but she didn't take them back. She meant every word. She didn't want to be the only one wild with desire. Even if it wasn't real, she needed Charlie's hands all over her. Anything to fan the flame burning in her.

And with the borderline feral gleam in his eyes piercing her to the wall, she'd say that was exactly what she was about to get.

Charlie suddenly grabbed both of her arms, yanking her toward him and placing them on his shoulders. A silent command as she obeyed and wrapped them around his neck.

His nostrils flared at her. "Don't be a gentleman, huh?"

His fingers slowly traced their way down the column of her spine, leaving a wake of goosebumps in their path. She was near breathless when he finally rested his hands on her hips, squeezing her gently before bringing her lips to his.

If the first kiss between them had been a tender and gentle exploration, delicately testing all the subtle ways that their lips could meet, this was light years beyond that. It may have started out with a couple of soft pecks, testing the waters between them, but it quickly escalated the moment Charlie angled her mouth against his to make the kiss deeper, harder.

Then all bets were off.

It became a flurry of hot, open-mouthed kisses that felt sloppy and dirty all at the same time. The slide of lips tangling against one another in a frenzy all its own. Nothing had ever felt this incredible, and Sam was completely at Charlie's mercy—exactly where she wanted to be, feeling the hard contrast of his body as it pinned hers against the wall.

He nipped at her lower lip as they changed the angle of their lips once more, their breathing becoming labored, almost tortured, as if every moment their lips parted were the worst moment of their lives.

All she wanted was to keep kissing Charlie like this until the world collapsed around them.

Had Charlie always been this good at kissing? Because, if so, every woman that ever entered his life was in immediate danger of eagerly spreading their legs for him—including her.

Her body arched into him, craving to fill every inch of space between them until nothing remained. A groan reverberated from him, an almost guttural sound that both surprised and delighted her. Oh yeah, she *really* liked that.

She wanted to hear him make it again.

But their moment came crashing down by the sound of laughter entering their periphery, a group ascending the stairs below them. Though it appeared that they stopped at the floor just below them, the jarring shift back to reality caused the two to part, albeit reluctantly. They were both panting, fighting to catch their breath.

"Are you alright?" Charlie asked, his lips a tantalizing shade of well-kissed that made Sam want to lean back in for more.

"Y-Yes. I'm good," she replied, a little more breathlessly than she meant to.

Good was the understatement of the century. Sam was on cloud nine.

"I guess I'll see you later, then?" Charlie said, as if he weren't sure what else to say, and she honestly didn't mind at the moment. She wouldn't have known what to say to him either after that, at least not until after she calmed her still-fluttering heartbeat.

"Yeah, see you tomorrow, *babe*," she added, the kiss leaving her unexpectedly weak and dazed.

He smiled in return, leaning forward to press a kiss against her forehead before turning and walking away.

She let him go, unable to stop him even if she wanted to. Her body still remained glued firmly against the hallway wall, pinned there by the invisible echo of his body. She watched him just long enough to see his footsteps fading into the distance, up the next flight of steps.

Now alone, she hovered there, taking a moment to collect herself. The lingering traces of their kiss tingled her lips.

Absently, she raised a hand to touch her mouth, finding that they, too, were as swollen as Charlie's had been.

That was… Well, that was by far the best kiss she'd ever had. Hands down.

Adjusting her tank top, she picked her bag up off the floor, which had fallen from her shoulder without her even noticing. She ran her hand across it, dusting off a bit of lint, before she picked up her two baskets of strawberries and turned to make her way to her apartment.

Though the day hadn't been nearly as warm as they had expected it to be, Sam's heated skin cried out for a cold, cold shower. A call she was more than eager to answer.

But as she rounded the corner, she suddenly realized that something was wrong.

She was sure… no, *positive* that she had locked her door before they'd left that morning.

She'd checked it several times because she'd worried her brain fog would make her forget. *Had* she forgotten? No, that wasn't right. Charlie would have told her if she'd left her door open like this.

Standing before her apartment door, wide open and practically hanging off its hinges, Sam froze in place. Splinters of wood caked the floor in front of her, remnants of what *had* once been a door trailing further inside.

Her bag slid off her shoulder once more and clattered to the floor.

"C-Charlie!" she screamed.

CHAPTER 18

CHARLIE

This woman was going to kill him.

Or he was in serious trouble of becoming Icarus.

If it meant he could kiss her like *that* again, though, he was almost willing to let it happen.

He had no idea what had come over him. Well, actually, that wasn't entirely true. Hearing those words, that *challenge* she'd issued him, blind desire took hold.

Don't be such a fucking gentleman about it.

Goosebumps raced down his arms and through to his nerve endings at the memory. If he'd continued the way he wanted to, he certainly *wouldn't* have been one.

His movements felt almost robotic as he made his way up the stairs, forcing himself to place one foot in front of the other just to keep himself from turning around. Every inch of his skin cried out from where he'd touched her, begging him to run back into her arms. Burning with a need that would likely take him hours to settle down.

He had a long series of ice cold showers in his future at this rate.

A sudden, shrill scream shattered Charlie's train of thought. It was so loud and piercing that he almost tripped over himself at the way his body instantly froze.

But it hadn't been *just* a scream.

Someone had screamed his name.

The flicker of recognition instantly turned his blood ice cold in his veins, piercing him straight to his core.

Sam.

Charlie flew back down the stairs, barreling around each landing as he took two, three stairs at a time. Blood roared in his ears, every ounce of energy he had propelling him forward and his mind singular on whatever caused her to scream like that.

It took him mere seconds to get back down to her floor, but it felt like a lifetime as he quickly rounded the corner to her apartment, nearly running straight into her as he did.

But upon seeing him, Sam reached out and latched onto him, burying her face into his chest as if her life depended on it. A grunt racked out of his chest from the shock of her fierce embrace. If she had put any force behind it, it might've knocked the wind out of him. Despite Sam's tall stature, she felt fragile as his arms instinctively went around her.

"Charlie," she whimpered, the sound almost completely muffled against his chest. "I'm-I'm sorry…" Her arms were tight, clinging to him as her body trembled against his.

White hot fear gripped him. He'd *never* heard Sam sound like that before. Shy, sure. Embarrassed, of course. Afraid? Not like this. Never like this.

She sounded so small, so broken, that it caused his chest to clench violently.

"Baby, what could you be sorry…" he started, but his attention was drawn to her front door.

The words died on his tongue.

A new fear ignited inside him as he attempted to gently pull her away from him. It had only been moments since he'd walked away, but in that narrow window of time, had she been hurt? Did something hurt her? He needed to check for himself. He needed to scour every inch of her.

His efforts to pull back only caused her to cling to him more tightly, as if she were afraid he would slip away if she released him. Yet, rather than this making him feel better, it only made him worry further. As if she were trying to hide something from him.

When he finally managed to peel her back enough to look into her eyes, his hands framed her cheeks. "Are you okay? Are you hurt anywhere?"

She shook her head, her bottom lip trembling. "No… I just found it like this…"

He pulled her back to him, shutting his eyes shut momentarily as he did. "It's okay. It's okay, Sam. I've got you."

She was okay. She wasn't hurt.

Charlie's heart felt like it finally began beating once more.

He tightened his grip around her. Her body shook beneath his touch, more pronounced as he held her there, and the fear that had stabbed into him—the one that had consumed his entire being—slowly began to morph into something else. Something much darker.

His gaze turned back to the door.

It had been split down the middle, as if forcefully kicked in. The tattered remains of one half hung precariously from the door frame, dangling uselessly in the air by its hinges while the other half lay discarded inside the apartment.

It couldn't have happened that long ago, given the nature of the destruction. No one would be able to walk down this hallway without seeing it—or hearing it happen. It must've been just before they'd gotten there. Meaning that there was a chance that whoever did this was still inside. That they were inside waiting for Sam to…

There was no way in *hell* he was going to let her check it out. His self-control teetered dangerously on the edge as he leaned back and saw the tears glistening down her heart-shaped face.

"Let me go in and see if anyone's still in there. I'll be right back," he said as he flicked a loose tear from her cheek.

"N-no!" she shrieked, the sound surprising coming from her, and it somehow only managed to add fuel to the fire swelling in his gut. "Don't go in. What if someone's still inside with a gun or something?"

He almost hoped that they *were* still inside.

It would give him something to hit.

He shook his head, unable to stop the hand that came up and rubbed his thumb across her cheek. "I'll be fine. You stay here, and I'll go check it out real quick."

"No, Charlie…"

"Call the police, and let them know someone's broken in," he instructed, forcing a calmness in his voice that he didn't really possess at the moment. "I'm just gonna check it out. I'll be *right* back."

"But…" She attempted to protest once more.

It took everything in him to pull away. "I'll be fine, promise. Just stay here. I'll be right back. Okay, baby? Just stay right there."

He stepped over the remains of the door, the sound of Sam's voice growing distant behind him as he walked inside.

The place was wrecked, no two ways about it. Almost everything lay in ruins. What was left of her furniture was scattered across the apartment in splintered wreckage. Only the couch appeared to be relatively intact, though the cushions had been torn apart like a rabid dog had been set on them. Feathers blanketed the area like a flurry of snowflakes strewn about. Even Sam's clothing hadn't been spared, with torn fabric intermixed amongst the downy chaos.

What in the living hell happened here?

Charlie crept from room to room, being sure to check behind doors, inside closets, just to make sure no one was there. All the while stepping over the leftovers of Sam's entire life in the process.

But, thankfully, no one was there.

He went back to stand in Sam's living room. It was eerily quiet, despite the destruction laying at his feet. The whistle of wind filtered through the broken glass windows lining her living room, the sound sending a chill up his spine despite the warmth of the sun pouring through. The sunlight cascaded through the empty void, causing the living room floor to almost twinkle from the shards of glass littering it.

It became abundantly clear that whoever had done this had no intention of stealing anything. There wasn't much left *to* steal from the looks of it. That would've been less jarring.

No, whoever had broken in had *intended* to destroy everything in their path.

And, Charlie feared, they had likely wanted Sam to be in that path.

When he returned to Sam in the hallway, finding her with her phone pressed to her ear, another woman was now standing next to her. Older than both he and Sam by quite a few years, the little tottering woman stood next to Sam, patting her back gently. One of Sam's neighbors, likely, though Charlie couldn't pinpoint which.

He wanted to thank her, but upon seeing him exiting the apartment, the woman protectively pulled Sam away.

"Hey, stay there! She's on the phone with the police!" she

called out, grabbing a walking cane leaned against the wall behind them and pointing it at him. "Don't you move!"

Charlie opened his mouth, about to explain, but Sam quickly placed a hand on the woman's shoulder. "No, no, he's with me. He was just… He was just checking to see if anyone was… if anyone was still inside. He's with… He's my… He's my boyfriend."

The other woman eyed Charlie but softened. She took a step backward to allow Charlie to cross the few remaining steps and scoop Sam back into his arms, tucking her safely into his body.

The woman remained there next to them, looking between the splintered door and the two of them in concern.

Charlie mouthed a thank you to her as Sam tucked her head beneath his chin.

"There was a tenant's meeting downstairs…" she explained, voicing an answer to the question lingering in the air. "It wasn't announced, but there was a dispute between two neighbors down the hall this morning. Everyone's still downstairs. I just came back to grab my medicine."

Well, that explains why there wasn't anyone nearby.

Sam's phone was still pressed to her ear, the faint echo of another voice on the other end as she continued answering questions. He listened to her struggle to suppress the tremble in her voice. The strong, opinionated woman he always knew and loved sounded as if she were ten years old all over again. Afraid and hiding underneath his kitchen table after another fight with her family.

A fierce protectiveness ignited in him in a way that made him feel particularly murderous at that moment.

Whoever had done this now had a much larger problem to deal with.

Him.

CHAPTER 19

SAM

"Are you sure about this, Charlie?" Sam asked as he tossed the small duffle bag that she'd packed onto his bed.

It felt a bit strange as she sat on one of the bar stools in Charlie's apartment. Unlike her own apartment, Charlie's two-bedroom apartment offered plenty of space to ward off the sense of claustrophobia plaguing her at the moment. She'd been here more times than she could count, but the current circumstances made it feel awkward and uncomfortable.

When Charlie had insisted that she stay with him, after it was suggested that she find somewhere else to stay for the time being, she hadn't had it in her to protest. Not that she wanted to in particular—other than that sense of pride at not wanting to put him out.

There had been no hesitation on his part, and if she thought about it, she had a feeling that he wouldn't have entertained any other suggestions. He'd watched her like a hawk when the cops had shown up, when they'd gone to the station for her to give a statement, when they'd been escorted back to her apartment so she could pick up a few of the remaining items left to take with her. The whole time, he'd watched her. Hovering so close that she was in constant danger of bumping right into him.

So, she had a feeling that he wouldn't be letting her out of his sight anytime soon.

She clutched the blanket that Charlie had draped over her shoulders, nursing the warm cup of tea he'd made.

"For the hundredth time, yes," he replied, returning to the kitchen and leaning against the kitchen counter as he folded his arms across his chest. "I'm not comfortable leaving you alone. Staying here with me for the time being makes the most sense."

"Still, thanks for letting me stay. I really appreciate it," she said.

"Of course, Sam. You didn't even have to ask."

She did, but it still didn't ebb the guilt that currently wracked her.

Once the initial shock had worn off, it hadn't taken a rocket scientist to figure out who had done it. There was only one person who came to mind.

She should've known better. It was laughable now, in hindsight, for her to *hope* that he would leave her alone. She felt stupid for thinking any differently. A youthful naivety that assumed the best of people had still tried to flicker to life inside of her through all the layers of doubt and mistrust.

After all, the cops were out looking for him as it was. For him to do something like this, it showed he had no intention of giving up.

Sam had never expected much from anyone. She knew all too well just how quickly the rug could be pulled from beneath her feet. But this was different. This was *dangerous*.

"I'm glad I decided to bring my laptop today…" she whispered, mostly to herself.

Charlie shifted. "I'm just glad that you weren't there when it happened…"

If she'd known that Paul had been on the way to her apartment when he had called her, thinking she was there…

"This is such a disaster." She sighed heavily, resting her head in her hands.

Sam hated being fussed over, always had. She knew how to take care of herself and had done a damn good job of fending for herself in whatever ways she could. But any argument she might have had quickly died down whenever her thoughts drifted back to her ruined apartment.

"It'll be okay," Charlie offered, a soothing lilt to his words that didn't seem as confident as it normally would have.

"How do you know that?"

"I just do. I'll take the couch while you're here." He motioned toward the bedroom when she looked at him. "You should go get some sleep. It's been a long day. We can talk about everything in the morning, after you get some rest."

She knew what he meant. He wasn't going to press for details right now, despite how much he probably wanted to. How much he *deserved* to.

It was easy to see the swirl of emotions, the curiosity, the worry, the *anger*, blazing in his eyes. Even when he averted his gaze from her, she could see it. She saw it in the way he shifted his weight, moving his arms to hold onto the edges of the counter behind him like he was trying to hold himself back. She saw it in the tight set of his jaw, the way he clenched it shut as if to keep the words from bursting out.

And while it was a very sweet notion that, even now,

Charlie was being so considerate, the thought of even trying to sleep seemed impossible.

"I… I don't know if I could rest right now," she said honestly, pushing the mug of tea away from her, "and you deserve to know, so ask."

He looked pained, as if unsure whether he should.

Sam hated this. She hated this feeling pulsing in her chest, stabbing into her with each breath that Charlie wouldn't look at her. It was absolute torture, seeing all the things he probably wanted to say to her pass over his face.

If he was mad at her, she was going to have to live with that.

Hell, she was mad at herself.

Eventually, a frustrated breath wheezed out of him. "Sam, why didn't you tell me what was going on?"

She found it hard to meet his eyes when they pierced her once again—those harsh blue eyes of his. She could feel the barely restrained heat in them, as if he was a breath away from igniting.

"I didn't want anyone to know," she said simply.

"Even me?"

"Especially you!" she cried out, the emotion catching in her voice. "You have enough on your plate with the charity coming up, the *anniversary* coming up. I thought I could handle it on my own. I know how protective you can get, and I didn't want to worry you. I was going to tell you about it tomorrow, which I know probably sounds like…"

Charlie scoffed. "You didn't want me… to *worry*? That you had a *stalker*?"

Well, when he put it that way, it did sound ridiculous. She'd known it had been. But hearing the words coming back at her didn't exactly help.

She shrugged shyly. "I didn't... I was handling things."

"Handling things? Sam, some lunatic broke into your apartment! Who knows what could've happened if you had been home when…" Charlie stopped and clenched his eyes shut before swallowing thickly, his Adam's apple bobbing in his throat from the effort. "How did this start?"

Strangely, this was the part she felt most awkward about. It felt weird having to tell Charlie—who she was currently fake dating for *her book* and who she had literally just made out with against the wall in her hallway only hours earlier—that she had gone on a date with another guy.

She sighed. "Angel suggested I try getting out there and go on a date, so I met him off of a dating app. We went on one date, and… well… it didn't go well."

Only leaving out a few details as to *why* Angel had made such a suggestion, but that was semantics right now.

He nodded thoughtfully, something she couldn't place flicking across his features as he worked his jaw once again. "Did he do something to you?"

She shook her head. "Not at the time. He was just a pretentious jerk, and I wasn't interested in seeing him again. I told him so and went home."

"Then what?"

"He didn't like that I'd rejected him, so he kept calling and messaging me to try and convince me that we were meant to be together. I blocked his number, and he started calling me on random numbers. It's why I changed my phone number."

Charlie cocked his head back. "Which time? You've changed your phone like three times since…" He paused, blinking his eyes a few times before clenching his fists against the counter. "How long? How long has this been going on?"

She licked her lips. "I met him earlier this year… I didn't want to worry you…"

"Well, mission *not* accomplished. Look… I get that you have this insane need to take care of yourself, but—Don't *even* start with me," Charlie stated as Sam went to protest, "—but someone wanting to hurt you tips the scales a bit, don't you think?"

"I honestly thought he would stop after what had happened at the cafe the other—"

Charlie held up a finger to silence her. "Hold on, what? What happened at the cafe?"

Shit. *Shit.* He was about to be *really* pissed off at her.

Sam pushed her mug forward and rubbed her face. "He… Look, I don't know how he found out where I was, but he showed up at the cafe the other day while I was there working."

"What did he do?" Charlie growled, his voice taking on a dangerously low tone, deeper than she'd ever heard from him before. It was enough of a difference that it caused her to meet his gaze again. He hadn't changed his posture at all from a moment ago, but something about his stance now felt carnal— like a wolf pacing at the edge of its enclosure.

And she'd been pushed inside without the key.

"Charlie…"

The intensity exuding from him should have unnerved her. But for some odd reason, it didn't.

It was Charlie.

It only made her feel… safe.

"What. Did. He. *Do?*" he repeated slowly, carefully releasing each word.

She squeezed her hands together to try to stave off the tremble threatening to come on, not from the intense look on Charlie's face but from the memory that rose.

"He just showed up. Sat down at my table when I was distracted and tried to get me to talk to him. I got up to leave, but he grabbed me and…"

"He put his *hands* on you?" Charlie seethed.

He would see them anyway at this point if she was going to stay. It was better for her to yank the metaphorical, and literal, bandage off now.

She reached for the bandage on her left arm, unwrapping it as Charlie watched on.

He fell into a deathly silence as the bandage fell away. Worlds could have collided together in the silence stretched between them, but not a word was uttered. His pupils were blown out now, chasing the sea away with a storm of darkness. He released his hold on the counter and took the few steps separating them to hold her arm in his hands.

His touch was surprisingly soft. Gentle even—as if he feared that she were made of glass, prepared to shatter at a moment's notice.

He turned her arm to look over the extent of the bruising. It was an ugly shade of purple and yellow, even more so than the last time she'd looked at it. The outline of fingers could be easily made out, like an imprint forcefully etched into her skin.

Charlie rubbed his thumb over one of the darker spots gently. She flinched, even the feather-like touch of his finger causing her to wince. His eyes met hers for a fraction of a second—a mixture of worry, panic, and rage swimming in those ocean depths—before he eyed the bandage on her other arm.

He didn't say a word as he took it and unwrapped it, letting out a curse as he saw that it matched the other.

It felt oddly intimate, despite the energy radiating off of Charlie in droves. He touched her arm as if it were something precious, as if *she* were something precious. It was so heart-breakingly tender that it caused tears to well in her eyes.

"I'll kill him," Charlie finally growled, more to himself than her, the fierceness of his words in total opposition to his gentle touches.

"You don't mean that."

His eyes pierced hers. "He put his hands on you. You have no *idea* how much I fucking mean that."

She tried to swallow the lump forming in her throat. "Look, I'm sorry that you got dragged into all of this, and I'm really sorry I didn't tell you about this sooner. Please don't be mad at me."

Charlie recoiled as if she'd struck him. "I'm not—Sam, I'm not mad at you."

"Not even a little?"

Finally, he gave her a small smile. "Okay, maybe a little, but more because something could've happened to you, and I wouldn't have..."

His voice trailed off, but she immediately realized where his thoughts went.

Erica.

She clenched her eyes shut for a moment as the guilt kicked into overdrive.

Of course his mind would go there. He'd already lost someone that he thought he should've been able to protect. By her not telling him what was going on, she'd run the very real threat of doing that to him all over again.

"Charlie, I'm sorry. I didn't even think…"

He shook his head and shushed her softly, wiping a rogue tear from her cheek with his thumb. "Don't. It's okay. The important thing right now is that you are safe. That's all I really care about."

She tried to laugh, the sound that came out sounding

muffled and wet. "I'm sorry for not telling you sooner, really. There's just been so much going on lately, and I thought I could take care of myself, and I … I promise that I won't take up too much space here, and I'll go back to my apartment the second I'm able to. I know this is going to put you out, having me stay here, but I promise I'll chip in with the bills and groceries. I've just… I've *always* been able to take care of myself, so I didn't think this was any different. But I was wrong. And I was scared, and I…"

Before she could finish, Charlie closed the gap between them and pulled her into his arms.

The suddenness of it startled her for a moment, her body freezing instinctively. But the second Charlie's heat, his warmth, registered in her senses, she melted into him.

It was exactly what she didn't know that she needed… until now.

Charlie buried his face into the crook of her neck as he hauled her off her stool and up against his body, her feet dangling in the air behind her.

"You can stay here as long as you want, Sam. You are *not* an inconvenience to me, and this situation is *not* your fault," he said, his words muffled in her neck. "I'm just sorry you went through all of this alone until now."

Any embarrassment or shame started to melt away under his touch.

When had Charlie's embrace turned into the thing she needed most in the world?

She squeezed tighter, unable to voice the words longing to break free.

It was a long while before he finally set her back down, but he didn't let her leave his embrace. Instead, he placed her on the counter, so he could continue holding her, moving to rest his forehead against her stomach.

"We'll figure this out. I promise," he said.

She smiled, giving another wet-sounding laugh. "Thanks, Charlie."

He remained there for another moment before pulling back. "You want to stay up and watch a movie? I don't think I'll be able to go to sleep for a while either."

The thought of doing something normal to take her mind off things was too tempting to turn down, so she nodded vigorously.

He chuckled and released her. "Good. You pick out a movie or something you want to watch on the TV. I'll go make up the bed for when you do get tired later, so you can get some sleep. I'll be right back."

She watched him go, the ache in her chest curling around her for an entirely different reason now. A new realization slamming into her senses and rendering her mute.

Sam didn't just have a silly little long-standing crush on Charlie.

She was *in love* with him.

CHAPTER 20

SAM

"You know, the next time I come down, I'm absolutely kicking your butt, right?" Angel declared as she sat across from Sam on the screen. "In fact, do I need to fly down early to cash that in? Because I absolutely will."

Sam had avoided this call for as long as she could, wanting a bit more time to put together a more well-thought-out explanation, but Angel had other ideas. Words were her bread and butter, but she didn't always have seven to ten business days to come up with a prepared speech for everything.

With Angel's bloodhound sense for trouble, any hope for that went down the drain. She had immediately narrowed her eyes at Sam the second the camera had turned on and demanded to know what the hell was going on.

How she'd managed to know so soon, she wasn't sure.

Sam had only woken up moments prior, so she couldn't be sure of much just yet.

When she had finally managed to wrench her eyes open, it had taken her a few to process where she even was.

She'd hadn't remembered going to bed after staying up talking with Charlie. They'd watched movies and talked into the wee hours of the morning, up until she apparently passed out from sheer exhaustion. Blinking sleepily, she'd taken in her surroundings as she realized that the soft pillow beneath her head was Charlie's lap, and the comforting blanket across her midsection was Charlie's arm. His head slumped back against the couch, dozing from where he'd also fallen asleep.

He had looked so… peaceful. Content, even. His light-brown hair was tousled messily atop his head, in desperate need of a combing. A few strands of it had fallen to frame his face in a boyish look that suited him for this time of day.

She'd been afraid of waking him up, not wanting to disturb him.

It had taken a bit of careful maneuvering, but she managed to sneak away into the bedroom to take her call without waking him. Yet the picture of him in that early-morning light was one she would hold onto.

Despite the lecture she was currently receiving.

The words had barely left Sam's mouth, a terribly put together explanation of what had happened, when Angel launched into a verbal deluge of half-veiled threats of violence and outright promises of what she was going to do to Sam when she got hold of her.

It was both terrifying and touching all at the same time.

Despite the topic, Sam couldn't help but laugh. "I don't think that's necessary."

Angel pointed at her, with Sam practically feeling each jab in her chest through the screen. "Oh, you don't get to call the shots here. I'm absolutely going to strangle this guy with my bare hands but not before I strangle you! Sam, why the hell wouldn't you tell anyone about that? Are you *nuts*?"

Sam shrugged sheepishly. "I didn't… I don't… You know how much I fucking *hate* worrying anyone."

A loud groan reverberated through the speakers as Angel threw her hands up in the air. "Yeah, this is a *much* fucking better way to find out about all of this."

"You're right. I'm sorry…"

Angel shook her head, pointing at the camera with one hand while reaching for something off camera. "No, keep your apologies. I'm gonna pack a bag right now, and I'll catch the first flight down, so we can figure out…"

"Please, Angel, I promise I'm okay!" Sam said quickly. "I'm staying here with Charlie until they find Paul. It's bad enough that I pulled him into this situation. I don't need you getting involved as well."

Angel froze mid-motion, and for a moment, Sam thought that her screen had frozen, but that was before Angel's head whipped back in her direction. "Charlie was with you when you got to your apartment?"

Yeah, her explanation definitely needed some work, as she'd only been able to give a few basic details before Angel had exploded in a fury, but she nodded. "Yeah, he was with me, and he's having me stay here with him."

Angel's body slumped back into her chair. "Thank *God*. I thought you were still there."

"I was getting to that part, but you got ahead of me."

Angel closed her eyes and pinched the bridge of her nose. "Well, *lead* with that next time, for God's sake. I thought I was gonna have a heart attack!"

"Don't worry. Your little writing machine is still up and running," Sam said, trying to joke to lighten the mood, but she instantly regretted it when Angel's eyes shot back open.

"That's not funny," her friend snapped. "People care about you—you fucking idiot."

Sam deflated. "Sorry."

She desperately fought the tears forming, only barely managing to keep them in. She deserved every word she was getting; she knew she did. If the roles were reversed, she'd be telling Angel the exact same things.

Angel made a strangled sound, a rush of air coming out of her. "As long as you're safe, that's all that really matters. But you need to knock that shit off with the agent stuff. You know you're more than just my fucking client… right?"

"I know. I'm sorry. I was just trying to lighten the mood…" Sam said. "I guess this part was just easier with Charlie because he was there when it was happening."

Angel settled back into her chair. "It's okay. Just please promise me that you won't keep stuff like this from me? Or from Charlie at the very least?"

"I won't, I promise. I just… I don't know… I told Charlie this, but I really thought I could handle it on my own and that it wasn't going to *be* a huge thing."

"People are nuts," Angel offered, her shoulders easing down from where they'd bunched up next to her ears, "so never underestimate a crazy person, but I get it. Especially knowing that sick sense of hyper-independent streak of yours."

Sam sighed. "Is it really that bad?"

Angel scoffed. "It can be. *Clearly.*"

"Sorry. I know it's a lot right now—and you also have a lot of feelings on it, which are totally valid—but is it okay if we talk about something else for now? I just… I just really don't want to think about it anymore."

The gaze from across the screen softened, and Angel nodded. "Sure, though don't be surprised if I text you with some follow-up questions."

"Of course, I'd expect nothing less." Sam laughed. "And I

promise I'm not putting you into the agent slot right now, but I've been focusing on my book to try to distract myself and do something productive. Did you get a chance to read the first couple of chapters I sent you?"

Angel narrowed her eyes, but whatever fight she had left in her deflated when she smiled. "Yes, I read it."

"And?"

"I loved it," she replied, her lips stretching into the first genuine smile today. "You've got a great setup, and I really liked the opening."

Sam pumped a fist into the air. "You think *they* will like it too?"

Sam yawned and stretched her arms above her head, relaxing more now that the worst of the conversation was over. It was surprising, but last night had been the best she'd slept in a while—feeling more rested and alert than she had for weeks.

Angel laughed. "I know they will. Their romance department is going to absolutely eat this up, especially with your name attached to it. I've gone ahead and sent them over the chapters you gave me, so I'll let you know what they say when I hear back."

"Okay, that's good. Gives me more time to work on it."

"Well, and speaking of... have you thought any more on a pen name? You mentioned it a while back, so I wasn't sure if you still wanted to go with that angle."

"I do. I haven't given the name much thought under the circumstances, but I'll definitely start working on a few options. You think they'll care too much about what I choose?"

Angel shrugged as she flicked a stray lock of raven hair out of her face. "They'll want to know what your options are, I think, and they will definitely have opinions on the matter.

But I'll make sure you get the final say. Keep working on the book itself, and we'll check in about it next week at our usual time."

"Okay. Thanks, Angel."

"Of course," Angel replied, the bright-red nail polish she had on now contrasting with the cream sheer sleeve of her blouse as she rubbed a hand up and down her arm. "You know I love you, right? Even when I'm mad at you for being an idiot, I still love you."

Sam's chest clenched, but she smiled. "I know. I love you too."

"Good. Now, I have a few things I need to arrange because, despite your assurances, I'm still coming down to see you."

"But—"

Angel held up a hand to interrupt her. "I have a conference down that way coming up anyway, so don't start. I'll give you the details when I get everything sorted out, but don't stress about it, okay?"

"Where are you gonna stay? I'd normally let you crash at my apartment with me, but it's not exactly in working order."

Angel shrugged casually, eyes darting off to the side. "I have someone else I can stay with in the area, so I'll just reach out to them."

This piqued Sam's interest, raising a curious eyebrow at her. "Oh? And who would that be?"

Angel turned her nose into the air. "Mind your business."

CHAPTER 21

CHARLIE

Charlie stretched his fingers, sore from an entire day's worth of drafting case notes. Sam sat across from him on the adjacent couch. Her eyes had been glued to her own laptop, her fingers flying over the keys as she continued writing whatever it was she was working on with her book.

Their eyes caught one another, smiling as Sam pushed her laptop onto the couch and stretched her arms above her head.

"I think I've earned myself a shower," she announced as she stood. "I'll be back in a bit."

He waved over his head wordlessly, the wave turning into a stretch and yawn of his own. It had been quite a few hours since either of them had gotten up, so Charlie figured that she could use a break.

The bedroom door clicked shut behind Sam as he stood. The coffee pot had been emptied less than an hour ago between the two of them, but he was still in desperate need of that sweet, sweet hit of caffeine, so he set about getting another started. A quick check of the time and Charlie couldn't help but groan. Only noon.

He leaned against the counter, about to stare off into the

distance with the remaining bout of energy he had for the moment when his phone began to ring.

Peter's name flashed on the screen. The last time he'd talked to any of his family had been when he and Tyler had argued days prior, so he wasn't exactly keen for whatever lecture Peter had prepared about getting more involved in the charity. But he picked the phone up anyway.

"Surprised you even picked up," Peter said quickly. "Figured you were still screening family calls."

Charlie rolled his eyes and sank back onto the couch. "Doesn't make you any less persistent."

Peter tsked. "I'm hurt, little brother."

"I'm more trying to ignore Tyler right now, so… no offense."

"None taken… this time. Tyler's pissed at everyone right now. You know how he gets. But you know he's only trying to do what he can to help mom and dad for the—"

"Can you spare the lecture today, Peter?" Charlie asked sharply. "I'm not in the mood to—"

"No lecture from me on that," his brother interrupted. "Tyler will come around when he's not in such a mood. But I wasn't calling about that, anyway. I was calling to check in on Sam. How's she doing? What updates have you gotten about the perv?"

Charlie froze. "Who told you about—"

"Angel called me."

Of course she had.

"I would've thought that *you* would have told me what was going on before Angel had to call me about it," Peter added.

Charlie gritted his teeth. "I've got things under control."

Peter chuckled. "Yeah, I'm sure you do, knowing you— probably locked down tighter than Fort Knox over there."

"Just," Charlie started before lowering his volume, "just don't tell anyone else right now, okay? Sam already hates that I'm involved in all of this. The last thing I need is to stress her out even more with everyone else coming in and fussing."

"I won't. I just wanted to make sure the two of you were okay."

"We're fine. Just… getting by for now."

Peter sighed. "You getting any sleep at least?"

Charlie rubbed the back of his neck. The usual brotherly antics, Charlie was used to. But he had to admit that hearing the genuine concern in Peter's voice stirred a lot of memories he'd rather not deal with at the moment.

"Enough."

Another chuckle. "Which means little to none with you."

"I've got things under control," he protested again, weakly this time.

"I know you do, but I know *you*, so I know you aren't sleeping worth shit right now," Peter said gently.

Charlie chuckled. "How could you *possibly* know that?"

"You seem to forget we shared a room for nearly eighteen years. You've always been that way," Peter said. "You remember when Mom and Dad had that big fight back when we were kids? It was a few nights before Christmas, and it woke us all up, so we tiptoed to the top of the staircase to listen? They made up right afterward, but you didn't sleep for like three days after."

A smile tugged at the corners of Charlie's lips. "You remember the weirdest things."

Peter chuckled again on the other end. "I remember sharing a bedroom with you two idiots, so when *you* didn't sleep, none of us slept… You didn't sleep more than five minutes at a time for months after Erica died."

At the mention of her name, Charlie felt his entire body

tense, abruptly rubbing his sleep-soaked eyes. "Not this again. Is that why you're checking in? Because you thought I'd go off the rails like I did back then?"

Peter sighed. "No, you're a grown-ass adult. I know how much you care about Sam, and… well, you can see where my line of thought went."

Charlie understood, but that didn't make the sting lessen any. At neither the reminder of it nor the implication that he had anything less than a one hundred percent handle on the situation.

Charlie scoffed. "Don't pull the older brother card on me now. I'm bigger than you."

"Alright, just because I'm not built like a fucking human battering ram like you and Dad are doesn't mean I can't still kick your ass if I needed to," Peter stated firmly, though he couldn't seem to hide the touch of humor in his voice, which only managed to irritate Charlie further.

"I'd like to see you try," Charlie challenged but deflated almost as quickly, knowing he wouldn't hurt a fly, let alone his brother. Even if he did like to push his buttons.

"Look," Peter said slowly, "I just don't want to see you torture yourself like you did last time."

He shook his head. "It's not the same."

"No, you're right. It's not. You couldn't stop what happened with Erica, but you think you can with Sam? Tell me I'm wrong."

"Please don't start with me on this again—"

"You and Erica had that weird twin telepathy thing going on—" Peter said abruptly, the shift forcing Charlie's system to short circuit temporarily. "—always creeped me out how you two could always say what the other was thinking so accurately."

A strangled sound escaped Charlie, reverberating around in his chest in a way that made each breath feel strangled.

He knew what Peter was doing. It was what he'd been *trying* to do for so long that Charlie had lost count.

"We were thick as thieves for a long time," he finally agreed. "Though, Erica used to joke that because we were fraternal twins, it wasn't the same."

Peter chuckled. "She definitely had a mind of her own, that's for sure."

"Much to Mom and Dad's chagrin."

Another laugh. "Yeah, you remember that time when she tried to convince all of us that we should go camping on the roof of the house? Because she wanted to be as close to the stars as she possibly could?"

Oh yeah, Charlie remembered.

And he remembered how angry his father had been when they'd tried to start a campfire up there.

The coffee pot dinged next to him, his anchor to reality. He blinked a few times and grabbed the pot, tucking his phone between his ear and shoulder as he grabbed his cup and headed back to the couch.

"I remember how we all managed to get grounded for a week, but Erica managed to only get two days," Charlie said. "She really wasn't afraid of anything."

The tightness in his chest threatened to suffocate him, but he cleared his throat in an attempt to ease the pressure.

"Time is supposed to heal all wounds, but… I don't know. I feel like it hasn't. I still miss her every day," Peter admitted, something that surprised Charlie more than anything, but he decided not to comment on it. As much as everyone gave him a hard time about opening up, this was the first time he'd heard Peter say anything about it.

Charlie cleared his throat. "Me too."

"Charlie… You're doing the best you can to make sure Sam is safe," Peter added carefully. "She's not Erica… Don't run yourself into the ground over something that wasn't your fault."

"I know," he lied, still feeling that ache deep in his chest that said otherwise.

"Sam's a wildcat either way, so I don't expect that she'd go down without a fight."

Charlie chuckled. "Yeah, you know how she is."

"Not as well as you do, it seems," Peter replied. "There was another little detail Angel added when we were on the phone—something for Sam's book?"

Oh no, he *absolutely* wasn't about to go there with Peter.

"Is there anything else you need?" Charlie huffed.

"Fine, cranky pants. But at least let me know if you guys need anything, huh?"

Charlie snorted. "I will."

"Good. Go get some sleep, Charlie. You sound exhausted."

Charlie rolled his eyes. "Okay, Dad. Goodbye."

He ended the call and tossed his phone onto the seat next to him. He felt weary from the conversation, which was truly a statement considering how exhausted he'd already been.

Sam sauntered back into the living room with a smile. "Who was that?"

"Peter."

"How's he doing?"

Charlie rolled his eyes. "Being a giant pain in my ass, so, you know, the usual."

"Was he giving you a hard time about the auction? He mentioned he had a date, too, so he won't have to participate either, but he wouldn't tell me."

Charlie raised an eyebrow at her. "You've been talking to my brother?"

She shrugged as she lowered herself back into her seat. "I texted him, joking about Angel staying with him when she gets in town for her conference. She wouldn't tell me who, but he's the only other person I could think of who she would stay with."

"You think he's taking her as his date?" Charlie asked. It wouldn't surprise him if he did. It was far from the first time that he'd suspected Peter had a thing for Angel, but he kept that to himself.

Sam scrunched her nose. "I don't think so. She would have told me if she was going. And, more to the point, she'd already have an itinerary a mile long of all the shopping we would have to do to prepare."

Charlie laughed. "True, though you probably do need to get something for it yourself soon, don't you?"

"Yeah, anything that I would have worn for it was completely shredded, so I'll need to go shopping," she answered, a shadow passing over her as soon as the words left her mouth.

He hated that. That broken and frightened glimmer in those beautiful, meadow-colored eyes of hers. Nothing should be there but beauty and sunshine, and certainly not that. Charlie hated it so much that he wanted to flip the table over, but he held himself in check. It would take time for her to feel safe again, and he was going to do his damnedest to make sure that happened.

"I'll go with you when you do. Just in case," he said, his gaze unintentionally lowering to her arms. The bruises there were starting to fade, but even seeing the hint of them on her made his blood boil all over again.

"Let's cross that bridge when we get there," Sam replied. "First, however, we need to go have some fun."

"Fun? What, you don't think sitting here in my apartment all day is fun?" He chuckled again.

Sam rolled her eyes. "You know what I mean. We've been cooped up in here for a few days. I think we should get out."

"What'd you have in mind?"

She tapped her chin idly with her index finger as she chewed on her reply. "I just want to do something normal. What else do people do for dates?"

Charlie raised an eyebrow at her. "A date, huh?"

She tapped his foot with hers. "Yes, a date. You didn't think I was completely giving up, did you?"

He had wondered, and he wouldn't have blamed her if she had decided to call the whole thing off, given the circumstances. It had only been a few days since she'd moved in with him, and he'd been too afraid to even bring it up.

The relief he felt at the mischief tugging her lips into a smile was palpable, but he tried not to show it as he shrugged. "I don't know. You're the expert, right? You're writing the romance novel, after all."

"Maybe dancing? We could check out that club across town that just opened?"

Charlie knew he was in for trouble.

He raised an eyebrow at her. "Dancing? You?"

"Yeah! What's wrong with that?"

"Last time I checked, you had two left feet," he teased, earning him another tap from her foot.

"Your memory is too long. That was years ago." She pouted, jutting her lower lip out at him.

Also true, it had been quite a few years since either of

them had hit up a club. The last time he could remember was back when they were in college.

"Fine. How about we go Friday night?"

She smiled then, a completely infectious look that forced his own smile to widen. "Deal."

§

Charlie leaned against the kitchen counter as he waited for the coffee to brew.

He had tried, he really did, to fall asleep that night, but it proved to be in vain.

Again.

In all honesty, Charlie hadn't slept very well the past *several* nights.

Every sound, every voice that echoed from somewhere in the building, every creak from the nearby staircase, and Charlie would leap up from the bed he'd made himself on the couch. Rinse and repeat most nights.

Even when he did manage to get to sleep, he found no solace there. That was when the nightmares came. And each time, he'd violently wake to the memory of Sam screaming.

Much like he had tonight.

Once ready, Charlie poured coffee into one of his larger mugs, needing the extra room in it for the caffeine he so desperately needed. He didn't wait long enough for the steam to dissipate before swallowing down his first taste of it, almost needing that burn on his tongue to remind him that he was no longer dreaming.

Sam was safe.

She was asleep in the next room.

In his bed.

He lowered himself onto one of the kitchen barstools, cup in hand. He glanced down at his watch as he took another sip. Eleven o'clock on the dot. A new record for him. He'd only managed half an hour before giving up this time. It'd be another long, restless day, unfortunately.

The couch wasn't exactly the most comfortable for long-term sleeping, but it worked in a pinch. He'd insisted on letting Sam have the bedroom while she stayed with him—for privacy's sake, he'd argued.

In reality, it was because he could easily see the front door from the couch.

Sam hadn't said much about the change to her routine, though the two of them had fallen into a pretty comfortable one since that first night. They'd set up shop in the living room, both working on their laptops in comfortable silence until work time was over, and they would hang out as they normally would.

He'd caught her, more than once, looking longingly out of the nearby window as she nursed a cup of coffee. Her nose scrunched up, as if she were trying to imagine the taste of her favorite cafe drink but failing.

All because of Paul.

Even *thinking* that name caused Charlie to grind his teeth and force another piping hot sip down his throat, reveling in the burn that followed. He hadn't been able to go to the gym since she'd been staying with him, not wanting to leave her alone for too long, and it was starting to show how much he needed it at times like this.

Only at the gym was it socially acceptable to punch something until you were too exhausted to continue.

He made a mental note that he should probably order one for the apartment when he wasn't in such a brain fog.

Sam's face flashed in his mind, the frightened one she had when he'd first found her in that hallway—not the brave one she'd sprawled on her face since then.

He'd seen Sam in various stages of her, with all of the good and bad that came with that. But he'd *never* seen her look that afraid before.

A fact he wasn't soon to forget.

He hadn't wanted to tell her before how scared *he* had been. The thought that there had been a remote possibility he could've lost her was… Well, it was too awful to even think about.

The fact that it seemed like they'd just barely missed Paul… if they'd skipped ice cream and headed straight home instead, she'd have walked right into him...

Dread twisted down his spine like a poisoned vine at the thought, causing a shiver to wrack his body.

He mulled over his options on how to kill time and distract himself from thinking about *that*, knowing in his gut that he wouldn't be able to fall asleep again tonight. Pulling his laptop out of his bag to get some work done didn't feel very appealing, especially given the brain fog sweeping through his head at the moment.

His Kindle was perched next to the coffee table, where he'd last left it a few days prior. He'd still been working his way through one of the books he'd gotten after his and Sam's date to the bookstore. Continuing seemed like the logical thing to do, so he gathered his coffee cup and went over to the couch.

He wasn't entirely sure whether his sleep-addled mind would comprehend much of what he'd read, but it was better than sitting there with his own thoughts.

He didn't make it more than a few pages before the sound of laughter startled him, almost causing him to spill coffee all over himself. He jumped forward, quickly putting the cup onto the table before it sloshed onto him, and looked in the direction of the laughter.

Sam burst from the bedroom, vastly more awake than even he was, with tears streaming down her face. Momentary panic was instantly replaced with amusement when she doubled over, the sound of laughing bubbling through. Her top lip clenched down over her bottom as if trying to prevent herself from being too loud, but with a loud puff of air, she began laughing anyway—hooting and howling loud enough that it would definitely wake any neighbors trying to sleep nearby.

"Oh my God, babe, I *have* to show you this," she wheezed, trotting over with her laptop in hand and dropping down onto the couch next to him.

His arm closest to her lifted and went to rest on the back of the couch, an opportunity she took advantage of as she scooted in close, practically nestling into his side as she propped her laptop on his lap.

"I thought you were asleep?" he asked.

"Nah, I was up reading when Angel sent me this," she said, pointing eagerly at the screen. Charlie turned his attention to the laptop, perusing the contents for a second until a few keywords caused his face to flame. Upon seeing the change in his gaze, Sam rolled her eyes. "Just read, I promise I'm not trying to be weird."

It was a quick read, only a paragraph long, but the content was… confusing, to say the least. Despite the sexual nature of it—which, granted, it had been a while since he'd last had sex—it felt as if he'd read an entirely different language. Nothing made sense.

He paused, flicking his gaze back to the top of the paragraph and read it a second time. His nose scrunched, trying to make sense of the jumbled mess of words.

"Who the hell wrote this?"

Sam giggled. "I've seen a few posts like this on those *men writing women* threads, where men are trying to write sex scenes, but this one takes the cake."

"A *man* wrote this?" he asked incredulously. "I mean, I've heard of those threads, too, but yeah, you're right, this takes the cake. I thought this was something an AI might have spat out."

It would've honestly been less surprising if that had been the case.

"I know. That's what I thought, too! But no, this was by an officially published author. Like… someone had to edit this."

Charlie's eyebrows shot up. "An editor saw *this* and gave it a pass?"

Sam's head fell onto his shoulder as she held her stomach and laughed again. "I'll never complain about the editors I've worked with ever again, I swear!"

Narrowing his eyes on a particular part of the paragraph, Charlie couldn't help but laugh along with her. "For refer-ence, a dick can*not* do that. They're not garden hoses."

That statement sent Sam into a deeper spiral of hysterics, falling fully into Charlie's lap from the force of her undiluted laughter. Her body pushed the laptop perched there so much that it almost fell to the floor before he caught it.

It was the first time he'd seen her smile like that since the break-in, and despite how amusing the article was, it was nothing in comparison to seeing her laugh like that. The sound of it rippled through the air like waves in a tide pool, both enchanting and comforting. It tugged on something deep in Charlie's chest, and it was exactly what he needed.

"I mean, alright, I know this whole fake dating thing is for you to learn, but this is *not* the kind of material to study from," he finally stated before pausing. Oh, that's right, they weren't supposed to bring it up. What had she called it? Fight club rules?

Sam didn't say anything for a moment, and he feared he might have said the wrong thing until she patted his leg. "It's a good thing, then, that you're such a great teacher."

"Yeah?" he asked, now more curious than anything.

She nodded, looking up at him from where her head rested on his lap and biting her lower lip to likely stop herself from laughing so hard, but the effect it had on him was much different. He fought to keep a hold of himself as she shook in his lap. "Yeah, I think you're more of a romantic than you let on."

He grinned; he couldn't help himself. "The highest compliment coming from the writer."

"Well," she continued as she turned her head to point out a particularly awful sentence from the selection on the screen, "as my current fake boyfriend and resident romantic, what are your thoughts on the kissing part of the scene he has written?"

Charlie glanced at the screen, rereading the section once more before chuckling. "That's *not* a kiss."

"It's not?" she asked.

"No, that's an *insult* to kissing."

Sam bit her lip. "What would you consider to be a better kiss, then?"

There was a hint of mischief twinkling in those smoldering green eyes of hers, a silent challenge issued. He had to admit that it surprised him, but it was a challenge he absolutely wasn't about to back down from.

"This," he replied as he leaned down and captured her lips with his.

How on earth someone's lips could be this soft, this addicting, he would never know. But kissing Sam felt like the worst kind of addiction that he feared he'd never break. Memories of their kiss in the hallway burned in his veins. He wanted to feel more of her, taste more of her.

He deliberately kept this kiss slow and gentle—soft pecks that left a promise of more. Though, when a little delighted sigh entered his mouth from hers, Charlie feared he'd snap in two.

He pulled back, albeit reluctantly, to kiss the tip of her nose and forehead. "Better?"

A touch of pink had risen in her cheeks, but she smiled in return. "Yeah, much better."

That contented smile was worth its weight in gold, and Charlie had to force his thundering heartbeat to settle down.

"Not hard to beat, though, if this is my comparison," he stated, squinting at a different passage on the screen. "Also, I think he used the word 'and,' like… twelve, thirteen times? Jesus, take a breath, dude."

Sam shrieked out a sudden laugh, slapping a hand over her mouth, as if she could pull back the volume. It was infectious, the way she immediately devolved into hysterics, grabbing her stomach to unsuccessfully fight the laughter off.

When he joined her, he felt as if the stress of the past few days melted away.

"I can't breathe!" she squealed, wrenching a hand from her stomach and grabbing Charlie's arm. "But good news! If I need inspiration, I know exactly where I should go if I want to describe someone's dick!"

Charlie, in turn, choked on his own laugh. "Please, no, think of humanity. Don't turn to this man."

"No!" she insisted, her voice tight as she fought for a breath. "To a car dealership! That way I can see one of those waving inflatable things they have out front since that's *clearly* how you describe an accurate dick according to this guy."

That was the end of chatter for quite some time as the two flew into a complete fit of hysterics.

CHAPTER 22

SAM

"Are you sure about this?" Charlie asked, the vivid neon lettering of the nightclub across the street flashing brightly enough that it lit up the dark night sky.

It had been quite a few years since Sam had last stepped foot inside of a club, the last time being back when they were in college. As she stood there—with the chatter of the throng of people queued up in line out front, the booming bass of the loud music vibrating through to the pavement—she had to admit that she *wasn't* so sure about this.

A pulse emanated from within that almost guaranteed a hangover to all who dared to enter.

All she had wanted was to go out and have some fun. Let loose a little so that they didn't feel quite so stir-crazy sitting in Charlie's apartment.

Standing there next to Charlie, she was starting to second guess herself.

"I think so. It should be fun. Right, babe?"

Charlie chuckled. "Absolutely—so long as no one pukes on me."

She laughed, wanting to promise that she would do her

best to steer clear of any green faces in the crowd to avoid such a fate, but she didn't feel confident enough to say so.

A light breeze tousled his hair as he stood there next to her, unwavering as he waited for her to make her decision. The black T-shirt and jeans he'd thrown on before they left made him look more like one of the bouncers stationed at the club's entrance rather than someone trying to get inside, but she had to admit the simple combination worked for him. The material of his shirt clung to his broad shoulders, flaring out at his waist and emphasizing the muscles of his back.

Given her limited choice in wardrobe from the break-in, and unfortunate timing for laundry day, she'd been left with two choices for tonight's adventure. Two dresses that hadn't seen the light of day in a few years but managed to survive the break-in because they had been relegated to the far reaches of her closet.

The first dress had been swiftly dismissed due to its length alone, barely reaching past the curve of her ass thanks to her tall frame. At the time, she'd justified that she could turn it into a cute top with the right pair of pants, but that vision never came to be.

Left with no other option, she had turned to the second dress—a ruched bodycon dress that hugged her curves a little too well, its hem skimming just behind her knees. A birthday gift from Angel one year that she'd never had the confidence to wear before now. Its deep, jet-black color perfectly complemented both Charlie's shirt and the only pair of heels she happened to own, so it worked out well.

She'd tried to ask Charlie what he thought of it, but he hadn't looked at her long enough since they'd left for an answer.

"Let's do this!" she said finally. "Worst case scenario is that we go in for a bit, get a drink or two, dance for a while, realize we're not cut out for this kind of scene anymore, and head back to your place."

"Sounds like a plan to me, babe—on one condition, though," Charlie said as he extended a hand toward her, flexing it. "You are required to hold my hand tonight unless otherwise stated."

Despite herself, she giggled. "Charlie, I'm not five. I think I can manage."

Charlie shook his head. "Nope, you can see how packed it is in there, and I'd rather not lose you in the crowd if I can help it. It's nonnegotiable."

"Charlie—"

"Just hold my hand, dammit," he demanded, flexing his hand more dramatically in her direction. She laughed once more, but she obliged, intertwining her fingers with his. It was more comforting than she thought, the warmth of his hand radiating up to her chest.

Charlie stuck to her like glue as they made their way inside, through the crowd, and over to the bar—his grip never leaving hers.

Even when they finally had drinks in hand, and the two retreated to a more secluded corner of the club, his hand remained in hers. They stood off to the side, leisurely sipping their drinks while watching the lively crowd.

Sam had no intention of getting drunk, but she gratefully welcomed the first few sips of her mojito, the alcohol's mildly soothing effect easing the spike of nerves that had threatened to rise at the pressing crowd of people. Everyone was packed in like sardines around the dance floor, so the sequestered corner they found themselves in was a welcome respite.

She hadn't expected to feel uneasy in the crowd.

Her fingers tightened on the glass before taking a large

gulp. She'd hoped that a night around other people would help ease that tension coiled inside of her—but it was currently having the opposite effect. As if she were searching, looking for *him*.

She shook her head and took another healthy swig. No, she didn't want to think about that tonight. Tonight was for fun. No thinking about Paul; no thinking about book stuff even.

"You think this is the UNC crowd tonight?" she shouted, trying to be heard over the music.

"I'm amazed you can *think* with the music this loud," he shouted back, flashing that cocky smile of his. "I feel like it's jackhammering right into my head."

Sam laughed. "Are we just getting old?"

Charlie placed a hand on his chest "Excuse me. I'm thirty, flirty, and thriving. You want another drink?"

She nodded, pointing at the almost empty glass in her hand. "Another one of these, please?"

"You got it," he said as he took the glass from her. "Stay here. It'll be quicker if I run and grab them. I'll be right back."

Charlie's towering frame effortlessly parted the crowd as he navigated his way to the bar. Standing head and shoulders above most of the others around him, it was like watching a beacon parting the sea. The image of it made her laugh.

She turned to look back out at the crowd, hating how her lips still tingled from the way he'd kissed her at the apartment. It was sweet, a delicate whisper of the kiss they'd had in the hallway. And it was exactly what she'd needed.

She'd pushed for it, she knew. She'd been about as subtle as a freight train at the time, but she'd needed to remember that feeling. Of his lips on hers. Of the sensation that sparked to life between them whenever they kissed.

Anything and everything to not think about the situation with Paul.

But it had backfired in an entirely different way.

She didn't want this to end, this arrangement of theirs. The problem was that she was enjoying it a little *too* much. Her book was halfway done, and she knew that her time with this would be dwindling to a close when it was finished.

She wasn't ready to let go of this, but she knew she would have to.

She could always ask him. See whether his feelings toward her had changed throughout their time together, but she decided against it for one very big reason. Two decades of friendship. That was what she'd be putting on the line if his feelings *hadn't* changed. If he was just *that* good at making her believe that it was real, and she told him how she felt, she ran the very real risk of ruining everything between them. She could lose him, and she couldn't bear the thought.

This had been a terrible idea for her heart.

A sudden jolt from her right sent her lurching forward, barely managing to steady herself with the nearby high-top table. A man stood beside her, reaching toward her as if to help stabilize her. He hovered there as she regained her foot, his hazel eyes glazed over yet fixated on her, a telltale drunken grin adorning his face as he leaned closer to her ear.

"Sorry," he shouted, a notable slur to his words. "I hope I didn't spill your drink?"

She shook her head. "I'm fine! No drink right now, so nothing to spill."

She smoothed her dress out, which had ridden up slightly by her sudden movement, and she sensed his hands still lingering near her hips.

The guy's grin widened. "Would you like one? I'd be more than happy to buy you one."

She laughed, shaking her head. "No, thank you."

The man eyed her up and down, licking his lips like he'd found his next course. "You're pretty cute. Are you here alone?"

"No, I—" she started, pausing when he took a step closer.

"Come on, let me buy you a drink," he pleaded, edging his body into her personal space with each word.

The overpowering scent of tequila wafted from his breath as he attempted to inch closer, but she extended her hand to halt his advance. "No, thank you, I'm here with—"

"Just one?"

She shook her head. "No, I'm good, really…"

The guy grabbed her wrist and turned without another word, as if his mind was already made up. He started making his way through the crowd to the bar, tugging her along behind him. Sam was taken aback by the suddenness of his actions, but in the loud and crowded nightclub, she doubted he could hear her protests.

She searched for Charlie amidst the sea of faces to see if he had returned, but he was nowhere to be seen in the chaos. She focused, instead, on not falling on her ass in the heels she had on.

The guy dragging her suddenly stopped, catching her off guard and causing her to collide into his back. She turned, expecting to find that they'd gotten to the bar, but instead, she saw that he had collided with someone else.

A familiar face obstructed their path, and Sam released a relieved breath.

Balancing two drinks in his hands, Charlie peered down at the guy wedged between them. The surprise in his eyes was quickly replaced by a heat that threatened to set anyone too close aflame.

Sam simply waved at him, unsure of what else to do.

"I suggest letting go of my girl right about now." His voice came out gruffly, a low rumble in his chest that made him sound as dangerous as his eyes implied.

My girl.

Sam felt the rush of relief as she was promptly released, the guy in front of her holding his hands up defensively. "My bad, dude."

As quickly as he appeared, the guy disappeared into the crowd before either her or Charlie could say another word.

She stole a glance at Charlie, noting the scowl etched into his face as his eyes remained in the direction the guy had fled in, a lethal calmness swirling in his eyes. As if he had half a mind to follow but had ultimately decided against it. It was such a stark contrast to how Charlie usually was that she couldn't help but laugh.

She patted his arm. "I think you scared him!"

Charlie blinked a few times before pressing one of the drinks into her hand. "Good. That was the intent."

"He was wasted, probably harmless."

"Doesn't matter," he grumbled. "Shouldn't need to be sober to know to keep his hands to himself."

Charlie sloshed back a few healthy swigs of the beer he'd gotten, a drop of it escaping and dribbling down his chin. Sam watched it with unabashed intrigue as it ran down his sharp jawline, across his Adam's apple, and disappeared into the black void of his shirt.

Shit.

Would she be a bad feminist if she admitted that seeing Charlie's protective side spring into action like that, like a sleeper soldier activating, was far hotter than she was ever willing to acknowledge openly?

After quenching his thirst, Charlie turned back to look at

her, the angry crease across his forehead disappearing. "Did he hurt you?"

She cleared her throat and shook her head. "Unscathed, as you can see."

"Good."

S am found herself pleasantly tipsy after indulging in a few more cocktails than she had originally planned. She teetered on that delicate balance where fine motor skills remained intact, yet she basked in a newfound sense of chilled-the-fuck-out that had eluded her for far too long.

With every sip from each entirely-too-sweet drink she had, layers of awkwardness seemed to melt away. The more she had, the less she cared about all of her other worries and troubles. All her concerns, worries, and doubts evaporated into a blissful haze, carried away on the winds of the night's energy.

She was just having fun now.

As the alcohol coursed through her veins, she and Charlie danced along to the music. They switched from increasingly wild and chaotic dance moves to nearly bursting at the seams laughing at one another. Their laughter bubbling over as the crowd gyrated around them to the pulsating rhythm blasting.

Despite her earlier shyness over the memory of his kiss, Sam found herself surprisingly unaffected by the closeness like she might have been if sober. Charlie's hands remained at his sides, only coming up occasionally to shield her from strangers bumping into them. She craved being closer, though. The feeling of his hands on her like a drug she couldn't get enough of.

The longer the night went on, the closer she and Charlie were pushed up against one another, with the crowd around them swallowing up the remaining space. The ability to be heard over the booming music—for even the simplest of exchanges—became increasingly difficult and caused them to further press together like all the other couples on the dance floor.

The beat shifted into something more carnal, animalistic almost, and the couples around them began to grind against one another in an unspoken dance of flesh and fire. The change made her *very* aware that her breasts were pressed up against Charlie's chest from how close they were to one another now. The scooped neckline of her dress showed how intimately they were positioned against him.

A fleeting expression crossed Charlie's features as their eyes met, quickly masked as he leaned in close. "We can leave if you want?"

The faint hiss of logic in Sam's mind agreed, the side of her brain that had been steadily drowned out by the multiple cocktails in her system. They probably *should* leave, but her feet remained planted firmly on the floor, rooted in place with Charlie's body pressing against hers. She felt far braver than she normally would have, thanks to the alcohol, which is why she instead took one of his hands.

"We came here to dance, right?" she said, her words drowned out by the ever-changing pace of the melody.

Are you flirting with me?

She'd asked him before when he'd pushed her against the wall and kissed her until she was left breathless. She wanted to flirt with him too. She wanted him as delirious with want as she had been, as she still was with him so close.

It had been a long time since she'd ever *tried* to flirt, so wasn't entirely sure how. Her hands gravitated toward his shoulders, finding an odd sense of comfort at the familiar touch despite the liquid heat pounding in her veins.

His hands found her hips, hovering there, as if he were afraid she would smack his hand away at any moment. If only he knew she didn't have the willpower to push him away even if she wanted to. She wanted him to touch her, to ease the ache inside of her.

Sam caught a glimpse of one of the other couples dancing next to them and a surge of nerves prickled at her once more. Their movements were more reminiscent of the kind of intimate act reserved for the privacy of a bedroom, as if she shouldn't even be watching.

Charlie drew her closer, a shiver coursing through her at the feeling of his lips so close to her ear. "You okay?"

She nodded. "I'm fine."

"We can still go if you want?"

"No, if I'm going to write smut, I can handle being here," she rationalized, shaking her head and feeling the world spin ever-so-slightly at the motion. "I'm fine."

Her desire to stay had little to do with her book, but her mind felt the need to offer an explanation as to why she would want to stay instead of what she really felt. Holding onto the last thread of rationality with a vice-like grip before it completely snapped.

In her hazy mind, she couldn't think of a time when she wasn't fully in control of herself. In control of her emotions. When she'd just let herself fall into the abyss and hope something, or someone, was on the other side to catch her.

Charlie threw his head back and laughed at that. "Your ability to write *smut* has nothing to do with this. This is dancing."

"It does, though! How can I expect to write a believable, sensual, romantic scene between two characters if I don't have a sensual bone in my body?" she argued, intrigued by whatever emotion suddenly crossed Charlie's features at her statement.

"Fuck all of that if it means putting you in a situation you're not comfortable with. We can—"

She shook her head vehemently, grabbing his hand before he could turn away. "No! Please, I want to stay. Please, babe?"

Though it was nearly impossible for her words to be quiet and be heard, her words came out barely a whisper. Charlie didn't seem to need to hear them to understand, however, as he yanked her closer against him. "Keep your eyes on me, then."

Charlie pressed her body against his from hip to chest, watching her carefully with each movement.

They began with a deliberate slowness, each movement a silent exchange of words, their eyes never leaving one another. Every touch, every shift, became a test of boundaries, a silent negotiation between them. A question offered, a response given, as if their bodies knew the answers all along. Their bodies began to move against one another, grinding together with increasingly frantic movements.

It was vastly more intimate than anything she'd ever encountered before, that was for sure.

"Let me know if you want to stop," Charlie said, not needing to lean in for her to hear him. She nodded but held on tight.

She wouldn't stop if she had a choice in the matter.

Her hips grinding against Charlie's was the closest to heaven she'd ever been.

His hands squeezed into the flesh of her hips, tight enough that it should've hurt but didn't. Desire pooled in through every pore, simmering deep within her until she was nearly boiling over with it. Her body became hyperaware of every single touch, every single movement against one another.

Their bodies moved together, mimicking the movements of those around them but also the unspoken act that caused that desire to flare low in Sam's belly.

The music continued, amplifying and engulfing them in a way that Sam stopped noticing anyone else around them. In that moment, it was only the two of them, ensnared by the hypnotic heartbeat of the music. Drawing nearer with each passing second until they were desperately clinging to one another.

Charlie's hands shifted, her dress obediently trailing the motion of his fingers. The material rode up her hips with his movements before dropping back into place. This motion repeated several times until Sam realized that she had started to pant.

"Dammit," Charlie grunted close to her ear. "Of all the times you'd wear a dress like this."

The rest of the world melted away, and all she wanted was Charlie to throw her against the nearest hard surface and have his way with her. But… there was more to it that stirred in her chest. The air between them was thick with unspoken desire, but something else lingered there. Intangible, but she felt it. She'd *always* felt it, and there was no denying it any longer.

"I think I'm in love with you."

The words slipped from her lips so effortlessly that she scarcely noticed their departure. Yet she saw the shift in Charlie's eyes. The surprise, the heat. She didn't feel embarrassment like she would've thought she would. Rational Sam left the building with whatever primal sensation overtook her.

Their bodies continued to move, but each movement

seemed to slow as he studied her. "You don't mean that, baby. You're drunk."

Baby.

He'd called her that before, but it shocked her just how quickly that lightning bolt of arousal slammed into her. It sent flickers of heat and electricity straight down to her toes and pinging in all the right... or wrong... places. *Babe*, she'd started getting used to. Only just, though. *Baby*, on the other hand... with the way he said it, sounding strained, as if it was pure torture... As if *she* were pure torture to him, and that knowledge did wicked things to her. It lingered in her senses —tingled in a way that demanded relief.

"I think I do. I think I've always been in love with you, and it took this experiment of ours for me to do something about it," she admitted, the words continuing to fall so easily from her lips.

She clenched her lower lip between her teeth, holding back whatever else threatened to spill from her.

It felt like they stood on the brink of something beautiful, something extraordinary. All she wanted was to tip them over the edge into paradise.

Charlie's eyes widened, her second statement settling between them more than the first. The expanse of his blue eyes blown out into a mere river of blue around the darkness swallowing them. A warmth emanated from the depths, a tenderness that threatened to overwhelm him, but there was also a separate heat pulsing through to the surface. One that more accurately reflected the movement of his hips against hers.

She felt the groan rumble through his chest, vibrating straight into her. "You're gonna be the death of me, Sam."

So far, during their time together, Charlie had been the one to lead. He'd been the one to flirt first, the one to kiss her first, the one to touch her the way she always dreamed he would.

This time, it was her turn.

She grabbed Charlie's face and dragged it down to hers, sealing their lips together. Charlie froze against her for a fraction of a second before clenching her body in his hands, fingers digging into her skin.

The music hammered around them, and other partygoers didn't seem phased by their embrace, seemingly lost in their own worlds as well.

It took mere seconds for Charlie to overtake her, taking control as her body yielded to him. The overwhelming pull to get even closer than they already were awoke a desperate hunger in her gut, erupting in a fiery blaze.

Charlie's hands trailed down her body and found a comfortable resting spot on the curve of her ass, holding her body snugly against his. Sam held on for dear life, completely lost to whatever had taken hold of her body. They had kissed before, so the act wasn't new, but this feeling certainly was. It was the first time that she felt like he was kissing her because *he* wanted to. Not because of their arrangement but because he *wanted* her.

Genuinely, truly, passionately, wanted her.

Charlie managed to lift her feet off the ground, holding onto her so that she felt as if she were floating on a cloud.

Who knew? Maybe she was—maybe she was floating in this little bubble they had created together.

It wasn't until she felt a wall pressing firmly against her back that she realized that they had stepped out of the crowd and to a more secluded back corner of the bar. Unsure how he'd manage to navigate the crowd, her body demanded her full attention once more as her legs instinctively wrapped around his waist, holding on for dear life.

Her head rolled back, desperate for air, as if it had been sucked from her lungs, but she found no escape. Charlie's lips ghosted along the line leading up to her throat, pressing hungry and yet surprisingly gentle kisses as he moved upwards.

Oh shit, she *really* liked that, feeling her core throbbing tortuously between her legs.

Lost to the sensations swimming through her, something hard and hot began to press urgently against her, only adding further fuel to the fire. She let loose the sound trapped in her throat and felt herself tense.

It was probably why she barely registered the feeling of his arms retracting from her, only to snatch both of her wrists with one large hand from where they had been resting. With one quick motion, he shoved them upward and pinned her wrists against the wall above her head, held down with his hand.

Good God, Sam feared she had truly died and gone to heaven. A sense of urgency drove her as she gasped into his mouth, with him immediately swallowing the sound by crushing her lips to his once more.

"Touch me," she whispered into his mouth. "Please."

Charlie wrenched his lips from hers and brought them to her neck, finding and latching onto a spot that had her toes curling. Teasing it with his lips and tongue. It forced her hips to grind against his involuntarily, her clit desperately seeking relief. The hard length of him straining against his jeans provided just the right friction as she moved her hips against his once more.

"*Fuck*, baby," Charlie ground out hoarsely, the groan in his voice like liquid heat, and she wanted more. She wanted more of that breathless, husky quality to his voice. The fire in his eyes scorched her before capturing her lips again.

It felt so incredible that Sam wasn't sure whether the butterflies swirling in her gut would explode.

Well… it wasn't the butterflies that were swirling around in there as a sudden, violent stomach cramp forced Sam to tap rapidly against Charlie's shoulder.

As if sensing the sudden panic in her, Charlie released her just in time for Sam to make a beeline to the nearest trashcan and violently vomit the contents of her stomach into it.

Her hair was swept back from her face, whether by her own hands or Charlie's, she couldn't tell. It had been far too long since she'd last gotten drunk, and her stomach protested vehemently against the string of numerous cocktails that she had consumed over the course of the night.

Once her stomach finally relented, she wiped her mouth with the back of her hand—trying to ignore the sour taste in her mouth as she took in a deep breath.

When she turned, she saw that it had, in fact, been Charlie holding back her hair. The raging inferno that had been in his eyes now replaced with worry and concern.

"Time to go," he stated, bending over and catching her just behind the knees so that he scooped her into his arms.

She was still a bit delirious at what had just happened, the feeling of his bruising lips on her still lingering. Her normally racing mind seemed focused on the feelings that had been dangerously stirred to life inside her.

She wanted to continue. She didn't want to ever stop kissing Charlie. In fact, she was determined to find exactly what his mouth could do to her in other ways.

The heat radiating from her instantly chilled, however, as they exited the building and spilled out into the cold night's air, prickling goosebumps on her skin.

Charlie lowered her to the ground gently, helping her to steady her feet before releasing her altogether. Something in his eyes pulled her from the dreamlike state she'd been in and into the real world.

"I'll call us a cab," he said quickly, turning away and pulling out his phone before she could respond. Hearing the distance in his words, and seeing the physical distance he now put between them, Sam sobered. Her bubble finally burst.

What had she just done?

CHAPTER 23

CHARLIE

hit.
Shit.

Shit.

This was bad.

Next level kind of bad.

It's true what they say about the morning after a night of drinking—it always sheds clarity. But Charlie hadn't needed to sleep to know he'd messed up. Big time.

He sat on one of the barstools in his kitchen, the hot cup of coffee untouched between his hands, as he repeated the previous night's events in his head.

He'd had a few too many, and that alone had been a mistake. One of them should have remained sober, or at least relatively so. And it should have been him. At least then Sam could have had fun without worrying.

What the hell had he been thinking?

Well, Charlie knew what he'd been thinking about.

I think I love you.

He was going to make sure he had those words engraved on his tombstone to showcase his utter stupidity.

He should've known better. *Would* have known better if he'd been sober.

She had been drinking. The probability that she'd gotten as lost in the moment as he had was too high to count. If she woke up and remembered last night, the very real possibility that she would regret everything was too much for him to bear. By the time he had realized his mistake, it had been too late.

Sam headfirst into a trashcan puking her guts up had been a fabulous wake up call.

It didn't matter who started what. He'd still had enough of a right mind to…

Touch me.

A shiver tingled along the column of his spine, leaving him momentarily breathless at the recollection. Even with hindsight knocking at his door, the words sounded like a sweet siren's call beckoning him into the abyss.

He ran a hand roughly through his hair, scouring his brain for the precise moment he should have known to turn around and take her home, before they'd gone past the point of no return—before his higher brain function was about to take a vacation day.

Well, if he was truly honest with himself, he knew when —and it was well before she'd ever put her hands on him.

He shouldn't have left her by herself, even if it'd meant dragging her through the crowd with him. At least then, whatever primal part of his brain wouldn't have kicked into overdrive seeing that asshole yanking Sam like some sort of caveman dragging his club behind him.

It hadn't mattered that the guy was clearly intoxicated, three sheets to the wind with how much he appeared to struggle putting one foot in front of the other. Once he'd seen the way she stumbled and recoiled, trying to pull away, everything else fell away.

One word had been on his mind as he'd shoved his way through the crowd.

Mine.

Clutching both drinks in his hands had been just about the only reason that he hadn't knocked the fucker flat out.

He should've known he was toast from then on.

He coughed, attempting to stoke the growing fire in his gut—and in his pants.

No, he *really* didn't need to think about that. Especially not with her sleeping the night off in the next room.

A text chimed from his phone, abruptly and mercifully pulling him from his thoughts. His eyebrow quirked up at the name on the screen.

Mom got that parking pass you need for the gala - let me know when you want to swing by and grab it

Right. That was looming closer with each passing day as well. Creeping up on him like a loaded bomb just waiting to implode.

God, his head hurt.

Luckily, before he could fall down that particular rabbit hole, he heard Sam stirring in the next room. He turned, mug in hand, as she shuffled into the kitchen. Covering a yawn with her hand while offering him a sleepy smile. She was wonderfully disheveled, a blend of the remnants of sleep and hangover mingling together. Her hair was hastily tied up in a knot atop her head, loose strands of it falling uselessly around her face. She scrunched her nose as one of the strands fell forward, tickling the edges of the little bags settling beneath her eyes. It was frustratingly adorable in a disarming kind of way.

That is, until his gaze landed on the baggy shirt she had on. It wasn't one of hers.

It was one of *his*.

His stomach lurched into his throat as his body desperately fought to mask the arousal that clawed to escape him.

Mine.

Fuck.

"Oh, thank God," she said, the sound crackling around the rough edges of sleep lingering in her throat. "Is that coffee?"

Despite everything he'd been thinking and fretting over that morning—the whirlwind of thoughts swirling around in his head at the sight of her standing there, barefoot and in *his* shirt—he smiled warmly.

He offered her his untouched cup, watching with amusement as she eagerly snatched it and took a generous swig. She swallowed the liquid down and leaned back against the counter, facing him, a little sigh escaping her as she did.

If she remembered anything from last night, she gave no indication of it—and he wasn't sure if that was a good or bad thing.

"How are you feeling?" he asked.

She shrugged. "About as good as anyone with a mild hangover would be."

"Mild?" He chuckled softly, unable to stop himself from enjoying the sight of her pout in response. How she could possibly look adorable at this time of the morning with any kind of hangover, he had no idea. But there she stood, with a slight indignant twinkle in her eyes.

"Yeah, it's not as bad right now as I feared it would be," she continued after taking another generous sip. "I think I threw up most of it after we got home, though I don't really remember that much of what happened. All I know is my tank is empty now."

He wasn't sure if he was relieved or not, but he forced a smile. "Hungry, then?"

"Starved," she moaned, her eyes rolling into the back of her head as if the mere mention of food sent her to another plane of existence.

He laughed. "We're a bit low on stuff in the fridge again, so I'll need to run out and grab a few things. I can grab you something on the way back?"

"Can I come?" she asked, perking up further.

Part of him wanted her to—for them to return to some semblance of normalcy since it appeared she did, in fact, not remember last night if she was this calm about it.

He needed a few minutes to himself because even if she forgot, *he* didn't. Their current living situation made taking a breather nearly impossible, and he still didn't want to leave her alone for too long, just in case, so a drive to and from the store sounded like exactly what he needed.

"I need to get gas for the car and a few other quick errands," he said instead of the truth. "You'll be bored. Besides, don't you have a book to work on, missy?"

Her pout deepened, casting doubt over whether it stemmed from his comment or his dismissal. He chose to believe it was the former.

"I do," she relented. "But first I'm going to enjoy this cup of coffee."

Charlie nodded in the direction of the pantry as he grabbed his car keys. "Well, there should be some scraps to hold you over while I'm gone, but I'll be back quick as I can."

He walked out before she could protest, not pausing until he was a few flights down from the apartment. Some fresh air would do him some good. Clear his head a bit. He'd grab some food, maybe even run by Tyler's place over in Cary to get that parking pass, and come back with a fresh new attitude.

He would not let last night ruin everything.

CHAPTER 24

SAM

*S*am's fingers hurried over the keys of her laptop. Her stomach was still a bit uneasy from last night, so she needed any distraction she could possibly get. She'd woken up from what felt like the most vivid dream that inspired a brand new scene in her book, and she had been more than eager to get it out of her head and onto paper. After Charlie had walked out to run a few errands, she'd practically sprinted back to the bedroom to grab her laptop and get to work.

She typed the final word of the scene she'd come up with, staring down at the page with satisfaction. With Charlie's help, writing this book had felt like an absolute breeze. They had agreed to not talk too much about the logistics of their fake dating, but it was yielding far more creativity in her than she'd expected.

But, then again, how could she not when she had Charlie as a model of what a romantic lead would be like?

He was everything—and then some.

As the cursor blinked in front of her, wondering if there

was anything else she wanted to add to this new scene, her mind began to drift.

What *had* happened last night?

When she'd woken up, groggy with a headache pounding behind her temples, she couldn't remember most of the night before. She'd laid there for a while, racking her brain, but nothing came.

She remembered getting to the club with Charlie. Getting a drink or two. The guy she'd bumped into. Charlie scaring him off. A few more drinks. Some dancing. But, after that, nothing.

It was as if someone reached in and had taken a chunk of her memory with them. It certainly felt that way, too, with the way her head still throbbed behind her eyes, pulsing there with a monotonous beat that even painkillers hadn't managed to fully dull.

It wasn't hard to miss how off Charlie had seemed when he left earlier, though she'd hadn't thought hard on it at the time.

Her stomach coiled in on itself, wondering if it was because of something *she* had done. She desperately hoped not. She'd already put this poor man through the wringer with all of her other drama—between helping her with this book of hers and letting her crash with him because of her whole stalker situation. The last thing Charlie needed was for her to do something else to make him uncomfortable.

She licked her lips, dry from the lack of hydration the past several hours. Her body sank back against the couch, the sheer weight of life the past few weeks making her body feel as if it suddenly weighed a ton.

It had been a bit since she'd had proper sleep, and despite the fact that she'd completely passed out the night before, it still didn't feel like enough. A year's worth of sleep didn't feel like it would be enough. It surprised her just how much everything had started weighing down on her over time, only now aware of it from the raw exposure a night of drinking had uncovered. But she felt it now, weighing her down like a ton of bricks.

She could use a nap, but she knew she wouldn't be able to fall asleep now even though she was so exhausted.

Charlie wasn't there.

She wouldn't be able to fully relax until after he got back. The only time she *had* managed to get any sleep recently had been when he was nearby. As if her body sensed him near and was able to fully let go, knowing she was safe with him there.

Until he got back, however, she would try to dive into her work. She was so close to the halfway point that she could practically taste it. It was the one thing in her life, currently, that made the most sense, and she wanted to cling to that. It had been a lifeline even in some of the darkest periods of her life, and now was no different.

First, though, she needed to get some water and her chapstick. Dehydration was starting to kick in a bit as dryness tickled the back of her throat and crackled across her lips. She had been particularly bad about drinking water throughout the night between bouts of running to the toilet, and she definitely felt the effects of that now.

Water was her first stop as she meandered into the kitchen and pulled a bottle out of the fridge. It was perfectly cold as she tore the cap off, gulping down the liquid. A trickle of it escaped through the side of her mouth in her haste, slinking down her throat and soaking into the collar of her shirt.

With a satisfied gasp after finishing the entire bottle, she glanced down to see how badly she'd gotten herself wet—immediately blushing when she realized what she was wearing.

It was one of Charlie's shirts.

A long, now wrinkled gray T-shirt that came down to just above her thighs. The bottom of it skimmed along the edges of whatever pajama shorts she'd thrown on as well. She must've grabbed whatever was closest last night when she tore that tight-ass dress off to get more comfortable.

Hopefully, he didn't mind too much that she'd borrowed it. After she took a shower in a bit, she'd wash it and give it back.

Before that, however, she needed something to stave off the dryness running across her lips. She went in search of where she'd last stashed her chapstick, finding her purse haphazardly tossed onto the floor near the bedroom door entrance—likely having been tossed there in a desperate attempt to get to the toilet the night before.

Her phone started ringing before she could apply it, trotting back to the couch where she'd left it to answer.

The cop, the one she'd spoken to last, chimed a greeting from the other end. Sam tried to remember what his name was, as it was different from Robert, the first one she'd spoken to. What was his name? Tom?

Regardless, Sam could hear the tension leaking through the phone. His voice was clipped, tight, like he was looking forward to this phone call just about as much as she had.

Which meant he probably didn't have good news to bring.

Dread snaked itself deep into the pit of her stomach as reality slammed back into place. She knew it'd been coming, but she wasn't ready for it. She'd almost convinced herself that this whole living arrangement with Charlie was more about their fake dating experiment than what it really was— that she was staying with him for her safety against some crazy stalker. How the *hell* was this her reality right now?

Too much of her life was slipping out of her control, too

much was changing, and she was struggling to grapple with that.

Charlie. She wanted Charlie right now.

Her entire being cried out for him, for his comforting arms wrapped around her, but she cleared her throat instead. Her gut instinct to shield him from this awful thing, knowing damned well how pissed at her he would be if she did, nipped at her heels. She'd update him later when he got back. She could take care of herself until then, like she always did.

For now, she steeled herself for what was to come.

Tom, as she'd guessed correctly, continued when she didn't say anything. "Is your boyfriend there with you? Might make you feel a little better for what updates I have for you."

"He's not…" She stopped herself, finding it harder for her to say *he's not my boyfriend*, than she thought, and—even more troubling—she didn't want to. "He's not back home yet."

"Should I call you back when he gets back? I can—"

A sound from the front door pulled Sam's attention away, turning to see Charlie coming through the front door, a paper bag tucked beneath one arm and another smaller one clutched in his hands.

Relief barreled into her, and she felt herself let out a quiet gasp seeing him. He was here.

"You're back." She sighed.

"Did your boyfriend get back?" Tom echoed, sounding a bit more hopeful, likely for Sam's sake, which was appreciated.

"He did," she replied, turning her attention to Charlie. Upon seeing the relief that must've been stamped across her face, he dropped the bag onto the counter and made his way toward her.

"What's going on?" Charlie asked.

Sam hovered her hand over the phone. "I'm getting an update on Paul."

Charlie's eyebrows furrowed as he came into the living room and sat next to her on the couch, the smell of grease and salt wafting from the smaller bag as he placed it on the coffee table. "Put him on speaker."

❧

*P*aul's *real* name, as it turned out, was Jonathan Handley.

And Jonathan Handley apparently had a history.

There were at least three other women he had done this to, changing his name each time and disappearing until he inevitably cropped back up again.

Sam now sat perched in Charlie's lap, hardly noticing that Charlie had slowly dragged her into his lap over the course of the phone call. His large frame enveloped her like a blanket made entirely of warmth and steel. Comforting and protective wrapped in one—like he knew that she would need it.

And he was right.

A stormy expression had plagued his normally soft features since they'd ended the phone call, giving him a hardness that she had rarely ever seen.

She hated that it was there because of her.

"What happens now, babe?" she asked quietly, not bothering to pull out of Charlie's grasp as she let the name slip between her lips. Sam found an odd sense of comfort there, even if she knew in her heart that it wasn't real. She needed it to feel real at this moment. She needed *something* to be real, something solid beneath her feet.

He gave her a small smile and squeezed her gently. "You continue staying here with me. Simple as that."

Part of her had hoped that this whole situation would just blow over eventually. That Paul was just a creep who would eventually leave her alone and move on.

Knowing that he had a pattern like this, however, changed things. This wasn't just a blip.

Paul, or whatever his real name is, was dangerous.

She knew that, she did, but she had almost started to believe that with enough time, this would all just be a distant memory. A story she could laugh about years down the road in a "You remember the time I had a crazy stalker? Yeah, that was wild, right?" kind of way.

She hated having one more thing in her life right now that was out of her control.

"Tell me what you're thinking," Charlie commanded quietly, his voice soft and comforting.

It would be easy to lie right now, knowing Charlie wouldn't push her, and that in and of itself was a slight comfort. That right now, she could say anything, and Charlie would still hold her in his arms. He would still be there to help keep the pieces of herself together, even when she didn't have the strength to.

But it would still be a lie.

"I don't know what to think," she replied honestly. "I think I really just wanted this whole thing to be something that would go away quickly. Stupid, huh?"

Charlie shook his head. "I don't think it's stupid."

"Naive, then?"

"Sam, this isn't exactly a normal situation to be thrown in. Stop beating yourself for not knowing how bad it was going to get," Charlie stated a little more firmly.

"Well, what are *you* thinking?" she asked, turning her head to gaze up at him.

A little wrinkle had formed between his eyebrows, where they were furrowed together. It had been a few days since he'd last shaved, so the stubble along his jaw was thicker than usual. It tickled her face as she looked up at him. The dimples she loved so much were tucked away from view as his lips formed a frown. A complete contrast to the fun, goofy Charlie that she was so familiar with. Replaced with this serious and worried one.

"I'm thinking," Charlie said after a few moments, "that I hate that you're in this situation too. That if I ever get my hands on this guy, I'm gonna beat him senseless."

Sam couldn't help but chuckle. "You're too sweet, but you wouldn't harm a fly, Charlie."

Something flickered in his eyes, like dark clouds gathering over the ocean just before a violent storm. "For you? I'd make an exception."

A lump lodged itself in her throat at that, knowing that he genuinely meant that.

It was troublesome for her heart. She could too easily mistake that expression for something that it wasn't.

This whole dynamic between them right now wasn't real.

Her stalker situation complicated things considerably, but if Sam didn't remember the fact that she and Charlie weren't *really* dating, that this whole thing between them was fake, she'd break her own heart.

And it would be all her fault.

If she was smart, she'd call this whole thing off between them. At least until after the situation with Paul was dealt with. Right now, however, she didn't want to be smart. She wanted to continue pretending that this was more than what it was.

Her sense of control was slipping away, and she wasn't ready to wake from the dream just yet.

Despite the fact that it would likely be a while before sleep even entered her mind, the thought of being completely alone suddenly felt more daunting. Far too many conflicting thoughts and emotions tried to fight their way to the surface to tell her it was probably a bad idea right now, for her heart, for her to ask this of him, but the overwhelming need for his warmth, to feel safe in his arms, overruled.

"Charlie?" she said softly.

"Hm?"

"Would you… Would you mind if we shared the bed tonight? Say no if you feel like it'll be too weird, or if that would make you uncomfortable, since this is your place, and I'm just a guest. But I don't think I want to sleep alone tonight."

He seemed surprised for a fraction of a second before his lips ticked upward into a warm smile. "Of course."

CHAPTER 25

CHARLIE

*C*harlie opened his eyes groggily, blinking the sleep
out of them as best as he could as he heard the birds
chirping just outside. Light had trickled in through the curtain
directly onto his face, tickling him awake.

The first thing he saw upon fully registering the living
world once more was Sam.

She was completely out of it, peacefully curled up into
him, as if she'd been there all night long. Her long arms were
slung around him, as if he were a giant teddy bear she were
desperately clinging to.

He hadn't blamed her for not wanting to sleep alone last
night. When she'd made the suggestion, he'd felt relieved. He
wanted nothing more than just to hold her—ensuring that she
was safe there in his arms.

Despite himself, he chuckled and tucked a loose strand of
auburn hair behind her ear.

She must've migrated from where she'd fallen asleep
before. She'd been adamant that she didn't want to take up
his entire bed since they were sharing. Sleep, however,

seemed to have other ideas for her. She'd migrated across the border and clung to him like her life depended on it.

There was something endearing about it that settled deep in Charlie's chest. She was such a fiercely independent creature, to a fault sometimes, that seeing her like this was a wholly new experience.

It felt precious, sacred almost.

He rubbed an errant thumb across her cheek, following the line of freckles across it and reveling in the softness greeting him. Even in sleep, she was stunning. Her long eyelashes fanned across her cheeks, just barely kissing the top of her freckle line. Her all-too-tempting lips were slightly parted, showing off their soft fullness. An absolutely picture of beauty that he couldn't believe was right in front of him—curled into him like an alley cat having found the perfect ray of sunshine.

It would be so easy to give in to what he really wanted, to sink back into the bed and hold her until the world collapsed around them. It was so tempting that he felt the itch of it down into his core.

Feeling her warm, supple body pressed against his, he had to suppress a moan at just how much his body *yearned* for her. Remembering the way her lips, hands, body had felt on his…

The lingering desire from it simmered in his veins, coming back with vengeance. Upon adjusting his position to try and untangle her limbs from him, he discovered a *new* problem that had, quite literally, risen.

He forced himself to scoot to the edge of the bed, swinging his legs out and placing his feet on firm ground. Something, anything, to ground himself in reality.

There were too many things up in the air for him to lose himself to that.

Sam shifted in her sleep, flopping onto her stomach and coming closer to the edge of the bed, where he sat. The long strands of her hair fanned out, the light of the morning sun causing it to shine like fire flaming around her.

A perfect metaphor if there was one about what she was to him right now.

Fire.

This experiment of theirs was destined to burn them both if he wasn't careful. He knew that, but there was a part of him that didn't want to care. Let them go up in flames together. He'd welcome it. All he wanted was to burn with her—scorch them both until they were completely ruined for anyone else.

"Charlie…" she exhaled on a sigh, scrunching her nose a bit before a blissful smile carved through the freckles.

Blood roared in Charlie's ears. This woman was definitely going to be the death of him. He was dying to know what she was dreaming about, what caused her to say his name so contentedly like that.

The need to touch her was too great, too undeniable that he found himself reaching out to rub her back. The expanse of it was uncovered from the tank top she'd thrown on right before bed, and his finger lazily traced the lines between the freckles dotting her back and shoulders.

An idea occurred to him, one that he couldn't deny.

He could say it once, just to get it out of his system. The words that desperately clawed to be released but he could never say if he didn't want to lose her forever.

He traced the letters along her skin slowly, deliberately. Writing out the one thing he shouldn't, in the only way he could, while savoring the feeling of touching her like this. It felt intimate, almost magical.

When he finished, he rubbed her back once more and finally tore himself away.

He made his way into the kitchen and set about getting coffee ready, trying his best to remain quiet so he didn't disturb Sam in the process. She deserved some extra sleep today.

The pot whirred to life as he sat on one of the bar stools while it brewed—barely making contact with the seat when his phone began to ring. It was still too early to get any work calls, so Charlie pulled it from where he'd tucked it into his pocket.

Charlie raised an eyebrow at the caller ID before answering. "Didn't expect to hear from you anytime soon, or at all actually."

"I hope I didn't wake you," Tyler said on the other end, his voice sounding much more awake than Charlie's. Charlie tried to remember how long ago that last conversation had been, but his sleep-soaked mind couldn't remember. The only thing he *could* remember was Tyler angrily hanging up on him after refusing to take over catering responsibilities.

"No, I'm waiting for my coffee to finish brewing. What can I do for you?"

Tyler scoffed. "You don't have to sound so formal."

Charlie shrugged, though he knew Tyler couldn't see. "Well, considering we haven't spoken since our last call, I didn't know what else to say. You were pretty pissed at me."

A dramatic sigh rang through. "Peter told me about Sam's situation. I just wanted to know if there's anything either of you need."

Charlie's jaw clenched. "Well, you can start by telling Peter that he needs to stop telling other people things that aren't his business to begin with."

"Come on, man. You know he's just worried about both of you," Tyler argued.

"I wish everyone would worry a little less. I've got it

covered," Charlie snapped a little more curtly than he intended.

Another sigh. "Charlie, I didn't call to fight. You and Sam have your own thing going on, the fucking dynamic duo, but you often forget that Peter and I do *actually* give a shit about both of you."

Charlie scoffed. "Rich coming from you since you threw a temper tantrum because you signed up for more than you were capable of and then got angry at me for not taking some of it off your plate."

There was a pause on the other end, and for a moment, Charlie wondered if Tyler had hung up the phone again. "You're right. That's on me."

Charlie blanched in his seat. He hadn't expected that at all. "I'm sorry, could you repeat that? I don't think I heard—"

"You heard me just fine, jackass. Don't push it," Tyler snapped. "I just don't want you to go ape shit like you did when we were at the sentencing. I think it's the only time I've ever seen you *that* angry, and I'd rather you not end up six feet under over it."

Unable to help himself, Charlie jibbed, "You sound almost like you care."

"You fucking—" Tyler started before letting out another long sigh on the other end of the phone, the sound distant, as if he held the phone far away. "I'm just worried, alright? Peter and I both are. Regardless of how much you fucking annoy me—which you do, by the way—you're still my little brother. I'm not trying to be all buddy-buddy with you. You have your life, and I have mine, so I'm totally fine seeing you a few times a year for holidays because you're *such* a pain in my ass... But I can't lose *another* fucking sibling, man."

It was so easy, especially this time of year, for Charlie to forget that he wasn't the only one who lost Erica. She was his twin, so the pain had always felt double, especially with the additional guilt he carried. But she was also Peter and Tyler's little sister too.

A pang of guilt rippled in Charlie's gut. "Tyler…"

"Don't get all mushy on me now. Just be fucking careful, alright? I've already talked to Mom and Dad about it and—shut up before you interrupt me," Tyler replied quickly before Charlie could protest, his voice tighter than it was before. "—and they're gonna hire extra security to keep an eye out for this guy while y'all are at the event."

Coming from Tyler, that meant more than Charlie could say. "Thanks, Tyler."

Tyler cleared his throat. "Yeah, yeah, sure. Tell Sam I say hi and I hope she's doing good. She's the only one between the two of you worth a damn, anyway."

The call dropped immediately after, forcing a laugh out of Charlie. Not because his emotionally-lacking brother showed actual human empathy but because he definitely wasn't wrong on that account.

CHAPTER 26

SAM

The time had finally come for the news Sam had been dreading.

She was confident about how her book was going, channeling all of her energy the past few days into a writing frenzy to distract herself from everything *else* going on in her life.

Things between her and Charlie were normal… ish. She'd rationalized, and rationalized more, about what Charlie had written on her back when he'd thought she was asleep. She was still half asleep herself, so who knows if that was actually what he'd written? Who knows if he was writing anything at all? He could've been just connecting the dots with the freckles on her back for all she knew.

It was fortunate that Charlie had to run into the office for a few hours—something about an outage and the data lab. It had taken most of the morning to reassure him that she would be perfectly fine by herself, especially after the most recent update, but she was secretly glad for the few minutes to herself to talk to Angel.

She just needed a little girl time, that's all.

Plus, she wanted to calm herself as much as possible before this call.

She positioned her laptop on the coffee table and settled onto the floor, crossing her legs. She was doing anything and everything she could think of to calm herself.

Grounding herself to the floor?

Check.

A warm and fluffy pillow nearby that she could clutch if she needed to hug something?

Her fingers traced the seam of the pillow she'd borrowed from Charlie's bed, ensuring it was strategically positioned within arms reach.

Check.

A cold and fizzy drink to sip on if the nerves started making her stomach feel sour?

She reached for the bottle of seltzer Charlie had given her before leaving and took a preemptive sip to get ahead of the curve.

Check.

She was as ready as she could be for whatever news Angel brought. The black video screen in front of her displayed the "waiting for host" message at the top as she settled into her spot.

Her phone dinged next to her, startling her from the thoughts running rampant in her head. A smile finally spread across her face as she opened the message.

Relax, they'll love it

She laughed and quickly shot off a reply, keeping an eye on the screen as she did.

Easy for you to say!

How did you know I was sitting here,
freaking out?

I have met you recently… haven't I?

Rude

You know you've got it in the bag

You said Angel loved it

I did, but Angel is biased

She's not the one publishing my book

You've got this. We'll figure it out even if
they don't

Sam laughed, trying not to let the butterflies in her gut mean anything more than the anticipation of the news she was waiting on.

Tell Angel I said hi

As soon as Sam put her phone back down, the screen finally lit up with Angel's sunny disposition.

The background was different from Angel's usual view of Manhattan behind her. Instead, she'd opted for what appeared to be a green screen. Angel's form melded in with an angelic-looking scene of clouds floating around her, the olive-colored turtle-neck she had on contrasting starkly with the dream-like purples and pinks surrounding her. A golden halo glittered above her head in the most ridiculous—yet very stylistic—choice that already had Angel giving Sam a self-satisfied grin.

"I hope this was on purpose and not just because your nickname is Angel?" Sam immediately asked.

Angel's grin widened somehow, appearing far too pleased with herself. "You know, I honestly didn't think of it that way, but thank you for making this choice even better. I think I'm gonna add it to my repertoire."

"Definitely quite the sight," Sam agreed, unable to hide the eye roll she gave her friend.

"Well, I just wanted to do something special, so you remembered how much of an *angel* I am."

Sam laughed. "Only if you come bearing good news?"

"I had a nice *long* conversation with the team, and they are *thrilled* with the pages you've sent," Angel confirmed, shimmying her shoulders.

The tension in Sam's gut finally unraveled. "Oh my God, really? They liked it?"

"They fucking ate it up!" Angel exclaimed, emphasizing each word with a clap in between. "They loved the idea of you trying your hand at romance. And, on top of the many other reasons why you love me, they also agreed to let you pick whatever pen name you want to use."

"Angel, you've outdone yourself!" she squealed, bouncing in her seat.

Angel fluffed her hair. "I know."

"Does that mean that my contract is safe?"

"It means they're updating it with this current project of yours as we speak."

Sam pumped a fist into the air. It was a dip in the pool in comparison with all the other things going on, but the relief she felt was swift. The sheer weight of it washed over her like a tidal wave with tears stinging the back of her eyes.

She wouldn't lose her dream job after all.

On the verge of celebration, she noticed Angel was holding up a tentative finger. "There's just… one catch…"

Of course there would be—it had sounded almost *too* easy.

"This should be a walk in the park for you," Angel added quickly, as if she could see the gears in Sam's head turning.

Sam narrowed her eyes. "And that would be?"

"The book is supposed to be a spicy romance… So, they just want to see one of the spicy scenes just to make sure they're totally happy with everything, especially since the book isn't *technically* finished yet."

Sam groaned and ran a hand through her hair. "Great. I haven't gotten to that part yet."

"Well, I'd hop along to it."

"How soon do they want it by?"

Angel grimaced. "End of the week."

Sam's eyes bulged. "That's in three days, Angel!"

"If push comes to shove, I'll see if I can do some publishing magic to convince them to drop the matter, but you know I can't guarantee it," Angel stated, quickly adding in, "And if you decide to cut the scene later, you always can. As long as they have *something* to read for the time being, I think they'll be satisfied."

It made sense, and the fact that it was *all* they wanted was far better than what she'd feared.

"Tell me what you're thinking," Angel prompted, snapping her bright-pink manicure in front of the camera.

"Sorry, no, you're right—something is better than nothing, and I don't have to keep it if it doesn't make sense with the story."

"But…" her friend drawled.

"But… I just… I mean… You know that I've read my fair share of spicy romances over the years…"

Angel nodded. "More than your fair share."

"But now that I'm at the point where I actually need to write that scene, it's a little daunting," Sam admitted.

"Well, speaking of," Angel started as she waggled her eyebrows at Sam. "Think that's something your experiment partner might be able to help you with?"

She rolled her eyes and tried to ignore the flutter in her stomach. "Don't *even* start with me on that."

Angel shrugged, a mischievous gleam in her eyes. "Why not?"

"This is sounding eerily less like talking me through writing a sex scene and much more like a fucking pep talk," Sam snapped, rubbing her forehead.

"Well, who else are you gonna talk to about it? I'm putting my self-appointed *other* best friend hat on now. Stop talking to me like your agent. Tell me what's going on. You look… stressed."

Sam *was* stressed. Everything was so muddled down that she suddenly wasn't sure *why* she was hesitating. Was it because there had been so much going on lately that her body felt constantly on alert? Maybe it was that she was still trying to discern whether Charlie had told her something significant with his finger drawings or if she had completely lost her marbles? Or was it because she'd have to say what *her* feelings were out loud, and that prospect suddenly terrified her more than she thought.

"I think… I think this fake-dating thing of ours was a huge mistake."

Angel cocked her head. "Why do you say that?"

Sam bit her lip. "Because I knew my feelings would get in the way, and they are… Big time."

Angel clapped her hands excitedly. "Oh my God, *finally*. Tell me everything!"

"I'm not telling you *everything*; that's private."

The speakers nearly burst as Angel squealed. "You *slept* with him?!"

Sam waved her hands. "No! No! We haven't slept together! Jeez, Angel."

Angel immediately pouted. "No fun. Why not? Sweetie, he was a teenager when he told Peter that he didn't see you as more than a friend. Don't you think there's the remote possibility that his feelings have changed?""

"Because," Sam hissed, "Charlie and I started this experiment as friends. We're ending it as *friends*. That's all he sees me as anyway, so it doesn't even matter."

The sting that accompanied that statement was overwhelming.

"Jesus Christ, you are so fucking *dense*." Angel groaned as she pinched the bridge of her nose. "I love you, you know that, so I say this with love, but you are so *dumb*."

The bluntness of that statement forced a strangled laugh out of Sam. "Rude."

"Okay," Angel started after noisily letting out a breath. "Put that aside for a minute. You *clearly* have a hard time separating different aspects of relationships—but you said *he* only sees you as a friend. What about you?"

Sam blinked a few times. "Wait, what is *that* supposed to mean?"

"It means that I've been your best friend since college, but you have the *worst* time sometimes towing that line between us being friends *and* working together. I'm not Charlie-level best friend, but you're still *my* best friend nonetheless."

Sam's entire body shrank in on itself. "That's different."

"How?" Angel asked, folding her arms across her chest.

Sam shrugged sheepishly. "It just is."

Angel laughed, but there was a sudden venom in her eyes that surprised Sam. "It really isn't. We used to tell each other everything! Hell, you get a fucking stalker, and it didn't even cross your mind to tell me until days later?"

Sam flinched at that one. "In my defense, I didn't tell Charlie about it either…"

The chocolatey depths of Angel's eyes softened as she relaxed her shoulders. "I know you didn't. And don't get mad at me, but I told Peter about it, and I think he might have told his parents and Tyler, just to make sure everyone is safe."

"Angel—"

"Don't—let other people worry about you for a change, okay? My point is just that—on top of the fact that you have this insatiable desire to never ask for help when you need it, which I'll never fucking understand—you tend to have a hard time when relationships change."

Ouch. That one stung.

"Admitting that you're in love with him," Angel continued when Sam remained silent, "and that he is *definitely* in love with you—don't you *dare* try to tell me otherwise—would mean that your relationship together might change, and I think that's what actually scares you."

Tears pricked in Sam's eyes, but she grunted in an effort to fight them off. "Okay, Dr. Phil, chill out."

"What I don't understand," Angel went on as if she hadn't heard Sam, "is why? Why would a change in your relationship with Charlie, or hell even with me, scare you so much?"

A sob tore through to the surface. "Because I can't bear the thought of either of you leaving me!"

Sam couldn't see the expression on Angel's face through the haze of tears, but she could hear the delicate change in her voice. "Sam, sweetie… why would you think we're going to leave?"

"Everyone always does!" she squeaked out, desperately rubbing her eyes in hopes it would make the tears stop. "My parents died and left me here. My family leaves me any time I'm not fucking useful to them…"

"Hey," Angel snapped. "Don't put me and that *witch* even *remotely* in the same category."

"So, yes," Sam continued, "I'm terrified that if things change between us too much, and between me and Charlie, that you'll both leave! It's what everyone does when they don't need me anymore, and I can't stand knowing it would've been my fault if it did."

Sam didn't stop the sobs as they tore through her. Her body doubled over as she wrapped her arms around herself, hoping that it would be enough to help keep the broken pieces of her together.

"Sam, I know I'm not gonna be able to talk *decades* worth of therapy into your head with all of that, but what I *do* know is that neither myself, nor Charlie, are going anywhere. We both love you. Just, in a different way for Charlie that probably includes a lot of naked time," Angel said, a hint of humor in her voice at the end.

Despite herself, despite the tears as they continued to stream down her cheeks, and despite all the conflicting emotions and feelings still raging inside of her—Sam laughed.

"I don't know about all that," Sam sputtered back.

Angel rolled her eyes. "Sam, you have this gorgeous man who proposed a whole fucking experiment just to help you do research for your book. Please open your eyes."

"I—"

Angel shook her head. "Talk to him, *at least*. Tell him how you feel."

"I'll… think about it," Sam said slowly.

"You better," Angel scolded as she pointed her finger at the screen, "because I'll kick your ass from here to Timbuktu if you don't."

❧

Sam leaned back against the couch, staring up at the ceiling. Processing her conversation with Angel.

Everything she'd said was right. She *was* afraid of things changing too much.

When Angel had become her agent, she'd overcompensated and leaned so heavily into Angel's new role that it had affected their friendship. Even if she hadn't meant for it to. And Charlie was no different.

Sam and I are just friends. I don't see her like that.

It had been so many years since she'd overheard that stupid conversation between him and Peter. They were still teenagers, and it hadn't been but a few months after Erica had died. He'd finally started acting more like himself, but with the trial going on at the same time, she'd known even then that he was overwhelmed. If she were in his shoes, she could see herself saying something similar just to get people off her back.

Right now, however, she didn't want to think about any of that.

Right now, all she wanted was to focus on writing. If she was on a deadline now to get that scene to her publishers, she would need to get started as soon as possible. Even if she had no fucking clue what she was going to write for it.

Already settled into her spot on the floor, she snagged a pillow from the couch and shoved it beneath her. She then began to click through the files on her laptop until she came to the open manuscript and hovered her fingers over the keys.

The last she'd left her characters and story, she was no where near the start of where the spicy scenes would begin. Though well into the story, she'd gone for a slow-burn kind of romance between her characters—meaning that writing a spicy scene now would be a bit out of left field.

In order to satisfy her publishers, she'd probably just have to write something smutty and see if it actually would work in the story when she got to that point. Otherwise, she could toss it. Simple enough.

That said, she'd need a few minutes before she could work up to trying to write it. She wasn't exactly in the head space for that kind of thing at the moment, so she simply picked up where she'd last left off.

She was heavily invested in the current scene when her phone started ringing.

Thinking it might be Angel following up, she picked it up without looking.

"You made your point the first time, you—" she started before being interrupted by a surprising voice.

"Come again?" Aunt Emily asked on the other end. Sam winced, regret setting in immediately. It felt like a lifetime ago since she'd last talked to her, but she was fairly certain the conversation would take a similar track.

"Sorry," she said, losing any enthusiasm she might've had in her voice. "I thought you were someone else. What's up?"

Aunt Emily cleared her throat. "I was following up to see whether you had talked to your little friend about Tommy's book."

Yep, exact same trajectory as last time. The unwelcome tension stretched between Sam's shoulders as she squirmed uncomfortably on the pillow beneath her.

"I've been a bit busy, Aunt Emily," she said.

Aunt Emily scoffed. "You can't *possibly* be that busy that

you can't just put in a good word for him. He's your *only* cousin, after all."

She was in no mood for Aunt Emily's antics today. "Let me ask you this, has Tommy actually even written a word of this supposed book yet?"

"Well, no, but—"

"Then there's nothing for me to tell *anyone*. But besides that—I've been busy," Sam said, trying to tamper down the anger slowly rising up in her throat and heating her cheeks and ears.

"We're all busy, dear, but I can't see what would be taking up so much of your time that you can't even pick up the phone. It'll take five minutes, and it'll really help Tommy out a great deal."

Nothing about this conversation was surprising to Sam. It was how her aunt had always been—and would likely always be. She'd pester her until she got her way and then disappear into the ether until she needed something else. It made Sam wonder why the hell she even put up with any of it. The number of times she'd run, crying, to Charlie's house, just to escape them, was too many to count. But for some reason, she always found herself picking up the phone anyway.

In fact… why *was* she putting up with any of it? They'd essentially stopped all contact with her after she went to college. She had no obligation to speak to any of them, especially how they'd treated her growing up.

When the silence dragged on for too long for Aunt Emily's taste, she scoffed. "What on earth could be more important than helping *your family* out?"

"I've been dealing with a stalker," she snapped, "so I'm sorry Tommy's book has been a bit low on my fucking priority list." She'd had no intention of telling her family anything about the situation with Paul, but the words slipped out before she could quell the anger rising in her throat.

"A *stalker*? Who on earth is stalking you?" Aunt Emily asked, and—unless Sam was hearing incorrectly—it almost sounded like concern in her voice.

It softened Sam enough to continue. "Some guy I met earlier this year. He broke into my apartment and tore everything apart."

"Oh my… Are you alright?"

"I'm fine," she said. "I'm staying with Charlie until they find the guy."

A rustling sound echoed in the background on Aunt Emily's side. "I'm grabbing a pen and some paper, hold on a second."

Sam raised her eyebrows. "What for?"

"You can just give me your friend's number, and I'll call her for you," Aunt Emily said quickly. "I already know what to tell her, so I won't have to trouble you again about this."

Un-fucking-believable.

Laughter bubbled out of Sam before she could stop it. Literally nothing changes.

"No."

"N-no?" Aunt Emily sputtered.

"No," Sam repeated. "None of you give a shit about me. Didn't when I lived with you, and it's very clear you still don't. I don't understand why, as I'm literally your only niece, but that's neither here nor there. Be honest… Do you even like me? Like, if you never got another single thing from me, would you even still bother talking to me?"

She could hear Aunt Emily flustering on the other end of the phone, starting and stopping a million times before one word finally came through. "No."

It was odd how one word could feel like a knife straight

to the chest, even if she knew it was coming. Sure, it hurt like hell, but at the same time, she felt like a weight was lifted. It was the strangest sensation, but it felt freeing.

"Then let me make this simple, so we don't waste each other's time going forward. Do not call me ever again. I'm done. I don't want anything to do with you or your family," she said firmly, ending the call immediately after before any objections could come through.

Sam grinned, prouder than she'd ever been of herself in a moment like this, going through her contacts before her aunt recovered enough to try to call her again, and blocked each and every contact of her family.

It was probably something she should've done years ago, but better late than never. Almost giddy now with the newfound freedom she had, she turned back to her laptop to pick up where she'd left off.

CHAPTER 27

CHARLIE

Charlie opened the door, paper bag swinging at his side. "Hey! I bring offerings of food."

"Welcome back!" she called out, her gaze firmly on her laptop.

He'd hated leaving her here by herself earlier, the unexpected relief tingling across his skin as he placed the bag on the counter. "What'd you get up to while I was gone?"

She smiled at him. "Well, it's been an interesting day, that's for sure."

"Yeah?"

"My publisher accepted my book."

Charlie pumped a fist into the air, earning a giggle from her. "See, I knew it! I told you they'd love it."

"And then," she continued, "I talked to my Aunt Emily."

Record scratch. What an awful way to celebrate something so great. "What'd she want now?"

Sam smiled once more and shook her head. "It doesn't matter. I finally told her to stop calling. Blocked her and everyone else on that side."

Quite the eventful day, indeed. Charlie wanted to cheer

but restrained himself. Even if she was happy with her decision, which she absolutely should be, he wasn't sure how she felt about it all. They were, at the end of the day, the only blood relatives she had left. And the last thing he wanted was to make her feel bad with some over-the-top reaction.

"Proud of you, babe," he finally settled on, meaning every word.

"Thanks. It felt really good," she admitted coyly. Her lip pouted out when she glanced back at the screen, a tension there that didn't match what she'd just said.

Charlie dug his hands into his pockets. "What's with the sour face, then? You look like you've been sucking on a lemon."

"Glad my face reflects my mood." She pouted, leaning back to stretch her arms above her head, a sliver of skin peaking out from beneath.

He shook his head and patted the counter space in front of him. "Come here. Tell me what's up."

A hint of pink seemed to color Sam's cheeks, but it could've been the sunlight against her face just as she turned to face him.

"I'm… I'm finding myself stuck on a critical part of my book, but I'm having a really hard time with it, so I'm frustrated. Nothing to worry about."

Precisely something Charlie should be concerned with, as helping her with this book was what started everything. Something he seemed to keep forgetting.

He motioned again for her to join him in the kitchen as he pulled two large bottles of seltzer from the bag. "Come hither."

She laughed. "For what?"

"Get away from your computer, and talk with me," he

replied, leaning back against the counter. "Clear your head for a bit, and have a drink with me."

It had been a few days since the nightclub debacle, and, while Sam hadn't given him any indication that she remembered anything, Charlie was exhausted from feeling awkward about it. If she didn't remember, he could pretend like he didn't either.

Beyond that, he missed her. Their conversations had been minimal between the chaos of Sam in the thick of writing, work, and the latest with Paul. Yet it felt like an eternity. He yearned for the effortless and laid-back manner they shared with one another over a hot cup of coffee.

Sam stood, giving one final stretch before joining him.

She accepted the seltzer he extended, popping the top of it off and clinking it against his.

"So? Tell me what's on your mind," he prompted.

She wiped her mouth with the back of her hand, the effect bringing a flush of color to her lips. She puckered them as she swallowed the sip she'd taken with a grimace.

He really needed to stop staring at her lips.

"I told you, it's just book stuff."

He laughed. "All the more reason to talk to me about it. It can't be that bad."

"Seriously, Charlie, it's fine."

"Sam," he egged with a grin, drawing her name out, "you can tell me anything."

There was something about the way her eyes darted to the side as she rubbed her arm that piqued his curiosity.

She shook her head. "Not this. It's embarrassing, and it has to do with the romantic parts of the book but…"

"All the more reason to talk to me about it, right? I'm still helping you in that department."

"Charlie…"

"Spill it, babe. It can't be that bad," he said before taking another swig.

"I don't—I don't have a lot of sexual experience."

Charlie choked on his drink, slapping his hand over his mouth to prevent spraying her in the face. He coughed as he tried to force the liquid down the correct pipe—and to hide the intense wave of arousal that statement brought on. "Fuck, sorry."

Sam seemed completely oblivious to the latter, instead starting to giggle, as if she realized how ridiculous this whole thing sounded. "I tried to warn you!"

He laughed, wiping his mouth. "You did. I'm sorry."

"See? Now it's weird. Let's talk about something else."

"No," Charlie interjected for some reason, unsure why he would push her on the topic. "You can't say something like that and not expect me to wonder what the hell that has to do with your book?"

She didn't meet his gaze as she took another sip from her own drink. "Well, I'm finally at the *smut* part of my smut book, but now that I'm here, I'm at a total loss. I thought I'd have all these great ideas on how the scene would play out, what they would want, what they would do, what they would do to *each other*, but nothing."

One, two, three.

One, two, three.

One, two, three.

Nope, that wasn't working. Charlie leaned forward on the counter to hide the reaction his dick was having right now.

"And your lack of experience is what you think the problem is?"

She shrugged. "Maybe? I don't know. I just think it doesn't help that I've only had one less-than-stellar, quasi-intoxicated sexual experience that lasted a grand total of ten minutes before the guy unceremoniously asked me to leave."

"How romantic," Charlie stated flatly, fighting the growl out of his voice.

He didn't remember this particular event, and she'd certainly never told him about it—not that he blamed her. Granted, he'd never exactly been forthcoming about the handful of one-night-stands he'd had over the years, but that never seemed to be a topic either of them touched.

But the fact that anyone was less than *eternally* grateful to even be in her presence like that made his blood boil.

"Exactly. So, I currently have a smut book with no smut in it," she stated. "And I'm not exactly drowning in dick right now, so it's not like I could figure it out that way either."

Charlie blinked a few times at her, surprised at her statement, when she seemed to realize what she'd said and clapped her hand over her mouth. Her green eyes were wide, a shocked gasp reverberating through her hand. "I can't believe I just fucking said that."

A nervous laugh tore out of her throat as her eyes met his, and he knew he'd do anything to make her laugh more.

He'd do anything she asked of him.

He cocked his head to the side. "How does one swim in dicks, exactly? Is that something you'd even want? Doesn't sound all that pleasant for anyone."

"Probably not logistically," Sam rationalized, a giggle still lingering in her voice. "Which do you think would be better —swimming in a pool full of flaccid dicks? Or a bunch of hard ones?"

Charlie thought on it for a moment, of this ridiculous situation, before responding. "Flaccid for sure, it'd be much softer."

She let loose the giggle she'd been holding back and

nodded. "Very true. But we haven't even established dick size. If we're talking about a bunch of hard twelve inchers, that would be intensely uncomfortable. But if they're flaccid, it might be pretty soft."

Where this woman got her sense of humor, he had no idea, but he loved it.

"Oh, but a bunch of three-inch hard on's wouldn't be?"

She tapped her finger against her chin, staring up at the ceiling as she considered. "I guess it would be like swimming with a bunch of thumbs."

At that, he threw his head back and laughed. Really and truly laughed. The kind that only Sam ever seemed to pull from him.

God, he'd never get over her, would he?

"What it must be like to live in your brain," he offered instead.

She shrugged. "It's made for some interesting reading material, I'm told."

"I'm sure," he replied, his smile feeling easy as it tugged at the corners of his mouth.

The temptation was there, right there dangling in front of his nose like bait. Kiss her, hold her close, tell her all the things he wanted to do to her. The things he'd been wanting to do to her for so long that he'd lost count. But he held himself there, firmly on the other side of the line they'd etched into the sand.

He wanted so desperately to believe she'd meant what she said that night. That all these years of torture on his end were at an end. That it hadn't just been a drunken confession on the heels of what they were doing.

The sting in his chest the night he'd overheard her and Angel talking, back when they were in college, ripped through him once more. He'd been so sure back then, after leaving home, that he'd almost convinced himself that maybe she *did* think of him in that way.

It had all come screeching to a halt with those six little words. *I've never liked him like that.*

If he didn't repeat that in his head, he'd make that same mistake again. He'd convince himself that maybe her feelings had truly changed, that she saw him more than what he was, but he couldn't bring himself to do it. He was too afraid.

"Charlie?" Sam asked, concern etched into her features as she watched him curiously.

Shit, had he been standing there staring off into the distance?

"Hm?"

She glanced down at the ground before meeting his eyes. "Why haven't we talked about the other night?"

Oh no. Did she remember something? Was she going to call everything off? Had he messed everything up?

Charlie forced a smile onto his face. "What about it? You had fun, right?"

She nodded, but she cleared her throat. "We did. I just… I-I feel like I should apologize."

He blinked a few times. "What?"

Sam pointedly looked away. "You wanted to leave when things started getting a little crazy, and I made you stay. And… I… I, well, I feel like I had this dream about saying something to you, and… I don't know… I don't know if I said it out loud?"

The embarrassment and shame in her gaze was too much for him to bear. He'd rather rip his heart out of his chest and serve it to her on a fucking silver platter than see that glimmer in her eyes.

He was about to respond, to deny it, but she held up her hand. "You've been so good to me. You've gone above and beyond to help me out, took me in when I didn't have anywhere else to go, and then I take advantage of the situation…"

Okay… Now he really was confused. What the hell was she talking about? How could she have possible been taking advantage of *anything* in this situation?

"Sam, what on earth are you talking about?" he asked slowly.

"This experiment! Fake dating!" she cried out, throwing her arms in the air as she did. "I took it too far. I never should have proposed any of this stuff if I couldn't even keep my own stupid feelings out of it, but I haven't done a very good job at that, and I've made things awkward between us, and I'm so sorry Charlie, I really am…"

Charlie stood there completely frozen in place, trying to dissect the words as they tumbled out of her mouth, but she continued.

"I should have never suggested we throw in the physical stuff. I thought I could handle it, but I couldn't. I know kissing me hasn't meant anything to you, I know that was part of our deal and I'm the one making things weird, so I wanted to apologize if I've been making you uncomfortable in any way. I've been trying really hard not to let all of this mean anything to me, but it has. I know you've been avoiding me a bit the past few days since the night club, so I'm sure I did or said something stupid there. You probably didn't want me to feel bad, so you didn't say anything about it, which I appreciate, but I don't want you to feel like you can't be honest with me."

Charlie stood, frozen in his spot, feeling his eyes widen. Her hands clenched into fists at her sides like she was prepared for anything he was about to dish out. He was so lost on exactly how he could salvage this situation that he almost missed something else twinkling in her eyes. It was faint, hidden under the layers of embarrassment and behind the shame spiraling in her eyes. Something he'd never seen before.

Charlie shook his head, struggling to find the words until a frustrated breath hissed out of him. "*That's* what's been going on in that head of yours? Sam… I've been worried that I've been the one making *you* feel uncomfortable."

She opened her mouth, closed it, and opened it again. "W-why would you think that?"

Charlie ran a hand through his hair. "Sam… Every time I've touched you, I've kissed you, I've held you in my arms, it's gotten harder and harder to let all of this *not mean* something. Not when…"

He forced himself to stop. Clenching the last few words between his teeth with a vice-like grip.

"Not when what, Charlie?" Sam prompted, but Charlie couldn't look at her right now. Not yet. He was too afraid that whatever he saw could ruin everything between them. That he would lose the one person who meant more to him than anything else.

"Nothing. Forget I said anything. We're fine. Everything is fine between us, okay? And you're gonna tell me if that changes, right?"

"R-right." She wavered.

"Good, now let's move on. Are you hungry? I grabbed us something on the way back because it's—"

"Charlie?"

Charlie rubbed the back of his neck, any way to distract himself. "Hm?"

The heat of her body stepping closer to his sent tingles shooting down his body. Gentle taps of her feet against the hardwood floor reverberated around the quiet apartment as she slowly came toward him.

"What were you gonna say?" she asked, quieter than she'd been before.

"Sam," he hissed, his tone warning, but she ignored it as she took another step forward, the heat of her singeing him to the point now that he feared he'd combust.

"Tell me."

Finally then did he raise his eyes. That stunning green gaze of hers glittered in the light as it narrowed solely on him. Nothing else in the world mattered but the space between them.

He sighed. "You may not like it."

She shook her head. "I don't care. Say it anyway."

That pull, those hypnotic eyes of hers, they were his undoing. Searching, gazing up at him as if he had all the answers she needed to hear. As if he had all the answers *he* needed to hear.

"Sam, I can't bear hearing you think that everything that's happened between us hasn't meant anything to me."

"What do you mean?" she asked, the breathless quality to it only spurred him on.

"Baby, I'm holding on by a thread here..."

"And you think I'm not?" she whispered. Something shifted in her gaze, that flickering flame that had burned bright that night at the club. It burned with an overwhelming intensity, with a fusion of want and need.

Charlie took the remaining step to close the gap between them, their bodies barely a breath away from one another.

"I think I need to be clear, as it doesn't seem communication hasn't been a strong suit of ours," Charlie started, unable to mask the husky quality his voice took on. "I can't lose you. Even if it means holding back the feelings I've had for you for *years*. I'll shove it away and continue to the end of this thing we started, so you can write your book. We'll go to the gala because I *need* you there with me, and everything will be as it was. I will walk out of this room, take a walk. Our slate will be wiped clean, and we'll never speak of it again. But I need you to be honest with me right now about how you feel."

He held his breath.

"I think I'm in love with you."

CHAPTER 28

SAM

Sam could be brave. She could be bold. Or, at least, that's what she told herself when Charlie walked in the door. Now, seeing the almost shocked expression on his face, she wasn't so sure.

"You mean that," he said. A statement, not a question. Something about his tone, the softness and vulnerability reflected back at her through his eyes, stopped Sam from sputtering some lame excuse about her nerves. This was real. This was raw.

And she wanted nothing more than to drown in those gorgeous pools of blue.

She nodded slowly. "I mean that."

Sam remembered when she was a little girl, dreaming of her happily ever after. She'd talked about her wedding, the dress, the flowers, how cute the groom would be. How they would run off together over the horizon and into the sunset.

Her aunt and uncle had been the worst role models for that. There had been days, living under their roof, that she wasn't sure why they were ever married in the first place. Her aunt would roll her eyes at him in disgust. Call him names.

Tell him he was worthless. Her uncle would stick his tongue out at her when her back was turned, threw obscene gestures her way.

But she remembered how much love and affection her father had in his eyes any time he looked at her mother. That adoration and joy plastered to her mother's face when she looked back at him.

It had been the model she'd referred to her whole life, even long after they were gone.

Standing there now, Charlie looked at her exactly the same way—like she was the answer to all his prayers.

"You… You said that the other night," he whispered, his fingers touching her arm so gently that she barely felt it.

A resurgence of embarrassment flooded her. "I did?"

He nodded, a slow smile lazily pulling his dimples into place. "You did."

"I did," she repeated slowly, scouring her memory. Why the hell didn't she remember something like *that*? She remembered the club. The lights, the music pulsating around them like a heartbeat. The guy that had bumped into her. Charlie's eyes when he intercepted them at the bar. Then… nothing. Everything after that had been a blur.

Charlie chuckled, as if he could read her thoughts. "I take it you really don't remember that part?"

She was absolutely horrified that no, she really didn't remember that part. What did she *do*? How the hell had she had that much to drink that she couldn't remember telling him something like that?

"Want me to fill in the blanks?" he asked, his fingers now tracing lazily circles on her arm.

She nodded, his words words like honeyed silk that wisped around her in a warm embrace. Embarrassment still flared low in her belly, but it was now intertwined with desire.

God, she loved his smile. She watched it widen and wanted nothing more than to drink from those dimples of his until this insatiable thirst of hers was quenched.

"The other couples started dirty dancing, and you wanted to try it."

Her eyes bulged. "I did?"

"You did."

"Oh God. You can kill me now." She groaned, reaching up to cover her face with her hands, but Charlie stopped her.

"We started dancing, and you said that to me," he continued.

"What did… What did we do after I said that?" she asked. Her brain was having a hard time keeping up.

He quirked a thick eyebrow at her. "What do you think?"

It was her turn for her eyebrows to shoot up her forehead. "Oh my God! Oh my God, Charlie, did we have fucking *sex* in a nightclub? Oh my God, I can't believe I —"

While she was about to panic, Charlie, on the other hand, threw his head back and laughed. That hearty kind of laugh that always tickled a part of Sam's soul, that she couldn't quite put her finger on. Part of it held the little flame she'd always held for him there, fanning into a inferno now. But it was his. Whatever it was in Sam's soul, it was his. It would always be his.

He chuckled once more, low in his throat. "No, baby, we didn't. Heavy petting and making out? Yes, absolutely fucking yes. Sex? No. What kind of monster would I be taking advantage of you like that?"

There was that name again. *Baby*. It was alarming how just hearing him call her that, in that low, sultry tone of his, made her to want to shed every article of clothing she had on.

And his.

She blinked a few times. "Remind me… not that I'm not thrilled to not have thrown myself at you in a drunken stupor, but… why didn't—why didn't we… You know?"

"I did not want the first time I fucked you to be against the wall of some dirty club," he gritted out as Sam's back met the kitchen wall. It took her a moment to realize that they'd been moving, that Charlie had slowly been leading her to the nearest kitchen wall and now had her pinned there in front of him. She had nowhere to go, and from the fire dancing in Charlie's eyes, that's exactly where he wanted her.

It was also, conveniently, exactly where she wanted to be.

How had she never seen this side of him before? This feral, carnal creature that talked smooth as silk and touched her like it was in his job description. Where the hell had *this* Charlie been hiding?

"That's—That's good," she said before licking her parched lips. "I just… I didn't think you… You know. I didn't think you thought of me that way."

"You didn't?"

She shook her head. "No. I thought you offered to do this fake dating thing with me because you just didn't want me to get taken advantage of by some random stranger. I thought you were just trying to be protective."

He chuckled darkly.

"Do you really think I could stand the thought of someone else touching you like I have recently? I just… I just didn't want to ruin everything between us."

She shook her head, almost not believing what she was hearing. Charlie actually wanted her? All the touches, the looks, the kissing, it had been… real?

"I didn't want to ruin our friendship either," she offered.

"I was afraid you wouldn't want to be around me anymore if you knew how I felt and…"

His bright smile filled her vision. "Not possible. You are my favorite person, Sam."

"I didn't think any of it was real," she continued. "I thought you were just trying to do what you thought a romantic lead would do."

"How'd I do, then?" he asked, that cocky grin of his shining through once more. He was enjoying this.

How the hell was he able to do that? It was as if he could simply flip a switch, and she was absolute putty in his hands. The Charlie she knew, the goofy one that always knew just what to say to make her laugh, instantly replaced with this effortlessly smooth-talking one that made her thighs clench together before she instinctively opened them for him.

"Very convincing," she admitted after swallowing the moan at that being this close to him elicited. "I thought you just felt bad for me because I don't have a lot of —"

"Felt *bad* for you?" Charlie interrupted indignantly, reaching up to rest his forearm above her head. "Sam, keeping my hands *off* of you has been the fucking *bane* of my existence."

She diverted her gaze away from his just so he wouldn't see how affected she was. Her heart fluttered in her chest with how close he was, the heat of his body radiating through to her core. That and… other places a bit further south.

Her brain was short circuiting to the point that she began to fear this was all a dream. A beautiful, lovely dream that she would wake from at any moment.

"Did you mean what you said the other morning?"

He furrowed his brows at her, appearing confused. "The other morning?"

"After I asked you to sleep in the bed with me. The next

morning I thought you… I thought you wrote something on my back when I was asleep.”

Charlie’s eyes lit up. “You were awake for that?”

She nodded. “Did you mean what you wrote? Do you love me?”

She dug her nails into the palm of her hand in a desperate, final attempt to make sure she was grounded in reality. This was really happening. Charlie wanted her, and she wanted him. Emotions whirled like a cyclone within the depths of his piercing gaze, anchoring her in place. She would happily swim laps in his eyes if she could get away with it, and if she played her cards right, perhaps she could.

The smile on Charlie’s face somehow grew. “Sam, baby, I’ve been in love with you since the day I met you.”

The words she didn’t know she needed to hear, so beautifully laid out before her. It was real. All of this had been real.

What had started as a silly little fake dating experiment to help her get research for romance had turned into something real. She hadn’t been imagining when he’d touched her, kissed her, held her like she was everything he’d ever wanted.

“I feel like, if this was in my book,” Sam said nervously, the words leaving her lips before she could stop them, “which I am totally not going to add, just to be clear, this would be the start of a spicy scene?”

She clenched her eyes shut, feeling stupid for saying something like that right now. However, she was met with the sound of his hearty laughter instead.

“Tell me what *you* want, Sam,” he demanded a little breathlessly.

His forearm strained above her as he lifted his other hand to cup her hip, as if it was always meant to be there. Her skin practically sizzled under his touch, and she could no longer remember why she hadn't peeled his clothes off with her teeth before now—because she certainly wanted to now.

When she felt something hard poking her hip, demanding attention, her clit throbbed tortuously between her legs.

What planet was she on again?

"I think you know what I want. Is that a gun in your pocket, or are you just glad to see me?" she asked while simultaneously willing herself to shut the hell up, but her voice failed altogether when he leaned forward and pressed his lips against her neck. Goosebumps prickled to the surface beneath his lips, his mouth teasing her as he drew a long, delicious line from the bottom of her ear to the nape of her neck.

When he pulled back, she was trying desperately not to pant.

"Not just about that—I need to hear the words, Sam. I'm in this if you are."

She blinked at him. In what? What was he asking again? The effect of his lips on her neck like that made her forget what her name was temporarily. "In what? What are we in? If it's my vagina, then yes, please, I'm in. Or… You're in? I don't know which, but yes please."

He chuckled warmly again. God, she loved his laugh. "Focus, baby. Us. Together. In a relationship. A very, *very* sexual one."

How the hell she was still functioning, she had no clue.

"You're-you're serious?" she asked, and she could see the amusement splayed across his face. Laughing without sound at the complete and utter way he had her in shambles. If her brain could stop doing somersaults over the feeling of his body pressed up against hers like this, the lingering sensation of his lips on her neck, it might've functioned enough for her to realize he'd already covered all of this.

He'd told her he was in love with her.

He wanted to be with her.

So, why the hell was she malfunctioning right now?

"Yes, I am," he said slowly. "I want this. Do you?"

His face was so close to hers, so close that she could feel the heat of his nose as it almost pressed into hers.

She tried to force it away, but a sudden sense of panic quickly gripped her. She wanted this more than anything, but… she couldn't deny that it frightened her. Things would change between them. For the better, obviously, but there was the distinct possibility that things might not work out. Then what?

She couldn't live without Charlie by her side.

As she stood there, mulling things over, she realized she was standing there completely silent, staring up at him like a statue. But Charlie didn't push her. He didn't pester or guilt her into responding before she was ready. Instead, he stood there patiently. Watching her with this adoring softness as he waited for her to come to her own conclusion.

So, she said the one thing she *did* know. "I'm—I'm scared."

Charlie released her hip and brought it up to cup the side of her face, the warmth of his hand like a comforting embrace all on its own. "I know."

"Everything will change, and… and as much as I *want* things to change between us, it still scares me a little," she admitted.

"I'd be lying if I didn't say I wasn't, too, which is why it's taken me so long to say it."

She licked her lips nervously. "But… But what if you change your mind and decide that you don't actually want this? That you don't want me? I can't lose you."

Charlie swiped a thumb across her cheek, his gaze filled

with such warmth that it felt as if Sam stood directly in the sun's light. "I *want* this, Sam. I want *you*. You will never lose me, ever."

"You promise?" she asked, wanting more than anything to believe him.

He nodded. "I promise. You will *never* lose me."

"I want this, too," she whispered, melting a little at the gentleness in his touch.

"Then we give this a real shot. Deal?" He pulled his hand away and put it out for her to shake. She laughed but give it a firm squeeze, sealing the deal.

"Yes," she confirmed. "So, what do we do now?"

The predator circling its prey emerged once more as Charlie pressed her body more firmly against the wall. "Well, for starters, I'm going to do *exactly* what I've been wanting to do to you for years, and then we can worry about semantics later."

Consider her a rapt audience. What exactly had he wanted to do to her for years? She knew a few of the things she'd imagined him doing to her, and if it was anything close to that, she absolutely was on board. The possibilities made her quiver in his hands.

She gulped. "What exactly would that be?"

Charlie's lips came down to her ear, the tickle of his voice as he whispered in her ear the final nail in the coffin. "I'm going to make you come as many times as I can until you pass out on my cock."

CHAPTER 29

SAM

Sam forgot how to form words, so instead of trying, she raised herself up on her toes and pressed her lips urgently against his. Needing him to deliver on that promise as quickly as humanly possible.

Charlie yanked her into his arms, lifting her effortlessly from the ground and trapping her against his body. The warmth of him like fire pressed against hers like this, and she wanted to burn with it. Burn with *him*.

She wrapped her legs around his hips, needing to ease the ache there. The slippers Sam had on dangled from her feet, one slipping precariously low as she lost herself in his kiss. In the fire consuming her from head to toe.

Their lips were frantic at first, each kiss heated and demanding. The only sound in the air coming from their lips crashing together over and over again. Desperate sounds ripped from both of them in their need, the urgency that had been long denied apparent.

Charlie caught her bottom lip with his teeth, slowing them down for a moment. This time softer, gentler. Savoring each touch, each glide of their lips against one another, as if they had all the time in the world.

Electricity crackled up and down her body. They *did* have all the time in the world, and she was damned sure she'd spend all of it drowning in him.

Each kiss became exploratory, testing to see the exact way they could angle their lips to taste, to drink in the sensation of one another.

A clatter reverberated behind them as Sam's slipper finally slid off the end and fell uselessly to the floor. The sound seemed to startle Charlie as he stopped. He pulled his lips away, much to her annoyance, but the thickness in his voice when he spoke stirred something feral in her blood. "I want to, so fucking badly, but we can stop if you don't want to. We can stop here tonight if you need some time. I've waited this long for you; I can wait a bit longer."

As incredibly romantic as the notion was, such a Charlie thing to offer that her lips tugged into a kiss-swollen smile, that wasn't in her plans for the night. Unless Charlie indicated otherwise, she was sticking with her original plans for the foreseeable future.

All of which included Charlie's body.

She shook her head, trailing her hands up to capture his face. "I want you to make love to me, so unless you want or need to stop, please don't. Don't ever stop."

His fingers dug into her hips. "Hold onto me, baby. I'm taking you to bed."

He adjusted his grip and carried her into the bedroom, as if she weighed nothing. His time at the gym was paying out in spades, and she made a mental note to join him the next time he went.

Her feet barely touched the ground before she was grabbing his shirt, pulling at it to expose the toned muscles of his stomach. Desperation licked at her heels—she wanted to touch him, to feel him against her in the ways she'd only ever dreamed of late at night.

The flat expanse of his stomach flexed under her hands as she lingered. The steely muscles beneath her fingers were firm to the touch, with only a slight tremor indicating how much he was trying to hold on to his self-control. She had no interest in that. She wanted him feral, absolutely ravenous for her. Her fingers grazed his skin there, following the trail of hair as it led down further and disappeared into the waistband of his pants.

They undressed one another, coming together in gentle, teasing kisses between each garment that was removed. It was a slow and sensual dance that felt almost as intimate as the act they were about to do together.

When she finally removed Charlie's boxers, she took a moment to admire him. She'd always imagined what his dick would look like, not that she'd ever admit that aloud, but nothing beat the real thing. Long and hard with a slight upward curve, Sam's mouth watered. It had been quite a while since she'd last had sex with anyone, and his size made her briefly wonder about the logistics of fitting it inside of her, but the burning need in her demanded she try.

Charlie pushed her back onto the bed, the image of a dark god of pure masculinity as he stood there in the shadows of light from the bedroom lamp behind him. Every bit of him was highlighted starkly against the light, showing off every inch of his glorious form. Sam had known Charlie was handsome, but he was downright *divine* without clothes on.

Openly ogling him felt dirty in a way that was unexpected, but she liked it.

But she liked the way he was looking at her almost as much.

Charlie hovered there in front of her, his broad shoulders blocking out the light and casting a shadow over her. His chest rose and fell as if labored—as if he were having a hard time holding himself back, forcing himself into a statuesque state as he drank her in like he was sipping on a vintage wine.

She splayed against the sheets, unable to hide her nakedness from him. Not *wanting* to hide it from him. Normally, she would have clasped at the sheets to cover herself, found something to shield her body. Anything to hide the embarrassment at being so open and vulnerable in front of someone like this.

She did none of that in this moment.

In fact, she wanted him to see her, to touch her, to taste her. She wanted it all, and she wanted it now—nearly delirious with need and desire.

Sam had never felt like she was a particularly sexy or sultry person, but she felt like the sexiest woman on earth with the way Charlie watched her. His hungry eyes roved over her from head to toe, his nostrils flaring at her exposed breasts and the soft curls between her legs.

"Fuck, if you're not the most beautiful thing I've ever seen," he rasped before falling to his knees before her. He crawled to her, hovering in a way that caused the hair on his chest to tickle her nipples, pebbled and begging for his touch.

First, she wanted to touch him. She'd spent far too many years imaging what his body would feel like, and she wanted to touch him before she lost all sense of reason.

Before he had time to process what she was doing Sam's hands trailed and took his cock in her hand, giving it a gentle squeeze. She luxuriated in the way it felt, the shaft pulsing with need.

Charlie squeezed his eyes shut, his mouth agape with a silent *Oh*. She'd replay that image in her mind for years to come, the sheer lust and desire etched into his features at her doing. He was making these expressions, these delicious sounds, because of her. She was drunk on that knowledge as she stroked his length, watching carefully from beneath him.

The velvety hardness of his erection felt magnificent in her grasp. The length of it was impressive enough, seeing it stand so erect and at attention, but the feeling of her hand barely encapsulating around it made her only that much wetter. Sam knew that she would formulate many, *many* plans with what she wanted to do with Charlie's cock in the time to come.

He allowed her a few slow, languid pumps of his heated flesh. Testing, teasing. His body shuddering under her fingers was the most incredibly arousing sensation she'd ever known. Sam squirmed underneath him as she fought her own arousal just so she could continue watching.

A low groan rumbled through him when she picked up speed and tightened her grasp. The sound made her feel like a queen, but when he let out a low *"Fuck"* next to her ear, she felt like a goddess.

Teasing him, she angled his cock to rub the tip of him against her slick core, but he immediately grabbed her hand and wrenched it away, appearing almost pained with desire as he did.

"Baby, I'm not gonna last very long if you keep doing that," he rasped, the little breathless hitch at the end of his statement more arousing than Sam expected. His bare skin against hers was wholly divine when he finally pressed her down into the mattress, and she wanted more.

But the sensation didn't last long when he immediately pulled away and started to lower himself down her body. His lips pressed gentle kisses along her heated skin as he slid lower and lower.

How she had not already exploded at how incredible it felt for him to touch her like this, she'd never know.

A soft gasp left her unexpectedly when Charlie's tongue trailed from her navel down toward her soaking pussy. Fire danced along her skin with each movement of his teasing tongue along her all-too-sensitive body.

He easily spread her legs and settled between her thighs—opening her like a feast for him to devour. She bit her lower lip to fight the protest she was about to make. No one had ever gone down on her before, but the hunger and voraciousness in his eyes had her losing the will to argue.

Words couldn't explain the feeling of his tongue burying itself in her pussy other than *bliss*. He swirled his tongue around her sensitive clit, lapping at it with enough pressure for her to already start panting in need, her toes curling. A twinge of jealousy coursed through her at whoever taught him how to do *that*.

At the same time, she wanted to thank whoever it was.

When he suckled and growled against her, she decided she might send whoever it was a basket of roses, as well, just to be safe.

A moan escaped her lips when she gazed down at him between her thighs. He looked like a man starved, his sandy-brown hair tousled wildly and his blue eyes sparkling as they met hers, watching her every reaction as if he derived pleasure from just watching *her*.

He greedily yanked her back to him when the movement accidentally pulled her away. The sound of his hungry growl vibrated through him and up her nerve endings. She was dangerously on the edge, and she knew she wouldn't last if he continued.

Part of her *wanted* him to continue, to ride his tongue until she was at heaven's gates—but that's not how she wanted her first orgasm with Charlie to be. She wanted the first time Charlie made her come to be when he was fucking her into the bed. With his glorious cock plunging into her like a deranged beast so blind with pleasure that neither of them could stand it.

"Charlie… Please, I want you in me now… Please, put it in…" she begged. It didn't even sound like her, despite knowing that it was. The words sounded desperate, the edges slurred from her own desire.

He moved without question, leaving her soaking pussy open to the cool air. A whimper of protest escaped her from his withdrawal, needing to feel his skin against hers once again. She felt so sensitive from his gentle, yet somehow bruising, touch that she wanted more. Needed more.

Charlie fished a condom out of the nightstand, his movements nearly as frenzied as her thundering heartbeat. He tore the foil packet open with his teeth, something about the action feeling erotic. Another moan ripped from her throat at the sight, surprising her that he wasn't even touching her, and her body was literally crying out for him.

He flashed her a mischievous yet knowing smile as he rolled the condom down his length. His fingers trembled just enough for her to notice as he sheathed himself. The weight of him settled back on top of her, pressing her firmly into the mattress. It was a sensation that felt both comforting and reassuring one moment, then fiery and lustful the next.

Charlie pressed his forehead against hers as he grabbed his cock and positioned himself.

"Last chance?" he whispered fervently, the last semblance of his self-control apparently on a thread.

Sam's throat felt tight as her entire body focused solely on the feeling of his thick cock pressed at her entrance. She couldn't haven't spoken if she wanted to, all she wanted was his sweet heat inside of her. Her body was already lingering on the edge of bliss from his previous ministrations, so she simply nodded.

Those beautiful eyes of his were on her, watching her, gauging her reactions as he began sliding into her. Inch by painstaking inch, he stretched her nearly to capacity. Her body welcomed his length eagerly, despite his size and girth. There was a dull ache as he pushed in, but it was well worth it. It felt so right, so incredible, that Sam was simply gasping for air.

He paused whenever she tensed, her body accommodating him as if it always knew it belonged to him, but he didn't stop. Every inch that sank into her pussy was nearly her undoing just to watch the pleasure erupt across Charlie's face as he pushed tortuously slowly into her. His eyes hooded over in pleasure.

A groan escaped him when he finally buried himself to the hilt, rolling his head back as if it were too much even for him to experience such pleasure.

His Adam's apple bobbed up and down, and Sam couldn't resist the urge to touch him. She leaned up and ran her tongue along the length of it—wanting to taste his pleasure, to taste the sounds he was already holding back. To her delight, Charlie let out a helpless cry and bucked his hips against her.

He seemed to have liked that.

He began moving above her, with her, but she felt the dull ache inside her sting as she clenched around him. He was large, and it had been a while, so she let out a gasp.

"Fuck—Charlie," she whimpered.

Upon hearing her, he stopped. "Are you okay?"

His gaze was intense beneath half-closed eyelids. He remained unnervingly still, with tender caution, as if he was afraid that he had hurt her. His arms trembled with the effort, and it only sent a little thrill of pleasure down to her core.

She nodded. "I'm okay. Don't stop."

She lifted her hands to cup his face, framing it with a loving touch as she kissed him. Oh, the hours, days, weeks, she'd spend kissing this man. She would make it her life's mission to do so. That and finding out more ways to elicit the sounds he was making, swallowing his moans of pleasure like the sweetest drink she'd ever tasted.

Charlie wasted no time before he began moving, the slow drag of his cock pulling from her body before pushing back in —their pace luxuriously slow and deliberate as their bodies acclimated to one another in a deliciously wicked dance that Sam couldn't imagine ever doing with anybody else.

Her body was his—it always had been.

"More," she begged as she started clawing at him. "Please, Charlie…"

Charlie lifted her hips with his hands, changing the angle and increasing his pace as he began thrusting harder, deeper, forcing a moan to barrel out of her.

Was this what sex was supposed to feel like? If so, she had been missing out on a *lot*. She held onto him, her hips greeting his in loud slaps of flesh against flesh, the sound dirty and passionate as they soon became frantic for one another, feverishly thrusting together.

It felt as if they were making up for the many years that they could have spent doing *this* together.

Lights flickered behind her eyelids when he adjusted her in his grip once more, his cock slamming straight into a particular spot that had her eyes rolling into the back of her skull. It shocked the hell out of her, the pleasure blinding as the tip of his cock repeatedly pounded against this magical spot that she didn't even know existed until then.

Holy shit. What the hell was he doing to her?

Her body was no longer her own, responding only to him. Spasming around him as if it were wild and wanton with the promises his body was making hers. Incoherent words spilled from her lips, though she wasn't sure exactly what they were.

Charlie's grin appeared through the haze of pleasure quickly taking over her senses, as if her delirium had been his goal the entire time.

"Charlie," she cried out, arching into him as she began hurtling toward release, so close now that she could practically taste it.

She began clenching around him, gasping with each movement barreling her forward. Charlie angled her hips to help him focus on the spot he'd found inside of her, continuing to hit it until stars began to shine beneath her eyelids. She let out more helpless cries, unable to contain her voice as she moaned and cried out feverishly.

"You feel so…" His voice was quiet for a second before he exploded in a rough growl, *"Fuck."*

That did her in. Her reaction was swift and violent as she came apart—crying out in ecstasy as wave after wave of pleasure slammed into her with such an intensity that she had never experienced before.

Her entire body convulsed around him and sizzled through each nerve ending. Choked, helpless cries rang out of her. Her voice felt rough as she realized she had started chanting Charlie's name, unsure how such a sound could be wrenched from her lungs without her knowledge.

He whispered praises into her ear as she rode out her orgasm—telling her what a good girl she was coming for him like that, telling her good her pussy felt wrapped around his cock, how close he was to his own release. Like hushed, silent prayers honoring her very being. His voice had never sounded so sweet—or so darkly sexy—before, but his words somehow extended the electricity pinging around her nerves, her orgasm lasting far longer than she'd experienced before.

Of course she'd gotten herself off plenty over the years, but all of that paled in comparison. And it didn't stop there, as only a few more quick thrusts and Charlie followed, his body quivering around her with the force of his own release.

The sound Charlie made as he came was, by far, the most incredibly sexy thing she'd ever experienced in her life.

Her own orgasm still thrummed in her veins, her body threatening to send her barreling down the gauntlet once more. His cock pulsed wildly inside of her as his hips lazily thrust into her once, twice more, before he slowed. His head dropped to her shoulder, his breath so close to her ear that it caused her to shudder.

His eyes were on her as they recovered, both of their bodies still humming with pleasure.

"Am I…" Sam started as her heart slowed enough for her to speak. "Am I dead?"

Charlie chuckled breathlessly. "I don't think so, but they do call it the little death for a reason, I guess. But… I'm sorry…"

She stared up at him with confusion. She was still returning to planet earth after such an out-of-this-world orgasm that she had no clue what he meant. Much less what the hell he could possibly be sorry about.

Giving her the best orgasm of her life?

Turning her into putty?

"What could you possibly—" she started, swallowing. "What could you possibly be sorry about right now?" He moistened his lips with his tongue, a tongue that had only moments ago been buried in her pussy, sending a flicker of the memory straight down Sam's body.

"I didn't—I mean, I didn't last very long," he panted.

Unable to contain her surprise, Sam burst into laughter, the sound nearly catching in her throat as she struggled to breathe momentarily. She turned her head to the side, a hand pressed to her mouth to stifle it the best that she could. "What, were you *timing* yourself? Or better, you thought I'd have the wherewithal to even *think* to?"

"Don't laugh!" he protested, though he couldn't suppress his own laughter. "I was trying to last long enough to make you come again, but I couldn't do it."

This man was too cute for his own good, she was sure of it.

"Don't worry, your secret is safe with me," she panted. "Besides, I was a little busy having the best orgasm I've ever had, so I was a bit distracted."

"Is that a fact?" he hummed, his voice dangerously thick with renewed interest and seeming a little too pleased with himself for her liking.

"Shut up. You know it was."

His pupils were dilated when they locked eyes again, appearing almost completely black with how blown out with desire they were, and she felt another wave of lust course through.

How the hell could she possibly want him again so soon afterwards? She was completely spent, but seeing the way Charlie was gazing at her again made her want to do it all over.

She really needed to pace herself, or she wouldn't last the night.

"You will be the death of me, Charlie Backman," she teased, giving him a quick kiss. "Give little Charlie a break first before you kill him."

Wickedness flickered in those dark pools of his. "Little?"

She giggled. "You know what I mean. You can't possibly have the energy for another round already."

"You wound me. You think that's all I have in me? I could do this all night long—*will* do this all night long."

She grinned. "Is that so?"

"It is. I've wanted this for a long, *long* time—to be inside of you, feeling your pussy quivering around my cock," he purred into her ear, kicking her pulse into high gear.

She was about to protest as he pulled away from her, but before she could react, he grabbed her and rolled her onto her stomach. With a firm grip, he yanked her hips upward, positioning her on her knees in front of him, ass in the air.

She gasped in surprise, quickly turning into a moan when he ground his pelvis against her ass, feeling the unmistakable length of his cock already pressing urgently against her.

"Where do you think you're going?" he growled, toying with her entrance with a lazy finger. The feeling forced her face into the mattress as her pussy quivered under his ministrations, ready for them to start anew.

He circled her clit with his thumb, earning a groan. She pushed urgently into his hand as he teased her. Lust and desire had long overridden her, and she was needy for his touch, for his cock, for his lips on her skin once more.

He leaned away just long enough to reach into the nearby drawer to fish out another condom, holding her down with one hand like he was afraid she'd run if he didn't.

As if.

She'd squirm under Charlie Backman's touch for as long as he let her.

Despite her position, she couldn't resist glancing over her shoulder to watch him. A light sheen of sweat coated his chest from their previous round, and she had a mind to turn and lick it off him. If only she could, but with her ass in the air for him, she decided to mark that in her to-do list for next time.

A list that grew with every passing second.

He took another foil packet and ripped it open with his teeth. The heat in his eyes, the barely contained hunger, burned there as he rolled it on. She took the moment to appreciate the length of him again. Her teeth dug into her lips, knowing that something *that big* had fit into her and was about to be in her again.

She had a lot of ideas about what she wanted to do with that cock in the future.

Charlie returned to rubbing her entrance, replacing his finger with the tip of his cock. Her answering purrs of pleasured seemed to egg him on, continuing his torturous path against her.

"Tell me what you want, Sam," he growled, the barely contained self-control once again teetering on the edge.

She didn't want his self control, though; she wanted him to snap and plunge mindlessly into her like there was no tomorrow.

She let out a breathy laugh, amazed that she could form words at this point. "You really need to ask me at a time like this?"

Another gasp escaped her when he leaned over to run a string of kisses down her spine, leaving a trail of goosebumps in his wake. "Communication is going to be important for us going forward, so I need to hear the words. I need to hear how much you want this. How much you want *me*."

"Please, Charlie," she whined, barely above a whisper.

"Please, what?"

She dug her nails into the sheets beneath her. "Please fuck me again."

"Good girl," he ground out, entering her in a fierce thrust

that had her seeing stars again. She thought he would take her hard then, fucking her down into the mattress, but he didn't. Each slow thrust was calculated and laced with desire. His. Hers. Theirs together.

When she whimpered, desperately wanting to feel more of him, he chuckled low in his throat. "Baby, I'm going to fuck you stupid tonight, so just hold on for the ride."

CHAPTER 30

CHARLIE

The early morning light coming up over the horizon caused Charlie to squint as he walked across the street, headed back to his apartment. He had a coffee in one hand and another coffee with a bag clutched precariously in the other. The crispness in the air felt starkly satisfying against Charlie's skin, cooling him from the heat that had been practically radiating from him when he snuck out earlier.

He'd had to pinch himself when he woke earlier that morning—fearing he'd dreamed up the whole thing.

It had been real.

Sam was in love with him. He was in love with her. They were in love.

And he'd spent the entire night trying to show her exactly how much—making love until they literally collapsed into sleep, both of their bodies giving out.

She was back at his place, still asleep in his bed. The picture she'd made when he opened his eyes was enough to pull a contented sigh from him as he hustled down the street.

It had been hard to tear himself away, but he wanted to

get them some breakfast before she awoke. A few of the hickey's he'd left in his wake the night before had started to appear on her skin, and he felt a bit guilty.

But who could blame him? She was everything he'd ever dreamed of.

Long strands of her strawberry-colored hair had spilled across the pillow like a fiery river, each wavy strand catching the soft light peeking through the curtains in lazy, looping patterns. The light freckles that dusted her nose and shoulders like little golden flecks of sunlight had crinkled as she adjusted herself on the pillow next to his. Her eyelashes, impossibly long and delicate, fanned across her cheeks and fluttered ever-so-slightly as she dreamed peacefully. Even the little grumbled protest she made when he had pulled away to get up was adorable.

He couldn't believe that she was *his*.

It was the all-consuming thought he had when he quietly crept back into the apartment, clicking the door shut as quietly as he could. She was *his*. And if he had his say in the matter, she was always going to be his.

He wanted to leave the coffee and bagel on the nightstand, so she could continue sleeping peacefully, but when he opened the door, she was already awake. At least, mostly awake. She blinked groggily at him and pulled herself to sit up in the bed like she'd already heard him come in.

The bedsheet was clutched in one hand as she held it against herself, the shape of her body outlined deliciously in the thin fabric.

Down, boy.

She smiled lazily at him. "Good morning."

"Hope I didn't wake you?" he asked.

She shook her head and adjusted herself, stretching her arms languidly above her head. The sheets she had clutched to her body pooled at her waist at the effort. Without a shred of clothing on from the night before, her breasts were on full display. The soft, creamy curves of them stretching along with her in a way that immediately had Charlie's cock at attention.

He extended the coffee and bag, with the bagel inside of it, to her. Her eyes lit up before moving to eagerly snatch them from him. Mid-motion, she paused, as she seemed to realize her chest was exposed and clutched at the sheet. Reaching out and taking the items from him with her free hand instead.

"It's not like I haven't seen them at this point, baby," he teased, leaning forward to press a kiss to her forehead.

She hummed a giggle. "I like when you call me that."

"What?"

"Baby."

He smiled. "I like calling you that."

Sam tucked the sheets into her armpits before taking a healthy sip from her cup. "In the meantime, at least let a lady have some modesty."

It took everything in him not to scoop her into his arms and kiss her senseless, so instead, he laughed. "Do forgive me, fair lady."

"How long have you been up?" she asked, fishing out the bagel from within the crumpled bag.

"About an hour. Figured you'd be hungry when you woke up."

"You figured correctly, but that was thoughtful of you," she said before quickly hissing out a sound of protest as she adjusted herself, her eyes clenching shut at the movement.

"You okay? Sore?" he asked, sitting on the bed next to her.

She nodded sheepishly. "Yeah, just a bit."

Images of exactly what caused her to be so sore flashed in his mind. The flash of pride was swift, but he pushed that aside for the regret at being so… rough… with her the night before. "Sorry, I guess I got a little carried away."

"I'm not complaining," she replied with a wink. "If this is the death of me, then I lived a good life."

He chuckled. "I hope I'm not that lethal?"

She shrugged casually, but the expression on her face was wicked. "I don't know. That was only night one. I need more data before I can come to any conclusions."

Oh yeah, he could definitely get used to this.

"Research I'll be more than happy to facilitate," he said, attempting to hide the arousal creeping into his voice but failing miserably with lust lacing the tip of his tongue.

She bit into her bagel. "Easy, tiger. let me finish my bagel at least."

A chuckle rumbled through him again. "Don't worry; I won't ravish you straight off the bat after you just woke up. I'm not an animal."

"Last night's events would tend to disagree."

As would the nearly empty box of condoms that sat on the nightstand.

He scrunched his nose. "Sorry, again. Besides the soreness, you feeling okay?"

"I am, actually," she hummed, a softness in her gaze that had his heart skipping a beat.

"Not freaking out about… you know… us?" he asked. It had been a lingering thought that snuck in. What if she woke up and changed her mind? What if she freaked out and decided to hell with the whole thing?

His worries disappeared when she placed the bagel onto the crumpled bag and cupped his face with her hand. "No. I've been thoroughly ravished, so I think I'm good."

Unexpected relief whooshed out of him as he stole a quick kiss, relishing in the soft heat of her lips, and pressed his forehead to hers. "Sounds like I'm going to have to keep you thoroughly ravished, then, to keep you from over-thinking, huh?"

"Most definitely," She practically purred, "Right now, though, there's something I want more than that."

Anything. Charlie knew without a shadow of a doubt that he'd happily give her whatever she wanted. Served up on a silver platter for her if she desired.

"What's that?" he asked.

She took her free hand and patted the spot next to her in bed. "Get your coffee and come cuddle with me. Don't you have any fucking manners? You can't leave a girl in bed by herself after a night like *that*. Cuddles are required."

He threw his head back, the laughter bubbling out of him and filling the room with his girth and warmth.

God, he really did love this woman.

He rose from the bed and circled over to his side, unable to look away from her as he did. It felt like a cardinal sin to look away with *that* look in her eyes. The one that twinkled up at him, as if she were watching him just as closely. The one that certainly didn't hide her own arousal as it steadily rose to color her cheeks.

He pulled back the sheets and eased himself beneath so as not to jostle her sore body too much. The last thing he wanted was to disturb the little cocoon of peace she'd created in his bed.

With a tender touch, he drew her into his embrace. The contrast between her deliciously naked skin and the fabric of his clothing felt torturous, and he wished he'd stripped himself bare just to feel her against him again. The notion seemed impossible, though, as she practically melted against him, the comforting warmth radiating from her body shedding any desire to leave her even for a second.

Her head rested lightly on his chest, rising and falling with each steady breath he took. She settled there, letting out a contented little sigh as she did.

He let his fingers delicately trace the curve of her spine, the need to touch her far too great to keep his hands to himself. They trailed up and down her back in a quiet rhythm that felt as natural as breathing. The simplicity and ease of lying there together like this was pure magic.

Yeah, he could *definitely* get used to this.

"When do you think we should tell people?" she asked after a few quiet moments.

Charlie would run out of the room and shout it from the rooftops if he could, but he didn't think that would be appropriate so soon.

"Whenever you want to, I guess?" he replied warmly. "Though, maybe we give it some time for it to be just the two of us?"

She nodded against his chest. "Good plan. I'd like to keep you to myself as much possible right now. I have a lot of time to make up for."

He turned the groan that vibrated in his chest into a chuckle. "I think you'll actually be the death of me, Samantha MacMillian."

"Put a pin in that for now, big boy," she teased as she leaned away from him to sip from her coffee. "I didn't even know you *had* that side to you until recently. I gotta let my little heart catch up."

"What side is that?" he asked, letting his finger continue its path up and down her spine. He felt the little shiver that followed and smiled. He was going to really enjoy undoing her at every turn, leaving her in shambles as he had his way with her.

She was the writer of the two of them, but he could easily write sonnets about what hearing her gasping his name, just as she hurtled over the edge into bliss, had done to him.

Sam nudged him affectionately. "You know exactly what side I'm talking about. One minute, you're my normal, goofy Charlie. The next, you're some smooth-talking flirt who talks like he knows *exactly* what you want in bed."

His lips found her shoulder, and he nipped her there, adding to another mark he'd left there the night before. "But I *did* know exactly what you wanted in bed."

"And I have no idea how," she said a little breathlessly. "It's a very stark, yet very sexy, contrast between the two versions of you that I know."

"Should I tone it down?"

She shook her head vehemently. "Don't you dare. As long as I'm the only one who gets to see that side of you."

Charlie's heart shot up his throat. "Baby, it'll only ever be you."

CHAPTER 31

SAM

Charlie had lived up to the promises he'd made.

In fact, if Sam thought about it, he undersold himself.

Dramatically undersold himself.

Reading about it in books was nothing in comparison to being at the mercy of Charlie's greedy hands. He'd made her come so many times that she had literally passed out on him, only for him to wake her up and start all over again until they were both delirious.

She hadn't lied when she said she had lived a good life if it meant dealing with the aftermath of sex *that* amazing. The initial ache of soreness had already died down considerably from when she had first woken up, now barely noticeable as she laid there in Charlie's arms.

She wondered what it would be like to wake up next to him like this every day. To see his sleeping face next to hers in the early morning sunlight. To hear his steady breathing as he slept peacefully with her tucked into his arms.

Charlie brushed his lips to her forehead. "So, do you still

need to work on stuff for your book? Because I have *quite* a few ideas that might come in handy."

She laughed. "I think we're done, Charlie, and I think *this* will help inspire the scene I need to send to Angel. Though, I know I'll never hear the end of it from her."

"How's that?"

"Well, we started out fake dating, so I could do research for a romance book, and we ended up falling into bed together. I feel a bit cliche."

He laughed, more boisterously this time. "I guess it is a bit cliche, but you won't see me complaining."

"Me neither, though I'm not one hundred percent sure what that means for us? I mean, I know we obviously touched on that last night, but my mind was a bit… scrambled."

"What do you mean?"

"Well, I mean, I don't mean to sound dense, but I don't know what to call myself in reference to you, or what we're doing now, and vice versa."

Charlie furrowed his brows. "We're dating now…? Should I make signs?"

She rolled her eyes and shoved him gently. "You know what I mean! We've been friends for how many years now? I don't know what labels to use. Are you my lover? My partner? Boyfriend? Orgasm giver?"

"Boyfriend," Charlie said softly. "Definitely boyfriend."

She relaxed into him. "I like the sound of that. Sorry, you know how I am."

"I do, which is why I think you need to be… oh, what was it you said you needed in order to *not* overthink things? Something about being thoroughly ravished?" he asked, his voice dipping an octave.

A shiver of delight raced up her spine, the heat in his eyes threatening to burn her alive, but in the best way possible.

"I still need to take a shower," she protested, his lips already tracing the shell of her ear.

"Then let's take one," he replied, shifting to rise from the bed and pulling her along with him. As they moved, the sheets slipped away from her body and pooled to the ground, leaving her completely naked for him again. His appreciative gaze roved over her.

Charlie rubbed his thumb across her jawline. "We don't actually have to… you know… if you're still sore, though."

She smiled. "I think I can manage. You think you can?"

His chuckle was dark as he hauled her against him. "Abso-fucking-lutely."

Their lips clashed as Sam's hands greedily finessed with his clothes, tearing them away impatiently. They only parted long enough to tear his clothing away, a hazy inferno in both of their gazes.

When nothing stood between them, they playfully began pushing and pulling one another toward the bathroom. Their bodies became a tangle of limbs and kisses. It was incredible that they were still so desperate for one another after how many times they'd had sex the night before, but Sam wasn't complaining. She needed him in mythically proportionate ways.

Charlie scooped her up and placed her on the bathroom counter without pulling from her, both driven by the feral need that felt like a drop in the ocean. Too many years had gone by, and they both had no patience for waiting anymore.

He left her long enough to clumsily find the shower faucet to turn the knob, letting the water spray as he returned to her. The steam drifting from behind the curtain floated around them like a blissful cloud.

He surprised her when he turned back, dropping to his knees and yanking her hips forward to bring her to the edge of the counter. Wordlessly, he latched his mouth to her already soaking core, their short time together like this already providing him with a road map of exactly where to go and what to do.

A helpless cry tore out of her when he found her clit, lapping at it in calculated strokes while his finger came up to delve into her pussy. Her spine arched against the counter. The contrast of the cold, hard granite against her soft skin made a shiver roll through her.

"I know, baby, I know," he purred against her sensitive flesh.

She squirmed under his skillful tongue, digging her fingers into the edge of the counter when he added another finger. She fought to find some purchase to make sure she didn't float off into space.

He moaned against her. "You taste incredible."

His eyes watched her carefully when she peered down. The image of her arousal soaking his face, his tongue drawing dangerous circles around her clit, was beyond erotic. If it had been a few days ago, the image would've forced a blush to her cheeks. But today? Today, she wanted more. She loved the way she could see the fire dancing along the surface of his ocean-blue eyes as he pleasured her with his mouth and fingers.

"What do I taste like?" she asked breathlessly. It sent a thrill through her core when the question ripped another moan from him, the feeling of it vibrating straight up her nerve endings.

He appeared to like that question a lot, his pupils dilating further to the point that the fire dancing there had disappeared into the void of his lust. His tongue became more insistent against her, flicking the sensitive bud in such a way that had her mouth open on a silent cry.

"Mine," he growled.

His finger curled inside of her, rubbing that magical place that his cock had discovered repeatedly, and she whimpered.

"Condom?" she begged, her voice keening as if she were begging for salvation. Maybe she was.

Charlie didn't protest, as if he knew she couldn't stand it longer, or *he* couldn't stand it any longer, and ran to grab one from the bedroom. He started rolling it onto his length when she leaned forward and held out a hand to stop him. "Can I?"

When he nodded slowly, she took the condom and tore the packet open with her teeth, as he had done the many times they'd made love the night before. The wild expression in his eyes felt dangerous, like she was teetering on the edge of being devoured, and she liked that. She liked seeing Charlie unhinged for her.

With her other hand, she took his length and gave it a few, tortuously slow pumps. The way his eyelids fluttered and clenched shut in pleasure, the little quiet whimper that was so low that it would've been easy to miss if she hadn't been paying such close attention, was so arousing that she had to clench her thighs together to ease the pressure between them.

Even more slowly, she rolled the condom onto him. He hissed out a breath, his hips bucking toward her like he couldn't stand not being inside of her any longer.

Without warning, Charlie spun her around, forcing her to lean over onto the bathroom counter. Her elbows banged against the cool surface roughly, but she didn't care. She'd worry about that later. All she wanted was the feeling of his cock inside of her again, slamming against that one magical spot until she cried out his name.

The head of his cock rubbed at her entrance, coursing its path through her soaking pussy up and down, up and down, until she was panting. Charlie shoved one of her legs further apart, forcing her to further open for him.

"Fuck, baby," he groaned. "Hold onto the counter. We're not making it into the shower."

The sweet torture ended with a swift thrust inside of her, tearing a helpless cry from the back of her throat.

Her eyes locked onto her reflection in the mirror in front of her. The woman she saw was disheveled, her eyes hooded and filled to the brim with lust. Her knuckles were white where they gripped the counter in a desperate attempt to keep her body from floating away. Her lips were kiss-swollen, deliciously full and open on a cry that wouldn't come. Sam's hair cascaded around her in loose tendrils that practically begged to be fisted in Charlie's hand and pulled on. Her breasts were full and heavy, peppered with the tell-tale marks Charlie had left over the course of the night, jostling along with the thrusts ramming her into the counter.

This woman felt like a stranger to Sam, completely foreign. Sam had never considered herself an overtly sexual human being. But this woman in the mirror was a wanton, sensual creature that lingered in the shadows. This woman took what she wanted and demanded everything of her lover. She knew what she wanted and went for it without hesitation.

And the man behind her was rabid, his cock repeatedly buried to the hilt as though he were on the edge of insanity. Charlie's hair was disheveled, ruffled to the point that it appeared wild. The scruff of his beard glistened from her desire soaking his face.

Her pussy clenched around him, both of them moaning at the action.

Charlie's hands trembled as they squeezed her hips, like the sheer will not to pound into her mercilessly was a massive undertaking that took all of his concentration. It was touching, knowing he was trying to be gentle with her, but she wasn't interested in any of that.

Their eyes found one another in the mirror, a new kind of intimacy discovered as they watched one another. Charlie changed the pace, giving her a few slow, tentative strokes inside of her. Watching her expression with intent until he hit the one angle that caused her to call out his name.

Target acquired.

Sam's eyes slammed shut on instinct, the pleasure so much that she wasn't sure if she'd died and gone to heaven.

Charlie released a hand, fisting a handful of hair in his grip. It felt intensely possessive, like a lightning bolt straight to Sam's clit, but Charlie managed to infuse it with a surprising tenderness. Devoid of pain yet still commanding her attention. With a firm tug, he drew her head back, forcing her to meet his gaze in the mirror.

"I want you to watch while I fuck you. I want to watch you come undone," he growled as his hips began slamming against hers, thrusting mercilessly into her. It was too good, too hard, too deliciously perfect that she was already peaking.

"I'm so close…" she whispered into the air.

Another tug at her scalp. "Don't close your eyes, baby. I need you to see how incredibly beautiful you look when you come on my cock."

It was her undoing, her pussy spasming around him as the orgasm rocked through her.

Their bodies were in unanimous harmony together as she took her orgasm from him, letting the wave upon wave of endless pleasure cascade through her. Her cries of pleasure intermingled with the slapping of flesh against flesh, only adding to the sensation bursting in her core like a firecracker.

She fought the urge to slam her eyes shut as pleasure

threatened to blind her—instead doing as he commanded and watching as she came apart.

"That's my girl," Charlie praised, following her into bliss as he let out a hoarse cry. He never let go of his hold on her hair, forcing her to watch as he rode out his own orgasm, and it was almost enough to send her over the edge again.

When he eventually slumped forward, he released his hold on her hair and braced his arms on either side of her. His body caged her as the two of them fought to catch their breath.

It had been so intense that she was too filled with emotion to speak, instead blinking slowly at him with a lazy smile. How could she possibly put into words what she'd just felt? What they'd just shared together?

Charlie kissed her spine lazily, his lips lingering there before finally pulling himself free to get rid of the condom. She mumbled a protest at the loss but without much energy left to do anything about it.

A haze had formed in the mirror, fogging up from both their efforts and the shower still running in the background. It was likely at the perfect temperature now, and she looked forward to it. Wiping off all the sweat and… other liquids that were currently running down her thighs.

The image excited her, letting some of her darker fantasies come out into the light. That maybe, one day, Charlie would fuck her completely bare. No barrier between them so she felt nothing but his hot length inside of her. That he would fill her to the brim until she was dripping with his…

Despite the powerful orgasm she'd just had, the thought had her clit fluttering.

She blinked a few times. It felt very naughty, very dirty, but it surprised her how much that prospect excited her. She wasn't sure if her lack of sex over the years meant that her brain was now kicked into high gear—like it was now hyper-aware of every sexual fantasy she ever had.

She didn't have long to worry about it, though, because Charlie returned and pulled her into his embrace. This man was both incredibly good and incredibly dangerous for her heart.

"I could get used to this." She sighed contently.

Charlie chuckled before pressing a kiss to her temple. "I could too. Now, let's *actually* take a shower, so we can get back into bed."

SAM

If there was a version of paradise, Sam decided that this was it. Currently snuggled up with Charlie on the couch, she couldn't think of anything better.

Well, scratch that. She *could* think of something better, but she didn't have the energy for it at the moment, being thoroughly sated and still a bit weak in the knees from earlier that day. Even now, however, Charlie casually holding her against him in the white T-shirt and gray sweatpants he'd thrown on was a dangerous combination.

She was more than pleased that despite the lingering worries looming—wondering if things were going to work out, whether this change would last—she found they became increasingly fleeting. Drowned out by Charlie's constant shows of affection, which continued to make her heart flutter. She wasn't sure how long that would last, whether it would eventually die out with time, or if he would always make it flutter like this.

Glancing from the screen up to Charlie's face, a touch of warmth heated her cheeks, and she smiled. He seemed so relaxed, so *happy,* that she couldn't help but snuggle in closer.

She wanted to check in with him to see how he was doing, knowing how close the charity gala was, but she didn't want to push. They'd talk about it when he was ready.

All she wanted was to luxuriate in this little bubble she and Charlie had managed to create.

The charity itself was less than a few days away, and she still needed to get something to wear for it. She wasn't in any particular rush, too content to leave the warmth of Charlie's embrace to even worry about it now.

Though it was the knock coming from the front door that finally burst their bubble.

"Did you order something?" Sam asked curiously. The words barely left her mouth, however, as Charlie disentangled himself from her to stand.

"Yeah, sit here, and I'll grab it," he replied, giving a quick stretch.

She pouted, already missing the blissful pocket of heat that had settled between them.

She hadn't been paying much attention to the movie they'd put on, so she turned back to see where they were. That is, until a familiar-sounding voice caught her attention.

She spun, practically leaping out of her spot when she spotted Angel, standing there next to Charlie.

"Surprise, bitch," Angel said, waggling her eyebrows. It took all of two seconds before Sam practically threw herself at her. Charlie, having seen the trajectory, had wisely gotten out of the way. He closed the door and stepped into the kitchen as the two women embraced, jumping up and down in spot like they were still in college.

"Oh my God! When did you get here?" Sam squealed, fighting the tears that threatened to escape.

It felt obvious, but she had missed her friend. A lot had happened in the past few weeks, both good and bad. Having her there now felt like the cherry on top for the good side.

"Alright, you fucking tree," Angel stated firmly from Sam's chest, her voice muffled into the fabric, "let me get some air!"

It was probably a good idea because Sam realized that Angel was just as eloquently styled as usual. Reluctantly, Sam released her, fearing that she might have accidentally crumpled the cream satin halter top Angel had on.

With a quick flip of Angel's raven hair over her shoulder, Sam couldn't tell if she had just gotten off the airplane or had just stepped out of a fancy New York boutique.

"I wish I could be you when I grow up," Sam teased.

Angel rolled her eyes at her before placing the rather expensive-looking purse on the counter next to where Charlie stood. Sam leveled a glare at him, appearing much too calm for this kind of surprise.

"You knew about this?" she asked.

His smile was coy, but he shrugged. "She might have texted me."

Sam turned back to Angel. "What are you doing here? I thought your conference wasn't until next week?"

Angel grinned. "Well... I might have lied about the conference. Peter here needed a date to a certain charity event, so I may or may not be going with you guys."

It was around that time that Sam even noticed the other individual hovering next to Charlie and startled.

Peter beamed at her, the same tell-tale Backman dimples appearing in the corners of his smile. Along with the newer crinkles around his eyes, he managed to somehow look older than when she'd last seen him a few months ago—more distinguished almost.

The height difference was more noticeable between the two siblings as they stood next to one another, with Peter just a few inches shorter. Peter looked like an older version of Charlie, so similar in a lot of ways, aside from the height. They shared the same sandy-brown hair, though Peter's was longer and curlier, and his beard was much thicker and more pronounced than Charlie's.

"Oh my God, Peter! I'm so sorry. I didn't even see you there!" Sam exclaimed.

She launched herself at Charlie's brother, giggling as he swept her up in a hug and lifted her off her feet.

Sam and Charlie had been thick as thieves growing up, but she would always have a soft spot for his brothers.

Peter chuckled, a warmth and affection in the deep timbre of his voice. "Chopped liver, I know, but I'll forgive you this time, knowing how much you two ladies have missed each other."

Angel stood next to Sam once Peter finally lowered her back to the ground. "I'm staying over at Peter's place while I'm here, but I wanted to come over here to say hi so that I didn't give you a heart attack when we showed up at the event."

"Much appreciated," Sam said gratefully. "With everything that's gone on lately, I might have."

Angel nudged her hip against Sam's. "I *also* happen to be in need of an outfit, and a little birdie told me that you might be in need of one, too?"

Sam grimaced. "Yeah, I'd been meaning to go."

"Then let's get going," Angel declared, looping her arm through Sam's as she began marching her toward the bedroom. "We're going shopping!"

Sam glanced over her shoulder. "Is this a group outing?"

"The boys are coming too. They'll just fuck off somewhere to get their suits, while we get our stuff. Can't let them see us in what we get—you know how much I like to make an entrance," Angel stated with a wink.

❧

*S*am attempted to zip up yet another dress, grunting from the effort as she shimmied her way into the material.

Charlie and Peter had wandered off to a different part of the store, while Angel and Sam had their little fashion show for one another. Trying on dress after dress and strutting through the dressing area as if on the runway.

"I think this is the one!" Angel announced in the dressing room next to hers.

Sam hadn't told Angel about the most recent update with Charlie. Angel would absolutely kill her for keeping yet another thing from her, but she vowed to tell her at some point while she was here visiting—just maybe not while the two of them were trying on floor-length gowns.

Sam pouted her lips as she stared at her own reflection. This most recent dress was a bit on the short side for her height. "I'll come out, so you can show me yours, but I don't think this is the one for me."

She kicked the excess of a previous dress she'd tried on out of the way and walked out into the dressing area. Angel's door opened next to her at the same time, and she strutted out confidently, sashaying dramatically as if she were, in fact, on a runway.

Yeah, Sam could agree that this was the perfect dress for Angel.

A floor-length mermaid-cut dress that showed off how slender her frame was, it was absolutely stunning on her. The gown had a dramatically low-cut neckline that went down almost to Angel's navel and which only someone like Angel, with her confidence, could pull off.

Sam gave a low whistle. "Hot damn."

If her suspicions were correct, Peter was going to have a hard time picking his jaw up off the floor with this one.

"That was the exact reaction I was going for with this one," Angel beamed, turning to angle a dramatic pose in the mirror.

Their shopping trips back in college felt like a lifetime ago these days.

Standing there, laughing, as Angel continued to make dramatic poses in the mirror, however, she remembered how much fun it had been. She wondered if she should suggest that their next stop should be to grab a ridiculously over-priced coffee from the food court like they used to.

It was vastly different from how their relationship had been the past few months.

All of their interactions lately had been centered around Sam. About her book, her career, her love life, her *stalker.* Sam wondered, watching Angel gleefully strike another fashion pose, when the last time had been that she'd asked about what had been going on in *Angel's* life.

"Thank you," Sam said after watching her friend finally get tired of posing in front of the mirror.

Angel quirked an eyebrow at her. "For what? I mean, I know I look fabulous enough that anyone would want to thank me for gracing them with my presence, but I don't think that's what you mean."

Sam chuckled. "For always being a good friend, even when I'm not that good of a friend to you in return. I'm sorry I haven't been checking in to see how you're doing as well.

I've been selfish recently." Sam winced when Angel immediately slapped her shoulder. "Ow!"

"First, have I ever been known to keep quiet if I needed to talk about something?"

"Well… no—"

"Then stop worrying about it. You've had a lot thrown at you lately. My life, in comparison, has been *exceedingly* boring, so there honestly hasn't been much for me to report on."

Sam tossed her a pointed glare. "Yeah, let's definitely not talk about the fact that you flew all the way down here from New York just to go as Peter's date... Nothing to report there…"

Angel averted her gaze back toward the mirror and fluffed her hair up. "Mind your business."

Sam shook her head. "Anyway, that doesn't matter. I still should have asked. You're my best friend."

Angel's eyes softened at that, swaying a bit where she stood. "I thought that was Charlie."

Well, technically, Charlie was her boyfriend now, but she wasn't quite ready to tell Angel that in a moment like this. "I can have more than one! There's no ranking here. You've been my best friend just as much as Charlie has. I'm sorry I leaned so heavily into our working relationship."

Angel took Sam's hand in hers, giving it a squeeze. "I appreciate the sentiment, I do, but please don't work yourself into a tizzy over it. Let's just be open and honest with each other going forward, okay?"

Sam nodded, but a lump had formed in her throat, preventing her from saying anything. She was trying to heed the words, but she couldn't help but still feel a bit guilty. Angel gave her hand another quick squeeze before waving Sam toward her dressing room. "Alright, I'm gonna get this one, so go back in there and try on that green one I gave you earlier."

The air around her felt lighter as she closed the door behind her.

She grabbed the green dress off its hanger, eyeing it with a hint of dread. Angel had spotted this one the second they'd walked in and insisted that Sam try it on.

It was definitely more outside of her comfort zone than the others she'd tried on. The others had been more traditional sweetheart-neckline ballgowns that ended up seeming too princess-wedding. This was a drastically different cut, one that would hug her a lot more snugly than the others had. Holding it in front of her, though, Sam could see the appeal.

It was an off-the-shoulder velvet gown with a slit cut up the side so high that Sam worried she might flash someone if she weren't careful. It was a tight kind of fabric, and she wasn't sure her ego could take the hit if it didn't hit her body in *just* the right way. Angel could pull off a dress like this in her sleep, but Sam wasn't so sure the same could be said of her.

"You sure about this one, Angel?" she called out, biting her lower lip.

"Absolutely!"

Her eyes fluttered shut when she started tugging it up her body, preparing herself for disappointment. It managed to zip up without a fuss, much to her relief, and she prepared herself for what she would see when she walked out. It was just a dress.

Angel was perched on a nearby stool, opposite her dressing room, when she finally mustered the courage to open the door. She was looking down at her phone, her own dress was laid out across her lap, and she was back in her regular clothing.

"What do you think?" Sam asked, standing there in the doorway.

When Angel glanced up from her phone, she beamed. "Damn, I love it when I'm right."

"Does it look okay?"

Angel nodded toward the nearby mirror. "See for yourself hot stuff."

She took the few steps out of the dressing room and turned, facing the mirror. Upon seeing her reflection, she had to blink a few times.

The brilliant emerald hue to the dress complemented the cool tone of her skin and fiery strawberry-blonde hair in a way she hadn't expected. As tall as she was, the slit up her right leg wasn't nearly as dramatic as she'd feared, but it was enough to show off the length of her legs. Even the fit of the dress itself surprised her. Despite the unforgiving fabric, it hit her curves in all the right ways, making her appear curvier and more voluptuous.

She looked *good*.

It made her feel like a lady. Classy, elegant, sophisticated, and—dare she say it? It made her feel a bit sexy, too. If this was how Angel felt on the regular with her elevated fashion sense, Sam could completely understand the confidence her friend exuded on a 24/7 basis.

Angel snorted. "We might have to tie Charlie's dick down, so he's not at full mast all night."

CHAPTER 33

CHARLIE

At exactly three in the morning, Charlie finally decided to give up the ruse of falling asleep.

He stared up at the ceiling with a frustrated huff. He wanted to get up and busy himself with something else, but he couldn't move. If Sam hadn't fallen so peacefully asleep curled into his side, he'd have gone into the other room so as not to disturb her. Instead, he watched her—her head rising and falling with each breath he took.

Even if things hadn't worked out the way they did, he wouldn't trade a single day with her for anything in the world. He loved her. Both now as her friend and her lover.

He flushed at the thought, cursing his body's instinctual pull toward her. Sam was a drug, and he was already an addict, wanting her with every waking breath even more now than ever before. He'd have to think about something else right now if he didn't want to pounce on her.

How could he be so lucky? It still felt like a dream—Sam was his girlfriend. Everything he'd ever wanted since the day he'd met her, finally come true. He wished they'd had that conversation years ago, so they'd have had more time together, but he also knew that it wouldn't have mattered in the end.

He would have waited the rest of his life for her.

She looked so peaceful sleeping there, clutching the side of his shirt, as if she were afraid he'd be torn from her. He tucked a stray strand of hair behind her ear, smiling when the motion caused her to sigh contentedly in her sleep.

Charlie's gaze returned back to the ceiling. There was so much to do later that day. So much so that the lack of sleep was frustrating. He would need the energy because, despite his mother relenting on the bachelor auction, he knew something else would inevitably come up.

It was the day he'd been dreading for quite some time. But… it was for Erica.

Despite how much he didn't want to deal with the circus, it was still all for her at the end of the day.

It was hard to explain to anyone else what it felt like losing a sister, a twin.

Erica had been the better twin; everybody knew it. Everyone liked her more, not that he could blame them. She was smart, cunning, talented at everything she put her mind to, and just overall a more fun person to be around. She was a bright light that had been snuffed out too soon.

The worst part was that he was starting to forget little pieces of her. Lost to the sands of time. The sound of her voice. Her laugh. The feeling of her presence right there next to him.

It was the first time in what felt like far too long that he let his mind wander to her. Shoving her memory aside so he wouldn't have to think about what he'd done. Or, more apt, what he *hadn't* done.

He could have prevented the whole thing. Erica would be alive today if he'd done things differently.

"Charlie?" Sam mumbled sleepily.

Charlie flinched at the suddenness of being pulled from his thoughts, but he recovered quickly and pressed a kiss to Sam's forehead. "Sorry. I didn't mean to wake you."

"Are you alright?" she asked, moving to prop herself up.

He was afraid that the sadness lingering from his previous thoughts would be all too apparent, trying to push her to lay back down. "Yeah, don't worry about it. Just go back to sleep, baby."

"Were you thinking about Erica?"

He stopped, glancing down at her. "How did you know?"

Sam's smile softened. "Considering we have to get all dressed up for a charity gala that was planned because of the anniversary of her death? I think I'd be surprised if you weren't."

"It's not a big deal," he stated quickly.

Sam's hand came up to cup his cheek, and its softness against his scratchy beard felt far more comforting than it should. He closed his eyes and relaxed into it, holding it there against him with his other hand.

"You know you can talk to me about her, right?" Sam continued. "I don't ask you about her more because I know it's not something you like talking about. And I know talking about her with your family is … complicated… but I knew her too."

A strangled chuckle escaped him, the sound reverberating in his chest with each breath now feeling tight.

He shrugged. "I don't know. It feels like if I think too much about her, that grief and guilt will eat me alive."

"Come here, honey," she whispered, pulling Charlie to lay his head on her chest. He didn't fight her, adjusting himself so that his arms were curled around her body as his head settled there right above her heart. The steady beating of it thumping beneath his ear.

"You take such good care of everyone you care about," Sam continued as her fingers began combing through his hair, "but you can't protect everyone all the time. It was *not* your fault that she got in that car, Charlie."

He sighed, wanting to believe her. Wanting to believe what everyone in his family had always told him. But he couldn't.

"I knew she was sneaking out that night to go to that stupid party," he whispered, the lump in his throat that had formed keeping his volume low.

Sam continued stroking his hair. "You were just teenagers, honey. And you know how Erica was; you wouldn't have been able to convince her not to go. She was young and wanted to have fun with her friends."

"But if I'd pushed harder," Charlie added, tears already welling in the corners of his eyes, "maybe she wouldn't have gone. I had a funny feeling. I knew something bad was gonna happen. I couldn't explain it, and she thought I was being dramatic about it. Yet I *knew* something felt wrong. But I didn't push. She begged me not to tell anyone she was leaving, and I just stood there outside and watched the car drive away."

It was his biggest regret in life.

He hadn't protected his own sister.

How the hell had he expected he could protect anyone else?

What was worse was the fact that not only had his own sister died, but the other two people in that car had as well. It made it all the more of a slap in the face that the guy driving the other car, drunk out of his mind after a bender at the bar, only got fifteen years of prison time for it. Fifteen years for three lives.

"Charlie, it wasn't your fault," Sam whispered, the sound of her voice like a soothing balm to the pain and hurt coursing through his chest. "There was nothing you could do. You've got to stop blaming yourself for something that you had no control over, baby."

The pet name proved to be his undoing for some inexplicable reason. The tender affection behind it was enough to forcibly snap him in two. But as he dissolved into tears that had long been trapped, he felt like a weight had been lifted from his shoulders. For the first time in many long years, he felt free of this weight. Even if it were only a few minutes, he'd let himself fall apart, knowing Sam would be there to catch him.

CHAPTER 34

SAM

Sam stood before the mirror, mascara wand in hand, as she delicately applied one more coat to her lashes. With a satisfied nod, she stepped back to admire her handiwork.

It had been a while since she had last taken the time to apply her makeup so meticulously or with as much extravagance. There was only a little time left before they all needed to leave, so it was a mad dash with four people getting ready at the same time.

"You need any help with your hair?" Angel asked from the bed behind her, her legs crossed in front of her and a curling iron held in place above her head.

It had been Angel's idea that they all got ready together at Charlie's apartment. The two of them had holed up in Charlie's bedroom, while Charlie and Peter had been banished to the smaller bathroom and office down the hall.

Sam smiled at her reflection before responding. "No, I think I'm going to do a side-swept half up-do. Pin one side and have the other side let down. What do you think?"

Angel gave her a thoughtful once-over before nodding. "Not a bad idea. It'll give Hollywood starlight vibes."

The exact vibe she had been going for.

"Are you still not going to tell me what's going on between you and Peter?" Sam asked, waggling her eyebrows.

Angel's eyes cut to hers. "I don't know. Are you going not going to tell me what's going on with you and Charlie?"

Sam's face heated. It wasn't that she *didn't* want to tell Angel; she just hadn't found the right time to do it. She hadn't wanted to say anything while they were trying on dresses, dinner with her and Peter afterwards was at a loud restaurant where they couldn't hear each other much anyway, and they'd been so busy getting ready today that they'd barely even had time to really talk.

She turned back to the mirror. Angel would kill her if she didn't tell her soon, though, so she decided that as soon as she finished applying her lipstick, she'd tell her.

That was until a sudden, high-pitched, scream pierced the air. Startled, Sam dropped the tube onto the counter and spun around.

Angel was leaned over toward the wall, close to the electrical socket the curling iron had been plugged into, but she seemed to be focused on something behind the nightstand. She snatched the offending object off the ground and spun on her.

"*Samantha MacMillian!*" Angel exclaimed loudly, stomping her foot on the ground as she held the object up.

It took Sam a second, but when she figured out what it was, heat abruptly rushed up her neck to her face.

Oh. Oh no.

At that moment, the bedroom door flew open, and both Charlie and Peter hurled themselves through the entrance. Charlie, leading the charge, gripped the door frame to prevent himself from colliding with Sam, Peter not more than a step or two behind him.

"What happened? Are you two okay?" Charlie asked, sounding as if he'd sprinted clear across the apartment. Charlie had managed to at least pull on his trousers and his undershirt, but the same couldn't be said of Peter as he shoved himself further into the room behind him in just a pair of boxers.

"Who screamed?" Peter asked, unapologetically shirtless next to her as Sam felt herself flush even harder.

Angel whirled on them, showing off the item in her hand.

A condom wrapper.

An *empty*, open condom wrapper.

"I fucking *knew it*!" Angel cried out. Quite the picture she made indeed, waving the condom wrapper above her head, as if it were some victory trophy, in nothing more than the bathrobe she'd brought with her. The rest of them in various states of undress as they stared.

Peter nudged Charlie from behind. "You dog."

Sam wished she could drop dead.

Charlie, to his credit, at least looked almost as embarrassed as Sam felt. His ears and face were red, growing redder by the second.

"Fuck, I wondered where that one had gone," he mumbled.

"Bitch, if you don't stop keeping things from me, I'm gonna fucking deck you!" Angel stated, though the smile trickling through hardly gave any weight to it. "You two finally got together?"

"Y-yes," Sam said. "Can you please put the condom wrapper down at least—"

Angel whirled around, facing Peter, and waved the

wrapper again in the air like it was a key piece of evidence to a crime she'd just solved. "You owe me fifty bucks!"

"What?!" Sam exclaimed.

"We had a bet going," Peter replied sheepishly, rubbing the back of his neck. Sam turned to look at him but immediately covered her eyes and rubbed at the tension that had so quickly formed between them. Peter was a bit leaner than Charlie was, but it was easy to tell that he was no stranger to the gym as well.

Charlie rolled his eyes and nudged Peter. "Dude, go put a shirt on."

Peter puffed out his chest. "I didn't exactly have *time* to grab one when I came running in here."

"Both of you, out!" Angel declared, shooing them with her hands. "I have to talk to Sam."

"But——-" Charlie started but retreated from Angel's sweeping hands.

"Your concern is duly noted, both of you, but shoo! I have to talk to my best friend. Get out!" she said, shoving at the two of them until she was able to close the door firmly behind them. She tossed the offending wrapper onto the nearby nightstand with a grimace and plopped down heavily onto the bed.

Angel patted the spot next to her. "Sit, I want all of the dirty details."

Sam giggled. "Are we just going to ignore the fact that you and Peter bet on my relationship?"

"We'll call it even for you not *immediately* telling me about this. Now, spill!"

Sam shrugged, suddenly feeling a bit shy about the whole thing. She'd planned on telling Angel while she was here visiting; she just hadn't formed the words she was going to say and was now at a bit of a loss. "It just sort of...

happened? We finally had a conversation about how we felt, and things just sort of happened from there…"

"Finally," Angel sang out. "I told you everything would be fine if you just told him how you felt."

She shrugged again. "I know. I was just worried that I would mess everything up."

Angel aimed a sarcastic grin at her. "And now that feels pretty stupid, huh?"

Sam laughed. "Yeah, a bit… Are you mad?"

"That we literally just had a whole-ass conversation about being open and honest?"

Sam winced. "Yeah, that."

Angel sighed, scooting closer and nudging Sam's shoulder with her own. "I'm not mad. I'm aware that protecting your peace is sort of your thing, and given how your family is with you, I can't say I blame you."

Oh yeah, that.

"I guess now's a good time to also tell you that I told my aunt off? Cut ties with her and the rest of them."

Angel's mouth opened wide before she smacked Sam's arm. "Okay, *now* I'm mad! How could you not tell me the *wonderful* news? Ding dang dong, the witch is gone!"

The laughter that burst out from Sam was unexpected but certainly not unwelcome.

"For real, though, I get it," Angel continued, sounding more serious. "I do. I would have loved for you to have told me about you and Charlie on your own before I found… that… but I get it."

"You do?"

"Of course. Regardless of how *obvious* it is for the rest of us how head over heels in love you two have been for each other, it's still something new to both of you. You had a lot of catching up to do, I'm sure. So, no, I'm not mad."

"Promise?" Sam asked. She knew she probably would deserve it if she was still angry after everything, but she wanted to start over. Clean the slate, so to speak. No more secrets between them.

Angel's expression softened. "Promise. Plus, I'm fifty dollars richer, so who am I to complain? But… I do have just one more question, and we'll be completely even."

"Okay?"

Angel waggled her eyebrows. "How's the sex?"

"Angel!" Sam exclaimed, shoving her playfully.

The only surprising part of Angel's question wasn't the question itself but more that she hadn't thought Angel would be curious about it.

"What? Am I not allowed to be curious? Is it good? You *promised* no more secrets!"

Sam chewed on her lip before letting a sigh hiss out of her. "It's fucking incredible."

CHAPTER 35

CHARLIE

harlie's grip tightened around the steering wheel, his knuckles almost completely white from the effort. He wished he could say that it was because of the worries and anxiety he'd felt earlier that evening. He'd felt lighter than he had in years after talking to Sam about everything with his family, with Erica, with this whole spectacle, but he'd still felt the flutter of nerves swirling around in his gut.

Those thoughts felt a million miles away currently.

No, what currently overtook all other thoughts at the moment was his body's reaction to simply seeing Sam in a fucking dress. This gorgeous, stunning woman—*his* woman —wrapped like a fucking gift in velvet.

He hadn't prepared himself in advance for that, cursing his past self for it, because his reaction had been swift. Even as he sat behind the steering wheel with a death grip, it took everything in him not to turn the car around and forgo the whole evening.

That fucking dress was going to be the bane of his existence tonight.

It clung to her like a second skin, the light hue of her skin cut against the stark, rich deep-green fabric. Its velvety texture highlighted every mouthwatering curve that she possessed. The neckline dipped just low enough to hint at the swell of her breasts—the fabric straining against their fullness. The dress's straps were delicately suspended off her shoulders, almost indifferent to their intended task and merely fluttering there.

When she walked out of the bedroom, arm-in-arm with Angel, it had taken just about every ounce of strength he had not to throw her over his shoulder and banish the other two from the apartment, so they wouldn't hear how loud he wanted to make her scream his name.

Even now, sitting here felt torturous.

All he wanted was to rip that dress off her body.

Thread by fucking thread.

It didn't help that—in this tight space, with no escape from it—the intoxicating scent of her perfume wrapped around the cords of his throat with a vise-like grip. It wasn't one she usually wore, but it made him nearly feral at how perfect it was for her.

It was subtle, floral, with a hint of citrus, and it managed to fit her just as much as her usual scent did. Reserved in a way that made him crave to see that wild side of her, a femininity that she was so clearly unaware of, one that could have him on his knees at her feet, and a punch of sweetness to make his mouth water. A siren's lullaby packaged neatly in a bottle.

What was worse for his psyche, however, was any time he stole a glance at her.

She seemed to sense his eyes on her every time, throwing him one of those hooded *come hither* looks. He was doing his best, he really was, but if she didn't cut it out, he'd have to pull the car over.

"Need help with that?" she asked innocently, her eyes lowering to his lap.

Shit.

"Behave," he ordered gruffly.

This woman was pure wickedness in an angel's form, and God save him from the things he was going to do to this angel later. He'd worship every inch of her body and have her sobbing by the end of tonight if things went his way—which he had every intention of happening.

She hummed low in her throat. "I'm just enjoying this a little. You're this excited simply seeing me in this dress, and you haven't even seen what I'm wearing underneath it yet."

He groaned, gripping the steering wheel even harder. "You're killing me, baby. We're gonna end up in a ditch if you don't behave."

"Sorry. It's just a little fun making you squirm." She giggled, batting those long eyelashes at him.

He laughed, the sound strangled. "I'm sure, but I'd hate to ruin that dress of yours, so I need you to distract me from ripping it off of you."

"I'd like to see you try," she replied, throwing him a smug wink.

Wicked creature, God help him.

CHAPTER 36

SAM

It wasn't the sheer volume of people heading toward the entrance that caught Sam off guard. No, Charlie had warned her about that—practically half of North Carolina had been invited.

It wasn't merely the grand entrance that Sam could tell had been meticulously crafted for the event, though it was incredibly impressive. A rolling red carpet unfurled elegantly, stretching all the way to the front door, like a scene straight from Hollywood.

The plaza leading to the museum's entrance had undergone a breathtaking transformation into a radiant red-carpet extravaganza. The already picturesque landscape had been elevated to new heights, adorned with lush greenery meticulously arranged along a walled-off barrier, offering a sense of privacy for those already inside the venue. A unique and welcomed feature, especially considering the museum's expansive glass windows that wrapped around the entirety of the building.

In the days preceding the event, Charlie had told her about the venue and a few of the things she could expect. So, she knew they were going to doll the place up to make it look even more grand and illustrious than it already was. With the museum's inherently sleek and contemporary design, Sam had figured that it wouldn't have been hard to elevate it into a captivating spectacle, its already pristine features serving as the perfect canvas.

No, what Sam hadn't anticipated were the relentless flashes of cameras, accompanied by the dull roar of photographer's voices barking instructions. They jostled amongst themselves, aiming for the perfect shot as patrons made their way along the carpet. And it wasn't just a couple of photographers to contend with either—there were scores of them lining the outer edge of the carpet.

Sam squeezed Charlie's hand as they waited for their turn down the carpet. "Paparazzi? Really?"

Charlie chuckled and squeezed back. "Just part of the experience; they're paid to take pictures of everyone coming in."

"Impressive," Sam murmured, the thought of the first pictures of the two of them as a couple igniting a flutter of excitement. "Do they give people the pictures afterwards?"

Charlie chuckled warmly, pulling her to him and pressing a kiss to her forehead before they were ushered along by a nearby attendant.

While this wasn't Sam's first time in front of cameras like this, it was certainly more than she had encountered previously. There had been the promotional tours that she had been on for some of her previous books, which had provided a taste of this kind of spotlight, though definitely not to this scale.

Thankfully.

Charlie, on the other hand? He was a natural. If he was nervous or anxious about it, it didn't show. His infectious smile, the one that accentuated the dimples pressed into his cheeks, never faltered. He kept her securely by his side, their steps steady and sure as they made their way down the carpet.

It came as no shock that the photographers gravitated to him. Who could blame them? Charlie in normal clothing was already attractive, but put him in a suit? Absolutely lethal.

It was tailored to perfection, highlighting his muscular frame and showing off the quiet strength he had beneath. His normally unkempt, tousled hair was combed back, save for a few rebellious strands left to frame his face. His scruffy beard was groomed and trimmed carefully, accentuating his chiseled jawline while managing to preserve the almost rugged appeal she loved about his beard.

Sam audibly gasped when her vision cleared from the slew of camera flashes enough for her to make out the inside of the museum.

Whoever had done the decorating for tonight deserved an award.

The museum managed to retain its timeless allure, every bit as sleek and elegant as Sam recalled from her previous visits there over the years. A series of signs adorned the nearby walls, beckoning patrons to explore the available exhibits at their leisure.

A number of guests were already navigating the halls with eager curiosity. The larger, more intricate sculptures that usually stood tall along the hallway appeared to have been relocated elsewhere to accommodate the influx of guests. A move that seemed to have worked, but only marginally, as the crowded space only swelled with guests with each passing moment.

Music drifted from a band stationed deeper down the hall, their harmonies weaving through the thrum of the crowd. The spacious layout had been sequestered off around the band, creating an inviting dance floor for interested partygoers. As couples twirled and laughter filled the space, the music served as a vibrant backdrop for most.

Charlie leaned in close. "You want to dance?"

She playfully swatted at him, eyeing the crowd to locate a few familiar faces. "We have to greet your parents first!"

He nodded as if in agreement, though she noted the disappointed twinkle in his eyes as he took her hand in his.

Towering over the majority of those around them, Charlie was able to effortlessly zero in on his family in no time. With a subtle nod in their direction, he guided Sam through the sea of people, their hands laced together in a casual intimacy that made her heart flutter.

As they drew nearer, Sam spotted Charlie's father amidst a small cluster of individuals, his infectious grin lighting up his face as he extended a welcoming handshake to another gentleman.

The Backman men were certainly easy to spot in a crowd.

While it had been a few years since Sam had last seen Charlie's father, Richard, the family resemblance was unmistakable. Richard's once sandy-brown hair was now adorned with peppered flecks of grey and artfully combed back sleekly. Even his beard, which Sam recalled having been much bushier and unkempt the last she had seen him, was now neatly trimmed back, lending to a softer expression in his eyes that somehow managed to also showcase the sharp slant of his jawline that he had definitely passed on to Charlie.

Richard spotted them approaching and waved them over enthusiastically. Charlie's mother, Amy, emerged beside her husband as they neared. A remarkable contrast in height, easily several heads shorter than her husband and sons, she turned in their direction, and an even wider grin broke out across her face.

While Charlie undoubtedly bore a stronger resemblance to his father, it was clear who he had gotten those stunning blue eyes from. The deep, ocean-blue hue shimmered in excitement as Amy reached her arms up for her son.

"You came!" she exclaimed excitedly, giving a little hop as Charlie lowered himself to give his mother a hug.

Lost in the sea of taller figures without her husband's assistance, Charlie's mother barely reached Sam's shoulder, easily making her the shortest member of the family.

It made Sam briefly wonder how this poor woman managed to survive giving birth to three large Backman boys.

"Of course I did, Mom. I promised," Charlie said, lowering her back so she was no longer on her tiptoes. The pale-gray chiffon gown that Amy had on swished around her feet. The material, which had pooled around them previously, lifted to showcase the black stiletto heels she sported, still not adding enough height for her head to reach her husband's shoulder.

Richard took Charlie's hand and pulled him in for a quick embrace, patting his back heartily before releasing him.

At the same time, Amy turned and held her arms out, inviting Sam in for a hug. "It's so wonderful to see you here, Sammy dear! It's been a while since we've seen you in town!"

Sam gave her a quick squeeze, feeling the familiar warmth she always felt when she was around Charlie's mother. "It's wonderful seeing you as well, Mrs. Backman."

"Oh, sweetheart, please call me Amy. I think we're past all that by now," she replied with a wink, looping her arms around one of Sam's to hug her to her side. It was such a familiar gesture yet so foreign after all these years.

There had been a time many years ago when, after another inevitable falling out with her aunt or uncle, such a gesture was everything she ever needed. The feeling of a comforting and loving parental figure who *didn't* stake their entire relationship on what she could do for them.

With everything that had been going on, Sam hadn't been able to reach out as much as she used to. It had been a while since they'd last spoken on the phone outside of the occasional text exchange.

"Well, well, well, what do we have here?" another familiar voice asked, pulling Sam from her memories. She turned, smiling when Angel and Peter strutted up next to them.

Sam wasn't sure that enough compliments in the world would be able to adequately suffice how amazing Angel looked in that dress—with the delicate black fabric kissed with lace accents that perfectly matched the color of Angel's hair, which she had done up into an intricate updo, pinned down with gorgeous little gold-and-crystal clips. The perfect picture of elegance and class.

Peter bent to give his mother a hug, though not having to stoop nearly as much as Charlie had.

As he did, Tyler, the more elusive of the Backman brothers, emerged from the crowd and flanked Charlie on the opposite side.

He swiftly reached out to grab Sam's hand, pressing a kiss to it before Charlie could protest. "Nice to see you, Sam. It's been a while."

Those Backman dimples creased into Tyler's smile, the one feature all three of them shared.

Standing together, the three brothers were practically mirror images of their father, with only a few features distinguishing them as their own. The three women—her, Angel, and Amy—stood back and giggled amongst themselves as the boys all exchanged greetings with one another, commenting on the similarities like a bunch of gossiping schoolgirls.

Charlie, the tallest among them, had at least a few inches on Peter, the oldest but second tallest amongst the brothers. However, unlike Charlie, Peter's ashy blonde hair was clearly the gift his mother had passed onto him, giving him a more youthful look.

Tyler, on the other hand, was the only brother to distinguish himself with a pair of thick-rimmed black glasses. If Sam didn't know him better, it would have added an air of intelligence and charm that made him appear like he was a more regular fixture of events such as this. Knowing how much of a stubborn, grumpy smart-ass he could be, it was an interesting combination.

Angel shook her head with a smile, nudging Amy with her hip. "You really made some hot kids, Mrs. Backman."

Amy laughed—the sound so familiar and warm that it was hard not to join her—and looped her other arm with Angel, the three of them forming a line.

"I'll take your word for it, but they certainly are some handsome boys for sure. I think they have their father to thank for that more than myself."

Angel shook her head more definitively. "Nope, Peter should send you a basket of fruit every year on his birthday for that ass. He clearly got that from you."

Definitely no filter on Angel tonight.

Amy beamed proudly. "Thank God one of them got it at least. Can both of you please just marry those two boys of mine and keep them out of trouble?"

Angel shrugged casually. "I think I'm further from that than Sam is."

Sam wanted to reach across and smack the smug smile Angel threw at her, but Amy lit up further.

"Did Charlie finally ask you out?"

Sam blinked at Amy a few times. "You *knew* he liked me?"

Amy tsked and rolled her eyes. "Honey, he wore his feelings like it was tattooed on his arm. I didn't want him to pursue you when you were both kids because of what happened with your parents, but he finally asked you out, I presume?"

She felt a bit embarrassed at the directness of it, still reeling from Peter and Angel finding out earlier that evening and not prepared in the least to tell anyone else for a while. But seeing the hopeful gleam in Amy's eyes, Sam couldn't help but laugh and nod.

Amy's arm tightened around hers. "At least one of my sons has some balls, then."

CHAPTER 37

SAM

"Mind if I steal Sam away?" Charlie asked as he broke away from the conversation with his father and brothers.

Amy and Angel exchanged a rueful glance. "Of course! We were just catching up. She's all yours honey."

Sam clasped Charlie's hand and followed as he guided them to the dance floor. A flush crept across her cheeks as she caught the looks they got from Tyler and Richard as they passed, with Tyler lifting a champagne flute in her direction.

Either Charlie had said some something, or they were indeed not nearly as subtle as they thought they were, and she was starting to believe the latter was probably the case.

Charlie gracefully twirled her around before pulling her back into his embrace. He took one hand in his as the other rested comfortably on the small of her back. A delicate touch that felt far more intimate than it should, and she couldn't help but smile.

They swayed along with the music, in perfect harmony with one another.

She had worried about Charlie tonight more than she was

willing to admit aloud. Worried that he would feel over-whelmed with everything going on. Worried that all of the people would overwhelm him. Just… worried in general.

The echo of his quiet sobs was a haunting sound that she hoped she would never have to hear tear from him again.

But, given the warmth in his eyes as he gazed at her, the gentle smile tugging his dimples into place, she was hoping that those worries would be a distant memory.

"I hope my mom didn't grill you and Angel too bad," Charlie said.

Sam laughed. "She didn't, though she knows you and I are together now."

Charlie grimaced, pushing Sam gently outward to spin her once more before pulling her back to him. "Nothing ever slips her notice, I guess."

"It certainly doesn't, though I think her focus is now honing in on the *other* couple here tonight," she said, nodding in Peter and Angel's direction, who had followed them onto the dance floor a short distance away.

"As long as I have you to myself, I'm glad for it," he teased, pressing a kiss to her forehead. "But I just realized that our official deal is technically over after tonight."

"I suppose it is," she hummed. "Feels a bit weird, huh?"

"A bit. Just think, all of this because you wanted to write smut," he replied, waggling his eyebrows at her suggestively.

"I don't see you complaining about research in *that* particular department."

"And I never will," he said, pulling her harder against him until there wasn't a breath between them. "In fact, I'm avail-able at your beck and call anytime you need notes."

Her chest rumbled with a laugh. "Well, you'll just have to wait for the next book. I finished writing it last night. But I'll keep your offer on standby."

"That's amazing! I hope I was helpful at least, then?"

"You were more than helpful. I got a lot of good material out of you," she teased.

Mischief overtook his features. "That so?"

Her arms went to encircle his neck. "I'd say so. You were the most romantic fake-boyfriend I've ever had."

He laughed, the sound of it causing the hairs on the back of her neck to rise deliciously. "How about as a real boyfriend now?"

"Hmm, not the same."

Charlie winced. "Ouch."

"You're even better," she added quickly, unable to keep the goofy smile from spreading across her lips.

He let out a low groan. "God, if I wasn't worried about the heckling we'd get from the peanut gallery, I'd kiss you right now."

"Patience is a virtue, honey," she teased as she rested her head against his chest.

Sam lacked the expertise to formally assess the event's success, but the packed dance floor and the loud chatter all around them suggested it was going well. She expected nothing less with Amy Backman leading the charge.

She sighed contentedly. Even if she was a little tired from staying up so late the night before to finish her book—well after Charlie himself had fallen asleep—she was glad for it. She'd turn it over to Angel after she got back to New York.

For now, she'd just revel in the fact that she'd not only met her goal but exceeded it in more ways than one.

Samantha MacMillian, pen name pending, had written a smutty romance novel.

She was no longer at risk of breaching her contract.

Her creative spark had returned with gusto, as she'd

already had a few ideas for new romance books she'd love to explore soon.

And, best of all, she'd gone into a fake dating experiment with Charlie and walked out of it with the most amazing boyfriend ever.

So, tonight, all she wanted was to rest easy and enjoy.

As the band concluded with their song, the singer took a moment to make a few announcements. The crowd around them parted, making their way off the dance floor and heading in various directions as the announcer listed off the locations of the different auctions that were about to start.

Sam pulled away from Charlie, nodding toward the throng of people. "Is there anything you have to do for this?"

Charlie shook his head. "Not that I'm aware of. I was told to be made available just in case they needed anything, but that's about it."

"What all are they auctioning off, do you know?"

"I don't really know all of it. There are actual items up for bidding, but there are experiences, too, at least from what my dad said," Charlie started before smiling. "Including a particular bachelor auction that I managed to get out of."

Sam laughed. "You and Peter, it seems, but what about Tyler? I didn't see anyone with him."

Charlie's smile widened. "He didn't bring one."

Her mouth fell open before she managed to throw her hand over it to prevent the laugh that threatened to spill out. "You mean he still has to do it?"

"Yep. As much shit as he gave everyone about it, Mom told him the rules applied to him, as well, so he has to participate later tonight."

Sam allowed the laugh to tumble out. "If you think for a second that I'm not going to record that—"

"You'll have to get in line," Charlie interrupted, "because Peter and I already called dibs."

As he finished his sentence, Charlie's eyebrows furrowed, and his gaze drifted over Sam's head. Following his line of sight, she spotted Richard amidst the crowd, beckoning him over with a wave. Seizing the moment, Sam decided to take the chance to freshen up.

"You go," she said as she patted his arm. "I'll catch up with you in a bit. Gonna run to the bathroom really quick."

There was hesitation in his eyes, as if he were trying to come up with an excuse not to leave her side, but she nudged him in the direction of his father. "Go. I'll be there in a bit, I promise."

She knew she had succeeded when he sighed, leaning forward to press a quick kiss to her temple. He let her hand go reluctantly as she pulled away, the faint whisper of his fingers lingering on her skin as she made a quick beeline for the restroom.

Once she finished and washed her hands, she took a minute to gather herself. She checked herself in the mirror, ensuring that her makeup and hair were still intact. Angel had been right about her hairdo, as the illustrious copper waves pinned off her right shoulder definitely *did* make her feel like a Hollywood starlet.

She quickly pulled out a tube of lipstick to reapply, blotted it once with a paper towel before checking her reflection. One final fluff of her hair and she made her way out of the bathroom.

She was only a few steps from the door when something grabbed her from behind and covered her mouth, pulling her back.

CHAPTER 38

CHARLIE

harlie glanced down at his watch for what felt like
the umpteenth time.

It had only been a small issue with one of the auction
items that had pulled him away from Sam, and it had been
solved quickly enough that Charlie made his way to stand
with Peter and Angel until Sam came back. They chatted
amongst themselves, eager conversation soon dying off into
distracted comments as they waited for her return.

He was starting to feel unease creeping up his spine the
more time passed.

It had been too long.

Way too long.

Of course she was an adult and had very likely just
bumped into someone she knew. Everyone they'd grown up
with, gone to school with, had been invited to this, after all.
Even he had spotted a few familiar faces in the crowd, so it
would stand to reason that she might have made a pit stop to
chat with someone. Maybe even more than one person.

It was just the night making him feel on edge; that
must've been it.

This whole spectacle, though beautiful and incredibly well planned on his mother's part, must've still had him on edge.

He tried to calm his nerves, rationalizing every which way he could. Even feeling a bit ridiculous about it.

He looked down at his watch again.

No, something was wrong. He could feel it in his gut. He couldn't quite put his finger on it, but something just didn't feel right.

Even Angel appeared to share his thoughts, occasionally rocking up onto her tiptoes to look over the crowd.

"She's been gone too long," he said finally.

Angel nodded, clutching Peter's arm for leverage as she once again stood on her toes to peer over the crowd. "I agree."

Charlie began threading his way through the throng of people without a word. He hoped that he'd bump into her on the way there, and she'd laugh about him overreacting again. Being overprotective again. That, he could handle.

Angel forged ahead and led the way into the bathroom, leaving Peter and Charlie behind for what felt like ages. When Angel walked back out moments later empty-handed, Charlie knew something had happened.

Panic choked him.

"Charlie!" Tyler called out from a short distance away. His father and two other individuals trailed after them, security guards, adding fuel to the fire burning in Charlie's throat.

"Where is Sam?" Tyler asked—something in his tone only confirmed Charlie's worst fears.

Paul was here.

Angel stepped forward next to Charlie. "We don't know. She went off to the bathroom earlier, but I just checked, and she's not in there."

The search began immediately.

Charlie's mother was asked to stay behind to keep everything running and prevent a panic—and just in case Sam did show up. Angel, on the other hand, refused to stay behind with her, despite Peter's protests. Not that Charlie could blame her, though his thoughts were pretty singular at the moment.

The group wandered out into the cool night's air through the back exit, closest to the restrooms.

Charlie cursed himself for separating from her at all.

He'd been too high on cloud nine with the most recent developments in their relationship that he'd almost completely forgotten about the whole situation with Paul. Or Jonathan, or whatever the hell his actual name was.

Fear twisted in his gut—with nothing but dense forest surrounding them, they could be anywhere.

They might not even still be here.

They could be long gone.

But that was when the silence around them broke. A voice. The sound was distant and barely just loud enough against the backdrop of the chaotic chatter, music, and loudspeakers blasting from just a few steps behind them. But it was just enough to have the hair raise on the back of Charlie's neck.

He spun around in the direction of the voice, waiting to see if he heard it once more.

Then he did. Coming just a distance away from the nearby park, he heard the voice again. Everyone around him seemed to hear it that time, all freezing in place as they listened. Angel even clapped a hand over Peter's mouth mid-order as he tried to tell the security guards something.

Then they heard it again.

Louder and a bit more clear, but suddenly cut off, as if

forcibly. The sound of it sent a shock of terror down Charlie's spine like a lightning bolt, the recognition immediate.

It was Sam.

She was screaming his name.

Charlie immediately broke out into a dead sprint.

His heartbeat was in his ears, pure adrenaline taking over. The shouts of the others behind him faded into the distance as he ran—there was no way in hell he was slowing down or stopping.

His girl needed him.

CHAPTER 39

SAM

Shock had given way to a surge of adrenaline as Sam clawed at the hand over her mouth, attempting to dig her feet into the ground but failing miserably. The pointed edges of her heels only managed to slide across the surface of the marble tile beneath her as she was dragged out into the open night's air.

The grip on her was vice-like, unrelenting and painful as an arm had circled around her waist and held her there, her mouth covered to prevent her from screaming.

She didn't need to guess who was behind her, who was yanking and pulling on her so hard that she'd surely have bruises from the force of it. It was Paul.

She had no clue where he was trying to take her. The museum trailed further and further behind them as he dragged her, passing beneath one of the large metallic arches dotted along the trail path. The nearest parking lot was in the opposite direction, and while she was only vaguely familiar with the trail they were headed down, she doubted there would be anyone nearby at this time of night.

"I bribed one of the waiters," Paul finally said, speaking

for the first time, "convinced him to take the night off, so I could use his uniform and blend in."

Light shimmered from above as they began to pass beneath another bronzed arch. Sam fought to turn her head to see where they were going, and when the nearby forest came into view, a renewed sense of fear clanged to life.

If they were completely out of sight, she wasn't sure what he would do.

"I just wanted us to be together," Paul continued, ignoring the protests she screamed into his hand. "Why did you have to be like all the others? I thought you might be different."

Sam managed to wriggle her face enough to free her mouth, taking the chance to immediately bite down on Paul's hand. His release relented enough that she pushed herself away from him but not enough to be completely free.

"I can't let you go this time, my love," he seethed, the stench of the whiskey on his breath wafting into her face. "I'm sorry, but if they catch me this time I'm going to go away for a long time. I can't do that. I can't go back to prison."

Sam didn't care to find out exactly what the hell that meant, going for the only thing she could think of to get him off of her. Her knee came up and slammed into its intended target, giving her enough purchase as Paul grunted and doubled over, to pull free of him. She immediately kicked off her heels and collected the hem of her dress, taking off like a shot back toward the museum.

She had no idea how long she'd been gone, but if she knew Charlie as well as she thought she did, he would be searching for her right about now.

It was hard to run in this dress, as tight as it was around her thighs, but she went as fast as she could. Her feet were screaming in pain from the rough asphalt beneath her, but she didn't slow.

As she made it beneath the next arch, a hand snagged her wrist and yanked her backward. Enough so that it caused her to lose her balance and fall backward into Paul's chest.

Paul shoved her against the metallic structure, hard. It clanged against her body, the force of it momentarily stealing her breath. He immediately jumped forward to cage her body in place with his, pinning her there.

"Let me go!" she shouted, the sound cut off as a sweaty palm found its way to Sam's throat and pressed her back further. A glint flickered in his eyes as he stared at her, something sinister lurking within. She began clawing at him again, using any purchase she had to get him off of her.

"Charlie!" she screamed as loud as she could, coughing as Paul's grip tightened.

"Shut the fuck up! We have to be quiet, or they'll find us, and we have to get on the road before they do. I'll take such good care of you, I promise. You just have to shut the fuck *up*," Paul hissed as he struggled to keep Sam in place.

Paul slammed her head back against the column behind her. "You *love* me!"

"Charlie!" Her voice echoed through the night, or that could've been the ringing in her ears.

"No one is——-"

The remainder of Paul's sentence was abruptly cut off as something slammed into him like a battering ram.

The impact was so sudden that it knocked Paul's hands from her, but it sent her tumbling onto the grass. She landed with a rough thud onto the soft earth just shy of the pathway, her knees slamming into the ground.

Paul, and whatever had hit him, had rolled away from the

light, making it difficult for her to figure out exactly what had happened.

Twinkling lights dotted across her vision, lightheaded from the lack of oxygen. Her neck was already throbbing from where Paul had his hands wrapped around her throat, further disorienting her. She squinted her eyes, making out two figures struggling on the ground a short distance away. The sound of grunts and fists colliding echoed through the air.

Despite the shock coursing through her, Sam recognized the figure now shoving Paul into the ground, nearly sobbing as hands grabbed a hold of her.

"Ch-Charlie!"

CHAPTER 40

CHARLIE

*C*harlie had blacked out for a moment as his body completely took over, surrendering himself to whatever force was taking over just as his body slammed into Paul's.

It felt like a blink, but in the next breath, when Charlie opened his eyes, he looked down to see Paul pinned beneath him. Thrashing there as he cried out and begged for Charlie to stop. Blood seeped across his face and coated Charlie's knuckles. That blood felt like a reminder. A red flag waved in front of a raging bull, and he felt his body continue where it had left off, now only aware of each fist as it raised up and connected with Paul's face.

He was a creature possessed, taken over by some feral, primal force, driven purely by his need to protect Sam.

Sam.

He had no idea how badly she was hurt when he had collided into Paul, but his entire being was currently focused on making sure Paul couldn't possibly get up to touch her again. Paul *tried* to defend himself, his arms attempting to block some of the blows, but he failed miserably. He cried out for someone to save him, to help him, but Charlie had other plans.

This was the man that had made Sam's life a living nightmare recently.

He'd followed her, harassed her, terrified her, destroyed her apartment, dared to lay a *hand* on her, so Charlie had other plans for him.

"Grab him, Peter, before he kills him!" A voice shouted somewhere behind him. One of his brothers most likely, if the small, conscious part of his brain was still functioning correctly.

He hardly even noticed as hands grabbed, trying to pull him off Paul but with little success. Charlie easily tore free and lunged again at the man pinned beneath him.

What could Paul have done to her if he hadn't gotten there in time? What *had* he done before he'd gotten there?

A few more minutes and he could have been too late.

Again.

"*You* grab him! He might kill us for holding him back," Peter shouted, latching onto Charlie's arm like a bull rider about to get bucked off. Charlie's father quickly emerged at his side as he slid in, reaching for Paul to try and pull the two apart.

"With a tackle like that, he might. Did you see that?" Tyler laughed, grunting as he held Charlie's other arm. "Tackled the fucker like his NFL career was on the line."

"This isn't the time for jokes!" Angel yelled somewhere behind them.

Security rushed in, swarming the scene until the group finally managed to pry Charlie off Paul. Peter was on one Arm, and Tyler apparently had jumped on his back—though in the chaos, he wasn't sure when. Even as they slapped the cuffs on Paul and began to drag him away, Charlie still fought to reach him.

One last punch for the road.

"Jesus Christ, Sam, what are you feeding him? He's supposed to be my *little* brother," Tyler chuckled in the thick of a grunt from where he clung to Charlie's back. "He's as strong as a fucking ox!"

His father stepped forward and gripped Charlie's face, giving it a firm shake. "Charlie, it's okay. They got him. He won't hurt Sam anymore. You did good, Son. She's safe. Calm down."

Sam.

His heart thundered in his chest as exhaustion threatened to overwhelm him, but the fog cleared away as a new panic overtook him.

Where was she? Was she hurt? Had he accidentally hurt her in the process?

He needed to see her.

"Note to self, never piss off Charlie," Peter teased as he and Tyler slowly released him, their hands hovering close by for several beats, as if they needed to prepare to grab him again if needed.

"Go check on your girl, man," Peter said quietly, pointing off to the side, as if he could sense the question lingering on Charlie's tongue.

He turned, finding Sam and Angel sitting in the distance. They were huddled together on the ground with Angel's arms wrapped protectively around Sam, rubbing her back as Sam leaned into her embrace.

She was safe.

He recognized the hesitation in Angel's eyes as he approached and stopped.

There was a high chance that they both might be frightened of him right now. He wouldn't have blamed them. He likely would've been afraid, too, if he were in their shoes. Yet his heart still ached at the flash of fear twinkling in Sam's eyes when she turned in Angel's arms, those soft green eyes of hers welling with unshed tears.

However, before he could say anything, Sam shot up out of Angel's arms and rushed forward, practically throwing herself at him.

Finally safe in his arms.

CHAPTER 41

SAM

"Well. That was… a night," Sam stated as she collapsed onto the couch. "Remind me to call your mom in the morning to apologize for the fuss… Again."

After the police had finally shown up to take Paul, she and Charlie had lingered long enough to make their statements, say their goodbyes, and head home. She'd have to go down to the station in the morning to wrap everything up officially, but after such an eventful evening, she'd been urged to go home and get some rest.

Her greatest fear had happened, and despite everything she probably *should* have felt at that moment, the overwhelming sense of guilt nearly drowned her. She'd brought her trouble to the only people who had ever truly cared for her, and the thought of Paul turning that rage and aggression in their direction, even remotely, left a sour taste in her mouth.

She'd attempted to bumble out an apology before leaving, unsure exactly how to apologize for something like this, but no one would hear a word of it. Richard insisted no one would even notice the chaos while Amy only took the time to berate Sam for even *attempting* to apologize. She was far from the first to do so, as Angel had also fussed at her when she tried to apologize for ruining her night.

Peter and Tyler, on the other hand, had been too busy taking bets on who could take Charlie in a fight to even notice them leave.

She had never felt more grateful.

An awkward silence had settled into the space between her and Charlie, even after they'd gotten into the car and shut the doors. The entire car ride home was intensely quiet, and that bothered her almost as much as everything else had.

She hadn't known what to say to him. Mostly because she didn't know what he was thinking, what he was feeling. He'd been so eerily quiet ever since she'd managed to peel herself off of him earlier. It was so un-Charlie-like that it unnerved her more than anything else.

Fortunately, due to the circumstances, they'd been assured that Charlie wouldn't be in any legal trouble for what had happened. It had been an immense relief, but she wondered if he still worried about it. She certainly was, especially if Paul tried to twist the truth. However, with his record and the warrant, she doubted he'd get away with it even if he tried.

The whole drive she worried—wondering if Charlie was taking stock of just how worth it the whole thing had been. If *she* had been worth all that trouble. If he didn't want to talk to her, she wasn't going to push him to do so, and she had been too afraid at the time to ask.

It had, of course, taken her by surprise, seeing both Tyler and Peter struggling to hold him back from Paul—knowing that Charlie was protective and strong but not really realizing the full extent until she'd seen it in action. But more than that, even with that strength, even with all of the advantages he had, there was still one reality of all of it.

Charlie could have been seriously hurt tonight.

Now in the safe confines of Charlie's apartment, she glanced over her shoulder at him, watching as he shed his suit jacket with an uncomfortable-sounding grunt. He casually tossed it onto the nearby barstool and began loosening his tie, all without looking in her direction. The unease in the air was palpable, and she didn't like it one bit.

Guilt ate at her as she caught a glimpse of his purpling knuckles.

Paul had taken the brunt of the fight, but there were traces of red and purple marks on Charlie that looked painful. It was easier to think about the logistics right now. It was less scary, less painful than what could have been. Those bruises might start to swell and become worse if they didn't get some ice on them soon.

She wordlessly walked over to the cabinet in search of a plastic zip bag, digging around until she found what she was looking for. If she couldn't bring herself to say anything, at least she could make herself useful.

Charlie watched her curiously, the intense energy that had been radiating off of him ebbing when she scooped ice into the bags and walked over to him. There was no exchange of words, but Charlie lowered himself onto a barstool as she handed him two bags, one for each hand.

She couldn't meet his eyes, worried that he might be angry over this whole ordeal. She wouldn't have blamed him —she was mad too. The endless cycle of "would've, could've, should've" had plagued her, reflecting on how she should have handled everything. Even going back all the way to the first time she met Paul. If she hadn't agreed to go on that date with him, none of this would have happened.

She refused to let her mind wander to earlier, before Charlie had shown up.

She couldn't bear to think about the angry purple bruises already marring her own wrist, the painful result of where Paul had grabbed her. Nor did she want to acknowledge the soreness in her throat from his choking grip, knowing it also likely bore bruises by his hand. All were just painful reminders.

Paul's eyes flashed in her mind. That gleam in them would likely haunt her for many years to come.

She shuddered but summoned a smile at Charlie when she was finally able to look at him. "Well, I'm gonna go get changed. After that, I'll make some tea for us if you…"

Her words trailed off when Charlie dropped the bags of ice onto the counter and rose. It was slow and cautious, watching her just as intently as she was watching him. He slowly reached for her hand without a word, taking it and guiding her to the bedroom.

He settled on the edge of the bed and gave a gentle tug, drawing her into his lap so that she straddled him. The slit in her dress eased the movement, though the fabric still hugged her tightly. She didn't care, even if it ripped in half. If it meant being in his comforting embrace, nothing else mattered.

His arms came up to wrap around her waist as he buried his face into the crook of her neck. He stayed there for a few beats without a word, his grip tightening around her as if holding on for dear life.

"You're okay," he whispered. Not a question, a confirmation.

She nodded, feeling the warmth of his body envelop her in a way that only he could provide. In the only way she wanted.

"You're not…" he started before she felt his fingers digging into her. "You're not afraid of me now, are you?"

Sam softened as understanding dawned on her. She pulled away slowly, gathering his face in her hands and forcing him to meet her gaze. "No, baby, I'm not scared of you. I could never be afraid of you."

The uncertainty in his eyes broke her heart. "Are you sure?"

"Of course I am. You could never scare me. Not like that. You saved me, Charlie."

"You haven't been able to look at me…"

She grimaced and let out an uncomfortable chuckle. "I've been worried that I ruined everyone's evening."

His eyebrows furrowed as he gave her another gentle squeeze. "How could you possibly think that? None of this was your fault."

"It still feels like it is—like if I had handled this differently to start with, none of this would've happened."

"Oh, baby," he soothed, releasing one arm from her side long enough to tuck a lock of hair behind her ear.

"Plus, I was more worried about you than anything else."

"Me?" he asked incredulously.

"Yes!" she cried out, trying to hold back the tears threatening to fall. "I didn't want you to get hurt."

He gave her a shy smile, a hint of humor in it. "I don't think you needed to worry about that."

"Well, I did. You could've been really hurt!" she said.

Charlie's fingers came up to trace the line of her neck, the softness in his eyes turning stormy as he did. "So could you. These bruises are already more than I can bear."

"It could've been worse."

He shook his head slowly, releasing a controlled breath as he did. "Sam, I think it took a few off of my life when we realized you were missing. By the time we found you, and I saw his hands wrapped around your neck, I just…"

Charlie leaned forward to press his forehead against her chest, as if he couldn't bring himself to finish that sentence. She understood how he felt, as that was how she felt when she watched the two of them wrestle on the ground. Afraid of what would happen.

She grabbed his face and pulled it back so she could gaze into his beautiful blue eyes once more. "That's why I can assure you that I'm not afraid of you, Charlie. You saved my life."

"Something I hope I *never* have to do again." He sighed, earning a wet giggle from her. "You have been the best thing to ever come into my life, Sam. Even before *us*. The thought of losing you is too much for me to bear. So, promise you won't scare me like that again, huh?" He brought his hand from her waist to cup her face, running his thumb across her cheek softly.

"I'm sorry I scared you," she murmured as he pulled her forward, kissing her.

"I love you," Charlie whispered when their lips parted.

A tear finally fell down her cheek as another giggle bubbled out of her. "I love you too."

Sam stared at the mounting stack of boxes before her and groaned. The pile seemed to grow each time she turned away.

"I couldn't have had this much shit in my apartment," she declared as Charlie walked through the front door, carting another box.

He placed it on top of the stack and grinned. "Last one at least."

"Thank God," she wheezed, bending forward to place her hands on her knees.

With her lease set to expire at the end of the week and Charlie's not ending for another few months, it had made the most sense for her to move in with him officially. At least until they could find a place of their own together. After all, it wasn't as if they hadn't practically been living together already, even after she had been cleared to return to her own place.

The trial was currently underway, and with her book's publication date drawing near, it had been a busy few months.

The trial was more of a formality at this point, as Paul had been on his third strike. He pleaded guilty, which surprised Sam more than anything, but she figured it was more so he could get as lenient of a sentencing as possible instead of leaving his fate to a jury. All the better. It meant she didn't have to spend a single day in court over the whole thing, so Sam considered it a win.

It had been the most liberated she had felt in a very long time.

The feeling had quickly been followed by her publisher's announcement. They were beyond thrilled with her book and, after a lengthy discussion, had decided to publish her debut romance novel under her new pen name, Sammy Smith. Not one of her most creative choices, but she was happy with it. Her book was slated to release in February of the following year, and based on the feedback she'd gotten from her early advance readers, it was projected to be a hit.

She even had a few more books under contract with her pen name, so Sam finally felt like she could take a breath. As if a weight had been lifted from her shoulders for the first time in nearly a year.

Now she had all the time in the world.

"Let's take a break," Charlie said as he took Sam's hand and led her into the bedroom. "I have something I'd like to try anyway."

She raised an eyebrow at him, curious as to what he could possibly have up his sleeve.

He guided her down the hallway and into the bedroom. She turned to raise an eyebrow at him before being pushed back onto the bed with a giggle. With a soft thud, she settled onto the surface, her curiosity piqued as she watched Charlie grab something from the nearby dresser. When he turned to her, he had a small stack of papers clutched in his hand.

Charlie cleared his throat as he began reading from the

top page. "Sally let out a moan as Connor's finger began to lazily trace her—"

Recognition flashed in her mind, and Sam launched herself off the bed. "*Charlie!* How the hell did you get that?!"

She jumped at him to snatch the papers, but he was quick and held them high in the air, well out of her reach. "I might have asked Angel to send it to me."

Traitor.

"Why?!" she squealed, starting to laugh at the ridiculousness of the situation as she continued jumping up and down to snatch it from him. "I told you that you would get to read the first copy I get before my publication day!"

Charlie shook his head decisively, a mischievous look in his eyes. "You're telling me that I helped you with the romance in this book, and I don't even get to have fun with it?"

"Nothing is sacred these days. Give that back!" she shouted and jumped up once more, but Charlie effortlessly grabbed her in midair and tossed her back onto the bed. Before she could even attempt to get back up, his body quickly covered hers, pressing her onto the mattress with a playful but firm hold.

It didn't take her long to feel the unmistakable length of him pressing urgently against her thigh, and she ceased movement, instead meeting Charlie's devilish glare. A mixture of arousal and amusement kissed each of his features.

"I think it's only fair, don't you?" he whispered, his voice already sounding husky.

She blinked at him. "You want to… You want to act out a spicy scene?"

His lips seared hers, forcing any rational thought out of her mind as she felt his hands rove over her body. When he pulled back, she was already breathless. "That's the idea. Now, be a good girl and follow along, huh?"

She nodded quickly, her ability to form words vacating the premises. As far as she was concerned, this was the most brilliant idea she'd ever heard.

In fact, why hadn't she thought of it sooner?

It didn't take long for the two to shed their clothing, Charlie practically tearing the material away from her body, as if it were a device designed to torture him. The pages splayed out on the bed next to them, almost forgotten, until Charlie pulled back.

His pupils had already blown out, but he grabbed the stack with one hand. His other hand went down to part her legs, leaving her open for him.

"As I was *saying*," Charlie stated as his focus returned to the words on the page, "Sally let out a moan as Connor's finger began lazily tracing her clit. His movements were methodic and calculated, like he already knew exactly what her body needed."

The moan that had been about to escape her was abruptly stifled as she bit down on her lip, wanting to refuse him out of sheer stubbornness. However, it proved to be a losing battle, as Charlie—like his counterpart in the book—seemed to know her body better than she did. He chuckled darkly as he increased the pressure on her clit, practically ripping the moan away from her.

"Good girl," he praised. "You keep making me lose my place, and we'll be here all night."

Her pussy throbbed at the notion. If Charlie kept calling her his *good girl*, she'd let him do whatever he wanted.

Before the vague threat could settle, Charlie removed his thumb. The sudden loss of friction caused her to whimper a protest. She tried to bring his hand back, but he chuckled darkly once more.

He seemed intensely amused at the mess he'd already made of her with just a few touches.

If she had half a mind, she would have remembered what she had written, to help her anticipate what would come next and prepare herself. Yet she knew that whenever Charlie's touch was involved, her brain inevitably turned to mush.

Charlie tossed the top sheet away as he continued to a different section. "Connor took a pebbled nipple into his mouth, savoring the taste of her as he suckled the sensitive bud."

He dutifully followed the character, leaning forward to take one of her nipples into his mouth, sweeping his tongue over it as his other hand massaged the neglected breast. Sam fisted the sheets around her, desperate to cling onto something as her toes curled from the sensation.

Her body burned with need, squirming beneath him.

He remained there for longer than she expected, rotating between breasts to make sure each had his full attention, teasing her nearly to delirium before finally pulling back. Her core pulsed almost painfully with how much she wanted him, *needed* him.

She wanted to tease him in the way he was teasing her, but the thought died in her mouth when Charlie fisted his cock in one hand, giving it a few generous pumps before wrapping it with the condom that she hadn't even seen him grab.

It was a deeply sensual and intimate scene that had her mouth watering, watching the condom roll along the length of him slowly. Imagining it was her lips wrapped around him, she was momentarily jealous of the condom.

The man had planned this, no question.

It was far from the first time she'd seen Charlie's cock by this point, but she still found herself wondering how the hell something like that ever fit inside of her. But boy, did she always enjoy finding out *exactly* how he fit—wondering how she had ever lived without this for as long as she did.

Charlie pressed his cock against her folds, wetting the tip and running it up and down the length of her.

"Look at how wet you are for me. Is this what you want, baby?" he asked, repeating the character's words perfectly.

She nodded wildly, the fierceness of her arousal so intense that she could hardly see straight, let alone respond coherently.

"Connor entered her in one fierce thrust," Charlie continued, punctuating the last word as he thrust himself into Sam's welcoming heat. The force of it rammed right into that sweet spot inside of her that caused her eyes to roll back in her head.

Charlie groaned as her body clenched around him, the edges of control starting to visibly slip as he shuddered against her. "Did you picture me doing this to you when you wrote that?"

"Yes," she whispered honestly, the heat in his eyes enough to set them both ablaze.

A low growl emitted from Charlie as he tossed the papers onto the bed next to them. One of his hands snaked around her waist as he teased her body with a couple of shallow thrusts. "I'll have to demonstrate the next part; I don't think I'll be able to read along for this."

"Good," she panted, digging her fingernails into his skin. "Fuck me, please."

Charlie chuckled. "You better hold on tight then, baby. We've got some more notes to take for the sequel."

ACKNOWLEDGMENTS

There are honestly way too many people to thank for helping me get this book into your (the reader) hands—but I'll give it my best shot...

Obviously, the first person I want to thank is my loving husband, Mike. You have continued to be my biggest pillar of support, the person who has listened to *way* too many mental breakdowns over this book, encouraged me when I felt like giving up, and the person who let me use them as a human dummy so I could figure out the logistics of a few scenes (not like that, get your head out of the gutter). Without you, everything was dark & grey, but you bring the color to my world.

Also, I warned you that it would start getting weird with these dedications once I started writing romances and smut so... here we are.

To my OG beta readers, Sarah Gasson and Alex Kolat, you two really are the true MVP's. If not for you two reading the MANY different versions of this book, it wouldn't have turned out nearly as coherent as it did. I will be forever grateful to both of you for that!

Additionally, Alex Kolat (my closest friend and mother to Theo) — you continue to be one of my biggest cheerleaders and supporters. Two husbands, a baby, and two books later—here we are. And for Theo, my god son—oh lord Alex please don't let him read this until he's much older, Aunt Liz still needs to be able to look him in the eye when he's older.

To my GTP friends who pretended like I wasn't writing

smut in the living room of their houses during Hobby Nights every month since I started this book—yeah we all know I lied but thanks for at least pretending.

For all my NC Indie Discord author friends — you all have been so incredibly encouraging and wonderful ever since I joined and awkwardly walked up to your author tables at author signings to say hi. Thank you all for helping to guide me to be a better writer and author by answering my thousands of questions in chat, your advice has truly been invaluable!

To my editor, Jamie — you have been an absolute godsend with this book. Thank you for helping to keep me sane and reassuring me that this book does indeed *not* suck (despite my brain telling me otherwise at times).

To my parents — please tell me you skipped right to this page and didn't read certain scenes I've written in this book. No? Alright worth a shot. Seriously though, thank you for always nurturing my love of reading and writing when I was growing up.

ABOUT THE AUTHOR

Leigh Creek is the romance pseudonym for author Elizabeth C. Cabrera. She spends vastly too much time daydreaming about the movie version of her books, drinking ungodly amounts of coffee, and pretending like she has her life together. When she's not writing and reading vastly too much, she's spending time with her husband and two cats (Link and Luna).

Sign up for the newsletter for behind-the-scenes, sneak peeks, and more authorly chaos!
www.substack.com/@eccpublishing

bsky.app/profile/authoreccabrera.bsky.social
youtube.com/@Author_Elizabeth_C_Cabrera
tiktok.com/@eccpublishing
instagram.com/ecc_publishing
facebook.com/eccpublishing